ALSO BY FIONA NEILL

The Good Girl

What the Nanny Saw

The Secret Life of a Slummy Mummy

Friends, Lovers, and Other Indiscretions

The
Betrayals

The
Betrayals

FIONA NEILL

PEGASUS BOOKS
NEW YORK LONDON

THE BETRAYALS

Pegasus Books, Ltd.
148 West 37th Street, 13th Floor
New York, NY 10018

First Pegasus Books hardcover edition September 2018

ISBN: 978-1-68177-850-1

10 9 8 7 6 5 4 3 2 1

Printed in the United States of America
Distributed by W. W. Norton & Company, Inc.

For Felix, Maia and Caspar

I

Daisy

Three is a good and safe number. I close my eyes and whisper the words three times so no one can hear. They sound like a sweet sigh. If Mum notices she might worry and *the days of worry are over.* I say this three times too, just to make triple sure, remembering how the words have to be spoken on the outbreath.

As I exhale, cold air blows in through the letter box into the hallway, making it flap against the front door. *An ill wind, ill wind, ill wind.* I look round to check Mum is still in the kitchen and bend down to examine the letter on the doormat, even though I recognized the large attention-seeking scrawl the instant it landed. Why, why, why is she writing to Mum after all these years? I don't touch it. Yet.

I hear Mum giggling. It's always a great sound. I can tell she's on the phone to my brother, Max, because he's so good at making her laugh. Much better than me. Even when I tell her entertaining stories about the Russian boy I'm tutoring or something that's happened at uni, there's caution in her response – as if she still doesn't dare trust in my happiness. Parents are the worst for holding you prisoner to the person you used to be. Or rather Mum is. Dad stopped being the resident jailer a long time ago.

I used to accuse Mum of being neurotic but now I understand that Dad's cool was a way of avoiding responsibility. Besides, it's in his interests to believe in happy endings and new beginnings because he got his.

Mum has an uncanny ability to notice tiny changes in me. She's like a meteorologist for my moods, collating and crunching information to predict subtle shifts in patterns. And she rarely makes mistakes. But, as she used to tell me back in the days when nothing was solid and reliable, you learn more by the things you get wrong than the things you get right.

I'm not sure I agree. If you are in Paris, for example, and you look the wrong way when you step out into the road you could get run over and even if you aren't killed you might end up quadriplegic. Generally death and disability don't provide good life lessons. If Max said that, Mum would fall around laughing. If I said it she would want to swab my soul for signs of impending darkness.

A big part of my mother's job is to observe people. She's a doctor, a breast cancer specialist, and she has spent years making sure that her emotions don't leach into her face. She's always trying to explain why empathy trumps sympathy. Patients need their doctor to appear under control, she says, especially when the news is bad. Any other response is self-indulgent. But I can tell when she's emotional because she chews the inside of her right cheek.

My attention returns to the letter. The inside of her cheek would be savaged if she saw this.

My mind is made up: it can't be ignored. I pick up the padded manila envelope and turn it in my hands, noting the following: 1) it is postmarked Norfolk, 2) she has written in baby-blue ink, 3) *truly, truly, truly a good and safe number*, she has included something heavy that feels like a small spoon. And 4) it is sealed with Sellotape. People only do that when they have given a lot of consideration to the contents. I also note that I make four observations rather than three. *Good work, Daisy*, I congratulate myself, although almost immediately I'm aware that counting is a retrograde step.

I head towards the shelf in the hall and randomly grab a hardback book that is big enough to conceal the envelope. Dust flies everywhere because Mum isn't the kind of woman who cleans to relax. It falls open on a well-thumbed page. 'Anxiety Disorders in Teenagers', reads the chapter heading.

Since Dad walked out on us when I was fourteen, Mum has become our responsibility. 'Look after your mother,' Dad always used to say when he dropped us back home from a weekend at his house after they split up seven years ago. Note I never called his house 'home'. The first time he said this, Max – who was only eleven at the time – told him to fuck off. He didn't like the implication that we didn't look after Mum, or the fact that the person saying it was responsible for causing the pain that meant she needed looking after. Dad told Max not to be so rude but it sounded half-hearted. And besides, Max had started crying as soon as the words were out of his mouth. Sometimes back then Dad cried too and I had to comfort him. Things have been calmer over the past four years. Or at least I thought they were. Until this letter.

I head into the toilet and lock the door behind me. It's designed so you can open it from the outside if necessary.

There are four holes above the lock where the old bolt used to be. I peer through one of these to check Mum is still in the kitchen. It's an old habit because I used to spend a lot of time in here: it was the one place no one could disturb me. At least I no longer check the lock three times. Reviewing myself in the mirror I see my face reflect the gravity of the situation back to me. When I'm emotional my lips always go cartoon rubbery. I run my finger across the hole at the bottom right-hand corner of the mirror where there is a tiny slice of glass missing. My fault. But let's not go into that now. The mirror came from the house in Norfolk where we used to go on holiday when we were children. 'Back in the day,' as Mum says breezily. She is all about living in the present. Even though she has spent the best part of a decade involved in the same clinical trial.

I turn my face from side to side to let the light fall on it at different angles and tousle my fringe and short dark hair in an effort to appear effortless in a French sort of way. Kit likes it like this. In fact, I think it's fair, if miraculous, to say that Kit likes pretty much everything about me. The timing of this parcel isn't great because he is about to arrive to meet Mum for the first time. She's been angling for an introduction since I first started going out with him eight months ago, but I wanted to wait until I was completely sure about him.

I close the loo seat and sit down. I'm not proud of what I do next. But who hasn't done the wrong thing for the right reasons at least once in their life? I honestly thought this would be the end of something, not the beginning. I carefully peel off the Sellotape and the padded manila envelope flaps open. I just knew Lisa wouldn't have licked it. She's as careless with things as she is with people. I breathe in and out, as deep as I can, one hand holding the envelope, the other resting on my diaphragm as it rises to make sure that my abdominal muscles are contracting properly on the inbreath. I know more about breathing than any yoga teacher.

In my defence I should say that at this moment I did try to reseal it with the same piece of Sellotape that I had peeled off a second ago. Privacy is a big issue for me. And there was no doubting who was meant to be opening it: *Rosie Foss*. It still surprised me to see Mum's surname because until my parents got divorced we all shared the same one. At the beginning Max and I made a big thing of this. We wanted to become Foss so she wasn't alone with her new name like she was alone with everything else. It felt strange to no longer have the same surname as my closest living relative but Mum argued, quite convincingly, that she had been Rosie Foss for most of her life before she married Dad and that at work she had always kept her maiden name. Max politely pointed out that just for the record, at thirty-nine years old, with two children, Mum most definitely wasn't a maiden. Mum had cracked up at this. Max doesn't have to try to be a light person. He was built that way.

I think about all this as I keep trying to stick the envelope back down. But of course Lisa has used cheap Sellotape. She's always dropping hints about how she and Dad don't have enough money, which annoys me so much because Mum has always worked so hard and Lisa hasn't had a job since she moved in with Dad. Part-time yoga teacher doesn't really cut it. Irritation makes me clumsy and the letter emerges tantalizingly from the top of the envelope so that I can see the uneven line of huge kisses beneath Lisa's signature.

I pull it out, taking care not to crease the flimsy paper. It's two pages long when it could have been one but Lisa's scrawl is big and confident, which is probably why I am even more surprised by what follows.

My dear Rosie,

I am writing to let you know that I have recently been diagnosed with Stage 4 breast cancer. (You know better than anyone that there is no Stage 5.) I thought the lump was a cyst or something left over from breastfeeding all those years ago. Do you remember those lovely, lazy days on the beach in Norfolk? But a recent biopsy proved otherwise and unfortunately the cancer has spread. I do not expect your sympathy. The reason for contacting you is simple: I want to see you one last time. I want to ask your forgiveness for the pain I caused you and tell you something that you need to know before it is too late. I am enclosing the key to the house so that you can let yourself in. I haven't told Nick about this letter and am increasingly too tired to get out of bed to answer the door. I have decided to keep my illness private for the moment and would be grateful if you could respect this final wish.

With fondest love, as always,

Lisa
XXXX

My emotions with regard to Lisa used to be pretty three-dimensional. Variations on the theme of animosity, angst and anger. Pretty textbook stuff. Since I met Kit, I have let go of the anger without even trying. As it pumps through my body again I realize that I haven't missed it. I can't stand the way Lisa assumes Mum will go running to her and cave in to her demands after everything that has happened. I even feel annoyed she has got breast cancer because that territory belongs to Mum. And then a further wave of rage that she has turned me into someone whose first response to a dying person isn't sympathy.

Why is she doing this after all this time? As far as I can see in my dealings with Lisa, she has never shown any signs of remorse for stealing Dad. But mostly I see this emotionally manipulative letter as a big threat to Mum's hard-won equilibrium. It will make her rake up the past and relive all the sadness and disappointment just so Lisa can feel better about herself. And I will do anything to protect Mum from harm. She is one of the most genuinely caring people that I have ever come across. She'll probably even try to help Lisa. Not that I want her to die, because then Max and I might end up having to look after Dad.

But just as quickly a new emotion takes hold. This is one I haven't felt for years. My skin feels clammy and my ribs no longer rise when I breathe. I'm properly anxious. Because I am as sure as shit that I know what Lisa is going to tell Mum.

I try to distract myself with the things that I don't feel: 1) sympathy for Dad, 2) sadness for Lisa, 3) regret at having opened the letter.

I try some breathing techniques but I can't focus, so I

allow myself a bit of tapping. Just three times on the bone below each shoulder. Repetitions in multiples of three. I stop at 21 because 24 is a multiple of a number I don't like. It helps. I don't need to do my toes, heel or the side of my foot. You have probably noticed a lot of my life now revolves around what I don't do rather than what I do. My ribcage settles.

'Daisy,' I hear Mum shouting. 'Can you get the door?'

Kit must have arrived. I look through the hole. Mum's halfway into the hall. With a wooden spoon in one hand and a packet of butter in the other, she looks uncharacteristically domestic. She doesn't notice when a sweaty lump of butter drops on the floor. For someone so well versed in infection control she is surprisingly slovenly around the house. Her bedroom floor is always littered with clothes and her toothpaste never has a lid. Max says she lives like a student. But I love her for it. 'Just coming,' I call back. She turns round and frowns at the toilet door, and I guiltily realize it spooks her because it reminds her of times past.

Judging by the black grains of rice that cover the spoon, she has reached what Max and I call 'the resuscitation of rice' stage of lunch. The smell of charred rice burning at the bottom of a pan that has run dry of water is to my childhood what the madeleine was to Marcel Proust. Actually, Dad said that. When they were still together and did funny banter. They split up in January 2008, almost exactly seven years ago, although according to Dad the marriage was over long before. I once asked Dad when it finished for him, and how come Mum didn't realize when she was living under the same roof. He said he couldn't recall the exact instant, which struck me as strange coming from a scientist who specializes in the nature of memory formation. I wish I were as good at forgetting as Dad. I remember everything.

I put the two sheets of paper face up on the toilet seat and take a couple of shots of the letter with my phone. I make a song and dance of flushing the loo and running water in the basin and put it all back exactly as I found it, except for one thing. I take out the key and slide it into the back pocket of my jeans. I'm not sure why I do this. Later Max pointed out that I had a thing about locking doors when I was ill. But I promise this is an impulsive rather than compulsive act.

Then I notice something else at the bottom of the envelope. It's an old photo of us all, taken in Norfolk, during the last holiday we spent together before the upheaval. When Mum and Lisa were still best friends. We are in the garden of the house where Mum grew up. 'My second home,' Lisa used to call it. Until it became her first home. Dad's part of the divorce settlement. There are fistfuls of irony in this story.

I have never seen the photo before. Lisa must have been running out of printer ink because it's sickly yellow. But it's not the colour that makes me feel queasy. I recognize the liverish lawn of my grandparents' house, dried out by the sun, and the garden shed in the background. It must have been taken on a timer because somehow all eight of us are in it. Mum and Lisa are centre stage, arms carelessly flung around each other, as though they are the married couple. Mum was fatter then. Lisa has always been thin. Mum is squinting at Lisa, whose eyes are shut, which is unfortunate because eyes are the windows of the soul and perhaps Mum would have known what she was up against if she could have seen into them at that moment.

Dad stands beside Mum but no part of his body is touching her. His right arm is around Max, who was probably ten when the photo was taken. His dark curly hair rests comfortably against Dad's thigh. Back then he loved Dad unconditionally. I am standing stiffly between Lisa's son, Rex, and his dad, Barney. I look tense because I was tense. Barney's hands are behind his back and his chest is puffed out so it appears as though he's standing to attention but he's probably hiding a beer can. His lopsided grin confirms my theory. Lisa's daughter, Ava, is on the edge of the frame. We used to be friends but not any more. After everything that happened, we were never going to make a model blended family. I touch Lisa's face with my finger and find myself scratching at it with my nail. Let it go, Daisy, Kit would say if he saw me. *Let it go.* But I can't. I keep scraping until she disappears. If I told him what happened he might understand. Because that was the summer my childhood stopped.

I come out of the toilet. Mum is offering Kit the hand that holds the spoon. He has the self-possession not to look alarmed. He's very calm, my man. Instead he deftly takes the spoon so they can shake hands.

'I'm Rosie,' says Mum, giving Kit the same reassuring but professional smile she uses on patients.

'It's so nice to meet you,' says Kit. His blond hair flops over his face, surfer style. He glances over to me and does that thing where he raises one eyebrow. That's all it takes. I realize this is meant to be one of those awkward moments but it really isn't. The good thing about having a super dysfunctional family is that there isn't a lot to live up to.

2

Max

My phone beeps. Twice in quick succession. When I see both voicemails are from Daisy I decide to ignore them. The days when communication from my sister required an immediate response are long gone. Or rather long, long, long, gone, gone, gone, as Daisy once might have put it. Occasionally, there was poetry in her illness, although she would never see it that way.

It's disappointment rather than indifference. I was hoping they might be from the girl I'd just left asleep in my room. Before I went, I decided to dress the skeleton I'd recently rented from the medical faculty Osteology Store in Connie's clothes and stand it at the end of the bed so it would be the first thing she saw when she woke up. That should definitely guarantee a response.

At the time it had seemed like a brilliantly original idea. But as my head clears in the early-morning cold, I realize she might find my sense of humour immature or, worse, freaky. Also I snagged her bra on a rib and when I pulled on her knickers over the skeleton's pelvis, I noticed a tiny coil of blood, probably not something she would want me to see. I've partially done an ob-gyn module, so I'm not fazed by bodily secretions, especially hers, but she might not see it that way. She isn't a medic like me and she's seven years older, which is a significant gulf when you're just nineteen and a second-year student with four years of study to go.

This girl, on the other hand, has a proper job I know nothing about, shares a flat I've never visited with a brother I haven't met and talks about future plans although I'm never given even a walk-on role in any of them. Last night she showed me a spreadsheet where she had done all sorts of calculations to work out how much money she needs to put away each week in order to save up for a deposit on a flat before she hits thirty. I had felt a moment of euphoria until I saw the figures were in dollars and she was talking about Brooklyn. At least it makes her account of living in the States with her father for four years seem plausible.

'If you bought a flat with another person you'd get there twice as fast,' I pointed out.

'I never want to be dependent on anyone else,' she shrugged.

'You sound like my mum,' I said, instantly regretting this response because it made me sound the age I am. 'I mean lots of women don't want to be financially dependent on a man.'

'I don't want to be dependent on a woman either,' she said, adding to my confusion. I think she enjoys it.

We were lying in bed together. She was on her side. She pushed her buttocks into my cock and so it began all over again. 'I only asked you to take a look because you're good with numbers.'

'Tell me you want me,' I whispered in her ear.

'I'll tell you anything you want but that doesn't mean I mean any of it,' she whispered back.

We had agreed after the first swipe right came good that each time we met we were allowed to ask one question about each other. There were two additional caveats: it had to be after we had sex, and you could only ask if you made the other person come. The first bit was my idea. I liked the idea of a single line of communication and keeping everything simple. There was a kind of purity to it.

At the beginning she turned me on so much that I didn't get to ask any questions. I apologized and she teased me about still being a teenager. So while I played catch-up I was a little loose with the truth a couple of times. When she asked me what was the worst thing that had ever happened to me I said it was my parents getting divorced but really it was Daisy getting ill. Even though divorce is terminal and my sister has recovered. But I share a big part of the blame for what happened to Daisy. And I told her I had one sibling and two steps, which strictly speaking isn't true because Dad isn't married and we never see Rex and Ava, so they only count intellectually, not emotionally.

I only say this to underline that although there is just a small part for me in all this I am at least a reliable witness.

I increase my pace. If I go back now I'll be late for my first lecture. Professor Francis is a moody bastard and is quite capable of refusing to let me in if I don't show up on time. I allow myself to think about Connie one more time and remember how I had lovingly straightened out her jumper, smoothed out the sleeves and pressed my face into it, inhaling her scent like a dog. Fuck, she smelt so good – like roses and lemon grass. Unlike my fellow students. We all have the whiff of formaldehyde about us. If it weren't so cold I would have stuffed the jumper in my bag so I could sleep with it tonight because I'm missing the scent of her already. If smell is the most powerful human sense then why can't memory trigger smell rather than the other way round? I wonder. I'll ask Dad when I see him later. He loves it when I ask him about work. It's a useful way to plug the gaps in conversation.

To take my mind off her, I start to think about microorganisms, specifically pathogens, the subject of Professor Francis's about-to-be-delivered lecture, and an idea starts to evolve in my head. Not the kind of thought that used to take hold in Daisy's head – although, thank God, even at her worst she had never obsessed about germs and contamination. But a very real and interesting idea about how pathogens are always stereotyped as the bad guys when they are so much more than simple hostile invaders.

'Hello, mate. Big night?' It's Carlo, one of my housemates. He puts his arm around me and ruffles my hair in a way that always feels more patronizing than affectionate. I'd told him about my girl in a moment of weakness when she hadn't responded to any of my messages for a couple of days.

'Have you ever considered that there are more bacterial, fungal and protozoan cells in the body than human cells, Carlo?'

'God, you know how to turn a guy on, Max,' Carlo groans. 'So did you get to ask a question this time?'

'All they want to do is exist and procreate. Live and let live. Like John Lennon.' Life was so simple.

FIONA NEILL

Carlo laughs. 'Try telling that to the woman with bed-sores that we saw yesterday. That was pure, fucking *Breaking Bad*. The pus was as thick as custard.'

I can't understand how someone with such a big empathy deficit has gone into medicine. He'd be far better suited to finance or tech.

We go into the lecture hall together. On the whiteboard Professor Francis has written *The Human Body: a complex ecosystem* and I feel as though I have arrived home. I told Mum this recently and she said it was exactly how she felt when she was at medical school. Carlo and I head for our usual seats beside the pillar in the fourth row. There's a very pretty Asian girl who sits at the end of this row. She wears a veil, which in my book puts her off limits, but Carlo sees it as a challenge worth rising to. He has a whole list of gnarly sexual experiences that he wants to tick off. That's why I haven't introduced him to Mum.

Professor Francis starts. He goes straight in with an observation about how microbes are usually limited to certain areas of the human body: the skin, mouth, large intestine and vagina. All the bits you want to lick and touch, I think to myself, although judging by the way Carlo winks at me, he's cleaving the same groove. I think about the girl in my bed again, imagining her lying on her front and the perfect arc of her buttocks and how it winds me just to look at her. She's probably got up by now, removed her clothes from my skeleton and drunk the takeaway coffee I've left on my desk for her. Skinny latte. One shot. We had agreed that didn't count as a question.

After half an hour Professor Francis opens the floor for any questions we want to throw at him for ten minutes before he starts the second part of his lecture. He's a cool guy. And I want to ask whether the purpose of sex might be to allow pathogens to colonize different parts of the human body, thereby increasing immunity. But I'm worried it might reveal too much about where I'm coming from or, worse, encourage Carlo to share his rimjob fantasies with me again. Not something I ever want to repeat.

I slouch in my seat. For much of my adolescence my body was so hard with tension that I assumed it was normal. But the past couple of years so many good things have happened that my muscles, tendons and ligaments are as smooth as honey. Daisy has been well. Mum has turned a corner. And now this girl has come along. Fucking is fucking. But this is something totally different. I've actually stopped thinking about anyone else.

I feel my phone vibrate again. I do that one-handed manoeuvre, checking the caller ID without removing the phone from my pocket in case Professor Francis catches me out. I get all excited when I see there's a photograph attached. I tried sexting her once but she said it's against the rules, so I think maybe she's sent a picture of the skeleton wearing her clothes or something she's seen on her way to work to tantalize me, because although she knows exactly where I spend my days, if she disappeared I would have no idea where to even start looking for her. I'm not even sure she's using her real name. Lots of people don't on Tinder. I don't.

But it's not from her. It's from Daisy. Carlo nudges me. I shake my head and try to focus on the teacher.

'Each individual pathogen causes disease in a different way, which makes it challenging to understand the basic biology of infection . . .'

The phone vibrates in my pocket. Daisy again. I switch it off.

I go the whole day without hearing from Connie so I'm already seeing a bad moon rising when I arrive at the restaurant to meet Dad and Lisa for dinner that evening. By then Daisy's messages have slipped off the bottom of my screen. I've spent most of the day indoors, including an hour and a half standing in the dissection room in the cloisters in the coldest part of the medical school.

I share my cadaver with four other students, including Carlo. Today we did the head for the first time. By the time it came to me, my hands were so cold that when I tried to make the incision to the supraorbital nerve, my scalpel slipped and I ended up prematurely severing the optic nerve, which will make it almost impossible to dissect the eye properly next week. I apologized to Jean. She's an old lady and deserves better than me. I looked up at the sign above the door for reassurance. '*Mortui vivos docent*,' it reads. 'The dead teach the living.'

When I get off the tube at Kentish Town, I try to call Daisy to apologize for my radio silence but it goes to voicemail so I head straight for the Indian restaurant. Usually Daisy and I meet up for a drink at the pub before we see Dad and Lisa. We always order Bloody Marys and place bets about how long it will take for Lisa to introduce yoga into the conversation. She used to be a corporate lawyer but she's retrained as a yoga teacher and is evangelical about healthy living in that way religious converts are. She's even learning Sanskrit.

Daisy is already sitting at the table when I arrive, still

wearing her jacket – a fake fur, stripy number that I immediately want to buy for Connie – so I know she hasn't been here long. She stands up when she hears my voice and gets up so abruptly that I have to steady her chair as she turns to face me.

'Hey, Maxi,' she says. Daisy is the only person who can get away with calling me this. She hugs me so close the fur from the jacket tickles my nostrils. 'Where've you been?'

'I spent the afternoon with Jean,' I say, deadpan.

'So when do we get to meet her?' Dad asks eagerly, standing up to give me a hug.

Now that I'm taller than him he does that backslapping thing a bit too energetically. One of the biggest changes in him since he got together with Lisa is that he sounds so enthusiastic about everything all the time. Like he's joined a cult or something. But he's also always primed for the disappointment of knowing that, whatever our news, he believes Mum got there first. So I assume he assumes that Jean has already been to Mum's house to eat burnt rice and dry chicken and feels hurt even though he gets he has no right. Or some such head fuckery.

'You should have brought her with you, Max. We'd be on our best behaviour.'

'Maybe in the afterlife,' I say, feeling sorry for him. 'She's my cadaver, Dad. And after today I can't take her anywhere because I severed her optic nerve, so she's got one eye hanging out. It's not a good look.'

Dad laughs a bit too loudly, and I feel guilty for Jean because we have real respect for her. Before the first shoulder-to-shoulder incision last year we all stood around with our arms folded and thanked her. Even Carlo. No one told us to do this. It just felt right. I can tell from the way Lisa puts a reassuring hand on top of his that Dad considers this further evidence of his distance from our lives. *Get over it. I have,* I want to say. It's probably true that I've spent more time with Jean than I have with Dad over the past eighteen months. But what does he expect? Who hangs out with their parents at my age? And when he could have been in our lives, he wasn't. He was with Lisa. This isn't judgement. It's fact.

'Don't I get a kiss?' Lisa asks huskily.

Recently Daisy has accused me of being susceptible to Lisa's attempts to flirt me into submission. It's just her manner, I tell Daisy. She's been like that since I can remember. I should introduce her to Carlo. She'd definitely tick his MILF box.

'*Namaste,*' I say instead, giving Lisa a low bow. I try to catch Daisy's eye but she's looking down at the menu, except I know she isn't really reading it because we always order the same thing.

'*Namaste,*' Lisa responds. 'I always say this at the end of my yoga classes.' I wait for Daisy's smirk but she doesn't react.

'We'll have our usual,' Dad says to the waiter when he comes over, as though we are a proper family unit with our own ancient rituals and habits and this waiter was present at my birth.

'Perfect, Mr Foss.'

I wince on Dad's behalf. The wrinkles on his face concertina as it dawns on him that we must come here with Mum too.

'Rankin,' Dad says. 'My surname is Rankin. My wife is Foss.'

'Ex-wife,' Lisa reminds him. There's no edge to her tone. She has never shown any insecurity about Mum.

'And please can we have one naan each –' Daisy says.

'Three will do,' Lisa interjects in a sing-song voice.

'Let's stick with four,' Dad insists because he is more afraid of antagonizing Daisy than Lisa. Sensible strategy.

Dad doesn't realize that Daisy orders as many carbohydrates as possible because she knows Lisa's life revolves around avoiding them. Samosas, pakora, biryani, egg-fried rice. I love the way Daisy's repressed fury is so wittily channelled. I was never very good at sustaining anger but Daisy's illness meant hers was dormant for a good few years and she has had to play catch-up.

Lisa squeezes some drops from a small brown glass bottle into her glass of water and tries to do the same to Dad's glass but he puts his hand over the top.

'Come on, Niko,' she urges him.

I can tell he wants her to stop. Daisy maintains they're trapped in contradictory urges: Lisa wants to show off about how much she influences Dad and Dad wants to demonstrate his independence from her. The truth probably lies somewhere in the middle. In many ways they make a good couple, not that I would ever admit that to anyone, although it echoes something Mum said recently. I try to imagine Mum and Dad being as besotted with each other as I am with Connie and then feel distraught that another guy could come close to making her feel the same way. I need to see her so badly that my body starts to ache.

'No thanks,' Dad says. 'I'll start again tomorrow morning.'

'There's only one week left,' Lisa insists. She turns to us. 'We're detoxing for a month. Maybe you should try it, Max? To purge your liver.'

Lisa seems to have this idea that I'm a big drinker. It's because of something that happened years ago, just after she and Dad got together. But the truth is I'm mostly too knackered to be a lush. I have eight hours of lectures almost every day.

'Your liver clears itself of toxins,' I point out. 'That's its purpose in life.'

'But it's good to detox to get rid of all those free radicals,' she persists.

'It'll take more than that to get rid of Jeremy Corbyn,' Dad jokes. He's trying to steer the conversation away from homeopathic remedies but for all Lisa's mindfulness, she doesn't pick up the hint.

'You must be an expert on free radicals,' she says, leaning in towards me.

She's wearing a floaty cream silk top. I lean towards her. I don't know if it's because I've spent the afternoon with Jean, but I notice her collarbone, sternum and a few ribs perfectly outlined beneath. She looks almost as cadaverous as my cadaver.

'Detoxing is a pseudo-medical concept to sell you stuff. But it's harmless, and if it encourages you to eat healthily and makes you feel good then that's great. Just don't stick anything up your arse. We saw a very interesting patient recently who got campylobacter sepsis from a coffee enema.'

Daisy looks up from her phone and giggles for the first time. It's a good sound.

'Max,' Dad warns. 'We're about to eat.'

We are halfway through the meal when I first notice. I stare at Daisy's plate. There are three small, neat piles of food. Rice, samosa and saag gosht. None of them touch each other. If you didn't know you would assume she was someone who had an artistic sensibility about how food should be presented. Except I know she doesn't because after Dad left I became the family cook, and she never complained about how my meals looked. Even when we were short on ingredients and I did things like mashed potato with gherkins.

I have just asked Dad the question about why memory can't induce smell. He has digressed into a long explanation about how an impaired sense of smell can be one of the earliest symptoms of Alzheimer's and Parkinson's.

'It's the first sense to go in cognitive decline,' he says. 'And it's worse in the left nostril.'

Usually this is the kind of thing that would really interest me but I am too busy staring at the small corner missing from each mound on Daisy's plate. For a long while I was utterly vigilant, even after the doctors gave Daisy a clean bill of health. How can you tell exactly what's going on inside someone's head? But over the past couple of years I have completely relaxed. So at first I think I'm being paranoid.

I try to remember whether she always does this. Daisy still is, if nothing else, a creature of habit. And Lisa has eaten even less, although she has chosen a different method for avoiding detection by hiding food beneath crumbled pieces of poppadom. I look at Dad's carelessly loaded plate and realize that I am the only one at the table eating anything. Dad tries to persuade Lisa to try a few mouthfuls of tandoori chicken.

'There's no sauce on it, darling,' he says, spearing a chunk on to his fork and trying to feed her like he used to feed us when we were little children.

She shakes her head. 'Please, Niko.'

I glance over at Daisy, waiting for her to mock-vomit at this display of intimacy between them. Because one of the new family rituals Dad is unaware of is our hyper-awareness of any physical affection between him and Lisa and our hyper-inability to tolerate it. In fact, Daisy still regularly refers to Lisa as Dad's 'fuck buddy'. It's an old joke but it can raise a cheap laugh. At the beginning it helped us to see it that way, especially since Dad kept insisting he still loved Mum but wasn't *in* love with her. 'He loves Mum but wants to fuck Lisa,' Daisy had impatiently revealed to me when I was eleven.

Dad gently takes Lisa's hand and presses the other tenderly against her cheek. 'You have to eat. It's so important to keep your strength up.'

Lisa's sleeve rides up and I see bruises and tiny puncture marks on the inside of her elbow. So far I've only been allowed to use a grapefruit to practise taking bloods but I recognize the signs instantly. *Fuck, she's pregnant*, I realize, trying to work out how old Dad will be when the baby is my age. Sixty-five. Must be IVF. Or a donor. And that's assuming Dad isn't firing blanks. I start to panic that if I take the baby out for a walk people will assume that I'm the father. And if I have a baby with Connie then it will be an uncle before it's even seen daylight. *Good detective work, Dr Rankin*, I congratulate myself. Then I berate myself for only thinking of me, because it's Mum who has most to lose in this scenario. I wonder if Daisy realizes. Maybe that's why she was trying to get in touch. To warn me. Daisy always looks out for me.

'Lisa and I have something we want to share with you,' I hear Dad announce. He puts his arm around Lisa and her top slides off her shoulder to reveal a bony shoulder blade. Lisa smiles. They both have tears in their eyes.

I sit back in my seat, smug that my diagnostic skills are showing such early promise. Dad clears his throat and looks down at the tandoori chicken. I nudge Daisy with my foot and nod my head to indicate that I know what is coming next.

'I have asked Lisa to marry me and she's said yes,' Dad says. His voice is all gravelly.

'We're going to do it in Norfolk. Just a small thing, for close friends and family. We'd really like it if both of you would come,' Lisa says. 'Rex and Ava would love to see you again. It's been a long time.'

Like hell they would, I think, as I try to absorb this unexpected news.

'Don't decide now,' Dad quickly intervenes.

I look at Daisy, waiting for her lead, but it doesn't come. She always has more words than me. Even if she's not talking they're running like a loop in her head, whereas I didn't speak until I was three years old. I wonder if it's a tactic. Her mouth looks as though she's trying to say something, but no words come out. I glance over at Daisy.

'Congratulations,' I say finally, attempting to fill the vacuum with enthusiasm.

'Oh yes,' says Daisy vaguely. 'Well done.'

My phone vibrates. It's Connie. She sends a Snapchat of my skeleton wearing her clothes. It's dressed in a peach-coloured shirt, buttons undone so you can see her bra, and a short skirt. One of its arms is draped around her naked body, the other holds up the skirt to give me a flash of black knickers. Ten seconds and it's gone. No time to take a screenshot. I feel breathless. I have to go. Carlo must have let her into the house. I don't trust him. He's a horny bastard.

'What's up?' asks Daisy.

'It's the curry,' I say, using my hand to fan my mouth. 'It's too hot.'

I scoop a spoonful of prawn korma from the dish on the table to speed things up but quickly realize I have taken too much. Half slops on to my already overflowing plate so I attempt to tip the rest on to Daisy's.

'No, Max!' She grabs my wrist away so violently that the prawns spill on to the tablecloth instead.

There is something foetal about their appearance that makes me feel slightly sick. Or maybe it's because they remind me of what's going on in Lisa's uterus. But actually it's because Daisy's small hands are squeezing my wrist so tightly that blood pools in the tips of her fingers.

'What the fuck!' I say.

'Stop it, Max,' commands Dad, who thinks we are fighting because that's what we used to do when he last lived with us and he enjoys playing the role of responsible parent instead of being Mum's understudy.

26

We have attracted the attention of the people on the next-door table. *You are such a loser,* I think. It's a calm thought, though, as if some underlying truth about Dad has suddenly revealed itself.

'Let me put it on your plate, Daisy,' I persist.

I am easily stronger than her and manage to tip the rest of the prawns on top of the small mound of saag gosht. She recoils. I see her lips move again. This time I know what she's saying because it's so familiar. *Three is a good and safe number.* There are now four mounds of food on her plate.

'Three is fucking irrelevant, Daisy,' I plead with her. 'Three is a big pain in the arse.'

'What's going on?' Dad asks. He always gets more demanding when he feels excluded. 'Tell me what's going on!'

'Would some of my drops help?' Lisa asks.

'We need to go,' I say abruptly.

Daisy is already out of her seat. I grab her jacket from the back of the chair, take her by the arm and leave the restaurant. I feel bad for Dad and Lisa, for trampling over their big moment.

'Sorry,' I shout back, 'let me know as soon as you have a date.'

We go into the street and walk for ten minutes until we find a bench outside the pub where we usually have the Bloody Marys. I am nettled with myself for not second-guessing Daisy's reaction to Dad and Lisa's news and in turn irritated with them for their clunky timing. At least they managed to keep quiet about the baby. Luckily it's a clear night. I instruct Daisy to look up at the sky and stare until the stars start to reveal themselves. I run through a few of the biggest constellations, including Cepheus and Ursa Major, and check her breathing is returning to normal. It's a well-rehearsed routine.

In *The Hitchhiker's Guide to the Galaxy* Douglas Adams says the cruellest thing you can do is show someone their exact place in the world, but when Daisy was ill I discovered that the opposite was true. She needed to be reminded of her insignificance in order to diminish the thoughts in her head, which told her that bad things would happen to the people she loved if she didn't do a million and one crazy things to protect them every minute of the day. It was as if she thought she possessed superpowers.

'I can't go through this again,' she sighs.

'Nor can I,' I say. And I absolutely can't. I suddenly imagine myself dead and a group of students, including Carlo, dissecting my body, trying to work out what has killed an otherwise perfectly healthy young man. But although I obviously haven't completed my medical degree, as far as I understand, no one can die of guilt. If you could I would have been dead long ago.

Carlo would probably talk about something completely banal like my dick size. It's such a funny thought. I think about sharing it with Daisy but it occurs to me that talk of dead bodies might trigger her bad words routine. I'm hoping like fuck this is a small relapse rather than some new reality.

'This is how unimportant you are, Daisy,' I say, pointing at the sky. 'You are not God. Nothing you do makes any difference to the way things eventually pan out. Nothing is your fault or responsibility. You don't have the power to make bad things not happen.'

'Can you say that again, please, Maxi?'

'No,' I say firmly, because she will make me repeat it three times. 'Do you know that Cepheus has the biggest black hole known to mankind at its centre?'

'Why didn't you answer my calls?' she asks calmly, still staring up at the sky.

'I was busy,' I say. I explain that I have girl trouble and a big test coming up on pathogens.

'We'll always be there for each other, won't we?'

Her anxiety has passed and now I'm itching to get back to Connie.

'Dad and Lisa getting married is no big deal, Daisy. They've been together for seven years. I don't think Mum will even mind that much.'

'I don't really care about Venus and Adonis,' she says, using her old nicknames for Lisa and Dad.

Then what am I doing here? I want to ask her.

When I finally arrive home Connie has gone. Carlo says she didn't say goodbye. Which implies that she said hello. I want to ask him if he tried to make a move on her but don't want to show him how insecure I feel. She doesn't get in touch with me all that day or the next. And in fact it's another week before I hear from her again.

3

Rosie

Long history. Poor outcome. It's a simple rule of thumb really. The first file sitting on my desk at Monday's clinic is so thick that there are now three separate folders stapled together and test results from various scans spewing out of the side. I recognize the name on the front right away. *Laura S.* Doctors aren't meant to have favourites but those who deny it are either lying or have an empathy deficit.

Some patients stay with you after they have left the consulting room either because there is an aspect of their illness that is particularly interesting – an anomaly or rare mutation of a tumour, for example – or because despite having had a whole pile of shit heaped on them they manage to retain a sense of humour and dignity. Laura S. belongs to the latter group. I learn more from most of my patients than they ever learn from me.

The day after Nick left me seven years ago (I found out on a Monday evening) Laura S. was the first patient I saw the next day. Nick had pleaded with me not to go to work that morning – mostly, I think, because he had booked a day off, anticipating it would be our last one together. *Big mistake to plan too far into the future*, I told him in between sobs, as the awful realization dawned that he had just completely sabotaged the one I had planned for us.

He kept repeating that we needed to put our affairs in order. *Are you dying?* I had asked. Everything he said sounded as though he was reading from a bad script. He needed space. *Don't we all.* He wanted to find himself. *That's a luxury unique to adolescence.* Our marriage had been over for years. *Then why hadn't I noticed?* He didn't mention Lisa once and I couldn't bring myself to discuss her betrayal with him. She had been a part of my life even longer than Nick. The week before this we'd even gone out together with a group of girlfriends and ended up in a karaoke bar duetting 'Sisters Are Doing It For Themselves', which I guess in a way she was.

It was too early for anger so it must have been survival instinct rather than petulance that propelled me towards the hospital that day. I told no one at work what had happened, although I went to the canteen for lunch with my team as usual and listened to them chat about who was sleeping with who and the worst mistakes they had made with patients. I didn't call any friends because who would I go to in a crisis apart from Lisa? Nick and I had agreed to tell the children together that evening because I wasn't sure I could find the words to explain what had gone wrong when nothing made sense. And there was something up with Daisy. She had been excluded from school a few months ago after an awful incident involving Lisa and Barney's daughter, Ava. The less said about that the better. Of course I didn't appreciate it at the time but the worst was to come with her.

Anyway, that morning in late January, Laura S. had sat in front of my desk with her husband waiting for her biopsy results. I had to tell her that not only was the tumour cancerous but it had already spread into her lymph nodes, so she would need her axillary lymph nodes removed as well as a mastectomy. This would be followed by months of chemotherapy and radiotherapy. The news was worse than I had anticipated.

'What would you do if you were in my position?' she had asked, when I outlined the treatment possibilities.

I gave her my professional opinion. She thanked me. And I knew right then that work would save me. Even if I had failed at everything else, I could still do my job. If Laura could face up to the challenges that lay ahead of her then surely I could too. The reason I want to explain this is that since then I have always irrationally associated Laura's survival with my own.

And now, having outlived the medical odds once, Laura S. is sitting in front of me again with her husband. But this time I have to inform her that the cancer has come back. I realize as soon as I look at the bone scan. The Swiss cheese appearance is a dead giveaway. And even before I check the blood results I know her calcium levels will be sky high.

It is the worst kind of news to deliver and I want to answer all of their questions as comprehensively as possible. Her husband always takes notes in a small exercise book with extra-wide lines, the kind children use when they are learning to write letters. But I notice this time that his pen isn't moving. Instead he is pressing hard on the page, tracing the same circle over and over again. He understands what this means. I feel as crushed as he does.

After this I catch up with my team in the radiology room where they are looking at MRI scans. The consultant radiologist, Deborah Goff, is one of the best there is. She's been part of my team for twelve years and I count her as a close friend. I blink as my eyes adjust to the darkness and join the back of the group staring up at the large screen on the wall. The first time I saw a radiology room as a medical student it was as mysterious as the control room at NASA. Now I can read the superhighway of fluorescent green and pink veins within seconds. I know right away that the barbed edges and opaque centre of the tumour under review mean that it's very likely to be malignant.

One of the new registrars, a high-achieving Oxford graduate, is in the middle of presenting the case. I have noticed that her fear of getting something wrong is seriously messing with her clinical judgement. I have spoken to her in private a couple of times about how we learn more from what we get wrong than what we get right, but it hasn't helped. I quoted from *Lady Windermere's Fan*: 'Experience is the name everyone gives to their mistakes.' But she didn't laugh.

Her first consultant has a reputation for being brutal and she's still traumatized. To her left is someone I don't recognize, most likely a trainee on rotation in oncology. I vaguely remember signing some paperwork. The way his T-shirt hangs down below the back of his scrubs reminds me of Max.

'What do you think?' Deborah asks.

'Clinical breast examination and more mammographic views?' the registrar tentatively suggests.

I encourage her to expand on her answer because she is partially correct. She jumps. She obviously hadn't heard me come into the room. She looks at me and then down at the clinical notes again. She's too hard on herself.

'Any other ideas?' I ask the group.

'Needle or surgical biopsy,' the man to the left of her replies confidently. 'As quickly as possible. The spicules are a dead giveaway.' Then he apologizes for his careless use of the adjective.

It reminds me of when Daisy was ill and used to try to neutralize bad words with good ones and how I only noticed when Max started referring to his favourite band as The Lifers instead of The Killers. I can almost laugh about this now. Almost.

As he goes on to describe the cloudy centre of the tumour I realize that I recognize his voice. It's the way the tone goes up at the end of a sentence in that slightly irritating American way. Deborah switches on the light. And suddenly StanTheMan is standing between Deborah and the trainee registrar, bathed in neon light from the screen, so he looks like a celestial vision. Except I can tell from the name tag on his scrubs that in fact he is called Ed Gilmour. So much more prosaic.

'Well done, Stan,' I say, giving him a slow clap. No one notices I get his name wrong apart from him.

'He's an F2, doing a six-month stint with us in oncology,' the registrar explains, also forgetting his name.

Not if I can help it.

Ed holds out his hand for me to shake it. 'I look forward to getting to know you better,' he says stiffly, then has the good grace to blush because few men know me as intimately as he does. He nervously runs his hand through his thick dark hair and holds my gaze for a beat too long.

It strikes me as strangely fascinating that something that is meant to be as precise as an algorithm on a dating site has the capacity to create so much chaos. After all, science is meant to create order. To be fair on Ed, he looks as appalled as I feel.

This goes some way to explain why I still haven't opened the brown envelope that I found stuffed through the letter box as I left home this morning. And why I didn't question how it had arrived when there was no mail at the weekend, or notice the fact it was postmarked two weeks earlier.

It is still sitting at the bottom of my bag after work as I head to the café at the Wellcome Collection museum to meet the person previously known as StanTheMan. We have met here every Thursday for the best part of five months before heading off to a standard room at the Travelodge in Farringdon. The ratio between time spent at the café and time at the hotel has dwindled and now we sometimes skip the drinks part altogether. Today we'll bypass the hotel bit because I am about to tell him that not only does he have to find a way to ask to move to a differ ent department, but that we can't see each other any more.

One of the best decisions I made when my friend Josie persuaded me to embark on this Internet dating malarkey was to always meet people here for the first time: if the conversation flounders or there's no hint of physical attraction you can head for the permanent medical collection where it's really easy to accidentally lose someone.

Especially if you hide behind the model of the obese man. And you can tell a lot about a man from his reaction to the porcelain fruit containing erotic scenes. Nervous laughter, confessions about foot fetishes, immediate propositions of anal sex. I've heard them all. It's pretty brutal out there.

When we first got a match online and had got through the preliminary chat, Ed had blindsided me by suggesting we meet here before I did. Strictly speaking I should have turned him down because, at twenty-eight, he was three years younger than the lower limit I had set myself, but I allowed myself to be swayed by this coincidence. Although of course I now understand that it was the metadata that made the connection between us rather than some beautiful synergy.

As I walk into the café and look for him at our usual table in the corner beside the gift shop, I berate myself for not realizing earlier that we share similar professional backgrounds. Looking back there were some pretty obvious clues: he talked about working shifts – and judging by his clean fingernails he obviously wasn't doing manual labour – and he used acronyms a lot. For example, when I accidentally revealed to him where I was born he asked if I was NFN (Normal for Norfolk).

'Stan,' I say dryly, sitting down in a chair beside him.

'Present,' he says, pushing a furry replica of a sperm cell into my hand. 'To say sorry. It seemed appropriate.'

I don't say anything but I do think how much I will miss the way he looks at me, all seductive tease, and the way he makes me feel when he fixes me with those grey-green eyes. The best is always left unsaid.

'Come on, Rosie. Not everyone uses their real name on Tinder,' he gripes. 'You don't.'

'Rankin is my married name and I'm called Rosie in real life.'

'Shit,' he says, shaking his head. 'I thought you might be married. I'd noticed your Caesarean scar. But then I saw you don't have that white line where you've taken your ring off so I couldn't work it out. But your skin is so pale everywhere. Especially your gorgeous arse.'

He slips his hand in the back pocket of my jeans and starts tracing circles. I allow it to stay there because I am about to end our relationship and I'd like to squeeze out one last moment of pleasure. He leans over to kiss me. I sit back in my chair.

'You've noticed this with other women?' I ask. 'The white line?'

'We're not exactly in an exclusive relationship, are we? So of course I'm seeing other women, and I guess some of them are in other more, er, formal kinds of relationships. You've got a husband, for God's sake.' He pauses. 'Now I have to feel bad for him. It's one thing suspecting but it's another knowing.'

'Don't,' I say, putting up my hand. 'Really don't. We're divorced and he moved in with my former best friend after he left me.'

'Grubby,' he says. 'So why do you use your married name?'

'I don't want any of my patients coming across me.'

'Why would your patients stalk you on Tinder?'

'I mean their husbands. If I came across their husbands then I would know something my patient doesn't know

37

and I would feel really sorry for her, and pity takes away dignity. I learnt that one the hard way.'

'You've thought this through a lot, haven't you?' he says.

'I read a fascinating piece of research,' I say. 'Twenty per cent of men leave their wives when they are sick, whereas only two per cent of women leave their husbands. It's a big problem.'

'God, I wish I'd realized you were a medic earlier. There are so many things I could have asked you. You could have helped me revise for my exams. That's why I was late sometimes. I've had a big struggle with haematology.'

'In that case, I'm glad I didn't,' I say, deadpan.

There is a lull in conversation. We have learnt more about each other in the past ten minutes than we have in the previous five months. It's a lot to absorb. We catch each other's eye, which is always dangerous.

'What did we use to talk about?' I ask, without looking away.

'We didn't do too much talking, Rosie. You seemed keener on the fucking part, and given my time constraints I was pretty happy to avoid the preamble.'

Harsh but true.

'So are you trying to get revenge on the male species by sleeping with as many men as possible without forming a lasting bond with any of them?' he asks, sounding curious.

'I don't feel vengeful towards you,' I say, pondering this idea. 'In fact, I feel quite grateful. It wasn't that well thought out. I want uncomplicated relationships with people without getting attached to anyone in particular.

After what happened with Nick, I don't trust my judgement any more.'

I don't tell him that my daughter was so ill with an anxiety disorder that for the best part of two years I didn't dare go out at night.

'Do you have any other regulars?' he asks.

'No,' I lie.

'And are you really forty?' he asks.

'Forty-six,' I answer. 'You?'

'Twenty-eight,' he says. 'You're the oldest woman I've ever slept with.' Then he realizes what he has said and attempts to backtrack. 'I mean you don't look the oldest. You're in pretty good shape.'

'Do you have many points of comparison?' I ask. 'You need a pretty big cohort to draw that kind of scientific conclusion.' Now he is completely on the back foot.

'My mum,' he says. 'But she's had four children.'

I burst out laughing. It is a ridiculous situation. I get up to go to the toilet. When I try to take my bag, he removes his hand from my pocket and puts it on top.

'I want this as collateral. You might do a runner.'

I allow him to keep the bag but take my phone. As soon as I am alone in the cubicle I log on to Tinder to see what's going on. Someone has messaged me. He's more age appropriate but I reject him because he uses emoticons. My phone beeps. There's a message from Ed: *Hope u not right swiping.*

I go back to the table and suggest we take a walk around the permanent collection.

'Too dangerous,' he says. 'You'll try to lose me there. Although at least I know where to find you now.'

'It's over, Ed. It can't go on.'

'What's over?' he asks in a faux innocent tone.

'Our relationship,' I say, exasperated that he is making this difficult when the outcome is so self-evident.

'If we don't have a relationship, how can it be over? It's an interesting philosophical question.'

'You know what I mean,' I say sternly, leaning towards him.

'You mean you don't want to fuck me any more,' he says loudly, so the people at the table beside us mutter disapproval. 'But we're so good at it. We've passed the sexual compatibility test.'

'That's enough,' I say in the same way I used to reprimand Daisy and Max in public to avoid making a scene. 'You need to ask to be transferred to another department. I can't have you working on my team.'

He gets up to go, and as soon as he leaves I feel a familiar sense of loneliness. Then I notice the letter that was in my bag lying on the table. He must have taken it out. The label where the address was written has been ripped off and the seal on the envelope is broken. I look inside and pull out two crumpled sheets of paper and start reading.

4

Nick

I usually prefer to write down a shopping list but I know better than most that negative emotion enhances memory function. And Lisa's diagnosis has certainly left a big scar on my cerebral tissue. I am still reeling. So when I get to the organic food store I have no problem recalling the exact ingredients she has requested for the juicing diet she believes will make her well and I believe will kill her. *Guava, Guanabana, Cassava, Curly Kale* . . . my recall is as flawless today as it has been each day since she started this hopeless regime.

This morning Lisa announced she wants us to spend our honeymoon at a clinic in Mexico that specializes in offering false hope to the terminally ill, and it is a measure of how much I love her that I have agreed to go along with this. I won't be telling my colleagues. So after our wedding at the end of the month we are off to Tijuana, heartland of the Sinaloa cartel, where she will undergo two weeks of intensive juicing and enemas, as recommended by Gregorio, her recently anointed spiritual healer. It's not exactly how I imagined life as newly-weds, but then nothing with Lisa has ever been predictable.

Last night I showed her a photo of two naked bodies

hanging from a bridge on the road from Tijuana airport but she said the one thing about knowing you might die is that becoming collateral damage in a drug turf war holds no fear. *What about me?* I wanted to ask. But I managed to resist because the question made me sound too much like myself. I'm finding it difficult to disagree with someone who is simultaneously preparing her wedding and her funeral with the same meticulous attention to detail that she applies to all areas of our life together. Lisa wants me to sing 'Happy Ending' by Mika at both. I have agreed because I will do anything for her and it's a song that has special meaning for us.

I have made many mistakes but falling in love with Lisa most definitely isn't one of them. She is the love of my life. Everything I am now she has made me. I have told her this every day since we have been together. I have learnt a lot from my first relationship. My ex-wife once said that one of the main reasons our marriage failed was because I intellectualized emotion rather than feeling it. I have tried to prove her wrong ever since.

'Can I help you, sir?'

I am aware that someone is trying to communicate with me. His hipster beard threatens to devour his mouth and, although I see his lips move, it is as if someone has turned down the volume and all I can hear is the voice in my head telling me that the woman I adore might die and there is nothing I can do. I wonder if this is how Daisy used to feel when the same mental flotsam kept washing up on the shores of her subconscious all day, every day. But of course this is different because my worry is real. I can't accept this is happening to us. I am going through the stages of grief and am stuck on disbelief.

Daisy's thoughts were about totally improbable events that most likely would never happen, like Rosie and Max being attacked by burglars wielding kitchen knives. I never featured in her obsessions, something I've tried not to take personally. I suddenly remember how, when she stayed with us, she used to attach a note to her pyjamas that said *I only appear to be dead*, because she was so afraid someone might think she had died in the night and bury her alive. Every evening before bed Max had to pledge three times that he would stick pins in her toes before allowing any undertaker to remove her body. Sometimes I wonder how Max has ended up being so well adjusted after everything Daisy has put him through.

'How can you be absolutely sure the watermelon is organic?' I ask the beard, wondering if my voice sounds as muffled to him as it does to me. People talk of having out-of-body experiences when they are in shock but I am pretty sure I am having an inner-body experience.

'We source everything directly from producers,' he explains.

It strikes me as curious that parallel to a world where women are required to be as hairless as pre-pubescent girls, the men they date now all look like cavemen. I'm transfixed by his womanly lips. They are as full and purple as the organic plums he is putting into my recyclable bag.

'We know each one by name.' He looks down at a label. 'This one is produced by Angel Gurria on a finca near Tijuana in Mexico.'

'What a coincidence! I'm going there on my honeymoon at the end of the month,' I say. 'Maybe I should go and check him out.'

'Cool,' he smiles. 'Congratulations.'

'Do you have any idea how much water there is in the average watermelon?' I persist.

He looks a little surprised. His mouth puckers into a perfect 'o' as if he is about to whistle.

'Ninety-three per cent,' I reply.

He whistles. 'That is a whole lot of *agua*,' he says. 'I guess Señor Gurria must have a good irrigation system.'

'So to be truly organic, the water used for irrigation would have to be fucking Evian,' I continue. The beard quivers. I feel bad immediately because he is good-natured, like Max. *Simpático*, I say to myself, irritated that he has infected me with his habit of peppering the conversation with Spanish words. I lean over the exotic fruit section, elbows resting on a couple of watermelons. 'Did you realize that human excrement is one of the most widely used fertilizers in Latin America?'

'Maybe the excrement is organic?' he suggests.

I assume he's joking. But we live in a culture where people believe in total quackery so it's possible he might think eating shit is healthy. When I laugh he takes a step back and says something else that sounds like birds whispering. People aren't used to even low-level aggression in organic food shops. Lisa would probably say it's down to all the yoga and meditation but I would argue that the mostly female customers look too carbohydrate deficient to protest about anything. Anorexia has been rebranded as clean eating. I doubt they consume the food they buy, apart from the seaweed. Frankly it all makes me want to eat a rare steak and chips cooked in goose fat.

A woman appears. She's his manager but she could be

the same age as Daisy. Or Lisa. I find it difficult to tell how old anyone is nowadays.

'Can I help?' she asks.

'I need to know whether the watermelon is properly organic,' I say. 'My fiancée has cancer and is on a very restrictive juicing diet. She can't afford to pick up a stomach infection from a bad one.'

The girl leans towards me across the counter. 'I'm so sorry,' she whispers.

I feel like crying and close my eyes to crush the pinpricks threatening behind my lids. She puts her hand on top of mine and squeezes my fingers. And yes, for a split second, I can see how a different man might exploit this situation to his advantage. I wonder fleetingly how that hand might feel around my cock but, contrary to what she later claimed, I wasn't trying to pick her up. Nor did I act in a threatening manner to her colleague. There is nothing more attractive to a woman than a man in extremis. After Rosie turfed me out women literally threw themselves at me.

'You realize no one recovers from cancer through juicing,' she says.

'I do,' I nod. 'But I guess everyone is entitled to hope.'

I walk with purposeful aimlessness for a while after this. The watermelons are so heavy that my arms feel as though they are being pulled out of their sockets and I hear myself panting like an old Labrador. I figure the exertion and stretching might help with the repetitive strain injury I'm getting in my wrist from chopping up nine kilos of fruit and vegetables every day. At least when we go to Mexico someone else will do the grunt work for us. I wonder whether we should go into the desert and try mescaline while we are there? Cactuses must be organic. And as Lisa keeps saying, she has nothing to lose.

Lisa has always been up for new experiences. It is one of the characteristics I find most attractive about her. She makes everything seem possible. Weekend in Copenhagen. Booked. Dinner for twelve. Cooked. Therapist for Daisy. Not that she gets any credit, but Lisa was the one who found the first therapist, even if he didn't work out. This is why I'm finding it so hard to come to terms with her decision not to have any proper treatment. Usually she has a solution to every problem. Rosie was always more conservative, someone who limited possibilities and saw problems where there were none. She's the kind of person who does things like unsubscribe from unwanted emails in the unlikely event she has any free time. She couldn't cook without following a recipe, and she applied the same methodical approach to love-making. Although I only ever mentioned this to Daisy's therapist, sometimes I think her illness might have been exacerbated by Rosie's uptightness and desire for control.

I pick up my pace and veer right down a side street. The early-morning light makes everything unnaturally vivid. I lurch from finding hope in the blood-red leaves of the Japanese maple to despair as I realize this might be the last time Lisa will experience autumn. The unseasonably warm sun shines in my eyes, making them water, and I don't see the small boy on a scooter careering towards me. He crashes headlong into the bag. There is a dull thud as his head hits a watermelon, which bounces into the road.

I notice the white stuffing leaching out of the boy's torn
blue anorak; the red blood from the cut on his hand as it
hits the pavement; the choking noise as he tries not to cry.
There is a drumbeat of wings flapping as a gang of pigeons
comes to fight over a bright pink piece of fatty bacon. I
get down on one knee to brush dirt and dust from the
boy's coat and offer him a prickly pear from my bag. He
takes it, turns it in his hands a couple of times, and scoots
away as fast as he can.

The watermelon lies on the road. It has split open. Its
inside is as fleshy as the lips of the man in the organic
store. For the second time that day I scrunch up my eyes
to stem the tears. In the space of a month everything has
turned from hope to fear.

When I recover, I realize that I am outside the main
door of the hospital where Rosie works. It's years since
I've been here and I'm confused about whether this is
where I was heading all the time. But it is obvious that
Rosie is the person I need to see more than anyone right
now. I tell myself that I have to let her know in person
about Lisa's diagnosis and our decision to get married. It
has to be in that order because the first piece of news will
soften the blow of the second.

I still carry the internal rhythms of Rosie's life and I
calculate that she will be coming to the end of her morning clinic. I can no longer recall her mobile number but
soon find it in my phone. I dial but it occurs to me that if
I announce my presence she might say she's too busy to
see me. No one can compete for attention with Rosie's
work. That's why she's so good at her job and so bad at
relationships.

I try to remember the last time we saw each other and am chastened to realize it was Max's last day at school, almost two years ago. We stopped doing family events together as soon as we split up. Her decision. Not mine.

When Daisy was ill, we communicated almost every day. We were at our best back then. Now it's months since we've even spoken on the phone. I think about the man at my memory clinic last week who had been married to the same woman for forty-five years but ended up moving back in with his first wife when he got dementia because she was the only one he could remember. Then it dawns on me that I won't ever be like this man because Lisa won't be around.

I go up the stairs into the old Victorian red-brick building and head towards the lift to take me up to the oncology department, checking the list on the whiteboard to confirm Rosie is the senior consultant on duty. I sit down and wait. It's less than five weeks since I sat with Lisa in a similar clinic in Norwich, trying to work out the prognosis from the expression on the doctor's face when our turn came. I called it wrong. The cancer had already spread into Lisa's bones, one lung, and there was something they didn't like on her liver. Aggressive seemed like an understatement. But it was manageable, if only she would accept their advice.

No one gives me a second glance. Everyone is too involved in the drama of their own lives to wonder why a solitary man carrying bags of exotic fruit and vegetables has appeared from nowhere at the end of clinic. I wait until every patient has been seen and head for the room with Rosie's name on the door. I have a brief internal debate about whether to knock, decide against it in case she says I can't come in, and then burst into the room with unintended strength to find that she isn't alone. Judging by the expression on the face of the red-faced young man sitting on the edge of her desk, he has recently borne the brunt of one of Rosie's searing put-downs. I still remember some of the things she said during our brief flirtation with mediation while we split up. ('It helps if I think of Nick as a collection of slowly deteriorating cells.' 'He intellectualizes emotion because he is incapable of feeling it.') There is a file on the floor with papers spewing everywhere. Seizing the initiative, I put down my shopping and hold out my hand to him.

'Hi, I'm Nick.' I smile sympathetically as he shakes my hand. *I know what you are going through*, I want to tell him.

'Ed,' he says, backing towards the door, obviously relieved I have provided the excuse he needed for an honourable retreat. He gabbles something to Rosie about coming back after he has read her draft of the presentation she is due to make during her keynote speech at the San Antonio Breast Cancer Symposium.

'Anything you think I should look at in particular?' He sounds completely flustered.

'The notes on the PI3K-mutation group,' says Rosie. 'Really interesting, Stan.'

She's got his name wrong but I don't want to embarrass her by pointing this out so I shoot the guy a sympathetic eye roll.

'So what can I do for you?' Rosie turns to me and speaks in the same professionally interested tone she might use with a patient.

Her politeness hurts because it highlights the distance between us. She crosses and uncrosses her legs but doesn't get up from behind the desk. She looks different but it's difficult to work out what has changed. Her hair is longer. Possibly a shade darker than I remember. Her face has softened and her skin has lost the sallow pallor it had when Daisy was ill. Or maybe it is simply that her complexion now compares more favourably with Lisa's.

'Do you remember that holiday where you insisted we should camp on the marshes and it rained so hard that we discovered Daisy and Max had floated out of the tent on an air mattress? They slept through the whole thing, didn't they? And then when I tried to make everything better by making bacon sandwiches, I used olive oil shower gel by mistake. So you took the bacon and washed it in the sea, but it was so salty we couldn't eat it.' I am taken aback to find myself awash with nostalgia. There aren't many opportunities for bacon sandwiches with Lisa. Especially now.

'Are you trying to do some test on the unreliability of flashbulb memories?' Rosie responds. 'To spot how our versions of the same event differ?'

She does that disapproving furrowed-brow expression that I used to call her signature look but instead of irritating me its familiarity is endearing.

'No,' I say, although a comparison of how divorced couples remember significant moments during the breakdown of their relationship would make for interesting and newsworthy research. 'I've been thinking a lot recently about when the children were small.' I pause and swallow a couple of times to disguise the catch in my voice. 'They were good times.' I remember how we used to have ridiculous

competitions over who could remember the most characters from *Thomas The Tank Engine* during long car journeys
and the time Daisy lost the car key in the mud on the
marshes in Norfolk and how Max had nightmares about
being trapped in a black hole.

'They were,' she says in a steady tone.

I wait for her reproach, but there is none.

'I read your paper about how memory shifts and
changes over time in relation to the bombing of the
London Underground.'

'Did you like it?' Even after all these years, Rosie's professional opinion still matters to me. I need her intellectual
approval. She remains the only woman I know who thinks
like a man.

'I thought it was very interesting that, within a year,
half the memories had completely changed,' she says. She
is distractedly opening and shutting the drawers of her
desk and peering inside.

'The purpose of memory isn't so we remember what
happened but what those memories teach us in terms of
how we react in the future,' I remind her.

'So what have you learnt, Nick?'

She looks up at me and I swear she can see the darkness
in my soul. I wince. She knows me too well. I immediately
regret fantasizing about the girl in the shop. She smiles
and I realize what is different.

'You've had your teeth whitened, Rosie.' I'm amazed.
Unfortunately Rosie never showed any symptoms of
vanity when we were together.

She stops smiling. 'What is it that you want, Nick,
because I'm pretty busy?'

I'm saved by the return of the junior doctor. He can't find the slides that he needs to load on to the computer for Rosie's presentation.

'Excuse me,' says Rosie, getting out of her seat. 'I won't be long.'

She's wearing a pair of jeans that wouldn't look out of place on Daisy, and I note the junior doctor catching a glance of her arse as he holds open the door for her.

'Hey!' I hear the word form in my mouth, but fortunately Rosie and her colleague are too wrapped up in the missing slides to notice. The door closes. I check my phone to see if Lisa has called. She hasn't. I'm desperate to hear her voice but I don't want to disturb her in case she is sleeping. Our nights are as broken as they were when Daisy and Max were babies. Lisa finds it difficult to find a comfortable position because her stomach is so swollen from all the juice and she wakes up in the night terrified about what lies ahead. *No one should make any decisions at 3 a.m.* I tried telling her last night, when she was worrying that Daisy's awful reaction to the news that we were getting married meant we should cancel. I think we should tell all the children what is going on – especially Rex and Ava, Lisa's son and daughter – but she is adamant she wants to wait until after we get back from our honeymoon to keep life normal for as long as possible.

Feeling anxious, I get up and pace around Rosie's tiny office. The outer edge of the linoleum floor is coated with a thin line of greasy dirt where it nudges the wall. The windows are filthy. Books are piled on the floor because there isn't enough room on the shelves. It never ceases to amaze me how these clever and dedicated medics work in conditions more suited to battery chickens.

Rosie's bag is lying on the windowsill because there is nowhere else to keep it. I'm touched to see it is the same brown leather designer handbag I gave to her our last Christmas together. Judging by the pockmarked leather and grubby stains on the side it has had a tough life over the intervening years. I remember buying it because it had endless compartments and pockets that I thought would help her become more organized.

I can't resist a peek inside to see whether it has fulfilled its purpose. But I'm disappointed. There are medical papers muddled with make-up, loose coins scratching a pair of glasses without a case, unopened post and at least two receipts from the same Indian restaurant where I went with Daisy and Max the other night. It shouldn't surprise me. Rosie is a terrible cook. But still it hurts.

There is a loose bank statement, which confirms to me that her financial situation isn't quite as bad as Daisy and Max have intimated and she is making some money from private practice. She's almost certainly solvent enough to take them away in the summer without any handouts from me.

But it is a crumpled brown manila envelope deep at the bottom of the bag that captures all my attention. I take it out and examine the sender's address on the back and immediately recognize the large confident brushstrokes of Lisa's script. In my grief-stricken state, I assume it must be for me. Holding it against my chest I decide from now on to keep everything Lisa writes, from text messages to funny notes, because soon she will be gone and all I will be left with are the unreliable memories.

I think about the survivors of the London bombing

that I interviewed over a period of five years. At the end, when I presented the results of my painstaking investigation, a few of them became incredibly angry with me for pointing out the inaccuracies in their description of what had happened. They thought I was accusing them of lying. I tried to explain that every time you retrieve a memory there is a re-storage process that means it shifts and changes over time. Even when I played back my interviews with them they couldn't accept the results of my research. I am determined to avoid this with Lisa by retaining as much physical proof as possible of our relationship.

It's difficult for people to appreciate how memory is prone to distortion. 'I know what you did, Dad,' Daisy once shouted at me during a row in the car after Rosie and I had split up and I was dropping her and Max back home at the end of their first weekend with Lisa and me. She flew at me after I told them I would always look after their mum. I didn't challenge Daisy because by that time it was clear she was too ill for reason, even if it wasn't yet obvious what was wrong. Instead I asked her simply to try to remember where she was when we told her we were getting divorced and when she said the sitting room, instead of the kitchen, I pointed out her inaccuracy. Max backed her up but he was just trying to protect his sister.

Puzzled, I turn the manila envelope in my hands. Why would Rosie have a parcel that is meant for me? There is a mark on the front where the recipient's name and address have been torn off but no clue to their identity. I look at the date and see that it is postmarked around the time Lisa had her first appointment with Gregorio. This is significant. The seal is broken so I take out the wrinkled letter, note our address in Norfolk on the top right-hand side and start reading. I am taken aback to see that Lisa is writing to Rosie. *My dear Rosie*, to be precise. I hear Lisa's voice in my head as she outlines the exact sequence of events leading up to her diagnosis. *Place, ongoing activity, informant, own affect, other affect and aftermath*, I hear myself mutter as I skim-read the first page. Lisa's letter perfectly reflects the six stages of a flashbulb memory.

I am filled with compassion and admiration for her. Apart from divorce, she and Rosie have shared every significant life experience with each other for years and death is the ultimate rite of passage. I'm just a little taken aback that she didn't discuss this with me. I rummage around the envelope and immediately find a photo.

I pull it out. It's a picture of all of us taken in Norfolk on the last holiday our two families spent together. I don't remember the exact details of who is in it because I am too upset by the fact that Lisa's face has been completely disfigured so that I only recognize her from the black leggings and white T-shirt that she is wearing. It's not simply a few gashes, her entire face has been carefully excised, leaving a perfect white head-shaped space: Rosie has taken a scalpel to her.

For many years I hoped that Rosie and Lisa might resurrect some semblance of the friendship I helped destroy but I realize now this is impossible. Rosie knows that Lisa is dying but she still hates her. There is no hope of reconciliation. I hear footsteps in the corridor and quickly stuff the letter and the photo at the bottom of Lisa's bag. I never get to read the second page of the letter.

When Rosie comes back in, she finds me sitting in the

same chair, scrolling down through emails. I can't do any more small talk.

'I have some bad news, Rosie,' I say. I explain everything in great detail because this is what she would expect, repeating the same phrases in the letter to gauge her reaction. As I speak, Rosie's body slumps into the cheap office chair with the broken arm, as if she is melting. There is the occasional flash of shiny white teeth as her mouth drops open and she searches but fails to find the right words.

'I'm so sorry, Nick,' she says simply, when I finish.

'I wanted to tell you in person that we're getting married,' I say.

The reason I am explaining all this is to demonstrate that, although doctors have a reputation for honesty, Rosie is as capable of dissimulation as the next person. She's a good actress. I'll give her that.

5

Daisy

I'm in bed with Kit at Mum's house when it starts again. We've stopped staying at his place because I need to be at home as much as possible to keep an eye on her. It's been almost a week since she first read the letter and I'm still watching and waiting for her reaction. Mum betrays nothing and I plan only to step in if it looks as though she's going to see Lisa.

During the week it's pretty easy to keep tabs on her because she's at work. But weekends are more complicated. I have explained to Kit that she's upset because Dad is getting remarried and she's feeling lonely. It sounds perfectly logical and Kit hasn't asked too many questions. Besides, he's closer to his office here and it's his turn on the sofa in the sitting room at his flat so, all in all, he's happy about our new arrangement.

Kit is really, really, really understanding, which makes me feel really, really, really bad for not being completely honest with him. He knows nothing about the bad thoughts and the lost years. I appreciate he wouldn't tell me to get over myself like some people did. It's more I'm worried it might infect our relationship with bad juju. I don't want to contradict his opinion of me because I am the best version of myself with him.

The following are qualities Kit believes I possess: 1) I am relaxed, 2) I am resilient, 3) I am cool. And when I first met him I was all these things, which gives me hope that I can be them again, once this problem with Lisa is out of the way.

The sour times start Sunday morning after we have sex. Kit is big into female pleasure – pretty rare in the age of the fuck boy – and I don't get bad thoughts about sex with him, which is my only piece of luck with the whole illness, especially given the incident that triggered it all in the first place. I'm not going into that now, though, because, for sure, it will make this setback worse.

Anyway, we're shuffling Spotify when a song by James from the album *La Petite Mort* comes on. Kit casually mentions something about how weird it is that orgasm is called 'la petite mort' when nothing makes you feel more alive. Not long ago, we'd have had a long discussion about this, I would have agreed with him and we probably would have ended up where we began, with his face between my legs. Now I immediately tense, clamping his hand where it's resting between my thighs, a gesture he misreads for desire.

'I guess it's because of that feeling of total disconnection and loss of consciousness . . . when you think about it, sex and death is a big literary theme,' he says. He reads a lot for a mathematician.

'Sex and life,' I repeat three times in an insistent tone as if I really am involved in the same intellectual debate. He disagrees and starts talking about *Romeo and Juliet*, *Dracula* and Victorian literature.

I try to focus on what he is saying, and usually I would

have a lot of my own opinions, but the thoughts in my head are louder than the words coming out of his mouth. All I can think about is that *mort* means death in French. I need to neutralize the word as quickly as possible by saying the opposite word out loud but I can't remember how to say 'life' in French. If I don't say this then something bad will happen to Mum and Max, and it will be my fault. The ifs, buts and mights are disappearing from my world. An image of Mum, lying motionless, naked and covered in blood, plays out in my mind. At first it's very impressionistic but the longer I fail to find the opposite word, the more vivid it becomes until I am part of the tableau, holding a mirror over her mouth to see whether she is breathing, while all the time hearing my own breath become more and more irregular. The anxiety is like a fire inside, burning the little oxygen I have left in my lungs. Even though I can hear Mum whistling the theme tune to *The Archers* on the floor below, I am convinced something awful is going to happen to her. I think of the drawer of kitchen knives and how easy it would be for a burglar to stab her with one. It's the same old obsession from years ago. I must lack originality.

Kit continues to circle the inside of my right thigh with his fingertip, a sensation that he knows I usually find irresistible. But it's as if he is touching someone else. I cross my hands over my chest and discreetly tap each shoulder blade three times. *Give in to the thoughts and resist the compulsions.* I hear the voice of my old therapist, Geeta, in one ear. But the voice in my head is more powerful. *Please keep Rosie Foss safe*, I say at the end of each set. I do the same for Max. Then I include Kit. This is a new one. There's a short-lived moment of pleasure as I realize that Kit has become one of the people I care about most in the world followed by the anxiety that with this comes great responsibility for keeping him safe. *Eleven threes are thirty-three.* It's weird shit but each repetition makes me feel calmer. All I need to do now is touch an object that belongs to each of the people I love three times and then I have finished –

'Are you reciting times tables?' Kit interrupts.

Shit.

I must have spoken out loud. I shake my head, close my eyes so Kit thinks I'm meditating and start counting all over again from the beginning. But when I finish, the thoughts have only made a half-hearted retreat. I push away his hand with unintended aggression because I'm scared of my inability to regain control.

'How do you say "life" in French?' I ask, wriggling away and doing my best to sound completely normal. My voice has that high-pitched tone I get when my breathing is too shallow. *Please, please, please don't let me have a full-blown panic attack in front of Kit.* I make a deal with myself that if I get out of this one I will tell him everything. My heart is pounding so hard in my chest that I'm surprised he doesn't notice. No one's heart should beat this fast. I'm going to die of a heart attack, and then who will look out for Mum and Max?

'Why?' he asks.

'Just curious,' I pant inelegantly. My arms are starting to go numb and I'm slippery with sweat. I smooth down my fringe over my forehead so he doesn't notice. Kit screws his eyes shut with the effort of trying to remember GCSE French vocab. Then at the point where I'm about to give up hope he opens them.

'I think it's *la vie*, like *la vie en rose*.'

'*La petite vie, la petite vie*,' I gabble. He tries to kiss me just before I say it for the third time. I push him away. '*La petite vie*.' I sound almost euphoric. Because three is a good and safe number. But I can't tell him that.

'What the fuck?'

He looks hurt and I feel bad but I'm confident I can turn this around. I'm good at thinking on my feet.

'I'm experimenting with one of Dad's theories,' I say. 'He reckons if you say things out loud three times then you remember them better. The more things you are doing when you try to recall something, the greater your chance of success. Or something like that.'

I've done it. Mum, Max and Kit will be fine. This time. Now I simply need to divert the conversation so that Kit doesn't mention any trigger words again. I congratulate myself for getting over this. No pats on the back because this might trigger a whole new round of tapping. But the relief is tinged with a sense of shame. I want to return to being obsessed with him, not my obsessions. Because that's a game I can never win.

I look at the clock and mutter something about being late for work. Weekends are always my busiest time because the children I tutor aren't at school.

'Will you keep a vague eye on Mum when I'm gone?'

He lies back on the mattress, puts his arms behind his head and groans in an indulgent way. I want to tell him that he has a beautiful torso but it sounds too cheesy. So I silently appreciate the curve of his chest, the shadowy outline of the muscles along his arms and the perfect line of his clavicle. It's still a couple of hours until I need to be in Chelsea to tutor the Russian boy I took on a couple of months ago. But tempting as it is to get back into bed with Kit, after a blue-knuckle ride like this I need some time on my own.

'I feel bad spying on your mum,' he says. 'She might think I'm coming on to her if I keep checking up.'

'Don't worry, Mum doesn't do relationships any more,' I say, getting out of bed and throwing on yesterday's clothes. 'You're helping me help her. Look at it like that.'

'Just to be clear, Daisy. I'm not going to update you every hour this time. If you don't hear from me presume everything is fine,' says Kit.

It's a reasonable request but he doesn't understand that if he doesn't message me the thoughts will come back again. I wonder if he could put out the fire in my head if I told him everything?

'Sure,' I say, leaning down to kiss him. I pick up the eczema cream that I use to rub on the points where the skin gets red raw from the tapping and put it on the bedside table, making sure there is a perfect triangle between the lamp, eczema cream and Kit's phone. Isosceles. Not equilateral. He pushes his phone beside the cream and I move it back into position. There's a stalemate as we both hold it. Kit looks at me intently. I feel his eyes boring into my soul.

'What does the number three mean to you, Daisy?' he suddenly asks. My body tenses. He releases the phone, turns on to his side, head leaning on one elbow. 'Have you always done that or have I only just noticed?' There's no recrimination in his tone. Just curiosity.

'What do you mean?' I avoid looking at him.

'I only see it because I spend so much time looking for patterns in numbers,' he says. 'I don't mind if you don't want to talk about it. But if you like I could check the door is locked at night so you don't have to get out of bed in the cold three times to do it yourself.'

He obviously hasn't noticed that I've started checking the knife drawer.

I'm not sure how to respond so instead I find myself asking him if he wants to come to Dad's wedding with me. I could use a human shield when I meet Lisa's children again. Especially Ava, because I haven't spoken to her since The Incident all those years ago.

'I'd really, really, really like to,' he says.

I give him a long look. He is definitely teasing me. Maybe if I tell him he won't leave me. The same song comes on again and he quickly switches it off, complaining that Spotify needs to develop a new algorithm to make its shuffle function feel more random.

I walk to work, telling myself I need to clear my head. But the truth is I'm avoiding getting behind the wheel of Mum's car. I only mention this because one thing I have learnt is the importance of ruthless honesty. So I can admit I don't want to drive because I might damage Mum's car, which could cause her to have an accident when she uses it later. And then instead of getting on with my uni coursework, I will spend the evening double-checking on Google for accidents and hospital admissions in the area to make absolutely sure she hasn't come to any harm. Or calling around police stations. I have done all of these in the past. So even though it takes longer to walk, it will save time in the long run. There is method in my madness. Craziness is very subjective.

As I walk I run through my lesson plan for the Russian boy, eleven-year-old Oleg. Similes, metaphors and proverbs. Comprehension, creative writing and words that impress. He needs to improve his creative writing if he's got any hope of getting into one of the approved schools on his dad's very short and very aspirational list. If he succeeds, I get a bonus, which helps concentrate the mind when I sit in their large, lonely dining room with their large, lonely child, wondering what on earth I am doing there when I could be with Kit.

He didn't want to have extra English lessons with me. This is no great insight on my part. Oleg told me very explicitly at the beginning of our first session together. 'To lay my cards on the table and clear the air,' he said, rolling up the sleeves of his shirt and resting his chubby forearms on the dining-room table. 'My last tutor but one taught me those phrases before he had to clear the decks.'

'Well, I don't particularly want to teach you either,' I told him truthfully, rolling up my own sleeves. 'I would much rather have a proper job but because I cocked up my exams I'm still at university and have to earn money teaching English to spoilt rich kids like you.'

We both burst out laughing at exactly the same time, which made us crack up even more. A bond was formed. The following week, during school interview practice, I asked Oleg what his hobbies were. He had no idea what I was talking about. I tried to find the word in Russian on Google Translate but it didn't exist. So I told him that they were things that you did in your free time that gave you pleasure.

'For example, I like to read and listen to music,' I explained.

He shook his head sorrowfully and his fat cheeks wobbled endearingly. He said he didn't like either, and that his favourite pastime was eating. I tried to explain that food was a basic human need rather than a hobby.

'Just make something up,' I said finally, in exasperation.

'I don't have a good imagination,' Oleg replied apologetically.

'Look, what does your dad like to do in his free time?' I said. 'Parents and children often end up sharing the same hobbies.'

He thought for a second.

'Prostitutes,' he said. I looked at the expression on his big round face and could see only sincerity in his eyes.

'And your mum?' I asked, not sure what else to say.

'Chemistry,' he said.

'That's very interesting, Oleg,' I said, grateful to have something else to talk about. 'What kind?'

'She spends a lot of time investigating which chemicals stop you having feelings,' he explained. Then he paused. 'That's why I don't want to pass the exam to go to boarding school, Daisy. I need to be at home to keep an eye on her.'

So Oleg and I share something in common.

Things start to go wrong the moment I reach his house. I find my usual route in through the basement is blocked. Apparently 'some idiot' has broken the back-door key in the lock so everyone has to come in and out through the front door, a situation that is making Oleg's dad 'very anxious', explains the Filipina housekeeper. It makes me anxious because as far as possible, if I'm having the bad thoughts, I like to take the same route in and out of buildings. At home, for example, I always prefer to step into the house on my left foot. In normal times I can cope with changes in routine but this literally puts me off my stride.

The housekeeper tells me that Oleg's mother has already made her book in carpet cleaners because of the mess. Doesn't she have anything better to worry about? But I still have enough self-awareness to realize that my worries are even more absurd because they are about things that haven't even happened. This gives me a chink of hope that I might be regaining perspective. The house-keeper puts forward theories about what might have occurred and says that Oleg's dad was the first one to find the broken key. *Which makes him the most likely culprit*, I think to myself. When someone is murdered isn't the prime suspect the person who last saw the victim?

'It's very dangerous, Daisy,' she says. 'Anyone could have come in.'

I have been here enough times to realize her worries have more to do with Oleg's dad's anger issues than anything to do with security.

'He never goes in the basement,' the housekeeper explains, as she leads me up the stairs. 'What would he want with washing machines?'

'Maybe he was doing some money laundering,' I joke.

She looks puzzled. It's lost on her.

I find Oleg sitting at the head of the long mahogany

dining table. He looks up at me as I come in. His eyes have a mournful bloodhound quality and as I get closer I see they are bloodshot from crying.

'What's up, Oleg?' I ask.

'I didn't get in,' he says, utterly despondent.

'It's just one school,' I say, putting an arm around him.

'It was the maths, not the English,' he says. 'So you're off the hook.'

'Good idiom,' I observe.

I notice a mark on the side of his face and don't ask how he got it because I might not like the answer. He tells me that he will be sent to boarding school and his mother won't be able to cope without him. He leans towards me.

'I ran away,' he tells me conspiratorially. 'I was going to keep going until I collapsed because if there is something medically wrong I will have to stay at home, but I bumped into this man who was carrying a bag of watermelons and fell over just round the corner. I can't even run away properly.' He starts to cry again. 'I really hurt my head. My coat got torn. A watermelon went into the road and was crushed by a car and the man hit me.'

'He hit you?'

'He slapped my face and then he started crying. I told him it was okay and he cried even more. Then he gave me a piece of fruit.' He pulls something that looks like a prickly pear from his pencil case.

'A complete stranger hit you?' I question him. But I don't press him for more details because I'm so relieved it wasn't his father. 'That's such bad luck. But you should remember all the details and use them in your creative writing.'

This seems to make him feel a bit better. He pleads with me to read to him for an hour instead of doing any work. Oleg is too lazy to pick up a book himself but he loves being read to. I started a George Orwell novel a couple of months ago because it's a good one for him to talk about in school interviews. But now I curse myself because the title of the book contains my worst number and is one of its multiples.

'I can't read it, Oleg,' I tell him simply. 'I want to but I can't.'

Oleg stares at me through his red-rimmed eyes. 'Why?' he asks.

'It will make me feel so worried I won't be able to concentrate,' I explain.

'Then I will read it to you,' he says, reaching out to hold my hand.

This is a good compromise because it means I can run through my rituals while Oleg does the work. We move to a sofa at the other end of the room and Oleg snuggles in to my side.

'*Thoughtcrime is a dreadful thing, old man . . . It's insidious. It can get hold of you without your even knowing it,*' he starts.

My body goes into immediate high alert. Why on earth did I choose a novel about people reading your mind? I wish I could tell Kit because the irony would make him laugh. But of course when I picked this book I was in a better space. Which underlines the fact I am no longer well, which reinforces my anxiety.

I line up my pen, notebook and phone on the coffee table, fiddling around until I am sure the angles are correct. I start my rituals and finish at the part where Winston

Smith faces up to his worst fears in Room 101. Which reminds me of my worst fears about Mum so I have to start the rituals all over again. And we might have gone on like this for the whole hour and a half if Oleg's father hadn't come into the room as his son reached the final chapter.

'What's going on here?' he asks.

Oleg and I both jump, which makes it seem as though we have been caught doing something wrong.

'I'm reading a book to Daisy,' Oleg nervously explains. He sits stiffly against the back of the sofa. 'It's good for my vocabulary and comprehension skills. And diction.'

Nice one, Oleg.

'I'm not paying you ninety pounds for ninety minutes for my son to read you stories,' says Oleg's dad to me.

All I can think about is that 90 is a multiple of 3, which is a good and safe number. And it's only when I notice Oleg is crying again that I realize I have been fired. The only upside is that the basement door has been repaired and I can leave by my usual route.

After this I go into a café and do the online Yale-Brown Obsessive Compulsive Test to monitor my symptoms. It's the first time I have done this in years. But I realize I need to get a hold of this relapse before it takes control of me. At least, that was Max's advice. After the dinner with Dad and Lisa he suggested I go back to see Geeta, but that seems too much like early surrender. I am convinced this is a temporary problem that will be resolved when Lisa is out of the way.

My hands are trembling as I answer the first of the ten

multiple-choice questions. *How much of your time is occupied by obsessive thoughts?* 1–3 hours, up from last week but way down on my personal worst of eight hours a day. This makes question six easy because my need for symmetry means I have to spend exactly the same amount of time on the compulsions. The people who devised the test clearly hadn't thought through that one. The fourth question makes me pause for thought. *How much effort do you make to resist the obsessive thoughts?* Should I count the sub-rituals, the short cuts I try to avoid the big ones? At the end I add up my score: 24 out of 40, nudging the higher edge of moderate symptoms. Both numbers are a multiple of the number I don't like, which means I need to go through all the counting and tapping three times. So it takes me a while to get home. But at least I won't have to repeat them again when I'm with Kit. I love the fact that his name has three letters.

I am just enjoying this thought when Dad calls. I don't pick up. He calls again. I don't pick up. But the third time I have to. Because three is a good and safe number.

'Hey, Daisy,' he says, doing his best to sound casual.

I tell him that I'm on my way to teach and don't have much time for small talk. Then I feel bad when I hear the hurt in his voice as he tries to kick-start a conversation with questions about what books I'm reading for my course, whether I would like some money to buy an outfit for his wedding and how many students I have on my books.

'The sea is very warm for the time of year,' he says in desperation when I fail to respond. It's not that I want to make it difficult for him. My attention has been totally diverted to a headline in the *Evening Standard*: a patient with Ebola has been transferred to a London hospital where Mum sometimes has a clinic. So all my worries about her being in danger suddenly seem completely legitimate. I pick up my pace because I need to get home to research exactly how the virus is spread.

'I wanted to check you were okay, Daisy, about me getting married again,' I hear Dad say.

Heavy conversation alert. I want to get him off my back so that I can attend to more pressing issues.

'We . . . I . . . understand it's difficult for you and Max. I tried to find the right way to tell you but perhaps I should have waited until we were alone.'

He's obviously rehearsed this conversation and I try to behave like a proper audience but I can't stop thinking about how I'm going to persuade Mum to cancel her trip to Atlanta because I'm pretty sure it's an airborne virus.

'Lisa and I have been together for seven years so it can't come as a total surprise.'

Eight years, actually. I don't get into that because I've just remembered that the Centers for Disease Control website will have all the latest news I need about Ebola, and if I can get Dad off the phone I can check out the stats right away.

'It's fine, Dad,' I say.

'Really?'

'I don't care.' And I don't. Marriage isn't worth the piece of paper it's written on.

'And how is Mum? I went to see her at work to tell her in person,' he explains, as though this was an act of great courage.

'She hasn't said anything.'

He hesitates for a moment in that way he does when he wants to ask a loaded question in a casual way. 'Do you think she has any plans to get in touch with Lisa?' he asks. 'If she does, perhaps you could give me the heads-up.'

And then I realize he must know about the letter too.

6

Max

It's Monday afternoon, which means it's Anatomy. Carlo
uses the electric saw to cut around Jean's skull. Our tech-
nician has helpfully plotted the route with a circle of red
string. Everyone falls silent as the bone squeals with
resistance when the blade makes contact. Carlo doesn't
flinch and makes steady progress. He likes an audience.
Even though his hands are encased in tight blue surgical
gloves they never shake. Unlike mine. He has enviably
steady, sensitive fingers. I made the mistake of telling him
this earlier this year and he claims it has become his most
productive chat-up line.

As I lean in towards Jean I note that the kind lab tech-
nician has tried to remedy my botched dissection of her
optic nerve and her left eye has been securely repositioned
in its socket. But her lopsided glance reminds me of my
limitations. I have talked to my tutor about my self-doubt
and he says it's not necessarily a bad quality in a doctor.
Just as well, because I have a lot of it.

Carlo asks me to pass him a chisel so that he can remove
the layer beneath the skull, holding out his hand without
looking up, as if I'm his assistant. He correctly identifies it
as the dura mater. Our anatomy teacher instructs him to

use both the chisel and his fingers to remove it. It peels off like a swimming cap and there is a collective gasp as, magician-like, Carlo theatrically reveals Jean's brain. For me this was always going to be the money shot. The embalming fluid might have changed the colour and texture so it has the pale colour and waxy texture of a pickled egg, but nevertheless it is a stunning moment.

'Everything we are, every thought, every urge, is contained within this structure,' says the anatomy teacher. 'This was Jean's identity. This is the essence of our being.'

We stand in awed silence.

The teacher points out a deep inky stain that we have all missed in the dura. 'Note the middle meningeal artery. Anything out of the ordinary?'

'It's ruptured,' Carlo says, leaning in. 'You can see where the blood has leached into the dura.'

I envy his certainty.

'Correct. What does this tell us?'

'She probably died from a head injury,' I suggest. 'Epidural haematoma?'

'Excellent, Mr Rankin,' he says.

Aisha chips in, pointing out that the pattern in these kinds of injuries is that the patient at first can seem lucid and awake but this is often followed later by seizures, coma and even death as blood pools between the dura and skull. 'Like Natasha Richardson,' she says.

The anatomy teacher gets out a plastic model of the brain from his cupboard, puts it on the slab and starts taking it apart in layers. He asks us to identify each structure and describe its function. He leaves me till last, removing the final piece of the jigsaw, a small area lurking in the depths of the forebrain.

'Max, your turn,' he says. 'Any ideas?'

So no reprieve from last week's public humiliation.

'I think this area is the basal ganglia,' I say tentatively, wishing I could be more confident in my opinion. I pick up the section and turn it in my hands.

'Correct,' he says. 'Anything more?'

'It's the deepest, most primitive area of the brain, one of the parts we share with birds and reptiles. It responds chemically rather than rationally to error and threat and goes into overdrive in patients with Obsessive Compulsive Disorder.'

'Elaborate, please.'

'OCD is an anxiety disorder. Sufferers have uncontrollable intrusive thoughts that cause intense distress and perform repetitive, rigid routines called compulsions to try to neutralize the anxiety and prevent the obsession from actually happening. On some level they know the thoughts and rituals are irrational but they can't stop them. The more they do them, the worse the illness gets.'

Thank you, Daisy, I say to myself, staring at the basal ganglia in awe. Because if Daisy hadn't been ill, the basal ganglia would never have featured in my life. How can such a tiny structure have so much power? I see Carlo making vomit gestures in the background. He can't stand it when he's not the centre of attention.

'Okay, folks, that's all for this week,' says the teacher, looking up at the clock. 'Good work, people.' He covers up Jean with the green plastic sheet.

I will miss her when we are finished.

*

We all leave together. We're a tight group. I switch on my phone and feel a surge of joy when Connie messages to say she is waiting for me outside my flat. Nothing's ever planned with her. Everything is last minute. Until recently I assumed it had something to do with her job. All her talk of buying a flat, financial independence and long hours made me think she was involved in some white-collar slavery, like law or finance, and I have to say that when I finally got to ask her what she did last week I was completely taken aback to discover she works in an organic fruit shop. It forced me to re-calibrate several of my assumptions about her.

'I manage an entire department,' she volunteered, even though it wasn't my turn to ask a question. 'Tropical fruit and veg.'

Maybe she sensed my confusion at her lack of ambition. I didn't press her for details. Sometimes the less you know about someone the easier it is to project on to them the idealized version of how you would like them to be. From what I've witnessed, most relationships are destined for disappointment.

And for the first time in my life I'm enjoying being obsessed by one person. Carlo says I've got it bad and he's right. I'd like to be exclusive but Connie's not interested. I guess everyone wants what they can't have. Just look at Dad. He must have sweated bullets for Lisa years before they got it together. The difference with him is he always gets his own way in the end. Otherwise how can you explain that he's ended up living in Mum's childhood home in Norfolk with her best friend from secondary school?

'Do you want to grab something to eat?' Carlo asks.

It's an ongoing joke in our anatomy group how full-body dissection not only makes us all ravenous but also makes us crave meat – apart from Aisha, who is veggie. Usually we all have steak and chips at a café round the corner after our weekly session. I make an excuse about needing to go shopping for a wedding present for my dad and then feel bad when the others look disappointed.

'You didn't tell me he was getting remarried,' says Carlo.

I pull off my lab coat and stuff it in my rucksack even though it will make it stink of formaldehyde.

'It's pretty recent news,' I say.

'So is she hot?'

'She's pregnant, Carlo.'

'Pregnant women can be hot.'

I don't want to fuel his fantasies by getting into any detail.

'Do you like her?' asks Aisha.

I turn gratefully towards her. It's weird but no one has ever asked me that before. 'If she wasn't with my dad, I might. I mean I used to like her before they got with each other.'

'What's she like?'

I think for a moment.

'She's one of those people who keeps her eyes open even when she's swimming under water.' I don't know why I say this. It has nothing to do with what happened after the wedding.

'You mean she never relaxes?' questions Aisha.

I nod. 'She's always alert to the next opportunity.'

'I actually slept with my stepmother,' says Carlo, changing the tone completely. I'm relieved because I don't like talking about my dad and Lisa. 'It seemed like the best way to screw things up between her and my dad. She was closer in age to me than him anyhow.'

We all make suitable noises of disgust.

'You are such a closet psycho,' says Aisha.

'Nothing closet about it,' I say.

'C'mon, guys, just jokes,' says Carlo. 'What kind of fuck-up do you think I am?'

I'm still not sure whether he was telling the truth. My phone beeps. There's an email from Daisy. *Subject: Yale-Brown Obsessive Compulsive Test.* I'm knocked off balance, even though I am the one who suggested she check out her symptoms after the scene at the restaurant. *2* out of *0,* says the email. I can tell from the date that she did it yesterday afternoon. I realize the missing number must be four or a multiple of four and the best-case scenario is that it's 20 out of 40, which isn't disastrous but is high enough to confirm that the illness is creeping back. My head starts to throb. I think about the clot we found in Jean's brain today and imagine the blood pumping through my own middle meningeal artery and wonder if it could rupture from the pressure. I vigorously rub my scalp.

'You okay, man?' asks Carlo.

My phone rings. I know it's Daisy.

'Sorry, got to take this. I'll catch up later,' I say, trying to sound relaxed.

I pick up the phone just before it goes to voicemail and Daisy does that thing where she starts speaking before I've even said hello. This is what happens when she has the thoughts. There are just too many words running like ticker tape through her head.

Her main headline is her certainty that something bad is going to happen to Mum. Or me. But mostly Mum. She's worrying about burglars again and whether it's possible for someone to get into the house without tampering with the windows. She read somewhere that people can put cellophane over the glass panes so that no one hears them shatter. In the bad old days, I would have tried to talk it through with her, to convince her that neither Mum nor I are in imminent danger, by running through all the evidence to the contrary and checking every window lock in the house. I would have pointed out that Mum is most likely at work seeing patients, I am in town having finished the best anatomy class of the year, and the window panes are too small for a burglar to climb through.

I zone out for a minute, wondering how much patience Connie has. Now I know it's not work pulling her away from me, I wonder exactly what it is that she's doing when we're apart. That will be my one question for her this evening.

'Ebola . . .' I hear Daisy say.

My heart sinks.

'. . . she does a clinic in that hospital where the nurse is being treated.'

'So what,' I say flatly, knowing full well where this is heading.

'All it takes is one tiny cell.'

'She's not even on the same floor, let alone in direct contact,' I say in exasperation. 'And the infection control team will be in overdrive. It's not an airborne virus.'

'Are you sure? What happens if they change the bedding, it rests against the door of the lift and Mum touches it? One cell can survive on a surface for hours.'

'Remember the therapist said you shouldn't go on the Internet or read newspapers when you're feeling fragile,' I point out.

She doesn't reply.

'Daisy, just because you think something doesn't make it true.'

Silence.

'It's anxiety. Nothing will happen. Focus on your breath.' I immediately realize my mistake. This is what she wants me to say.

'Say those three things again, Maxi,' she pleads. 'Please.'

'I've told you I'm not getting into that again. Nothing bad will happen whether I say them or not.'

'Please. Just this once. Until I've got the better of it again. If you say it three times I'll be fine.' It's so tempting to give in but I know from previous experience that she'll be back on the phone within hours. Three, to be precise.

'Have you tried that thing where you recite a crap song in your head?' I suggest. 'How about that one about getting a house in Devon and drinking cider from a lemon?'

'I'm in too deep. That doesn't work. Please just say it three times.'

Her voice is so tight that she doesn't sound like my sister any more. And in a way she isn't because she's being hijacked by the illness. But this time I don't want to play the role of hostage negotiator or, worse, get taken prisoner with her.

'The therapist told you not to do this,' I say.

My phone beeps and I know it's Connie, asking when I'll be home. I imagine her sitting on the wall outside my flat with her skirt hiked up so that I can follow the curve of her leg from ankle to thigh. She will be getting impatient and then punish me with silence when I turn up late. I start to waver.

'You'll get back to your girl quicker,' says Daisy, reading my thoughts.

'Don't involve me in your compulsions,' I say, trying to stand my ground.

I remember something interesting that a psychology student in my flat once told me about a paper he had read on how the rituals performed by Nepalese Sherpas resemble OCD rituals.

'Listen, Daisy. It's really fascinating. They make one hundred miniature clay shrines, one hundred food cakes and one hundred butter lamps. It all has to be laid out completely symmetrically to placate and soothe their demons. Try to imagine it all in your head.' I need to get her out of this loop.

'Please, Max. Just say it three times. Then I'll let you go.'

'Have you told Kit what's going on? Can't he help you?' Surely it's someone else's turn to pick up the slack with Daisy.

'I don't want to spook him. I should have explained before it came back. But if I tell him in the middle of a relapse he'll think I'm a freak. I don't want to mess it up with him, Max. He's the only thing standing between me and the darkness.'

'Believing something doesn't make it real, Daisy,' I say

resolutely. I tell her I'm going to put down the phone in three seconds, forgetting her thing about the number three. 'Try that thing where you ping an elastic band round your wrist.'

'Three is a good and safe number,' says Daisy.

Fuck this shit, I think. *Fuck this shit*. I resist the urge to say it a third time.

'I'm going to put down the phone in four seconds.' That was cruel but I can't help myself.

'Don't! There's something I need to tell you,' Daisy shouts. 'I wanted to keep you out of this but I can't deal with it on my own. I'm sorry, Max.' I assume she means the bad thoughts. My phone beeps. I don't want to read her email because I can sense that however difficult things are right now, they are about to get a whole lot worse.

'Open it up,' she commands, going all bossy older sister. She can sense my reluctance.

I open the attachment. It's difficult to read on an iPhone, especially because it's a copy of a handwritten letter. I have to enlarge the image until the words are big enough and then the screen is so small that I have to tackle each sentence in halves. I hear Daisy doing her breathing exercises down the phone. I recognize Lisa's loopy scrawl right away and for a moment am pleased that she is finally writing to Mum after all these years. But as I piece together the jigsaw of words on the first page I start to feel like a dirty voyeur. Lisa has cancer. She wants to apologize to Mum. There's something she needs to tell her. I hear myself say the words under my breath until the initial shock has subsided.

'She's dying,' I hear myself say, over and over again, as

I try to digest the news. Every time I say 'dying', Daisy mutters 'living' under her breath. I feel sorry for Lisa and Dad because they are so happy together. I feel sorry for Mum because Lisa is asking too much of her. And I feel sorry for myself because I want nothing to do with any of this.

Also from a clinical perspective I can't believe I got it so wrong. I mean what kind of dumb fuck mixes up the symptoms of cancer with the symptoms of pregnancy? It's a lesson that stays with me for the rest of my career. Evidence always trumps instinct.

'Where did you get this, Daisy?' I'm halfway between angry and scared.

'I intercepted the letter on Mum's doormat when it arrived,' she says, waiting for me to congratulate her.

'Why did you open it?'

'Because I don't trust Lisa.'

I can't argue with that.

'Do you know what she wants to tell Mum, Maxi?'

'No,' I lie. Because of course I do – and of course now that I realize, it can't be allowed to happen.

'What do you think we should do?' asks Daisy.

'Has Mum read it?'

'Yes. I think so. I kept it for a couple of weeks and then put it back.'

This must be what it's like working in A&E. Trying to ask the right questions to reach the right conclusions as quickly as possible.

'I thought she was pregnant,' I say. 'I saw the puncture marks on her arm and I thought that was why they were getting married.'

'I think you need to brush up your diagnostic skills, Dr Rankin,' says Daisy.

Without realizing it she always hits the nerve. She's right. I will make a crap doctor.

'Where are you? I'll come as soon as I can.' Daisy's relapse starts to make sense.

'Meet me at Mum's,' she says. 'I'm so sorry, Max. I didn't want to involve you.'

Not as sorry as I am. I find a park bench and for the first time in years I sit down and bawl like a baby. I try to work out what I'm crying for and am besieged by different free-floating thoughts that I can't anchor firmly enough to give them any productive analysis. *Slow down, Max,* I tell myself. I close my eyes and try to slice the thoughts into sections, as if I'm in my anatomy class.

First up, I don't want to lose my sister to the plague of obsessions again. I realize she's probably been downplaying the symptoms. My sense of self-preservation is overwhelming and I wonder if I could transfer to a medical school someplace like Spain, or even further afield, for the rest of my course so I can escape this time. I wipe my eyes and google European universities to see where you can do cadaveric dissection and then start to feel guilty that I am letting Jean down by disappearing halfway through the job. I start an email to my tutor but even before I have finished the first sentence I realize that the weight of my responsibility for Daisy's illness means that I can't turn my back on her: I am as trapped as she is. I am totally incriminated.

I get up from the bench and start walking to Mum's house. I walk slowly because I never want to arrive. I am struck with guilt that I could even have considered leaving Mum alone to deal with all this. I get out my phone and start reading Lisa's letter again, trying to gauge its effect on Mum. Because I sure as hell know what Lisa wants to tell her and the consequences will make an epidural haematoma seem like a head cold. How could Lisa do this, knowing how Mum struggled to keep everything together and get her life back on track after Dad left her? But it's simple really: Lisa only ever cares about herself.

I press the doorbell three times so Daisy knows it's me. I feel small and powerless, like the small boy who used to ring this bell every afternoon after school, unsure what he would find when his mum and sister answered the door. It's the same sensation I had when I got caught in a rip tide in the sea in Norfolk the first weekend we went to stay there after Dad left. I remember being dragged out by a current so strong that I felt as if I was being sucked down the plughole of a bath. At first I tried to fight it, screaming and yelling in protest, raging at its force and my impotence. 'If you want something badly enough, nothing can stand in your way,' Dad used to say. That weekend what I wanted more than anything was Mum and Dad to stay together and as I struggled against the rip tide I realized Dad was full of shit. There was no point in struggle. Because some things are just stronger than we are.

Then it strikes me as I wait outside the front door. Lisa is like a rip tide. Calm on the surface. But capable of dragging us out into open water and leaving us to struggle against the current until we all sink under. She's going to die but she wants to take us all down with her. I had always argued with Daisy about Lisa's true nature but now I realize that I was wrong and Daisy was right. Just as I reach this conclusion I get a message from Connie telling me that Carlo has let her in.

7

Rosie

It's late when I leave work. I'm based at a different hospital today, trying to finalize the details on a Phase III breast cancer trial that I've been involved in for almost a decade and the trial assistant has just noticed that one of the patients on the list has ulcerative colitis, which automatically rules her out of the treatment.

I double-check the notes and see that it is Laura S. My heart sinks. How could I have forgotten her history when I recommended her, especially since her stomach problems made it very difficult to give her the first chemotherapy regime that I prescribed?

I'm not as hard on myself as I used to be when I make mistakes but I feel terrible for offering up hope where there was none. I've had my fair share of pipe dreams because when Nick first left me, I truly believed he would wake up one morning and realize he had made a terrible mistake. *Mid-life crisis. He's having a moment. He'll come to his senses*, my friends told me.

I will call up Laura S. to explain tomorrow morning. It's never a good idea to deliver bad news in the evening. I wonder if I should speak to her husband? He knows full well that immunotherapy was the last weapon in the armoury for her. Their inevitably reasonable reaction will make me feel even worse, especially if I have to deal with one of my less charming patients in clinic tomorrow.

Also, from a completely selfish perspective, this leaves us more than a couple of patients short for the trial and I wanted to have everything in place before my trip to Atlanta next month. Finding women who fit the exact criteria can be very time-consuming. The assistant hears me sigh and offers to go through the file of prospective candidates again in case we have overlooked someone.

'Thanks so much.'

'It's an easy mistake, especially when someone works the hours you do.'

Nevertheless I'm still feeling mightily preoccupied when I leave much later than anticipated. I can't resist a quick trawl through Tinder on the way down in the lift, even though there's a risk the wrist flick might betray what I'm doing to the other people in the lift. My reward is immediate distraction.

StanTheMan has messaged to see if we can meet up but I don't bother responding because Ed Gilmour has come to represent reality rather than escape. Since he insisted on continuing his rotation in my clinic I have attempted to establish some professional distance from him. He says it's too difficult to find another placement at short notice and that he really likes oncology. His personality fits well with my team but doctors are an observant bunch and, although he's discreet, he's too open to be completely reliable. Also when he isn't out with me I'm now wondering whether he's with someone else and I don't want to ever mind about anything like that again. He's definitely flirting with the insecure junior doctor.

There is pandemonium on the ground floor when I get out of the lift at the back entrance of A&E. Security guards stand at the door. Photographers and television crews are lined up outside; there are nurses wearing full-body plastic protective gear and goggles. I bump into one of my best friends from medical school, a top infectious diseases consultant, who tells me that someone who has contracted Ebola has been transferred to the isolation unit at the hospital.

'I'd go out through the basement,' she suggests. 'It's a bun fight out there.'

I take her advice and stop in the stairwell on the way down to check my phone again just as MickyJ messages:

I'll go straight to it: do you want to have sex with me?

He's a bit young to have memory problems. *We already did. Good punctuation, though*, I write back.

Rerun out of the question? he responds.

Correct, I say.

I try a couple of right swipes and read some messages from novices who betray themselves by trying to be overly interesting and asking pointless questions like *Wot are your life aspirations?* or *U like it when a guy speaks French to you?* and a couple of overtly sexual messages of the *I want to come in your face* variety that I simply delete. I message less than I used to because I have learnt along the way that no amount of digital chemistry can will physical attraction into being. Anyone who calls me *hon*, writes a lazy bio, posts only group pics, looks like he spends too much time in the gym or has kids in the picture gets an immediate left swipe. And to save time I have reduced the search distance to one mile.

Half an hour later I'm sitting at my table in the restaurant at the Wellcome Collection with a 33-year-old whose real name matches his profile. I'm fascinated by the way Leo looks like a younger version of Nick, although this isn't consciously why I chose him over the more age-appropriate advertising executive who also suggested meeting up tonight. I have grown to prefer younger men because they live in the present and generally require less worship. I'm very much not looking for a relationship.

Leo has thick dark hair that flops over his pale face and a long, angular physiognomy that creates interesting shadows in the mottled evening light. He is more worn than his photo suggests. There are dark circles under his eyes and lines that indicate he is quick to smile. In my experience it takes between ninety seconds and four minutes to know if you find someone attractive so I never order anything more than a bottle of beer and packet of peanuts in case I need a quick escape. Also I have discovered the hard way that limiting myself to one Corona is the best antidote to regrettable alcohol-fuelled sex. And there's none of that embarrassment about who should pick up the tab. Because even though I would define myself as a feminist there's still something disappointing about a man who lets you pay your way too readily.

The reason I want to explain this is that although my private life might appear chaotic and random, it is in fact as well worked out as the mathematical formula that brought me face to face with Leo in the first place. In my experience, married life is far dirtier and unpredictable.

Anyway, Leo is definitely a yes. I know this within the first two minutes when he mentions Richard Dawkins and vaginal steaming in the same sentence.

'Vaginal steaming?' I ask him, wondering if I've landed a fetishist. They tend to reveal their hand pretty quickly.

'One of my matches had read about it on Gwyneth Paltrow's website and ended up with a mugwort-flavoured second-degree burn on her fanny in the shape of a teacup,' he explains. 'Someone like Richard Dawkins should take on the pseudo scientists, but maybe even he lacks the cojones.'

I laugh so much that I forget Laura S. and the letter from Lisa. Leo tells me that he is a Dawkins fan and that the fact *The God Delusion* has been unofficially translated into Arabic and downloaded ten million times, mostly in Saudi Arabia, is one of the things in life that make him truly happy.

'What are the others?'

He raises one eyebrow and I break eye contact. I rest the bottle of beer on the table. He rips open the bag of peanuts and tips them on to the packaging. We lurch towards the pile at the same time, his hand brushes mine and neither of us pulls away. There is a familiar jolt of connection.

'So what's your motivation?' he asks.

I can tell he's got form by the questions he doesn't ask. He's not interested in the process, how many dates have worked out or how long I've been doing this. Best of all, he doesn't want to hear what it's like to walk in my shoes.

'I guess I like that sensation of feeling without talking,' I say. 'Like a conversation without words.' It's more complicated than that but I know from experience the worst dates are when people talk about their divorce, and it sounds too bleak to explain that having sex with strangers was the only thing that made me feel alive again after I thought I had died. 'You?'

'I work long hours. When I get home I have to study so I don't have time to meet anyone or the energy to keep a relationship going. The usual London thing.'

As he talks I notice he massages the inside muscle on his right forearm, a displacement activity that I at first mistake for nervousness or boredom. He has long fine fingers and badly bitten nails. There are white chalky callouses on the fingertips of his left hand, which makes me wonder if he plays a stringed instrument. He catches me staring.

'I've got a problem with my arm,' he explains, pressing the offending muscle. 'It's so sore I think I'm losing sensation in my hand.' He tells me how he wakes up in the night unable to feel his thumb and index finger. I wait for him to say that he has googled the symptoms and thinks he has multiple sclerosis but he doesn't, which suggests a level of self-restraint that I like.

Brachioradialis muscle, I think to myself. Textbook. The good thing about learning anatomy in your early twenties is that it stays with you forever. He's almost inevitably suffering from repetitive strain injury. Possibly but not definitely caused by playing the guitar or violin, over and over again. I don't ask him what he does because if he's a halfway decent human being he will feel obliged to ask about my job and I don't want to think about work.

Also I learnt from early forays into digital dating that

revealing you are a doctor can quickly transform a date into a medical consultation. There are a lot of hypochondriacs out there. Although I did once correctly diagnose a guy with atrial fibrillation. He turned out to be a freelance journalist who subsequently wrote a piece for *The Times* with the title 'How Tinder Saved My Life'. He wanted me to appear on one of those crappy daytime TV programmes with him but I refused. It was at these moments ironically that I most missed my friendship with Lisa, because she would have loved this story and probably encouraged me to do the interview. She always made me leave my comfort zone. When she joined my school in sixth form, she was the person who got angry with me when I said I wanted to be a nurse rather than a doctor and encouraged me to ditch my first boyfriend because he was boring and in her book boredom was the worst fate of all. Whatever you say about Lisa, she was a lot of fun, the kind of person you want to have in your life forever. I used to imagine us in our old age, drinking and smoking too much, sitting in the pub by the beach in Cromer after a swim in the sea, her still wondering if she and Barney really were compatible while she eulogized my perfect relationship with Nick.

Back then I was the one blessed with certainty. Sometimes, when I compare the life I thought I was going to have with the life I now live, I feel like I might be swallowed up by the gulf between the two. I should have learnt from my patients that assuming you have control over your destiny is a delusion. The ones I know best tell me it's the worst part of the illness.

'Try stretching it out and pointing your hand towards

the floor,' I suggest. I lengthen his arm into the correct position and place the palm of my hand over his. His hand encircles my wrist, and his fingers weave their way through mine.

'Shall we go?' he suggests.

We get up. He slips an arm around me, I check to see if there is anyone I recognize but it's late and the restaurant is quiet. His arm slides down my back and pushes me towards him so our faces are almost touching. There is always something breathtaking about having a totally unrecognizable face so close. His sore hand touches the side of my face. He kisses me and I respond and there is that first hot jolt of flesh-on-flesh pleasure. He loops one arm around my neck and the other finds its way inside my T-shirt where it presses in the small of my back.

'Hey,' I say softly as we disentangle and appraise each other.

'Your place?' Leo suggests.

'That won't work. Too many people around,' I reply, deliberately vague even though he probably assumes I'm married. The truth is that Daisy and Kit seem to have moved in with me. Daisy explained that one month in four Kit has to sleep on the sofa at his flat because it's the only way he and his three flatmates can afford the rent. But that was weeks ago.

'There's a hotel off Gray's Inn Road,' I suggest.

He runs a finger down the inside of my arm from the elbow to the wrist and at that exact instant I notice a puncture wound on the fleshy part of the inside of his palm. It bears all the hallmarks of a needlestick injury from a syringe or something similar.

'How did you do that?' I ask suspiciously, unfurling his fingers.

'Work-related injury,' he says.

I run my hand along the callouses on his fingertips. I can read the human body like a blind man reads Braille. Then it dawns on me: he's a trainee surgeon. That explains the repetitive strain injury from performing the same movement over and over again. The Tinder algorithm for matching up people with shared interests has got too sophisticated and the chances are, given that my settings allow me to connect with men in a one-mile radius, he probably works in the hospital where I just came from. I suggest we have a quick look around the permanent collection and manage to lose him somewhere in the first room. It's a big shame because we probably would have had great sex. He messages me and I press delete.

On my way home in the tube I run through my usual routine. Checking emails, deleting the obsolete, prioritizing responses, skim-reading a couple of articles in the *International Journal of Breast Cancer* and making a list of what I need for my trip. Activity is always the best antidote to regret. At Hammersmith I glance around the men in the carriage and catch myself doing a quick mental left or right swipe. I clear out the pockets of my handbag, scrunching up old receipts and chewing-gum wrappers, and even make a makeshift hook for the broken zip with a paperclip. I discover a fluorescent pen without a lid that was responsible for the vivid green stain that soaked through the leather from the inside out.

I love this bag even though it was the last present Nick

bought me. I found it wrapped up without a card at the back of his chest of drawers on my birthday on ground zero plus two. I threw it away and it spent three days in the bin before I decided that even if the marriage was irretrievable the bag wasn't. There's still a small brown bloodstain on the side that dates from this period. And three scratches on the side that Daisy gouged out when she was ill. They're a good reminder of my shortcomings. My fury over what I had assumed was an act of sabotage turned out to be hieroglyphics created by Daisy to protect me. And the person who had innocently told me that Daisy had invented 'magic rituals' to protect us was Max, then just eleven years old. That's why I have a Walt Whitman poster with the quote 'Be curious, not judgemental' on the wall in my office. To avoid making assumptions about anything.

When I can find nothing else to usefully do with my time I pull out Lisa's letter from the bottom of the bag. The envelope is crumpled and torn and the address label is missing. It's a week since I first opened it. This time I'm hoping for clarity on how to respond. Time isn't on her side. Cancer is an expansionist enemy with its own temperament and personality. I read slowly, trying to remember the sound of Lisa's voice, the sing-song lilt and how everything she said, even the most mundane remarks, required an exclamation mark, but I can't because it's years since I last saw her. For a long time the only way I could deal with what happened was to pretend she had never existed, and everyone around me was more than happy to collude in that delusion.

I close my eyes for a moment and see her face clearly:

the slightly upturned eyes, inherited from her mother, her long dark hair and the overgrown fringe to hide the chickenpox scar on her left eyebrow, her perfectly drawn lips. And then I suddenly remember the last time we were all on holiday together, how we played a game where you pull a name out of a hat and describe someone's characteristics without giving away their identity. We were hunched around the wooden coffee table in the sitting room in Norfolk. For some reason Ava had written down Lisa's name, Nick pulled it out and spontaneously said, 'Cupid's bow lips,' and Barney immediately responded, 'Lisa.' I had never noticed Lisa's lips before. Daisy was studying Shakespeare's *Venus and Adonis* at the time and after Nick moved in with Lisa, she thereafter sarcastically referred to them as Venus and Adonis. Thinking about this again, I feel like one of those patients who ignored a whole raft of symptoms until it was too late.

Sometimes I blame myself for bringing Lisa into Max and Daisy's lives. But Lisa had been a part of my life for even longer than Nick and the children. I have known her for almost thirty years, since she arrived at my secondary school in the lower sixth after her father, an RAF pilot, was posted to a base in Norfolk. She had spent the previous three years at a base in Germany and was way more self-contained and sophisticated than the rest of us. She introduced us to the music of Kraftwerk, claimed to have seen David Bowie live in Berlin and immediately got asked out by the coolest boy in the year. I couldn't believe she wanted to be my friend. I met Nick through her when he and Barney were cast in the same play at university.

We lost contact for a while after we graduated, when

Barney was at the peak of his career as a rock critic and
they spent all their time at glamorous parties, then seam-
lessly picked up again when we were pregnant with Daisy
and Ava at the same time. When it looked as though Nick
might be at a conference for a week over my due date, she
offered to be my birth partner, even though she had only
had Ava four months earlier.

The train stops in a tunnel. Signal failure at Earl's
Court. I resolve to tackle the letter line by line. There is a
cat's cradle of hidden meaning. Lisa has always been
someone who conceals a precise nature beneath an apparently spontaneous surface. I remember once finding pages
of revision notes in her curious looped handwriting for a
history exam she claimed not to have revised for. So I
understand that there will be a connection between her
belated discovery of the importance of our friendship and
the secret referred to in the final paragraph, and that the
common denominator will almost certainly be Nick.

The memory of the lovely, lazy days breastfeeding
Daisy and Ava at the house in Norfolk is meant to induce
nostalgia, and it does. We had hatched a plan to get pregnant at the same time and amazingly, give or take a few
months, it had worked, so we spent a lot of time together
in Norfolk on maternity leave, waiting with a meal on the
table like 1950s housewives for our husbands to arrive for
the weekend on a Friday evening. Now I wonder if the
way she lay in the sun, all warm breasts and curves, was
intended to pique Nick's interest. I was naive back then
about the primitive nature of most men.

I have never asked Nick when he felt that first stirring.
He used to grumble about the way Lisa's relationship

problems with Barney absorbed so much of my attention, and her sloppiness around the house when they stayed with us drove him crazy, but maybe he was trying to throw me off the scent.

I inwardly curse Lisa for forcing me back in time but I know from my patients that when you have no future, the urge to focus on the past becomes overwhelming. Lisa's actions, I remind myself, are those of someone who assumes she is dying.

I also understand that the revelation about her illness in the middle section is designed to arouse both my sympathy and my professional interest because of course all she has to do is google me to realize there is perfect compatibility between her cancer and my specialist area of research. She wants to go on my trial. I knew that the first time I read it. I knew it when we were looking for prospective patients to fill the two remaining places today. And it was probably the reason Nick had come to my office, even though he couldn't ask me outright to save the life of the woman who came close to destroying my own, not because of my feelings, but because he knew that if Daisy and Max discovered, it could prove a cataclysmic setback in his carefully resurrected relationship with them. Nick is shameless, apart from when it comes to his relationship with his children.

I struggle with the last part of the letter the most. It is typical of Lisa to ask for forgiveness. She was always attracted to drama and overblown epic themes: heroes and heroines, acts of courage, nostalgia for the past. With its absolutist agenda, in most respects, cancer is the perfect illness for her. The first few years after Nick moved in with her, I half expected a letter like this apologizing for what had happened. At the beginning I even rehearsed the conversations we might have in my head. But instead there were years of silence. When I finally confronted Nick, he described what had happened between them as a coup de foudre, as though this absolved him of all responsibility, and then blushed when I told him he sounded like a character from *Gone with the Wind.*

I expected more of Lisa. But as time went by, I realized there would be no day of reckoning. I talked to very few friends about how I felt because I didn't want what had happened to define who I am and, in any case, for several years all my emotional energy was invested in trying to help Daisy. But I remember once explaining to Deborah, my closest friend at work, that I had come to accept Lisa's position because words would change nothing anyway.

And now this, the desire to be forgiven. Lisa isn't a religious person and, unlike honour and revenge, the concept of personal forgiveness is a relatively modern theme. I have little doubt that the idea of closure is something planted in her head by the therapist that Nick mentioned. I am a loose end that needs tying up. It has much more to do with how she feels than how I feel, and that perhaps reveals all too late the essential truth of our entire friendship.

The emotional cost will be much higher for me than it is for her, not least because I have to go back to the house that was once my home. But she won't have thought of that. She is thinking only about everything she is about to lose, not everything that I lost.

I understand why she wants to keep Nick out of this.

He loathes playing a leading role in any drama and will want to maintain the status quo at all costs. And in any case this is something between Lisa and me. I remind myself to resist the human urge to tend towards action. We fixate too much on the decisions we make without giving any value to those never taken, which in my book are often the best but are too quickly forgotten. Sometimes doing nothing is the best course of all. It's a concept that cancer specialists understand better than anyone.

So before my trip to Atlanta, I might decide to take a couple of days off to go and see Lisa in Norfolk, which means I probably should take the key she mentions with me. But equally I might not go at all. It's a decision of sorts.

When I tip the padded envelope upside down to retrieve the key, however, there is nothing inside. I rummage around my bag and the recently rearranged contents spew on to my lap but no key falls out. I must have lost it. The only thing in the envelope is the photograph. I don't get it out, partly because the train has arrived at East Putney, but mostly because I don't want to be reminded of the last time we were all happy together in case I find something in the picture that suggests we weren't.

It's almost half past nine by the time I get home. I close the front door behind me, stand completely still for a moment to collect my thoughts and massage my temples before noticing a couple of crumpled envelopes on the floor. There are footprints all over them. I bend down to pick them up, silently maligning Daisy and Kit for failing to execute even this minor domestic task. If they are going to live here full time I need to establish some ground rules.

I add the letters to the pile of unopened post on the hall table. One is a bill. The other is from the clinic Daisy used to attend but of course now that she is over eighteen it is addressed to her rather than me. It's probably something routine, a newsletter or plea for donations. There is a vague sense of unease, a residue of the anxiety I once felt, but it dissolves as soon as I hear the sound of her laughing in the kitchen.

What does occur to me is that I have no similar recollection of finding Lisa's letter on the doormat and still less idea of how it found its way into my bag. Nor can I be sure that I had ever actually seen the key she mentions in her letter. I frown as I try to remember the first time I saw the manila envelope. I know that Nick later described this as a classic case of short-term memory malfunction because picking up the post is one of those subconscious actions we repeat hundreds of times a day. In contrast, I think that finding a letter from Lisa on the doormat after seven years of silence is something I would remember forever. But I am too distracted by the noise coming from the kitchen to chase down this thought to its logical conclusion. And if I had, would it have made any difference to what happened later anyway?

I go into the kitchen to grab something to eat because one of the best things about having Kit live with us is that he compensates for the extra time I spend trying to pair odd socks and sort laundry into three different colours by cooking almost every evening. It's a fair trade even though the kitchen is a total mess. Kit tries to keep order but puts back everything in a totally illogical place. Daisy is just plain messy.

I find her perched on the edge of a stool by the kitchen island, expertly shredding the skin off a big purple grape. She's wearing my dressing gown over an oversized T-shirt belonging to Max and a pair of jeans that belong to Kit. When she has finished peeling the grape, she throws the fleshy globule high in the air and catches it in her mouth to loud applause. I join in until I notice there is a third person in the room who gets up with such force when he sees me that he tips over his half-drunk bottle of beer. He ignores the spillage and heads purposefully towards me, brandishing a handful of documents that he has rescued from the pool of beer.

'Rosie,' says Ed Gilmour. 'I've brought you the missing research papers. I thought you might need them.'

'Hi, Mum,' says Daisy through a mouthful of grapes as she and Kit try to stem the flow of beer on to the kitchen floor by damming it with my dressing gown.

Daisy and Kit are too busy sorting out the mess to notice the expression on my face, and I am too busy trying to reassemble my features to notice the expression on Ed's. So when we finally face each other we stare blankly for a beat too long, each waiting for the other to react. He's so close that I can feel the thick heat of his breath on my skin. He smells of beer and hospital and sweat mingled with hastily applied deodorant. I realize to my surprise that he smells familiar and that this is a good feeling.

He presses a pile of papers into my arms and for a brief moment his hands rest on top of mine. His left thumb trails slowly across my knuckles and I feel almost nauseous with desire. I stare at his hand touching mine to avoid catching his eye and when it pulls away I flick through the documents to disguise the sense of loss. They consist of a couple of copies of *The Lancet* from earlier in the year, a black-bound notebook that belongs to him, a *Guardian* and some other papers that he must have dug out of his bag to make it look as though this was a work-related visit when Daisy and Kit had startled him by opening the door. I had told him I lived alone.

'Thanks,' I say, putting down the papers on the kitchen worktop and finally meeting his eye. 'That's very considerate of you, but couldn't they have waited until tomorrow?'

'I found them on your desk when you left and thought you might need them tonight. But you obviously had other plans.'

'I had a meeting at the Royal Free,' I explain. 'About the clinical trial.'

He shakes his head, shrugs his shoulders and smiles to indicate that he doesn't believe me but isn't going to make a fuss.

'I was just leaving,' he says.

'There's still some beer in the bottle,' Daisy intervenes. 'Ed was telling us what kind of boss you are, Mum. How everyone finds you terrifyingly brilliant and longs for your approval.'

She turns towards me with an expression of shocked disbelief and the oversized T-shirt that she is wearing slides down to reveal a small red welt below her clavicle. She's laughing as she speaks, which makes the revelation even more bitter-sweet. I know from experience that I can't judge anything from the size of the walnut-sized stain across her skin. All that I can be certain of is that there will be an identical one of equal proportions and intensity on her opposite shoulder. She catches me looking and quickly pulls up the T-shirt.

'I need to go,' says Ed. 'I've got an early start tomorrow.'

'I'll show you out,' I say, leading him into the hall and closing the kitchen door behind me.

'I'm sorry, Rosie, I didn't mean to intrude.'

'How did you get my address?' I ask him.

He pulls out a ball of paper from his pocket and irons it out on the palm of his hand. I recognize Lisa's handwriting: it is the missing address label.

'I took it as insurance policy in case I felt a sudden overwhelming desire to see you.'

'Did you look in the envelope?'

'No. I'm not that nosy. But when your daughter answered the door and said you were about to come home, I couldn't resist the chance to observe you in your natural habitat.'

'I like to keep my private life private,' I hear myself say, although actually I would like to tell him everything. About the welt on Daisy's shoulder and what that might mean, the cock-up with Laura S., and my thwarted Tinder date. The sort of chat I used to share with Nick. Of all that was lost, that part is the most difficult to bear. Ed moves towards me and tilts my chin towards his face.

'I love your dark eyes, Rosie. They're so contemplative. But you move so quickly and impatiently that I never get to look at them for long enough.'

The unexpected tenderness of his words takes me unawares. I close my eyes and rest my head on his shoulder for a moment. The street light shines through the window and everything is hot and red like the sore on Daisy's shoulder.

'You need to go,' I say.

When I go back in the kitchen, Daisy and Kit have disappeared. I pick up the dressing gown and see that there are three knots in the cord.

8

Nick

I'm in the middle of a meeting at work when Lisa messages to remind me about our appointment with the alternative health practitioner. Or the alternative death practitioner, as I prefer to call Gregorio. How can anyone honestly believe that shooting a double espresso up your arse and drinking litres of watermelon juice stops cancer cells from replicating? Mind you, if I was paid £150 an hour to peddle tripe like that, I might believe in miracles. We no longer live in an evidence-based culture so I'm not that surprised. All that counts is how you feel about things. And although I've got much better at that since Lisa came into my life, it's still not always my strong suit.

Gregorio passionately believes chemotherapy is part of a pharmaceutical conspiracy to earn big money for drug companies. He also talks a lot of bollocks about cancer being caused by the stress of modern living when a) Ancient Egyptian mummies had tumours, and b) it's stressful living in Darfur but the cancer rates aren't any higher. It's a measure of my self-restraint that I haven't pointed out any of this to him over the past couple of months. If I did he'd probably accuse me of being out of touch with my spiritual side. Unlike Lisa, who is apparently so spiritual that Gregorio has offered to take her on as his sorcerer's apprentice once she recovers. I can't work out if he is criminal or delusional.

'Sorry, team. I've got to go to a meeting,' I tell everyone gathered around the pockmarked table in our meeting room. I am grateful they know nothing about Lisa's illness because at least for some of the day it feels as though life continues as normal. But also because I don't want them to discover how she has elected to be treated, which I think reflects badly on me. 'And thank you again for all your hard work. This is a big moment for our department.'

As I load papers into my briefcase, I congratulate them again on the publication of our ground-breaking research into false memory. It has generated a lot of interest because we have proved that it is possible to distort memory by planting misinformation in the human mind, a discovery that has implications for anything from the judicial system, with its emphasis on witness accounts, to memories of sexual abuse.

Our work shows that with the right technique you can convince innocent people they are guilty, or random bystanders they have committed a crime and the unharmed that they have been victims. Basically we have discovered that if you can get someone to imagine what something *could* be like, you can get them to imagine what it *would* be like and then these elements turn into what something *was* like.

Interestingly, so-called pseudo memory is more common in people who suffer from Obsessive Compulsive Disorder. In fact, one of my PhD students is researching memory impairments in OCD patients, which is of course personally very interesting because of what happened to Daisy. My student has discovered that people suffering from OCD have difficulty recalling a complex geometric shape they have just been shown as well as exhibiting a deficit in spatial memory, such as remembering places on a map.

When Daisy was ill, for example, she was very good at remembering how to do things, because her striatum brain structure was constantly over-stimulated. But her visual and episodic memory was totally crap. That's why she had to keep checking things over and over again.

With all this swirling around my head, I head out into the street. As well as forgetting the appointment I realize I have also failed to get today's supply of organic fruit and vegetables for Lisa's juicing regime. Sometimes I think the reason Gregorio came up with this diet is so that I don't have the time or energy to research any alternatives. It's like having another part-time job on top of what I'm already doing. So I duck into a Lebanese corner shop and stock up on melons and broccoli and put them in the Planet Organic bag that I keep in my briefcase for such emergencies. I admit it's a short cut but I also hope that if Lisa continues to refuse to have chemotherapy then perhaps the residue from pesticides will kill off a few of the bad cells. Also, if I'm being completely honest, it feels good to get one over on Gregorio.

Just before I turn into Harley Street something catches my eye in the window of a second-hand shop on the corner of the road. It's a gold pendant on a chunky chain with a large ruby in the centre surrounded by seven arms each with a different inlaid stone. It's not my sort of thing but Lisa would love it. The man behind the counter explains that it is a Navaratna, which apparently translates from the Sanskrit as 'nine gems'. It comes with a piece of paper also written in Sanskrit, which names each gem and describes what it represents. Ruby for the Sun, which is at the centre of the solar system, pearl for the moon, emerald for Mercury, and so on.

The vendor is the type of person who requires a lot of interaction before he does a deal so I'm forced to listen to a lot of guff about how pure, flawless gems can protect from demons, snakes, poisons and diseases. Thanks to Gregorio I have developed a good line in looking interested while completely ignoring what someone is saying. Lisa jokes that I have finally discovered my inner Zen when in reality I'm imagining interesting ways of inflicting pain on him.

So after all these diversions it's no surprise that by the time I reach Harley Street I have missed almost the entire first hour of Lisa's appointment. I'm directed straight into the treatment room by the receptionist and find Gregorio finishing up a ritual that involves flicking something that looks suspiciously like a feather duster all over Lisa's body, while making clicking noises with his tongue. I put the bags of fruit in the corner and theatrically pull a pen from my pocket.

'Expelianos!' I say, waving it like a wand. I remember from reading Harry Potter to Daisy and Max when they were little that there is a spell to get rid of illness that would probably be just as effective as Gregorio's mumbo-jumbo but unfortunately I can't remember it. Lisa opens her eyes, turns her head towards me and starts to giggle.

It's the best noise in the world. I adore the way her nose always wrinkles and her eyebrows disappear beneath her fringe when she laughs.

'Please, Niko,' she giggles. 'Put your wand away. You'll put Gregorio off his stride.'

'Here's hoping,' I mutter.

I love the sound of her laughter so much. Before this wretched diagnosis it was so close to the surface and I always felt a burst of self-satisfied pride when I managed to provoke it. Now she laughs less but when she does I savour it all the more, knowing that soon I will lie awake at night ransacking my memory to recall its sound. I walk over to her, trying to ignore Gregorio, and lift a strand of hair that has stuck to her cheek. I kneel down beside her so we face each other and kiss her beautiful lips, closing my eyes for a couple of seconds so she can't see the tears. I open them when I'm sure I have regained control. She has lost so much weight that her features have become her face. To me she looks lovelier than ever. I could stare at her forever.

'Darling Lisa,' I say, trying to keep my voice steady, but instead it sounds ridiculously husky. 'Sorry I'm late. I was meeting with my team.'

'Why so gruff, Niko darling?' she asks, gently stroking the hair on my forearm with her middle finger. Her voice sounds weak. The illness, the lack of sleep, the diet and the endless pit of worry have all sapped her energy. 'How was your celebration?'

'Good. Great. Everyone was in very high spirits. I even got a note from the vice-chancellor of MIT.'

'That's so wonderful,' says Lisa.

She is always really supportive of my work, much more so than Rosie ever was. I mean Rosie always professed to be interested, but it was difficult for my research to compete with the drama of the life-and-death decisions she takes every day.

'How were Ava and Rex?'

'I spoke to them both. Ava has agreed to fly over for the wedding. Rex isn't sure but I think he'll relent. He said he's meant to be in Glasgow on a course.'

'Did you say anything?'

She shakes her head. It doesn't surprise me, although I wish they were a little less self-absorbed. Lisa has decided to postpone telling them what has happened until we get back from our honeymoon, so it doesn't cast a dark cloud over our wedding, but I can't help wondering if she is putting it off until she hears back from Rosie. I think about the letter in Rosie's handbag again and feel a shiver creep up my spine. Bloody Gregorio keeps emphasizing the need to make peace with anyone Lisa has wronged. And I'm terrified what she might tell her.

'We're about to start the next part of the treatment,' says Gregorio seriously. He makes a big show of putting on a pair of surgical gloves to divert our attention. 'Lisa, please can you roll on to your side.'

I now notice that Lisa is wearing a medical gown that opens at the back, giving him a fantastic view of her wondrously shaped naked buttocks. I feel a stab of jealousy. It's a feeling I have had many times since her diagnosis, as if the cancer is my love rival, absorbing all of her attention and taking her away from me into the hands of strangers. I can't compete with its strength. I feel the now-familiar heat of rage creep up through my body. My hands start to shake and I put them behind my back so Lisa doesn't notice. I'm not asking for sympathy but keeping Lisa's illness secret from everyone apart from Gregorio has its own pressures.

He pulls a table on wheels towards the treatment bed, behaving as though he is about to embark on something medically incredibly complex, like spinal surgery. He puts one hand on Lisa's buttock and rests it there for what seems like a lifetime. I have never in my life hit anyone but the desire to split his upper lip is almost overwhelming.

There are some things no man should have to see. I remember Barney telling me how watching Lisa give birth had put him off sex for months. Not a problem I would ever have had with her. But that's nothing compared to what I'm about to go through. I eye what looks like a large pickle jar filled with thick dark coffee and a narrow plastic tube that will all too soon be inserted into Lisa. I remember what Max told me about infections, and wince.

'She always has a flat white, Gregorio. One shot,' I say, conspiratorially leaning over the bed towards him.

I have decided the best way to get her out of his clutches is through humour. Lisa starts giggling again. Her laughter instantly dissolves my rage. Gregorio puts down the tube and gives me a long soulful look.

'I don't think you are taking this seriously enough, Nick,' he reprimands me. 'The sooner Lisa starts the enema treatments, the sooner she gets better.'

I take a deep breath. 'Look, I'm a scientist, Gregorio. I have a systematic way of thinking. I believe in testing a theory with factual observation. And I have looked for evidence to support your theory because I really want to believe it but I just can't find it.'

'If you don't believe, the treatment won't work,' he says with a beatific expression on his face.

'Sort of like Father Christmas, then?'

'Nick,' warns Lisa.

She banned me from challenging Gregorio at the outset, arguing everyone has the right to hope (true) and that a positive attitude can overcome most adversity (bollocks). Lisa's love affair with pseudo science and self-help manuals used to be part of her charm, a quirky eccentricity that I adored in part because it underlined how different she was from Rosie. But now I wish I could transpose Rosie's brain on to Lisa's body. I note that Gregorio is testing the temperature of the coffee. My options are running out.

'Exactly what empirical evidence do you have for that statement?' It's a question I often pose to my students. I cross my arms defensively.

'I've explained this before,' Gregorio says impatiently, crossing his own arms. 'Cleansing the colon removes carcinogenic toxins. It stimulates the liver to produce more bile, which flushes out the toxins from the liver. It is a timeless tradition that dates back centuries.'

'So is blood-letting and applying leeches but no one is doing that any more,' I point out.

'Nick, I don't think your attitude is helping Lisa,' he says, stroking his whiskery chin. 'I understand your rage, Nick. It's very common. You must be feeling a lot of frustration but it's very misplaced. I see this a lot with the loved ones of people I treat.'

'I bet you bloody do,' I say.

'It's called transference, Nick,' he says smoothly. 'You are projecting your anger on to me. I am a lightning rod for your repressed emotions.'

'Please, Nick,' pleads Lisa. 'I want to give this a try.'

'Can everyone stop using my name so many times in a sentence,' I say, immediately regretting the way I sound like a petulant child.

'If you like, I could recommend a therapist for you to speak to,' Gregorio offers.

'And why coffee?' I continue, trying to rein in my anger.

'The coffee grains kill the bad bacteria,' he says to me, bowing his head. Gregorio always does this when he's trying to impress his ancient wisdom upon me and deflect perfectly reasonable questions. 'If your colon isn't happy then toxins accumulate.'

I have noticed in the past his habit of using black and white adjectives to describe his treatment. Everything is good and bad, happy and sad.

'I hope it's organic,' I joke, but it sounds like a snarl.

'Organic, hand-picked and Fair Trade,' he confirms.

The angrier I get the slower he speaks. It's so bloody passive-aggressive.

'And how do the coffee grains distinguish the good cells from the bad?' I ask. 'Do they do a Jeremy Paxman-style interview first? Or do they do something even more scientific like read their aura?'

His shoulders tighten. He is a man who is unused to having his authority questioned.

'I think we can both agree, Nick, that the last thing Lisa needs right now is any further tension caused by argument over her treatment. The relationship between stress and cancer survival rates is well validated.'

'Actually, there is excellent research to show stress plays no important direct role in either developing cancer or survival rates,' I say. 'My ex-wife is an oncologist and she can back me up on this.'

'Oh, Nick,' says Lisa.

I can't bear it when she's disappointed in me.

'Ultimately, it isn't what we know, it's what we believe that is fundamental,' says Gregorio, bowing his head.

Lisa shoots me a warning glance and I look away, turning towards the window overlooking Harley Street. I distract myself by trying to imagine how it looked in the eighteenth century when women had their tongues cut in half to cure hysteria and people believed cancer was contagious.

'Perhaps you should get in touch with Rosie,' I tell Lisa gently. 'She might be able to give a second opinion. I could speak to her first, if you like. Or we could go and see her together.' I see her eyelids flutter beneath her fringe for a split second as she weighs up her options and I'm hopeful that maybe she's going to come clean about the letter. I don't want there to be any secrets between us.

'Rosie won't want to see me. Not after what I did to her.'

It's a lawyer's response. It reveals neither the truth nor a lie. Silent tears start to stream down Lisa's cheeks and soak into the edge of the hospital gown and on to the treatment bed. It's the first time since the diagnosis that she has broken down in front of me and I find it very affecting and confusing.

Gregorio starts to tell us how it is good to cry because the tears contain toxins.

'For God's sake, man, just shut up for a moment!' I tell him.

Remarkably, he acquiesces.

I sit down on the bed and put my arm around Lisa. Her tears are all the more poignant because in all the time I have known her, she has never done self-pity. It's one of the qualities I most admire about her. I remember, when we first went public, how some of the mothers at school waged a pathetic vendetta against her, turning their backs on her in assemblies, refusing to return her calls, and Lisa never once flinched. Instead she held her head high and let it all wash over her. When Daisy lost the plot with Ava, Lisa was the person who restored calm to the situation, while the rest of us were losing our heads. Even when Ava and Rex asked to live with their father, rather than with us, Lisa said she could understand their anger and welcomed their decision because it might stop Barney from drinking. Which indeed it did. She is one of life's true survivors. At least I believe she would be if I could get her out of Gregorio's clutches and on to a conventional treatment plan.

I wipe away her tears with my thumb, accidentally smearing mascara across her cheek, and make a weak joke about putting on war paint for the battle ahead even though we both agreed at the outset that we didn't like bellicose cancer metaphors. I should change the subject but I can't help myself. Lisa would be the first to advise me never to shy away from the difficult questions.

'Have you tried to communicate with Rosie?' I ask,

tilting her chin towards me so that our faces are almost touching.

She looks into my eyes, holds my gaze and shakes her head. She always was a better liar than me. 'It wouldn't be right. Not after all these years.'

'Your illness changes everything. Rosie might be able to help you.'

'Don't you understand, Niko? This is a punishment for what I have done to her.' She waves her hand across the breast with the hateful lump.

I persist. 'If you could have five minutes with Rosie, what would you say to her?' I ask.

'This is karma, Nick. Look and learn. The truth catches up with everyone eventually.'

She doesn't mean it to sound like a threat but somehow it does.

'We fell in love, Lisa. It's an age-old story. Even Rosie understands that. Cancer is something that happens on a cellular level.'

'So do you have any questions about the centre in Mexico?' Gregorio interrupts, sensing victory. 'They are really looking forward to welcoming you there. They've never had a honeymooning couple before. It will be very special. There will be rose petals on the bed and watermelon juice on ice.'

I think for a moment. It's too irresistible.

'Do you get your money back if the cure doesn't work?' It's obviously a joke but these guys don't do humour.

'I think it would be better if you left us alone to continue the treatment, Nick. Lisa needs all her emotional energy to be focused on her recuperation.'

'Lisa?' I ask hopefully.

'He's right,' she says. 'And haven't you got to go and meet Daisy and Max to run through their reading at the wedding?'

I'd forgotten that too.

'Have you got the book with you?'

She has every right to sound exasperated.

'Yes,' I lie.

We agree to meet at Liverpool Street Station in a couple of hours so that we can get the train back to Norfolk together.

Feeling pretty deflated, I find a table outside a restaurant just in front of platform nine and type *readings for second marriages* into Google. There are almost a million results, which tells you something about the optimism of human nature. Lisa is insisting that each of our teenage children recites a verse from 'On Marriage' by Kahlil Gibran, even though it is the same poem I read at her wedding to Barney.

I've done everything I can to put her off but she is as adamant about this as she is about refusing chemotherapy. She says we are the only people who were at her first wedding and that we'll never find a poem that sums up our relationship so perfectly. She keeps quoting the line about love being a 'moving sea between the shores of your souls' and arguing that nothing could be more appropriate for a beach ceremony. I haven't seen this stubborn side of Lisa since she was married to Barney and at one point last week even considered phoning him up for advice on how to handle her.

It's difficult to have a rational argument with someone who is dying. I tried one of Gregorio's favourite methods by suggesting that it would be 'bad karma' to repeat the same reading. I spat out the word karma like an olive stone. She responded by telling me that Gregorio thinks the poem perfectly embodies the 'solemn sanctity' of our relationship. I couldn't believe she had discussed it with him. But that's not all. When Gregorio revealed that he is registered to conduct secular wedding ceremonies she asked him to officiate at ours without even consulting me. So I told her that if cancer is her punishment for what she did to Rosie then Gregorio is mine. She was so upset that I immediately backed down and agreed to her plan.

I look up and scan the crowds milling around the station to see if I can spot Daisy and Max. Daisy is incredibly well read and I'm hopeful she might come up with a good alternative. But given her reaction to the news of our wedding, we'll probably be lucky if she even turns up. I order a couple of beers for Max and myself and drink both of them.

In the immediate aftermath of the diagnosis, getting married to Lisa had made perfect sense. It seemed to me to be the natural climax of the epic journey we have taken together. I did it all properly: I went to our favourite antiques shop in Norwich and bought a ring and got up early the following morning to head to the beach to write 'Will you marry me?' in pebbles on the sand, leaving the ring as the full stop beneath the question mark. I filmed Lisa on my phone as we walked to the edge of the cliff, and as she realized what was going on she turned to me and said, 'Yes.'

But somehow when she insisted she didn't want anyone to know that she was ill, the grand romance and heroism of the gesture withered and with it my unerring certainty. That's the problem with feelings. They can be so ephemeral. I even deleted the film when I realized I had no one to share it with.

Then the few people we told about the wedding – her children, my children, her ex-husband and my ex-wife – were understandably less than politely enthusiastic. I tried to explain to my father, who is in the early throes of dementia, but he was completely shocked because he had forgotten I had got divorced from Rosie. Lisa's mother said she wouldn't come from France if Lisa's father would be there and Lisa's father refused to come without his newest wife. Ava said she didn't want to see Daisy. If I could have told them she was dying perhaps they would have stepped up to the mark, but Lisa said she preferred to run the risk of our wedding day being remembered for the ill humour of our guests rather than her illness. Brave is sometimes a byword for foolish.

I have to go through with it, I tell myself. *I have to go through with it.*

'Go through with what, Dad?' Daisy asks.

Max emerges from the crowd behind her. She bends down to kiss me on the cheek and gives me a quick hug. I didn't realize I had spoken out loud.

I hold Daisy in my arms until she shakes me off. I am always grateful for her affection because for so many years it was withheld, and it is always strictly rationed. For a while she even used to flinch when I touched her. She has definitely lost weight. Even through her sweater I can feel her upper body is all sharp angles. But I know better than to say anything.

'Are you having cold feet about getting married?' asks Max, pulling up a chair beside me and giving me a long hard stare with his strange dark eyes.

Max has always had this unnerving way of instantly assessing a situation and drawing (mostly) the right conclusions. It's a trait that all the best doctors share. He puts a hand on my shoulder and looks genuinely concerned. He is such a nice kid.

'No, no, no,' I say, laughing too long and too hard. 'Someone wants to interview me about my research. I'm feeling a bit nervous, that's all.'

'But you're a publicity whore,' observes Max. 'Why would you worry about that?'

His honesty cuts through the bullshit of the rest of the day. I laugh properly for the first time in ages. Daisy seems distracted. She takes out little cartons of UHT milk from a plastic container on the table and starts building three small towers. It's completely irritating but I need her co-operation over the reading so I pick up a carton and add it to one of the towers.

'They each have to have nine, Dad,' she says, immediately removing it.

'How's your course going?' I turn to Max. He has turned down my offer of a beer and opted for tap water.

'I'm in the middle of exams, Dad.'

There's no reproach in his tone. Max never was a guilt tripper in the way that Daisy was. But I feel an immediate pang of conscience that I didn't realize. Lisa would have organized a card at least. She's very good at things like that. She keeps a drawer full at home in Norfolk, ready for any event – births, deaths, marriages, good luck, congratulations – life is a series of occasions, really. I'm reminded again of Lisa's letter to Rosie. *There's something I need to tell you . . .*

'How are they going?' I ask Max, dragging myself away from these uneasy thoughts.

'Good. I think.'

I wince as one of Daisy's milk towers collapses and a carton falls to the ground.

'Next year should be exciting, you'll get to see patients, won't you?'

'I'm intercalating, Dad,' says Max. 'I'm spending a year doing an MSc specializing in dementia. I discussed it all with Mum and she thinks it's a good idea because it adds extra points to my final result.'

His tone is unerringly patient and polite, as if he's speaking to an elderly stranger. I know nothing of what is going on in my son's life. A wave of resentment towards Lisa washes over me for denying me the opportunity to explain to my beloved children why I have been so distracted of late. I glance at my watch and realize that the train is due to leave in less than twenty minutes.

'Lisa and I were wondering if you would do a reading at our wedding. She's very fond of the piece on marriage from *The Prophet*, by Kahlil Gibran, unless you can think of something else that you'd prefer? You might have a much better idea.'

It all comes out too quickly. Daisy finally looks up. I have her attention now.

'How many verses does it have?'

I'm heartened by her question. 'Three.'

'Three is a good and safe number, Dad,' she says. 'You know that.'

It's something she used to say all the time when she was ill and the fact she can joke about it now shows how far she has come.

I laugh. 'You can even do the third verse if you like, darling.' It feels good to tease her.

'Daisy,' warns Max. He nudges her with his foot underneath the table. 'Stop.'

I have to say that I'm amazed that Max is the one who is reticent.

'Lisa and I would like to ask Rex and Ava to read some of it too,' I say. I wasn't planning to introduce this idea today but Daisy's positive reaction has given me confidence. Besides, who knows when I'll have another chance to discuss this possibility with them?

'But that's two plus two people for a poem with three verses,' says Daisy.

She's got a point.

'Won't it be a bit odd?' asks Max.

I assume he's talking about the prospect of reading at my second wedding, which is the reaction I had anticipated.

'I mean we haven't seen Rex and Ava for years, not since –'

'The Incident,' chips in Daisy, finishing the sentence for him in the same way she used to when he was little. 'That's what Max is getting at.'

'Water under the bridge, water under the bridge,' I say, wishing I had Rosie's ability to soothe a situation with calm logic.

'Water under the bridge,' Daisy concurs.

I'm grateful for this unexpected emollience.

'Perhaps Rex and Ava should read a different poem. Weddings always have at least three, don't they?' Daisy suggests.

'Good plan,' I say, trying to sound jovial even though I don't feel it.

Max's phone beeps. He picks it up, looks at the message and smiles as his fingers flutter over the keyboard.

'Girlfriend?' I ask.

'Not sure,' he says.

I wait for Daisy to fill in the gaps as she usually does with Max but she's focused on building the little towers of milk again. I'm so relieved that we have resolved the issue of the readings that I no longer find it irritating.

'I'm really into her but I'm not sure if she's into me. When I'm not with her all I can think about is when I'm next going to see her, and then when we're together I can't enjoy the moment because I know soon she's going to leave –'

'You met on Tinder – what do you expect?' Daisy interrupts. 'It's not exactly an exclusive relationship.'

'Why do you need to meet girls on Tinder?' I ask. 'I thought it was for older people.'

'There are a lot of sad middle-aged people like you, Dad, but I don't match with them, although my girlfriend sometimes does,' says Max. He apologizes when he realizes how this sounds.

Daisy giggles.

'Why don't you make yourself less available?' I suggest. 'Or invite her to go away somewhere for the weekend. Bring her to the wedding if you like.'

'It might be a bit weird,' says Max. 'I haven't met any of her friends or family. And she'd be the only person who wasn't connected to you or Lisa.'

'No, she won't. I've already invited Kit,' Daisy announces.

'Who's Kit?' I ask. I hear the ache in my voice. I hate the way I'm always playing catch-up with my children's lives. Why hasn't Rosie mentioned him to me?

'My boyfriend of nine months,' says Daisy. 'We're living at Mum's together. He's a statistician, he writes algorithms.'

I swear she's enjoying my discomfort. 'It would be nice if you could let me know when there's someone import-ant in your life, Daisy,' I say, doing my best to curb my exasperation.

It reminds me of the time when she 'forgot' to tell me that she had won an English Prize at school so that I looked like a bad parent for not turning up at the award ceremony. There's a special place reserved in Hell for someone who goes off with their wife's best friend and I always felt Daisy did her best to confirm people's worst prejudices about me.

'Just like you did, Dad,' says Daisy in an acid tone.

She knocks down the little towers of milk cartons and they fly on to the floor. I see the people at the next table watching us. There are so many layers of sarcasm wrapped around each word that I feel winded by them. I can't understand why, after all this time, she suddenly feels so venomous again. Just minutes earlier she was completely relaxed. I put it down to the wedding and wonder if it's too late to call it off. But what kind of man jilts his dying wife at the altar? *The kind that fucks his wife's best friend*, I hear you answer.

'Daisy,' warns Max. 'It's not the moment.'

'When did you first tell Mum there was someone special in your life?' asks Daisy.

I have expected this question for years and have rehearsed my response well but it still sounds pathetic. 'I realize that it isn't good that I fell in love with Lisa after Mum left me, and I'm truly sorry for the pain it caused both of you, but as I'm sure both of you now understand, love is nearly always wrong-headed.'

'Dad, you don't need to talk about this,' says Max. There is a desperate edge to his tone.

'You are a liar, Dad. Just admit that you are a liar. Tell Max what you did,' commands Daisy.

And we are back where we began. Maybe this is what Gregorio means when he talks about life being circular.

'I don't know what you're talking about,' I say.

The train screeches into platform nine. I would rather wait in the carriage than be turned to stone under Daisy's cool gaze so I give them both a hug and get up to leave. When I get into the carriage I lock myself in the toilet like Daisy used to do, switch on the tap and splash water on my face. I look in the mirror but I hardly recognize the person looking back.

9

Eight years earlier
Daisy

We waited six long days for them to arrive. I remember this because it was the summer of the ladybirds. Thousands appeared each day, as if they were attending a summit on the North Norfolk coast to discuss the Drapers' absence. At my grandparents' house, they turned up everywhere: inside the fridge, the toes of my socks, the sealed cockpit of Max's *Star Wars* Millennium Falcon, even in the ear of the next-door neighbour's dog. They only lived for a few days and the ground crunched beneath our feet with the husks of their dried-up corpses.

Every afternoon Max collected up the bodies from around the house in small matchboxes that he labelled with the exact time and location where he had found them, to monitor the scale of the epidemic before stacking them into neat piles according to the date. It was the sort of productive scientific activity that Mum and Dad approved of, whereas moping around complaining about Ava's failure to show and even bigger failure to communicate with me was not.

By the end of the week there were six piles of matchboxes on the bookshelf in the bedroom we shared at the top of the house and still no sign of Barney and Lisa. A routine of sorts was established whereby the phone in the kitchen rang at the same time as Max's afternoon collection. Mum would give it a sad look before disappearing into the larder, pulling the cord as far as it could stretch and closing the door so she could speak to Lisa in private. And every afternoon Dad would come in after another failed attempt to tame the overgrown garden, forget about the tripwire across the kitchen, crash into the table and swear under his breath about the heat, the dust and everything that was broken, including the dishwasher and the downstairs toilet. But in reality he was angry with Barney and Lisa, his 'alleged best friends', as Max referred to them.

Sometime later Mum would emerge, like a mole blinking into the light, with an excuse that was proportionate to the amount of time she had spent in the larder. She would fix Dad with a meaningful stare, although the latest explanation for what they called 'the no-show' was clearly directed at us. *The first rule of lying is keep it simple*, I had once heard Dad tell Mum. She was never a good liar.

That was the summer I finally understood the grammatical use of the colon. Nothing was obvious: everything required an explanation.

Day One. 'Rex has an inner ear infection and needs to get antibiotics: they might leave later today, as long as they can get an emergency appointment at the doctor's but that depends on how busy the surgery is.'

Day Two. 'Lisa is waiting for some legal files to be biked over, then they can leave: there's some deal at work and she's hoping it will be postponed so she can go tomorrow morning.'

Day Three. 'Barney has to finish a piece he's writing for *The Times* about a new Radiohead album: he's waiting for some background from the manager and those music types don't get out of bed till the afternoon.'

Day Four. 'The brake pads on their car need fixing: the mechanic said he had never seen one as worn down on the back-left side of the car and it was a miracle someone hadn't died.'

'*Lived: lived: lived*,' I muttered under my breath. By Day Five I didn't even listen to Mum's excuses. I was furious with her for not being honest with us when she set such store by always telling the truth, but really I was angry with Ava.

At night, lying on the top bunk, with Max below, I tried to get him to guess what might be going on but all he wanted to talk about were the ladybirds. Apparently they were fatally lured to the coast by an epidemic of aphids. If this was true, why did we only see the *Coccinellidae* (he insisted on calling them by their scientific name) and not the aphids? Max kept asking Mum and Dad. They would usually have lapped up a question like this but they were too wrapped up in hushed conversations about Lisa and Barney to pay us much attention.

'Stop obsessing about the ladybirds,' I shouted from the top bunk on the fifth night after Max started telling me that their spots were to show predators they were poisonous. 'You're not a bloody expert.'

'Stop obsessing about Ava,' he shouted back. 'You're not bloody married.'

But the truth was that we had been best friends for almost fourteen years, which is longer than most relationships. We were born four months apart; we learnt to walk at the same time; we wore identical French plaits our first day at nursery and measured our skirts to make sure they were exactly the same length on our first day at secondary school. This was the first summer holiday that we hadn't communicated at least every other day, and it didn't take much insight to realize something was wrong.

I continued to help Max collect the papery ladybird wings that littered the house like pieces of giant dandruff. I hated the way they turned to dust between my fingers but I kept going because I didn't want to jeopardize Max's new non-speaking role in my magic rituals that had begun that summer. Each time I picked up a pair I had to whisper, 'I love you, brother of mine,' under my breath three times to protect him from bad stuff happening.

I still don't fully understand why I got him involved. Probably because we were sharing a room and he wanted to know why I kept getting out of bed to make sure the curtains touched each other in the middle. I decided that the best way to shut him up was to get him to help me with some of the less important tasks, like checking the windows and curtains were closed and making sure the tap in the bathroom was switched off.

He seemed to enjoy it. Maybe because it seemed like a continuation of the games we used to play together when we were little. I never told the therapist but Max is the only person I have ever fully involved in my illness. I'm not sure if this is significant. But it seems worth mentioning.

I can't remember what triggered the magical thinking

that summer. The first therapist made a link between my fears over something happening to Mum and the dying ladybirds. She was so pleased by her insight that I didn't want to disappoint her by saying that by the time we went on holiday to Norfolk, I was already like a stand-up comedian who had got together a pretty smooth routine that I ran through when the anxiety about Mum got too much.

Of course there was always room for improvisation and I added a few original flourishes to the evening schedule in light of Max's participation. I won't get into all the details. Compulsions are only interesting for about three seconds, but mine involved six repetitions of actions that included checking the bedroom windows were shut, making sure there was no gap in the curtains, and tapping the wall in a triangular pattern in multiples of three. There was a raised wallpaper pattern involving creepy oversized foliage that helped me plot these points with complete accuracy.

When this was finished I had to say the following nine times:

'Please watch over our family.
Please don't let me die in my sleep, but if anyone has to die let it be me.
I am a good person who hasn't killed or harmed anyone.
Mum is strong and healthy and will live a long and happy life.
Max is strong and healthy and will live a long and happy life.
Three is a good and safe number.'

If I made a mistake or it felt wrong I had to start all over again. Then I had to wait until Max was asleep so I could climb down the ladder of the bunk bed, put my hand on his hot little chest to feel it rise and fall six times. Only then could I relax. I had to lie on my back with the duvet no higher than my hips, even if I was too cold, and set the alarm to make sure that I didn't sleep more than nine hours. Max asked why just once and I explained quite simply that Mum was in danger and this was a way of protecting her. Later it transpired that I was right about Mum being in danger, just not the nature of the threat.

I probably missed vital clues through lack of sleep. My nerves were frayed from exhaustion and the effort of keeping watch over my family. Dad wasn't included. I knew he could look after himself. I was right about that too.

I hadn't seen Ava much that summer and the more she didn't arrive the more nervous I became that she hadn't been in touch with me. Mum had finally allowed me to get a Facebook account at the beginning of the holidays but Ava hadn't even responded to my friend request.

This wasn't completely unusual. I had noticed recently that, for Ava, life was increasingly whoever she was with that day, which made me a prisoner of a friendship that no longer delivered the intimacy I craved. I knew she and Rex had been sent to stay with her grandmother and her French husband somewhere in the South of France for a month so that Lisa and Barney could get on with their work. Although, when I think about this now, I realize the excuse about work was probably another untruth.

When their old blue Vauxhall finally wound its way up the drive at the weekend, music blaring and horn beeping, to shatter the relative peace of that holiday, instead of elation I remember for a brief moment violently wishing they had never come at all. We had got into a good family routine with comforting short cuts like eating cheese toasties in damp swimsuits on the sofa while we watched DVDs of *Friday Night Lights* in the evening and playing endless card games where Dad would let Mum win so she would keep going. I had enough time to tend my unwanted thoughts without anyone interrupting and was worried how I was going to run through my evening routines when we had to share the same sleeping space as Rex and Ava in the attic.

'Hello, people!' Barney shouted over the music when he got out of the car on the passenger side, as if he was the lead singer in a rock band addressing the audience from the Pyramid Stage at Glastonbury. He was wearing a pair of baggy floral swimming shorts, a Hawaiian shirt buttoned up the wrong way and round mirrored sunglasses. He held out his arms in a dramatic embrace waiting for someone to step forward and when we were slow to respond he lurched towards us, shirt billowing in the breeze to reveal a wobbly stomach pouring over the waistline of his trunks. I shrank back behind Dad.

'Mika!' said Barney to us all. 'He's going to be big, big, big! Remember you heard it here first.'

The music abruptly stopped. Someone in the car had turned it off. Unperturbed, Barney turned to Dad and hugged him tightly, pulling him from one side to the other so heartily that Dad had to put an arm on my shoulder to steady himself.

'Barney, it's great to see you,' said Dad breathlessly.

His mouth was laughing but his eyes were filled with something like tolerant contempt.

'Good journey?'

Barney didn't answer because his attention had turned to Mum. He used to adore Mum.

'Sorry about the delay, Rosie. Must have been like Geffen waiting for The Stone Roses' second album. I'll make it up to you. You look properly gorgeous, by the way.'

Mum danced skittishly from one leg to the other in embarrassment, but I could tell she was pleased.

'We're just so happy you made it at all,' she said, behaving as though they were doing us a favour by coming on holiday when it was obviously the other way round.

Barney bent down to kiss me on the cheek and I almost gagged when I smelt the sourness on his breath. It was like he was rotting from the inside out. His face was so shiny that it looked as if it was melting.

I don't remember much about Lisa. Over the years I have tried to cast my mind back to that moment. But unlike Barney, Lisa was always subtle. I remember her standing behind him wearing cut-off denim shorts and a pale pink T-shirt that might have belonged to Ava. If everything about Barney seemed louder and larger than I had remembered, everything about Lisa was smaller and quieter.

She got out of the car, gave Mum a smile that almost qualified as a grimace and mouthed 'sorry'. They hugged for a little too long, and when Lisa's sunglasses tumbled to the ground I could see she had been crying.

'Bloody hay fever,' she said, vigorously rubbing her nose when she saw me staring.

I looked at the car, expecting Ava to throw out her bags from the back seat, but instead Rex bounded out like a big, clumsy dog being released from a kennel that was too small. He stretched and I saw how his jeans hovered above his ankles and hair seemed to sprout from any part of his body that wasn't covered by clothes. When he came over and stood beside Barney I noticed that he was now the tallest in the group, apart from Dad.

'How did that happen?' Mum asked, craning her neck to speak to Rex as he gave her a quick hug before turning his attention to me.

'How are you, Small?' he asked, enfolding me in his arms.

'I'm good,' I said shyly. 'How's your earache?'

'What earache?' he laughed.

He had called me Small ever since I could remember. All the girls in my year at school fancied Rex and although I won a lot of points by declaring that I couldn't comment because I had grown up with him and he was like a brother to me, the sensation between my legs definitely wasn't sisterly. I tried not to breathe, so he would forget that I was in his arms. Rex always felt safe.

'You're not going to fit on the bunk bed,' I mumbled into his shoulder.

Mum gave him the once-over and quickly suggested he sleep on the sofa bed in the sitting room. 'You'll have more privacy there,' she said, eyeing Lisa for backup.

But Lisa was back at the car, leaning into the boot to get out bags with dirty laundry spewing out of half-undone zips. As she bent over Barney slapped her on the bum and said, 'I bet you look good on the dance floor.' Barney was always loud but this was something different. He was fizzing.

Max and I giggled, and Barney responded by doing a few more Dad-dance moves.

'My feet can hang over the edge of the bed,' said Rex self-consciously. 'Ava will just have to accept she goes on the bottom bunk.' It was an old argument whose familiarity made us laugh longer than the joke deserved and it occurred to me that during times of upheaval most human beings find comfort in rituals.

Ava chose to get out of the car at this moment – for maximum impact, I realized later. It was five weeks since I had last seen her at school and in that time she had transformed. She was sleek as an otter, taller, leaner and tanned in a way that is only possible after weeks in the South of France. Her hair was shorter and her legs longer. Everything about her had evolved. She was wearing a short striped crocheted halter-neck top that I had never seen before. It drew immediate attention to her breasts, which had grown so big that it was impossible to avoid them. I wasn't the only one who noticed. Dad ended up shaking her hand instead of hugging her, probably to avoid accidentally touching in case any contact might cause them to burst out of their skin. Max hung back shyly behind Mum, staring at Ava as if she was an exotic creature. Only Mum stepped forward.

'We're so pleased you've come,' said Mum, hugging her.

Why hadn't Ava warned me? I wondered. And then I

realized it would have diminished this moment of triumphant arrival. I glanced down at my own breasts and found them lacking. They were insecure and needy, requiring padded bras to make them stick out further than my tummy which, unlike Ava's, was coated in an extra layer of white blubber. I had been proudly wearing my new yellow-and-white striped bikini on the beach and knew immediately that I would hide it in my drawer and put on my old baggy navy swimsuit. I looked at her but all I could see were my faults reflected back. The fat calves and thick thighs. The red patches of sunburn set against pale skin that would never turn mahogany. Ava shot me a gloating smile that said she had made it to the other side of puberty to a place where her body worked in her favour and she had the power to bend the will of even men like my father. She had left me behind. This was her first act of betrayal.

'Greetings,' she said as everyone tried and failed not to stare at her.

I waited for her to come over and hug me but she didn't. Sometimes it's not the things people do that show you how they are feeling, but the things they don't. Usually after so much time apart we would have peeled off together and talked non-stop until we were convinced we had downloaded every detail of the space between us since we had last been together.

'Greetings,' responded Max, sensing an opportunity. 'Would you like to see my Lego Millennium Falcon?'

'Love to,' said Ava sweetly.

She slung a denim bag with French writing on the side over her shoulder, took Max's hand and they headed off into the house. She turned to me just as she reached the door.

'Coming?' she asked, and I followed them. Perhaps it was going to be all right.

I leapt up the stairs to the attic three at a time, hoping this would swing things in my favour, and when the clock in the hall struck three as I hit the top step I felt sure luck was with me. In the bedroom I waited for Ava to turn her attention from Max to me but she was too busy scrutinizing every single stormtrooper from his Lego ship, even though they were all identical. Then he told her about the ladybirds and she insisted on examining each matchbox and checking the details on the side.

'Daisy collects the wings every evening so that I can unite them with their bodies,' he explained. 'Daisy says they're like fairy dust sprinkled over the house.'

I felt myself go red with shame at being exposed as the half-child I was.

'That sounds like fun,' said Ava indulgently.

This was so far removed from Ava's usual idea of fun that even Max looked disbelieving. She began to climb up the ladder to the top bunk of the bed at the far end of the room, but before she had even reached the second rung, Rex charged into the room and rugby tackled her on to the floor.

'Not so fast, Average,' said Rex, using his pet name for her. 'I'm sleeping up there.'

'Rex, you total bastard,' said Ava, her face all stubborn bottom lip. Suddenly she looked and sounded like Ava again. 'I always sleep on top the first night.'

'I'll go on the bottom and you can go above me,'

suggested Max to Ava from the other side of the room. 'So you are comfortable.' He treated Ava like something breakable.

'Great,' said Ava. 'Rex can go on the top bunk of the other bed.'

Before I could say anything, Rex threw his bag on the top bunk of my bed. The idea of him sleeping above me was terrifyingly pleasurable even though I was already wondering how long I would have to wait for him to go to sleep so that I could run through all my stuff.

'I can put up with anything for six nights,' said Rex.

'Only six nights?' I said too quickly. 'I thought you were coming for ten?'

'It took us five days to get here,' said Ava, addressing me directly for the first time. 'Apparently Dad can only take a week off work, even though he hasn't got a proper job. And I've got a party next Saturday.'

'Whose party?' I asked, as casually as possible.

'I don't think you've met her,' said Ava, deliberately vague.

'Can't Daisy go with you?' asked Max. Despite the fact he was only ten he was old enough to smell betrayal.

'I've already got a plus one,' said Ava. 'I'm taking Molly.'

'But you hate Molly,' I spluttered, my voice coated with indignation and hurt. 'You said she was totally shallow and obsessed with boys.'

'Actually, that was me,' said Rex. 'And after a week with her in France I can confirm that is an understatement.'

'You took Molly to France?' I asked Ava incredulously. I couldn't believe it.

'Yeah,' she said. 'We share a lot of the same taste in music and clothes. Molly's cool.'

This was all the confirmation that I needed. My best friend had dumped me. Even worse, she hadn't even bothered to let me know.

'Shall we go and see the sheep?' suggested Rex, realizing his mistake.

It was his kindness that got me most. When we reached the field behind the house, we found the ewes forlornly bleating for their lambs that must have been taken away the same afternoon. That night, as I waited in bed for everyone to fall asleep, I listened to the sheep crying and understood that life was all about loss.

To stop the tears I pressed my fingers into my eyelids until I saw stars. My nose started running and I tried silent sniffing while I organized my thoughts. I needed to sort out which rituals I could run through without anyone noticing and leave the others till later. I arranged the alarm clock, glass of water and book in a triangle on the bedside table, made tiny adjustments and then started tapping out the triangular pattern on the bedroom wall beside the bottom bunk with the knuckle of my right index finger. Immediately I felt calmer.

Midway through the fourth set I felt a hand slide down from the top bunk to grab my wrist. It happened so quickly that for a moment I was paralysed with shock. I tried to pull away but Rex's grip proved too strong. He held my wrist in a vice for what seemed like ages. When I realized he wasn't going to release me without a fight I relaxed and his fingers slid away from my wrist and up on to my hand. I opened my palm in surrender and Rex began drawing small delicious circles that sent shivers up my body.

The same feeling stirred between my legs and spread over me until even my scalp tingled. My breathing got heavier but instead of counting the rise and fall of my chest I closed my eyes and gave in to the sticky pleasure of desire. For the first time in my life I didn't need words to articulate what was happening to me. I had kissed a boy from school at a party at the end of last term but it hadn't made me feel like this. I had explored his mouth with my tongue, conscious of the difference in texture between the softness of his gums and the hard white enamel of his teeth, but it was more like scientific research. This was totally different. It was so exquisitely pleasurable that I felt almost nauseous and when eventually he pulled his hand away the sense of loss left me feeling winded. I put my hand over my face and breathed in the smell of him on my skin. The same thing happened the following night, except the second time his hand was waiting and I searched for it with my own.

Tuesday was going to be the hottest day of the year and we decided to spend it on Mum's favourite beach because she had to get the train back to London the next day for work. It was within walking distance of the house but preparations to get there always took so ridiculously long that you would have thought we were travelling to the outback for weeks. We all assumed roles rehearsed over years and, for a short while, it felt like old times. Barney took charge of drinks, filling the cool box with water, cans of beer and a bottle of white wine; Dad made a tomato sauce with at least ten ingredients to put inside wraps that he would heat up on the beach in a frying pan; I stood beside him crushing garlic and chopping onions, debating whether we should leave out capers and include black olives. Cooking with Dad used to be one of my favourite activities. Lisa fried bacon for the filling and talked about how she couldn't wait for lunch even though she never seemed to eat anything, while Barney made bad jokes about the advantages of a mostly liquid diet. Mum and Ava got together all the equipment. Over the years this had got more and more elaborate to include a luxury camping stove, kettle, three windbreaks, beach chairs and a blow-up whale. I watched as Mum took out a knife from the kitchen drawer.

'What's that for?' I asked casually.

'To cut the cheese,' she said.

'Why don't we grate it instead and leave the knife here?' I suggested.

'Good thinking,' said Dad.

Mum put the knife back. I felt calmer than I had in ages. For the first time in around six months I hadn't gone through any rituals that morning. My head was too full of Rex.

I was hyper-aware of his presence. At breakfast he had sat down beside me on the wide-backed bench, close enough that I could feel the heat from his right thigh. The energy flowing between us was so strong that I was sure someone would notice. As he buttered toast I furtively observed his long, elegant fingers from beneath my fringe. I imagined them tracing a line from my hand, up to my shoulder, and then stopped in case someone could read my thoughts. I was certain he would engineer an opportunity to be alone with me, but after finishing four pieces of toast (unlike mine, his appetite was undiminished) he announced that he was going for a run.

'Are you listening, Daisy?' Dad asked, as he put the lid on his tomato sauce.

'Sorry?'

'I was asking if you want to come to the beach to help light the barbecue.'

'I need to look for my swimsuit,' I said, even though I was already wearing it underneath my shorts and T-shirt. I knew no one would notice my untruth. Everyone's focus on that holiday was someplace where it shouldn't have been. I went into the washroom and pretended to search through the laundry basket, waiting for the anxiety and the bad thoughts about Mum, but they didn't come. At the bottom of the basket I found a T-shirt belonging to Rex. I sat down on the floor between the washing machine and tumble dryer where no one could see me and lifted it to my face and inhaled his scent, a sweet mixture of sweat, cheap aftershave and smoke.

Ava had gone without telling me, Max trailing behind her like a devoted puppy. I could hear Dad and Barney heading out through the front door, complaining about the overloaded baskets that they had just packed.

'How's it going?' I heard Mum ask Lisa as soon as the front door banged shut.

I put down the T-shirt.

'Not good. I found an empty bottle of vodka in his computer bag this morning,' said Lisa. 'He tried to pretend it belonged to Rex but I pointed out that the label proved it came from an off-licence by his old office in King's Cross. He won't admit it, but it was the drinking that lost him the job.'

I was more taken aback by the savagery of Lisa's tone, like knives shredding Barney apart, than the revelation about his drinking, which frankly was anticlimactic. All adults drank too much. Period.

'It's not Barney's fault that the Internet is killing journalism,' Mum said. 'Why would anyone pay for something they can read for free?'

'So why did they get rid of Barney and keep on the guy he recruited two years ago?'

'Maybe he costs less,' said Mum without conviction.

'Maybe he drinks less, Rosie.'

'Did you mention the bottle?'

'He told me he could handle it, that my intense scrutiny made him feel as though he had a plastic bag over his head and was slowly asphyxiating, which is strange because that's exactly how he makes me feel.'

Mum didn't say anything and I guessed she was giving Lisa a hug.

'I can't go on like this, Rosie.'

'He must be feeling so bad about his job,' said Mum gently. 'What Barney needs is a plan. Has he put out any feelers?'

'His editor said he can freelance but they're not going to give him a contract and the word rate is piss poor,' said Lisa. 'Barney's kind of journalism is dead but he won't accept it and instead of doing something positive like going for a run or offering to write about something other than music, he's smoking and drinking himself into oblivion. Like Keith Richards without the bank balance.'

I couldn't believe what I was hearing. Lisa and Barney were one of those truly, madly couples who went to glamorous parties with famous people. They weren't like any of Mum and Dad's other friends who were, quite frankly, pretty boring. Barney and Lisa still kissed in public and had parties that people talked about for weeks. For my twelfth birthday Barney had not only got me a free ticket to see Girls Aloud but had also arranged for me to meet Cheryl Cole. I didn't realize the invitations dried up the moment he lost his job.

'Barney's only consistent quality is his ability to suck the joy out of almost every situation.'

'At least he's not going out late and shagging other women,' said Mum.

I sat up straight. I had never heard her speak like this before. It struck me that Mum and Lisa were more intimate with each other than I was with Mum. *Just like Ava and me,* I thought. Then I remembered our friendship was over. I waited for the stab of loss but it was already blunted.

'Anything would be better than this,' said Lisa. 'One of us might as well be happy.'

'God, I'd kill Nick if he was unfaithful,' said Mum.

'Everyone is susceptible,' said Lisa.

'At least if he was having sex I guess his mood might improve,' said Mum.

She giggled wickedly and so did Lisa and I admired Mum's ability to always make people feel better in any situation, although I was also wondering what susceptible meant. Was I susceptible? Was Rex? Was Mum? Were we all susceptible? She made it sound dangerous, like a transmittable disease.

'He blames me for everything. He says that if I was kinder to him then he wouldn't feel the need to kill his feelings with alcohol but I'm not good at infinite patience, Rosie. He falls asleep on the sofa most nights. The other morning I had to hold up a mirror in front of his mouth to see if he was still alive, and then when it steamed up I almost felt gutted. This is not what I signed up for.'

'You'll get through this,' said Mum gently. 'You guys have always had a great relationship. The foundations are strong.'

'Things haven't been right for a while,' said Lisa. 'The drinking has crept up on him.'

'Do you think it would help if Nick spoke to him?'

'I don't think so.' There was a long pause. 'Barney's got a problem with Nick.'

'What do you mean?'

'I didn't want to say anything. I feel so bad bringing all our problems on holiday. But Nick makes Barney feel inadequate. Nick represents everything that Barney isn't. He's the king of self-restraint whereas Barney has no willpower whatsoever. Nick has a great job. He takes exercise. He exudes a sense of responsibility. Barney feels like a loser beside him.'

'That's awful,' said Mum.

I couldn't believe Lisa was talking about my dad like this. I felt proud of my parents at this moment.

'Will you be all right when I'm gone?' Mum asked Lisa.

A few days ago Mum's absence would have made me so anxious that I would have had to go through an intensive bout of magical thinking to protect her while she was away. Now I felt almost liberated at the thought of her leaving.

'I'll be fine,' said Lisa. 'If anything goes wrong, Nick will help.'

The back door slammed and they were gone. I picked up the T-shirt, lay down on the floor, stuffed it between my legs and rocked back and forth until I was a hot soggy mess.

When I got to the beach no one seemed to notice I had even been missing. Ava was lying on her back on a boogie board, flicking through one of those magazines that promise better versions of yourself, as if every part requires constant self-improvement. Max was encircling her with a wall of sandcastles.

'I'm building them in groups of three, to protect Ava,' he explained, searching for my approval and then looking confused when I blushed. 'I know you think three is a good and safe number.'

'Why three?' Ava asked languidly, without opening her eyes.

She hardly spoke to me on that holiday and, when she did, it was only to emphasize the distance between us. I willed myself not to glance at her breasts and remembered how, just the previous Christmas, we had put satsumas in our trainer bras to try to imagine what they might feel like.

'Is it because Rex's name only has three letters?'

'Stop it, Ava,' said Lisa, who was lying on her front beside Mum.

I get she was trying to be kind but you lose even more dignity when people feel sorry for you. I couldn't help noticing the way Mum looked so soft and doughy beside Lisa, her swimsuit all baggy. She didn't stir from her medical journal.

'There's room beside me,' said Rex, patting the sand. 'Come on, Small.'

I carefully laid out my towel beside his, sucking in my tummy as I got on all fours to iron out the wrinkles before sitting in the furthest corner with my back to him, knees pulled up against my chest. How was it possible to feel so self-conscious and so invisible at the same time? I stared at the sea, watching out for seals, and wondered if Ava's magazine contained a cure for fatty knees.

Dad had lit the barbecue and was aggressively fanning the flames with a paper plate. Barney was sitting in a deckchair, legs splayed, with a bottle of beer in one hand while the other possessively rested on the cool box. An empty bottle lay tipped on its side in the sand beside him.

'Do you want a beer, Ava?' Barney asked.

Ava shook her head.

'She's fourteen, Barney,' said Lisa in exasperation.

'It's good to build up tolerance,' Barney said.

No one laughed. Even his jokes had gone off.

'Don't be angry with me, Lisa,' said Barney, resting his cold bottle of beer on Lisa's bum. She jumped. 'I can't bear it when you're angry with me.'

'Give it a rest, Barney,' said Dad.

'Don't you think my wife looks beautiful?' Barney turned to Dad. Dad ignored him. 'She's hardly got a wrinkle on her face.'

'That's because I don't have anything to smile about,' muttered Lisa. When she saw Rex and Ava were listening she tried to do that thing where you turn something that is truer than anything else you have ever said into a joke.

Barney flipped the lid of the beer into Lisa's face.

She flinched. 'Barney, it's not even midday.'

'We're on holiday,' said Barney. 'Why so uptight?'

'Why don't you go and have a swim before lunch, Barney?' suggested Mum.

Lisa shot her a grateful glance.

'Good idea, Rosie,' said Barney, his shoulders immediately relaxing.

I felt a foot poke me in the small of my back.

'Come on, Small,' Rex said. 'I'll race you and Dad.'

The three of us ran towards the sea and I didn't worry whether my tummy was jiggling or my flesh was the worst shade of pale pink because as long as Rex wanted to be with me it didn't matter. I threw myself into the water and felt my body pincushion with goosebumps as I dived into the middle of a wave that was about to break on top of me. I kept swimming underwater until I couldn't hold my breath any more.

When I came up I flipped gracefully on to my back, closed my eyes against the glare of the sun and porpoised, over and over again, pretending I was a seal. When I finished I looked back at the beach. Barney was lying in the shallows, like a beached whale. Ava was still stretched out on the boogie board. Her loss, being too cool to swim on such a hot day. Mum was reading. Dad and Lisa were crouched down over the frying pan, cooking tortillas for wraps. Their heads were bowed, foreheads almost touching as if they were praying. *They are susceptible*, I said out loud with absolute certainty, without understanding what I even meant. Rex chose that moment to grab my leg underwater and I shrieked so loudly that even Ava stirred to see what was going on.

'Time for the death roll,' Rex grinned.

We had done this a thousand times before. I took a breath so deep it hurt my lungs. Rex slid his arms under mine and wrapped them around the front of my chest from behind so I was pinned tightly against his body. Then he pulled me under. We twisted and turned along the seabed for what seemed like ages before surfacing together, breathless with exhilaration. He didn't let go. I pressed the back of my head into his chest, feeling the hair tickling my cheek, and let my legs float to the surface as he pulled me through the water.

'You're so sweet, Small,' he whispered in my ear.

I didn't trust myself to say anything because for once my head was blissfully empty of all thoughts.

We stuck to our resolution to be the last people on the beach, not even shifting when the tide had consumed so much of the sand that we were left sitting on a narrow ribbon with the sea lapping at our feet. Max frantically dug a moat around Ava, vowing to protect her, as if willpower alone could hold back the tide. But eventually he had to admit defeat. We were all subject to forces of nature stronger than ourselves that week.

I don't remember exactly how the row started after dinner. It was the hottest day of the year but we couldn't eat outside because we had reached peak ladybird infestation.

They flew into our eyes, our ears, our hair and the drinks we tried to sip on the weed-infested terrace. In the end we had to close all the doors and windows, and even then they came up through the plug in the sink and crawled in through keyholes. Max couldn't keep up with the scale of the invasion but when he tried to enlist Ava's help she refused.

Every surface of the house felt sticky, even the parts that shouldn't, like the old velvet sofa and the television controls. Dad said it smelt of domestic rot, which upset Mum because he was talking about the house she had grown up in. Lisa defused the situation by finding an old CD by a band called The Stranglers that turned out to be Dad's favourite album of all time. But this seemed to irritate Barney, who said he was fed up with Lisa's 'possessive insights' about Dad and the way she was undermining his role as resident music expert. It seemed even more pathetic than the arguments Max and I had.

It was Barney's turn to cook dinner but apparently he had suddenly been asked to write a review of the album that he had been playing in the car. So instead of making Bolognese sauce he took his computer up to the bedroom to work. Clubby beats thumped through the sitting-room ceiling but when Lisa went to check on progress he was asleep, which meant that Dad, the only person in the house capable of rustling up a decent meal involving three ingredients (a packet of pasta, olive oil and a few cloves of garlic), had to step in at the last minute. Lisa's gratitude was only matched by Barney's resentment. He came down to dinner long after we had finished. No one mentioned his absence. He tripped and fell down the last three stairs and when he poured into the sitting room, I wondered if he had drunk so much that he had actually changed state and become liquid. 'Let's get this party started!' Barney croaked. He got up, turned off The Stranglers and put on a dance track that even Max could tell didn't match the mood.

He headed towards the sofa and landed clumsily beside Rex and me and began ruffling Rex's hair with his hand in a way that I could tell was both irritating and uncomfortable.

'You're a good son, Rex,' he said, over and over again, panting gently, all droopy-mouthed.

Rex shifted away from him towards me and lifted my legs on to his lap to create more room. He put his hand on my knee and the sensation was so pleasurable that I didn't trust myself to speak. I wondered if anyone else had noticed because the air around us must have changed at a molecular level but everyone else's attention was focused on trying to ignore Barney.

'Dad. Please,' Rex said gently. 'Why don't you go back to bed?'

'Contrary to what some people might have said, I wasn't in bed, son. I was working. Putting food on the table. Trying to keep your mother happy. Not an easy task. She's a very demanding woman. Has high standards.' The more he spoke, the more he slowed and slurred his words until they were as sticky as treacle.

'Not here. Not now,' said Rex in a low voice. 'Please.' He sounded like a little boy.

I glanced over at Ava. She was wearing headphones and humming, painting her toenails with black nail varnish, impervious to what was going on around her.

'Get me a glass of wine, Rex,' said Barney.

Even my thirteen-year-old self could tell he was as thirsty for conflict as he was for wine. His face had darkened and his eyes narrowed to tiny slits. Lisa got up from the arm of the chair where Mum was sitting. She knelt down in front of Barney and put her hands on his knees. His hands were clenched so tightly that his knuckles were completely white.

'Please, I think you've had enough,' whispered Lisa. 'Let's go upstairs together.'

'Has anyone told you that sometimes you can be the tiniest bit really fucking boring, Lisa?' said Barney.

'That's enough, Barney,' Mum intervened. 'Max is here.'

She got up and removed the bottle of wine from the table beside him. He didn't protest. I realized that Mum was probably the only person in the room capable of turning this around.

'What do you think, Nick?' Barney turned to Dad, who was sitting at the kitchen table holding his head in his hands. 'Do you think I've had enough? Because you seem to be the big man around here.'

I put my hand on top of Rex's and squeezed it.

'Barney, please,' pleaded Lisa. 'These are our friends. All they want is for us to have a nice time together.'

'Are you sure about that, Lisa? Are you sure that's all they want? What empirical evidence do you have for that statement?'

'Barney, you've been coming on holiday here for years and whenever you leave you say it's the best week of your life. You're with people who love you more than anyone else in the world. Why don't you sit down at the table and eat some spaghetti?' Mum tried to reason with him. 'Get him some water, Nick,' she said.

Dad got up and went over to the sink. He slowly sliced a lemon and took some ice from the freezer and eventually brought the glass over to Barney. Barney stood up from the sofa to take the water from Dad. Swaying back and forth, he took a sip, gave a sudden smile and for a couple of seconds I thought everything was going to be fine.

But instead he wordlessly threw the water, ice and lemon in Dad's face, smashed the glass on the floor and stomped upstairs, slamming the door behind him. Mum got up to follow him.

'Leave him, Rosie. No one can do anything with him when he's like this,' said Lisa, her voice a whisper. She fetched kitchen roll and began soaking up water from Dad's drenched T-shirt.

'I'm so sorry, Nick' she said. 'We shouldn't have come. It's my fault for persuading him.'

I found the note from Rex a couple of days later, after Mum had gone to London. It was buried in a confetti of dead ladybirds inside one of Max's matchboxes hidden underneath my pillow. I carefully unfolded the piece of paper. *Bunker 3 p.m.*, read the tiny black writing in the middle. Hands trembling, I turned it over to read the other side. *You make me hard.* The matchbox slipped through my fingers and hundreds of dead ladybirds floated past on to the floor. I was alone in the bedroom but I felt the heat rise to my face and course through the rest of my body, until even the inside of my mouth, nostrils and ears burned. Although no one had ever come close to saying something like this to me, I knew exactly what it meant. It was the sort of thing the boys in my year dared themselves to whisper to girls like Ava, knowing she would laugh in their face.

I don't know why I was so surprised. Although it was the logical climax of everything that had occurred between us over the past week, it most definitely wasn't how Ross spoke to Rachel and it didn't conform to the romantic narrative I had imagined. A phrase from a sex ed class at school last term danced into my head. *The penis is made of spongy tissue filled with thousands of blood vessels.* Afterwards Ava and I had sung this line to the tune of a song by the Scissor Sisters and laughed until we cried.

I had always imagined that losing my virginity would be the culmination of a long-drawn-out process with endless footnotes along the way that I would discuss with Ava. I had anticipated weeks of preparation, involving exercise focused on what magazines identify as problem areas, the exact amount of depilation for someone who had only recently grown pubic hair and, most importantly, the purchase of appropriate underwear. Not this sudden explicit proposal. Even in my altered state I knew I was completely out of my depth. But it didn't occur to me for one second that I shouldn't turn up. Rex's lust was surely a measure of his love.

After finding the note I stayed upstairs for a couple of hours, trying to read the new Harry Potter. When I couldn't concentrate, I experimented with outfits, finally opting for my denim miniskirt with buttons down the front, a plain white T-shirt, bikini top and a pair of white knickers that were the wrong side of sexy but the right side of clean.

When I went down to the kitchen everyone apart from Barney was milling around. No one mentioned his absence. Max was still wearing his pyjamas. Unwashed saucepans from lunch, breakfast and the night before sat on the cooker and kitchen worktop. Someone had put dirty dishes into the dishwasher without checking whether the rest were clean but no one had bothered to sort out the muddle. This was what happened when Mum went away. All the boundaries got blurred. Clean and dirty, breakfast and lunch, loyalty and treachery.

'Hello, Small,' said Rex, patting the seat beside him.

I tried to avoid looking at him and blushed. Of course he wanted us to behave normally together so no one else would be suspicious but unlike him I was a complete amateur. I looked at the space and worried that if he found me so irresistibly attractive he might get an erection and Ava might notice. She would most definitely say something.

'He's not going to bite you,' Ava teased.

She would be ruthless if she sensed my fragility so I sat down at the end of the table and pretended to read my book again. '*Of course it is happening inside your head, Harry, but why on earth should that mean that it is not real?*' I read the same line over and over again, wondering if I had the same problem.

'Maybe she'd like him to,' said Max, who was playing Connect 4 with her. 'Did you know that ladybirds bite, Ava?'

Lisa was writing a shopping list and Dad was insisting

she didn't need to because he could remember everything off by heart using memory cues he had devised to help people with dementia. He showed off by reciting every team in the Premier League, the names and addresses of all the parents on the class list and the ingredients of the crab pasta we were planning to cook together that night. It occurred to me that by then my world would have turned on its axis. Would I even be able to eat afterwards? I wondered.

'Why don't you come with me and then you can see the empirical evidence for yourself?' said Dad. 'That's what a good scientist does.'

'I'm a lawyer,' said Lisa.

'It's still an evidence-based profession,' he teased.

I was pleased he was being so kind to Lisa, because she would be missing Mum.

Dad turned to Max. 'Can you keep an eye on Daisy, please?'

It was one of our favourite family jokes and we all laughed. I felt bad for Rex, and even Ava, because our happiness was in such contrast to their misery.

'I'm going to the beach,' I told Max when I found him in the kitchen a few hours later. He was lying flat on the floor using a pair of tweezers to pick out dead ladybirds from the gap between the floor and skirting board. 'Will you be okay?'

He didn't look up. 'It's exhausting trying to keep on top of all this,' he sighed, like a tired old man.

'Barney's here. If you need anything.'

'Like a glass of wine, you mean.'

We both giggled. I headed out the back door through

the garden, wondering if it was going to hurt and whether I should have downed a couple of sachets of Calpol from the bathroom cupboard. As I walked under the washing line, I saw a pair of tiny black knickers that belonged to Lisa hanging on the line and impulsively tore them down and stuffed them into the waistband of my skirt. I wondered why Lisa wore such exotic underwear. I was pretty certain that the new version of Barney that had turned up on this holiday wouldn't notice the way the lace felt like the wings of the ladybirds.

I headed towards the beach. It was really hot and I held up my arms so my T-shirt wouldn't get sweaty. I was drenched with Mum's perfume. It attracted clouds of ladybirds that I tried to windmill away. I increased my pace. When I got to the dunes I looked behind me to check that no one had seen me. I cut left through the marram grass and it whipped my legs red raw but I was glad of the pain because it took my mind off what was to come.

The old breeze-block pillbox had been built during the war for the Home Guard to defend the coast. It nestled in the dunes, camouflaged by folds of sand and plants that now threatened to obscure it completely. Over the years it had become our favourite location for elaborate imaginary games that sometimes took up the whole day: Viking invader, hide and seek, doctors and nurses. Even when he was tiny Max was always the doctor. Ava and I used to pretend the pillbox was our house and cook sand cakes that we served to Rex and Max on seaweed plates. Last year we had discovered the hexagonal roof was a perfect suntrap. I found the door straight away. The arch was even smaller than I remembered and I had to crawl through the gap, commando-style on my stomach, which filled my T-shirt and bikini top with sand.

It was dark inside, which was a blessing because Rex might not notice the way my skin puckered around my buttocks and the ladybird bite on my leg that had gone septic. The air was damp and musty and I noticed that the ground was strewn with rubbish left by other people. I buried some empty beer cans and half-eaten packets of crisps. Then I smoothed an area flat by the small slit window and unfolded the towel I had brought with me so that I could tell anyone nosy enough to ask that I was going swimming.

I sat down and waited. For weeks my head had been brimming over with thoughts and now I felt strangely calm, as if my entire life had been leading up to this moment. I remembered Rex lying on top of me, tickling me until I cried, when I was little; I remembered how he had come up to me in the playground on my first day at secondary school to whisper, 'Stand tall, Small,' in my ear, winning me the immediate approval of my new classmates; I traced back gestures of casual affection and saw that each had meaning. How many people end up marrying the first person they have sex with? I wondered, casually confident I would soon be able to contribute to such debates.

There was a noise outside the window. It sounded like a voice. He was here. I knelt on the towel and combed my hair with my fingers, waiting for him to crawl through the entrance. I felt something press into my stomach and remembered that Lisa's knickers were still stuffed down my skirt. I quickly pulled off my old white knickers, buried them in the sand beside me, and pulled on the pair I had stolen from the washing line. They were too big and blousy but mine were now covered in sand. I felt panicked by the obscene idea that he might notice I was wearing his mum's underwear. But it was too late. I heard another noise outside, this time more high-pitched. I wondered if it was an oystercatcher. They always made their nests in the dunes.

I looked through the narrow arrow-slit window. Outside the wind had sculpted a small, perfectly shaped shelter in the dunes. It was surrounded by clumps of grass and wild plants creating a totally discreet bowl that in a different time would have been perfect for nude sunbathing. There was something there. I pressed my face towards the window opening, imagining that I might see Rex beckoning me to come and share this new hiding place.

But instead I saw the back of a man's head facing the sand. Except he wasn't making human noises. He was grunting like an animal. The noises got louder, forming a guttural rhythm like ancient music. My eyes adjusted to the brightness and the man lifted his chin towards the sky. It was Dad. His swimming trunks were down by his ankles, and he was on top of a woman, grinding his hips into the centre of her being so hard that at first I was relieved that it wasn't Mum being subjected to such rough treatment. Then almost immediately I realized that it should have been Mum. The woman's legs clamped Dad's lower body to hers. I put my hands over my ears because I didn't want to listen to the obscenities coming out of Dad's mouth. The woman directed his rhythm. It sounded as though they were dying. *Sex is death. Sex is death. Sex is death.* The thought barrelled through my head in time with their rhythm.

I glanced over at the door, willing Rex to arrive, because surely he would know what to do, and then the noise stopped. I looked out of the window again. The woman beneath Dad turned her head to one side so she was looking straight at me. Her face glistened with sweat and I saw it was Lisa.

I'm not sure how long I waited in the pillbox after this. It could have been minutes or hours. Rex never appeared. I blamed myself for what had happened. If I had done my rituals that day then I would have saved Mum. It was all my fault. Anxiety cascaded through my body and I resolved to immediately improve my system to prevent any more catastrophes on my watch:

1. Instead of just tapping the ball of my foot I would tap the heel and the side.
2. As well as tapping my shoulders I would include my elbows and the inside of my wrists.
3. In addition to checking the curtains and windows, I needed to check every plug was taken out of its socket before I went to bed, every switch was off and the gas was turned off.
4. I would triple the number of times I had to say the special words at the end of all the movements.

I ran through this new routine once and for a while the anxiety subsided and my head felt clear. When I finally left to go back to the house I knew that I had changed completely. I felt as though someone had turned me inside out, exposing every cell and nerve ending, leaving me with no defences. *Three is a good and safe number.* I said it over and over again on that long walk home.

IO

Max

I was still collecting up dead *Coccinellidae* from the sitting-room floor when Daisy appeared in the garden. Outside thunder rumbled and lightning forked the sky but inside it was hot, sweaty work. The ladybirds stuck like Velcro to the bottom of furniture and their wings turned to dust between my fingers. I was almost overwhelmed by the scale of it all. There were 276 bodies under the coffee table alone. I quickly ran out of space in my matchboxes and had to use an old ice-cream tub for the spillover. Counting each body would take hours and I needed Dad's advice on how to estimate but he was still at the shops with Lisa.

Barney might have helped, but he had been asleep upstairs all day and after what he did to Dad the other night, there was no way I was going to disturb him. 'He's in exile,' Ava announced at breakfast. No one responded or even mentioned what had happened, even when Rex got a piece of broken glass in his toe and Daisy insisted she had to hold his foot in her lap for half an hour to prevent him from bleeding to death. If I had thrown a glass of water at someone, the consequences would have been catastrophic.

Nothing felt quite right on that holiday. And although

I had an idea of what was wrong, I just couldn't work out why it was wrong. It was like when I looked through the wrong end of Dad's binoculars and could see something in the distance without knowing what it was. But somehow I convinced myself that if I could keep on top of my ladybird research then everything else might feel less wonky.

I looked up at Ava, who had refused to move so I could reach the ladybirds under the armchair. Her feet were resting on my bare back while I lay flat on my stomach using a ruler to scrape out dead insects. She was watching *Friends* on a computer, listening through headphones, and lip-synching all the best lines. I could tell when each episode finished because she curled her toes in and out in time to the music, scratching my back with her long black nails. It should have been unpleasant but it wasn't. Either she hadn't noticed Daisy was standing in the pouring rain, gazing up at the sky, or more likely she was ignoring her. Ava specialized in psychological torture.

'Isn't that just kick-you-in-the-crotch, spit-on-your-neck fantastic?' she said, doing a terrible impersonation of Jennifer Aniston.

Then the toe-curling began again. There would be scratches on my back the next day but I didn't mind. They would remind me of her when she was gone. I understood for the first time on that holiday what Daisy saw in Ava. Being the object of her attention was like having a tiger for tea. It felt dangerous and comforting at the same time. Although it took years for me to realize, she was the prototype for all my adult relationships with women. I never truly fancied a girl unless she put me on edge.

I woke up each day tense with the need for her attention and couldn't believe it when she wanted to play with
me. She helped me fix the tiny helmets on to my
stormtroopers when they came apart; she didn't complain
when I wanted to pause *Doctor Who* to discuss whether the
Weeping Angels were more frightening than the Abzor-
baloff; and she let me watch any film she was watching
without mentioning my age. Best of all she saved me from
the new games Daisy wanted to play, which weren't really
games at all, because they weren't any fun and for the first
time in my life they made me scared of my own sister.

They involved things like repeatedly checking whether
the curtains in our bedroom were touching all the way
down the middle in exactly the way Daisy wanted. If I
went from floor to ceiling, for example, she would make
me start all over again. Sometimes when I finally got it
right she insisted I open them to check the window was
closed properly so I had to repeat the manoeuvre. While
I was doing this she often disappeared downstairs. I followed her once and saw her take out all the knives from
the kitchen drawer, count them three times, in a really
sinister way, and then put them back. I would fall asleep
to the sound of her tapping on the wall. Totally weird.

Even worse, Daisy acted like she was doing me a favour
by letting me join in. When I asked her why we had to do
all this stuff she explained that it was magic to keep Mum
and me safe, which was a good example of irony, because
the only thing that frightened me was Daisy with all her
weirdnesses.

The first time I was truly freaked out was a few days
after we arrived. I was on the bottom bunk, in total

darkness, drifting between sleep and wakefulness, when I felt something touch my upper body. It pressed down on my Shaun the Sheep pyjama top close to his head, and stayed there. I froze with fear and kept my eyes tight shut, convinced it was the ghost of my grandmother, who had died in this same bedroom when I was little. I imagined her dressed in her favourite pale-pink nightdress, naked beneath, with a big black hole where her teeth should be, because she always took them out at night. I had once caught sight of her pubic hair and it was thicker than Shaun the Sheep's fringe. Just considering this made me even more terrified because ghosts know exactly what you are thinking.

The hand stayed on my chest. I started to make all sorts of promises to myself about what I would do if only it would disappear: I won't take short cuts with Daisy's magic spells; I will never again take coins higher than 10p from Mum's purse. As it crept slowly to the lower seam of my pyjama top and gently peeled it up towards my chest the promises got more and more extravagant: I will learn to say my times tables backwards; I will eat cucumber; I won't stare at breasts. The hand rested on my bare stomach. Please don't let it drift any lower, I pleaded in my head, not because I was scared of it slipping inside my pyjama bottoms but because I didn't want even a ghost to know that I had wet the bed. That was my most shameful secret.

And then the low whispering started. 'Be safe, brother of mine. Be safe, brother of mine. Be safe, brother of mine.' I recognized the voice straight away. At first I thought she might be sleepwalking but then I realized she was counting my breaths in sets of three until she reached nine. 'Three is a good and safe number,' I heard her say. The same thing happened the following night. No surprise that when Ava and Rex arrived I instantly volunteered to go in a bunk bed with Ava. And for a few days at least things went back to normal.

The French doors crashed open and Daisy came into the sitting room, looking wild. The downpour outside had oiled her hair to her scalp. Her eye make-up was mostly streaked down her cheeks. As her calves stepped over me I noticed they were whipped red raw and that a small trail of blood had leached into the top of her favourite trainers, which were leaving a trail of sandy footprints on the pale-blue carpet. The cuts on her legs were a dead giveaway – only the razor-sharp grass in the dunes could savage you like that.

'Have you seen Dad?' I asked, trying to put a lid on the overflowing ice-cream tub.

She shook her head and her dark eyes bored into me like she was looking for an answer without asking a question. I shrank back into Ava, who kept up with the *Friends* riff: *'All right, look if you absolutely have to tell her the truth, at least wait until the timing's right. And that's what deathbeds are for.'*

Ava looked straight at Daisy and pulled off her headphones. 'Are you, like, practising for Halloween or something?' Ava asked, wrinkling her nose in a way that always made me smile.

Daisy brushed her hand over her face and when she saw the black streaks on her fingertips she started wiping more vigorously, spitting on her hand and scouring her cheeks until they were as red as her legs.

'Please don't, Daisy. You're making it worse.' I tried to get up to make her stop but Ava's legs pressed down on my back and the more I tried to wriggle away the deeper she dug in her nails.

'Don't worry about Rex seeing you messed up. He's not here,' said Ava flippantly.

It was the right thing to say because Daisy immediately stopped clawing at her face.

'Do you know where he is?' she asked Ava, trying to sound casual.

'He went to the caravan site to find that girl he met yesterday and the day before,' Ava said, holding Daisy's gaze.

My stomach tensed. I hadn't been expecting this.

'Which girl?' asked Daisy.

Don't make it sound as though you care, I thought. How could she be friends with Ava for so many years and not realize that?

'The incredibly cool girl with the wolf tattoo on her calf who comes the same week every August,' said Ava, finally releasing me.

I got up from the floor and rubbed the furrows in my back.

'Remember we spied on her and Rex in the dunes last year? She was sunbathing topless.'

I couldn't remember her face but I could remember her breasts. They were unavoidable. Like Ava's.

'Max remembers,' giggled Ava. 'Why do you remember, Max?'

I blushed.

'Rex didn't tell me that was where he was going,' said

Daisy, pushing her hands deep into the pockets of her denim skirt. Her gaze jumped nervously from Ava to me.

'What did he tell you?' asked Ava, raising one eyebrow. 'I didn't realize you were stalking him.'

This was a lie because the joke that holiday was if you wanted to find Daisy, you just had to locate Rex. Everyone knew she had a crush on him. She exposed herself on a daily basis by wearing make-up at breakfast and sitting too close to him and pretending to like things she hated eating, like crab, or knew nothing about, like rap music. Sometimes Ava would tease her and for a couple of hours Daisy would rein it in but then the humiliating cycle would begin all over again. Behind her back Ava referred to Daisy as 'The Limpet'. Lisa described her more fondly as 'Rex's little shadow'. But instead of feeling angry with them I was furious with Daisy for not being able to see she was making a fool of herself.

To be honest, if I was a girl I might have fancied Rex. What I hadn't realized until that moment in the sitting room was that Daisy genuinely thought she was in with a chance. She truly believed Rex was interested in her when it was obvious he felt sorry for her. Even worse, Ava understood in that way girls like her do, and she wasn't afraid to show Daisy the absurdity of her illusion. I wanted to protect my sister from this harsh truth but it was too late. She went wordlessly upstairs and, although part of me knew I should go after her, the other part wanted to stay with Ava even more.

A few minutes later, Barney lumbered into the room, slow as a giant Galapagos tortoise, and lay down on the sofa. I had almost forgotten he was in the house. He was wearing the same pair of swimming trunks as yesterday and it looked as though he had shaved one half of his face and forgotten the other. His trunks were splattered with purple spots that I guessed were red wine. I was relieved to see he was holding a glass of water, which he tried to balance on his stomach in between tiny sips.

'Hey,' he said. 'What's up?'

'Hey, Dad,' shouted Ava over her headphones. 'Do you want to watch *Friends* with me?'

'I've got work to do,' said Barney. He opened up a music magazine and told me how he was the first person ever to review an album by the Arctic Monkeys and should have been given first refusal on any interview with the lead singer, especially since he had just been one of their VIP guests at Glastonbury. I was flattered he wanted to discuss this with me.

'Maybe he thinks you're too busy,' I said, trying to be helpful.

'Correct,' said Barney, nodding so fast that his chins quivered. He frowned at the magazine. 'Whose turn is it to cook supper? I haven't eaten all day.'

'It should be Dad's,' I explained. 'But he ended up cooking the other night when it was meant to be you because of the ... the ... situation.' There was a long silence. My stomach rumbled and I realized that I hadn't eaten since breakfast either. 'Did you know that a ladybird consumes an average five hundred aphids during its lifetime?' Dad always said that the best way to deal with an awkward silence was to fill it with a good solid fact.

'Are they back yet?' He didn't mention Dad and Lisa by name but I knew he was talking about them. He rested the magazine on his stomach and put the glass on top, making me feel nervous because it was obviously going to tip over and then Dad would get angry with him for messing up the sofa.

'I don't think so,' I said, knowing whatever I said it wouldn't be enough. I tried to think what Mum would say in this situation. 'Maybe they can't find any Cromer crabs in Cromer.'

I felt uncomfortable without understanding why, which is probably the reason I so eagerly agreed to his next suggestion to go to the fish and chip shop.

'Then we'll have dinner on the table when everyone gets back,' said Barney, heaving himself out of the chair. 'Come on, Max. You can go in the front if you like.'

I realized as soon as we went into the driveway where Mum and Dad's car was parked that Barney wasn't in a good state. I had to show him how to unlock the door and then he kept miscalculating when he tried to put the key in the ignition.

'Are you allowed to drive Mum and Dad's car?' I asked politely when really I wanted to ask him if he was seeing double.

'We share everything,' Barney said emphatically. 'Everything.' He turned the key too far in the ignition so that it shrieked in protest.

The car lurched into action, and we shuddered up the driveway. As we turned left into the narrow country lane the wing mirror clipped the edge of the gatepost and drooped from its socket – like my arm did when I dislocated it playing football.

'Oops,' said Barney.

I started to giggle. Barney turned to me and gave me a wicked smile and punched the air with his fist. He put on the music at full volume and unwound all the windows, even though it was pouring with rain. Mika thumped out of the speaker: 'Relax, Take It Easy'. I hoped the words would have a positive effect on him.

'See. Your dad's even got the CD I gave to Lisa!' shouted Barney.

He pressed his foot down on the accelerator and the car groaned as it swept ever faster down the lane. He drove through puddles as if he was in a speedboat and the spray came in through the window, soaking the inside of the car. I put my arm out of the window and the rain on my hand felt as hard as hailstones.

'Can you see round corners?' I asked, leaning towards Barney when he swerved left, like I'd seen Jeremy Clarkson do on *Top Gear.*

'Sure,' said Barney. 'Don't worry. You're in safe hands.'

Even though I was only ten and pretty much believed anything adults told me, I realized everything he'd just said was an untruth but I was too worried he might think I was rude if I challenged him. As we raced past a field I saw some cows sheltering from the storm beneath a tree and wished I could get out and lie down beside them because they looked so sensible and Barney had obviously gone mad. For the first time ever I hoped Daisy was performing some of her magic spells to protect me. It occurred to me for a split second that perhaps she really could do witchcraft and this was what she had been trying to save me from. I closed my eyes and felt the wind and spray from puddles lash my cheeks. When the car weaved round another corner I opened them again.

'Barney, I feel a bit sick,' I shouted over the music. 'Please could you slow down?'

'Let's live a little!' Barney shouted.

I wished I hadn't said anything because he turned towards me instead of looking at the road ahead and a sour cloud of alcohol and cigarettes enveloped me. If only Mum hadn't gone back to London I wouldn't be in this situation. Somehow thinking of Mum reminded me to put on my seat belt. Barney gripped the steering wheel, crunched down a gear and pressed hard on the accelerator. He sang, loudly and out of tune, as if Mika had done something personally to offend him. The engine wheezed in protest. I watched as the speedometer rose, pleased to have something to distract me so I didn't have to look at the way the hedgerow outside the window had blurred into green and brown smudges. I retched silently and managed to swallow down the acidy bile without Barney noticing.

'Barney, if you don't mind, I need to get home to finish picking up my ladybirds. Today is a very big day for me,' I said, worried that he had actually forgotten I was in the car with him. 'It's the final day of my experiment.' My voice got caught on the bad taste at the back of my throat and I felt panicky that I was going to start crying.

There was a black and white blur outside the window as we passed another herd of cows.

'Stop staring at me like that!' Barney shouted out of the window at the cows. 'Cows are always so bloody judgemental, don't you think, Max?'

I nodded in agreement even though I didn't understand what he was talking about. 'Did you know George Washington's dentist made him false teeth out of cows' teeth?' I asked.

Barney turned towards me and started laughing. He shook his head from side to side so his cheeks wobbled and gradually slowed down until I could see each individual ripe blackberry in the hedgerow and a tractor ploughing the field beyond. It was a miracle.

'He also made a set out of hippopotamus teeth,' I doggedly continued. 'A lot of people assumed they were made of wood, but that is completely wrong. He drank too much Madeira wine and that's why they were stained brown.'

Barney swerved into a gap on the side of the road where there was a little stall that sold Cromer crabs. Something had shifted.

He turned off the engine and kept laughing and shaking his head without releasing his grip on the steering wheel. Then he made a strange noise like a reverse sneeze and his shoulders started shaking. He bowed his head and I thought he was about to start praying but instead enormous teardrops began to fall from his eyes and on to his lap, adding to the spots on his swimming trunks. Apart from in films, I had never seen a grown man cry before. Barney's sobs got louder and more forceful so that the car actually shuddered. I swear the tears came from his belly not his eyes. This was even more alarming than what had come before. I couldn't find any useful facts to fill the space between us. I thought about telling him how the fourteen spots on a ladybird's back represented the seven sorrows and seven joys but it didn't seem right in the circumstances. His sorrows definitely seemed to outnumber his joys.

'I'm sorry, Max,' he started saying, over and over again. 'I'm not a good person.'

'It's fine, Barney,' I said, unsure why he was apologizing. 'Nor am I.' I wanted him to ask me why because at that precise moment I would have told him. Instead I ended up living with my secret for the next eight years.

'I didn't mean to frighten you, Max. You're such a good kid. Ava says you're a complete original.'

I wasn't sure what this meant, but it was enough to discover Ava thought about me when we weren't together.

'I wasn't scared. Well, maybe a bit, but you're a good driver. Not as good as The Stig, but you know how to take a tight corner on two wheels. Better than Dad does anyway.'

This was completely the wrong thing to say because the tears fell harder and faster until there was a large wet patch in his lap that was the same shape as Australia. I wondered if this qualified as a good fact and was about to tell him but pulled back at the last minute because he might think I was weird for looking at his crotch.

'It's all fine, Barney. Nothing lasts forever. It will pass and everything will get better,' I said, stitching together phrases that Mum used with me when I was upset. Worried my words sounded a little rehearsed, I said them again with more feeling and put out my hand to touch his forearm.

He took my small fingers in his soggy fist and gripped them so tightly that I thought he was going to cut off their circulation. I tried to breathe through my mouth so I didn't have to inhale the air around him.

'You're a good kid, Maxi,' he said, and for a moment I almost believed him.

'Do you think we should forget the fish and chips, and get some crabs instead?' I suggested, remembering Dad wanted to cook crab pasta.

He pushed a crumpled twenty-pound note into my hand and I got out and negotiated a good deal for four cooked crabs so I could give Barney as much change as possible.

'They don't have any predators, apart from human beings,' I said as I got back into the car and took one of the crabs out of the bag so I could admire its glassy black eyes. 'Do you think human beings are born destructive or become destructive, Barney?'

'You've got an old head on those young shoulders, Max,' Barney replied. His nose was running and he wiped it on his T-shirt. 'Think that might be one for your dad to answer.'

I liked the way he thought Dad had answers to the difficult questions, because sometimes Dad seemed pretty boring compared to Barney.

When we arrived home, everyone apart from Rex was waiting for us in the driveway in the pouring rain. I was really pleased to see Mum had arrived, because she was good at diagnosing situations and coming up with treatment plans. But instead of Mum, Dad steamed towards the car, his mouth a straight line of anger. I got out quickly, assuming he was annoyed with me. I had done a bad thing that day and part of me was hoping someone had discovered so I could be properly punished. But instead he threw his arms around me and crushed me tight to his chest, which seemed a bit over the top because I had been gone all of an hour, whereas he had spent most of the day at the shops.

I watched Barney get out of the driver's seat and sway towards them, holding the plastic bag of crabs. He swerved into one of the flower beds that Dad had weeded and didn't seem to notice when his flip-flop stayed behind in the mud. Lisa went over to take him by the arm but he shook her off. Dad released me and took big threatening strides towards Barney.

'What were you thinking?' asked Dad, his voice all heavy. 'Taking risks with Max like that.' His hand hovered just above Barney's shoulder.

Barney turned his back on Dad. I couldn't see what Barney had done to deserve this reaction when he'd been the only adult who even noticed me and cared that I was hungry that day.

'We went to get crabs, Dad,' I said, unravelling myself from Mum's arm to put myself between Dad and Barney. I couldn't believe that Dad and Barney were about to get into another argument. They were beginning to remind me of the male water buffalo fighting over females in David Attenborough.

'We were hungry and you and Lisa had been gone so long that we thought you might never come back. You're the ones who should be in trouble.'

'The problem is Barney is over the limit,' said Mum, leading me away by the hand to the flower bed where

Barney's flip-flop lay on its side in the mud. She bent down on one knee until she was at my level and held both my hands. She only did this when she had something serious to say.

I looked over her shoulder and saw Daisy and Ava standing by the front door, watching us. It was the only time that I saw them alone together on that holiday. Even then, Ava was detached. I envied her indestructibility.

'Over what limit?' I asked impatiently.

'Over the alcohol limit,' said Mum calmly. 'It means that you can't drive safely because your reactions slow down. Barney shouldn't have risked driving, especially with you in the car.'

'It's called drink driving,' said Dad, sounding suddenly exhausted. 'He could have easily had an accident and you could have been hurt, Max.'

'Daisy had done all her magic spells so that was never going to happen,' I said cheerily, hoping that everyone would just calm down when they saw how unaffected I was.

Mum looked confused. I glanced over at Daisy for backup but she stared back at me, flat-eyed. Butterflies started fluttering in my chest.

'What are you talking about?' asked Mum.

'Daisy tries to keep us safe,' I tried to explain. 'It's hard work. Like a part-time job.'

'Look, he's crashed the bloody car,' said Dad, lifting the wing mirror and then dropping it so it flopped pathetically against the bonnet.

Lisa came over to Dad and touched him in that sensitive part on the inside of his elbow. 'Don't be too hard on him, Nick,' she said.

At last, someone was defending Barney but he would never realize because he'd gone inside the house. 'What Barney needs is a hug,' I told everyone. But instead of going after him, Mum and Dad hugged me instead.

Assuming there would be no dinner after all this drama, I dawdled up to our bedroom, tummy rumbling, feeling sorry for myself, stopping every few steps to collect up dead ladybirds from the stairs. I was completely behind schedule now. I thought about starving children in other countries and how they sometimes went for days without food, whereas at least I had eaten two pieces of toast with peanut butter for breakfast. And if I got really hungry I had my dead ladybirds with me. There's a lot of protein in insects.

I found Daisy sitting upright on the top bunk. When she saw me she put her finger to her lips to indicate she didn't want any interruptions and continued tapping the wall beside her in a triangle, over and over again. At the end of each set she muttered, 'Three is a good and safe number.' I felt embarrassed, as if I had caught her doing something private like going to the loo or dealing with her period. The butterflies started fluttering in my chest again until they were all I could feel.

I put the ladybirds on the bookshelf and distracted myself by picking up the photo of my grandparents that had sat there ever since I could remember. It had probably been taken soon after they were married. They stood stiffly, dressed in formal clothes that were at odds with their smooth skin and easy smiles. I wondered if all adults made their lives more and complicated until, in the end, this is what killed them. After all, Mum said Granny had died from complications.

'Everything will be fine, Maxi,' Daisy said firmly as she climbed down the ladder.

I jumped, wondering if my sister could read my mind, in which case she would realize what I had done that morning. I waited for her to say something but when I looked at her face there was nothing in her expression that made me confident anything would ever be fine again. She was so pale that her skin looked almost see-through. There were still bruise-like smears of black eye make-up on her cheeks and a remote look in her eyes as if she was somewhere else. It was a trait I would get used to over the years that followed.

'Actually, there's something I have to tell you, Daisy . . .' I began, but she was already halfway out the door.

'Actually, you say actually too much, Maxi.' For a second she sounded so like the old Daisy that I wanted to cry. 'But I can't stop now. There's a couple of things I need to do.'

Twenty-one things actually because I knew she was heading for the knife drawer. What would I have said to her? That it was supposed to be a joke? That I never meant for her to take it seriously? I assumed she would notice right away that the cream-coloured paper with the red lines came from the notebook where I kept my records about the ladybirds. I thought she would get angry with me for using her favourite purple pen. I imagined that when she discovered she would wrestle me to the ground, tickle me until I begged for mercy and we would roll around laughing like old times.

Why did I do it? I have asked this question of myself many times over the years but it is difficult to remember the thought processes of my ten-year-old self. I thought it was funny. I wanted to wind her up for making me feel uneasy. I did it to test how much she really fancied Rex, assuming she would be put off by his full-frontal proposal. I did it because I wanted to put a stop to Daisy humiliating herself in front of him and everyone else. I had lost too much of my sister already that holiday. Maybe I subconsciously did it to please Ava.

After all, the line came from one of the films that I had watched with her. When she had explained what it meant we both fell around laughing. We used it as a catchphrase when no one else was listening to describe anything exciting. It sounded particularly funny when Ava said it. *Ice cream makes me hard.* It felt innocent and deviant all at the same time, which is a heady combination.

If I tell you it took me less than three seconds to take a decision whose consequences would reverberate down the years, maybe you won't be so hard on me. I never thought that her reaction would be so cataclysmic. But I knew as soon as I saw her face that the person who went to the beach wasn't the same person as the one who came back and that this was all my fault.

Looking for something to distract myself from the butterflies, I found my rucksack and began packing up pants, T-shirts, random pieces of Lego, my Super Mario games and a piece of paper with Ava's favourite quotes from *Friends* that she had handwritten for me. Usually I felt sad at the end of our summer holiday in Norfolk but this time I wanted to go home so that everything would just go back to normal.

Mum called me down for dinner. I didn't deserve to

eat. I waited until she shouted again and then went down-stairs. The mood in the kitchen was weirdly upbeat, as if nothing had happened earlier. Mika was playing and Rex and Ava were using a baguette as a microphone. There was much discussion about how the plague of ladybirds had stopped just as the storm had started, as if the two events were connected.

'It's got nothing to do with the weather,' I kept saying, but no one wanted to listen to my theories about how the *Coccinellidae* must have eaten all of the aphids. I thought Barney at least would be interested but when I pulled at his sleeve, he shook me off like a dead ladybird.

He was standing in a circle with Mum, Dad, Lisa and Rex, listening to a story Dad was telling about when Barney had invited him on a press trip with him to cover The Rolling Stones tour in Japan. I'd heard this story so many times before that I knew exactly what Dad was going to say five seconds before he said it.

'I didn't realize Barney had this cult following in Japan and when we went to press conferences the journalists were more interested in speaking to him than Mick Jagger. I had no idea he was such a player.' Everyone laughed and Dad poured Barney another glass of red wine. 'He even made the cover of *The Japan Times*.'

'You missed out the bit where you have to share a dou-ble bed and Barney puts sushi in your mouth to stop you snoring,' I pointed out, but I must have been wearing my invisibility cloak because no one took any notice.

Dad enthusiastically asked everyone to vote on whether we wanted to eat his crab pasta outside and I was the only one who opposed the motion. I tried to argue that the benches and chairs were soggy and the terrace slippery with green algae but no one wanted to listen because they were so desperate to find something they could all finally agree on.

Parents make a big thing about children being honest but actually spend a lot of time pretending and telling untruths themselves. So when we sat down and Mum kept saying what a great week it had been, I knew what she really meant was that she was relieved we had all survived six days together without anyone killing each other. And when Dad said we and the Drapers were like family, what he really meant was that we would be trapped in a relationship with them for the rest of our lives.

11

Nick

I'm not going to pretend. To my complete surprise the best day of the holiday was the last because I spent most of it in Cromer with Lisa. Although we had known each other off and on for the best part of sixteen years, I couldn't remember when we had ever spent any length of time so intensively alone together.

You have to understand that by this stage in the week the atmosphere in the house was toxic. Although I could understand how a couple could infect a marriage with words, I hadn't grasped how they could also contaminate the air the rest of us breathed. All relationships require a certain degree of make-believe to dilute their reality but Barney and Lisa had stopped pretending. Unlike Rosie, I didn't believe there was anything that we could usefully do to interrupt their death spiral and I just wanted them to leave.

The house reflected the mood. Everything reeked of decay. I went to sleep to the sound of woodworm doing shifts drilling the ugly mahogany wardrobe in our bedroom and woke up to find dead ladybirds beneath the damp duvet. One night a dying ladybird weevilled its way up my left nostril and I almost choked in my sleep. Damp had peeled layers off the walls between the bedrooms and Barney's mad rants and Lisa's tears became the muffled soundtrack to the hours of doom between two and four in the morning.

As soon as I had breakfast I sought sanctuary in the garden, tearing out bindweed that was strangling the shrubs that Rosie's parents had once lovingly tended, worrying about how quickly bonds dissolve and things fall apart when unity of purpose disappears.

That Thursday I woke up alone in bed for the second day in a row. Rosie had got the train to London on Tuesday night and my heart sank as I remembered I was stuck with Lisa and Barney again. I had grumpily tried to persuade Rosie to swap holidays with a colleague, using the feeble argument that they were more her friends than mine, but she was adamant. Work always came first with her. How could it not? It was so humid that my body was covered in a slippery, salty layer of sweat. My head throbbed from the heavy atmosphere and I couldn't even arouse myself with one of my favourite fantasies about the woman in charge of research grants at work.

So when I stumbled into the kitchen and Lisa suggested going to the shops with her after breakfast, I was more than happy to escape, even though I knew I was most likely being used as a pawn in her propaganda war against Barney. This wasn't due to any great psychological insight on my part: Rosie gave me nightly bulletins on the state of play between Barney and Lisa and so I had recently learnt that the same qualities that once made me boring in Lisa's eyes were now being used to compare me favourably to Barney and he understandably didn't appreciate this sudden devaluing of his currency. So everything from my 'pedantic' cooking techniques, 'unfashionable' job and 'fascist' exercise regime were held up by Lisa as a mirror to reflect his inadequacies. Such was the alchemy of misery.

Frankly, although I was a bit hurt to discover after all these years that Lisa found me boring, even though Rosie insisted it was 'in a good way', I wasn't totally surprised. If I hadn't been married to Lisa's oldest friend, neither she nor Barney would have had any interest in me at all.

Rosie also informed me that Barney's recent broken knuckle wasn't really the result of a cycle accident – in fact, he had punched a hole through their bathroom wall – and he no longer had sex with Lisa because he could only get half an erection. I winced when she told me that, mostly because I felt sorry for Barney but also because like most men I was worried it might be contagious if I thought about it too much.

After this, I warned Rosie not to tell me any more, arguing that in a couple of months they would be fine again and we would have to look them in the eye, smile and pretend we knew nothing. Forgetting is one of the most important tasks undertaken by the human brain but I know from my work that sensationalist details have a tendency to linger way beyond their sell-by date. Thought suppression is very hard. I once assisted on a research project which showed that male participants who were instructed to inhibit erections as they watched erotic films were less successful than those who weren't told to do anything. So the chances of me letting something slip were pretty high.

I spent a lot of time that week wishing that Barney and Lisa hadn't come to stay. I still do in some ways. Although Daisy was a little subdued, everything had been fine before they arrived but by the time they left, their shame was a stain that had spread over us all. More than anything I wished things could go back to how they used to be, with Barney playing the ringmaster and us his willing audience.

I smiled as I remembered how last year he had made us all get out of bed in the middle of the night to examine the seabed during the lowest tide of the year. Lit by the full moon, we had lifted rocks to discover prehistoric creatures that none of us had ever seen before. There was a blenny, covered in slime, so it could survive out of water for up to an hour, short-snouted sea horses and weird and wonderful molluscs that looked like woodlice. Max even captured a spiny sea scorpion with a mouth so wide it looked like it was grinning at us. They were good times.

Then I remembered the first time I met Barney, when he and I both auditioned for the same role in a play our final year at university in London. Our paths had never crossed until then. It was something French and philosophical. He got the main part and I had a non-speaking role, which probably tells you everything you need to know about him and me. The director turned out to be a psychopath who insisted we remain in character all the time so Barney decided we should loosen up before the first night by taking magic mushrooms. When he came onstage, the drug had taken effect and instead of Barney, a pink unicorn stood in front of me. It was marvellous. Barney had an uncanny ability to take people out of their comfort zone to places he knew they wanted to be before they realized it themselves.

Even more significantly, he was responsible for introducing me to Rosie. He had just started going out with Lisa and she brought her old school friend to see the play the weekend it opened. Pure serendipity. It only lasted one night after the director was arrested for public affray for punching Barney at the after party. Rosie was three years into her medical degree and came back to my flat with Barney and Lisa. She held my hand and talked to me for six hours until I came out the other side of the trip. I think I would have gone mad without her. She had an air of calm authority that vanquished the demons in my head. When it was over we went to bed and had the kind of hallucinatory sex where orgasm has colours. That was the first and last time that I ever took drugs. I didn't see much of Barney and Lisa for a few years after that. We went to each other's weddings and parties, and Rosie and Lisa occasionally saw each other. But it wasn't until Rosie and Lisa discovered they were pregnant with Daisy and Ava that we began to spend significant time all together. We tried to outdo each other with stories of sleep deprivation; we shared a nanny, went on holiday, and bound ourselves together with experiences that camouflaged the differences between us.

I had quarried into a rich seam of memories. I reminded myself they were stories of what had happened. They didn't reflect exact events, just how I felt about them. And it made me sad to think that not so long ago we used to look forward to seeing Barney and Lisa. Their bickering, their edginess, their glamour, their ability to live in the moment made our own life seem a little less drab. Even better, whenever we left them, Rosie and I were always relieved that we weren't them.

'We need to take bags,' I reminded Lisa, wondering if this was the sort of trait that she found boring.

'Where are you going, Dad?' Max looked up, his face hamster-cheeked with toast. 'You promised to help me pick up the ladybirds.'

'I'll do it when I get back,' I said.

Max shook his head so vigorously that globs of peanut butter sprayed out of his mouth. He might be very good-natured but he knew when he was being fobbed off. He started explaining how he needed to pick up the dead bodies at the same time every day for the experiment to be true and how there were too many that day to collect within the time frame. I felt a complete affinity with his logic and knew I was letting him down.

'I'll step in for you, if you like, Nick,' Ava intervened.

'Thanks, that's very nice of you,' I said, trying to sound more enthusiastic than I felt because I didn't trust her motivation.

Ava was all hard edges and posture that week, trapped with her child's mind in her adult body, trying to work out how to respond to what was going on with her parents. Everyone tip-toed around her like a sleeping lion.

'I thought you were doing something with Daisy?' Lisa questioned Ava.

'Don't worry. I've got my own plans,' said Daisy quickly.

I noticed how Ava raised an eyebrow but fortunately Daisy didn't see.

*

As far as I could tell we were the only customers at the supermarket in Cromer. There was one person at the till, a young woman with a snake tatoo that wound from the top of her shoulder to her wrist, but she was reading a magazine. Everyone else had sensibly gone to the beach on what was to be the hottest day of the summer.

Lisa had ground to a halt in front of hundreds of cans of tinned peaches in the aisle that seemed most likely to deliver a positive result on some of our more demanding ingredients, like saffron and cayenne pepper. She stared at them for ages, dead-eyed, like a sleepwalker. They were strangely compelling, a voluptuous relic from a forgotten past where trifles and sponge fingers ruled the shelves, but even so they didn't warrant quite so much attention.

I looked at Lisa, wondering how I could get her to move on. The shop was badly lit from above and even the dark rings under her eyes had a queasy orange hue. I glanced down her body and saw her hipbones jutting out through her black leggings. She had lost a lot of weight since we last saw her. Unsure what to do, I picked up a can to check its sell-by date. How many recipes involved tinned peaches? I wondered. I could only think of one. Peach cobbler. I handed her the tin and she dreamily put it back on the shelf in the tomato soup section.

I tried to entertain her with a story about a woman I had seen at work the previous week who had a rare condition that meant she could remember exactly where she was and what she was doing every single day of her life since she was about five years old. It was one of the most fascinating cases I had seen in my career.

'She spends more time in the past than the present,' I said.

Lisa didn't respond.

'Are you okay?'

'Sorry I'm so out of it. I'm finding it difficult to sleep, Nick,' she said finally. 'I try to forget myself, forget the loose spring creaking under the pillow, forget Barney beside me, forget the tree scratching the bedroom window, forget that tap dripping in the bathroom sink next door. But the more I try to forget the harder it is.'

She gave a quick unconvincing grin that faded before it reached her eyes. Her fingers gripped the handle of the trolley as if it was a Zimmer frame and she kept staring at the tins. She sounded exhausted, as if crafting all these words into sentences required energy that she didn't possess.

'That's because sleep is a distraction from the world. You can't remove yourself from what's going on with Barney. So you can't switch off. You've got too much on your mind,' I said, wanting to weave sentences that would sweeten everything for her. Barney was the poetic one. Not me.

'Everything feels so fuzzy and out of focus. I can see the children are struggling but I don't know what to say to them. I'm leaning on Rex too much and he's trying to be the responsible adult when he should be out having a good time. Ava's got a boyfriend who we haven't met but I suspect he's older than her and I think they're having sex. When I get home from work instead of looking after the children, I have to deal with Barney, who's spent the whole day drinking, smoking and doing Sudoku. I haven't told anyone this, but the night he broke his fist, he wet the bed and Ava had to help me get him out of his clothes and change the sheets. The next day he claimed he couldn't remember anything about it and when I tried to talk to Ava she left the house.'

'He's having blackouts,' I said, my shock at what Lisa was telling me muted by the pleasure of being chosen as her confidant. 'Alcohol blocks the neural signals that create short-term memories. It's a complicated process but a simple result of drinking too much. He genuinely can't remember. How long do you think he's been like this?'

'I think he hid it for a long time. I mean he's always drunk a lot, and then when he started writing about music it seemed like part of the job description. His boss let him put mojitos on expenses because Barney always ended up getting a great interview out of an all-nighter. His other friends won't admit it because drunk Barney is much more fun to be around than sober Barney, but "party animal" is just a polite way of saying functioning alcoholic, isn't it?'

'Is he drinking on his own?'

She nodded. 'I'd like to do a four-day week, just to catch breath, but I can't because we need the money.' Her head dropped as if it was too heavy for her body and she stared at the worn linoleum floor. 'Have you ever gone through something like this and got out the other side?'

I was taken aback by the disarming honesty of her question. The air was sticky and tiny beads of sweat bubbled up in the channels either side of her nose and across her brow. She licked her upper lip with her tongue and looked up. Her hair was scraped off her face in a ponytail and a small strand stuck to her forehead, obscuring the tiny scar from when she had fallen off Rosie's bunk bed as a teenager. The same bunk bed that Daisy now slept in. I watched as my hand moved towards her face to remove the strand of hair and tuck it behind her ear. She didn't flinch. Her eyes narrowed as she stared at me. There was a searching honesty that I had never seen before during all the years we had known each other. It would be impossible to lie to her.

Unable to hold her gaze, I pushed the trolley forwards and fortunately it nudged the edge of a bumper pack of pale-pink toilet rolls at the end of the aisle, bringing down the whole display. They tumbled to the ground and by the time we had rebuilt it, Lisa had forgotten her question. I pushed on towards the trifle sponges and Angel Delight, noticing how our trolley was still completely empty.

'You're right that I can't switch off,' she continued, 'but the irony is that Barney finds it so easy to remove himself. Have you noticed how much he sleeps? How his morning nap merges into his afternoon nap? It's like he's gone into hibernation just at the point when he needs to wake up. The only time he's fully awake is when he's about to start drinking or when he starts one of his two a.m. rants.'

'He can't face up to the situation. That's what happens when people are depressed,' I said.

'That's what happens when people start drinking at midday,' retorted Lisa, bitterly. 'You can't separate one from the other. He's such a loser.'

'He's been made redundant. He needs our sympathy not our judgement.'

'It's not losing his job that's the problem, it's his reaction to the situation.'

'Maybe he needs to get some professional help? I can ask my colleagues at work for some recommendations if you like.'

'That's so kind of you, Nick.' She exhaled and the tension momentarily drained from her body. 'He used to be so funny and entertaining, didn't he?'

'And he will be again,' I said confidently.

'I think he loves the alcohol more than he loves me.'

I was feeling virtuous about my sudden display of empathy after days of low-grade resentment at the way Barney's mood had hijacked our summer holiday and upset the equilibrium between us all. I felt like a good person for having these feelings towards an old friend. At that moment in the supermarket I was truly sorry for him. I could see how his identity and self-worth were bound up in his work and how it was easier to sit at his computer and pretend to work, rather than face the reality that he was unemployed and, in his current state, utterly unemployable. The golden era of the rock critic was well and truly over. Curiously, I wasn't even that angry about the glass-throwing incident. In some ways I had deserved that. I had been treating Barney in the same way as I might Daisy or Max when they used to have tantrums. He was right to call me a patronizing wanker.

I looked at my watch and realized we had already been gone for almost two hours. If I wanted to fit in a run after the ladybirds I needed to speed things up. At least we had gravitated towards the 'three-for-diabetes-two section', as Rosie referred to the offers section of supermarkets, but it most definitely wouldn't deliver on the ingredients for the crab linguine I wanted to cook.

'Barney's always been out of control. That's part of his genius,' I smiled. 'He just needs a few things to go right and then you'll get into a more positive cycle again.'

'No one ever warns you about doubt, do they?' said Lisa, wiping the sweat off her face with the back of her hand. 'But I think of all the human emotions it is probably one of the most corrosive.'

I should have asked her what she meant but I think we both knew.

'The best cure for doubt is activity,' I said quickly, pointing at the empty trolley. 'I need to get back to help Max with his ladybird odyssey.'

'You're a good dad, Nick.' Lisa smiled and pulled out the list from her pocket.

I took the trolley from her hands and began wheeling it to the fruit and vegetables section.

'Okay. So what do we need?'

I closed my eyes and reeled off all thirty-seven items from Lisa's shopping list without any hesitation. When I opened them she was open-mouthed. There was such childish wonder in her reaction that I couldn't help beaming with self-satisfaction. She laughed and it made me realize how little I had heard that sound over the past five days and how good it made me feel to make her happy.

'How do you do that?' Lisa smiled.

'It's an old trick. Never to be divulged. It's a great way to impress my graduate researchers. I use it to remember their names from day one, like Cyrus of Persia. He knew every soldier in his army.'

'I won't breathe a word to anyone,' she pleaded.

'If I tell you, I'll have to kill you,' I teased.

We headed to the woefully stocked spice shelf and I stared at it for a minute, scanning each row. I closed my eyes and performed the same trick again, remembering every spice in alphabetical order from allspice to thyme.

'You're freaking me out, Nick Rankin!'

'Come on, we need to increase our productivity.'

I honestly can't remember whether it was Lisa or me who suggested we stop at the beach for a swim on the way home. I can see why the question warrants reflection but there's only so much a busy brain can recall. I'm not being evasive – all the science shows that people who claim to remember events in the greatest detail are the biggest liars. In fact, if you remember something often enough, even if it didn't happen, it will become real. It's a terrifying but beautiful notion that every day we wake up with a slightly different personal history. Remember that. It's important. The past is a vanished shadow.

From the car park, the sea beckoned beguilingly, all turquoise-blue promise, but as we walked on to the beach I noticed a frothy menace to the surface that made me wish Rosie were with us because she could read its unpredictable moods better than anyone I had ever met. There was an offshore wind but I couldn't remember how this affected the ebb and flow of the tide. We plunged in and I felt the indecisive currents batter my legs at cross purposes. Usually the shallow sea floor took most of the punch out of the waves but as I looked towards the horizon I saw the sky was streaked with bruise-coloured ribbons in purple, grey and yellow, indicating a storm at sea.

The noise of the waves breaking was so intense that we couldn't hear ourselves speak. Lisa's head rose and fell in the swell. I watched over her as she took a deep breath before diving into the waves just before they broke and whenever she disappeared from view I felt a surge of anxiety. She was completely fearless. I preferred to let the waves suck me beneath the surface and spit me out on the stony shore like a passive piece of driftwood. When we got out we were both completely breathless from the exhilaration and the sense of doing combat with a force more powerful than ourselves. We faced each other for a second, panting like dogs.

'You're right. I feel so much better,' said Lisa, shaking her hair so the cold drops rained down on my bare torso.

'Hey, get away from me!' I shouted, picking up my shirt and waving it matador-style to shield myself from her salt storm.

'Sorry, sorry, sorry,' she said. Then she grabbed the shirt from my hands and used it to dry her face and arms, sidestepping my feeble attempts to get it back. When she was finished she scrunched it up into a damp ball and threw it at my stomach, laughing when I dropped it on the sand.

I didn't want to put my trousers on over my soaking-wet boxer shorts because Max would realize that I had been swimming instead of rushing home to help him collect up the dead ladybirds. I felt guilty without feeling any regret. At that moment I didn't want to be anywhere other than here with Lisa.

'Shall we go and bake ourselves in the dunes for a while?' I suggested, pointing to a spot close to where the old pillbox was buried in the sand.

'Good plan.'

She carelessly rolled her leggings around her bra and flip-flops and carried the sausage of clothes under her arm. If anyone noticed we were in our underwear, they didn't give it away. We scrambled to the top of the dunes, using the marram grass to steady ourselves, oblivious to the scratches on our fingers.

When we reached the summit we stood for a while in silence like royalty, imperiously surveying our kingdom below. The wind had blown a perfect bowl-shaped shelter. I got down on my hands and knees to smooth out the bumps in the warm, silky sand until it was comfortable enough for us to lie on while Lisa hung our wet clothes to dry on the marram grass, using our shoes as weights to stop the breeze from blowing them away. It all felt strangely domestic. I lay down on one half of my shirt, enjoying the way the heat from the sand soaked into the back of my body. Lisa collapsed beside me, turtled on to her back and closed her eyes to block out the glare of the late-afternoon sun. We were completely cocooned from the world.

'It's strange how in life your good qualities always end up being your bad qualities, isn't it?' Lisa said with a deep sigh.

'What do you mean?' I shifted on to my side, and propped myself up on my elbow so that the sun was on my back. My right toe found itself resting on the soft flesh on the side of her foot.

If she noticed anything she didn't give it away. Her
T-shirt had wrinkled up, revealing a stretch of tanned
flesh on her stomach that drew my eye down to her knickers. For a split second I wondered what she would do if I
rested the flat of my palm between her legs. I would stay
still until she could feel the pulse beating in my hand and
wait until her legs parted. I sneaked a quick look at her
face, to check her eyes were still shut, because if she saw
me she would see nothing but hunger in mine. I noticed
how her hair had completely escaped from its noose and
her half-parted lips were dry with salt. Her left arm was
stretched above her head and the strap of her T-shirt had
slipped down, revealing the perfect round tip of her clavicle. It was shiny and hard like a boiled sweet, so close that
I could open my mouth and lick it. My stomach somer-
saulted and I felt my dick stir inside my boxer shorts. God,
what was I thinking?

I remembered a trick I had last used in my early twenties and ran through the bowlers and batsmen playing for
England in the last test against Australia. By the time I
reached Monty Panesar I had regained control. Thank-
fully Lisa kept talking.

'What I'm trying to say is that the things that make you
good also make you bad. Barney's irresponsibility makes
him really attractive but is also the cause of his downfall.
My optimism that everything will turn out fine means I
don't deal with problems until they've mushroomed into
impossible situations.'

'I get what you're saying but I'm not sure it always works.
Do the traits that make me boring also make me exciting?'
I was teasing her and she had the good grace to blush.

'I can't believe Rosie told you that. And I didn't mean it the way it sounded. What I was trying to say is that when you deal with complete uncertainty every day, being with someone who plans everything suddenly seems like a good thing. I'm so grateful to you for looking after me. It feels like such a long time since someone has done that.'

I had allowed reason to govern my heart for many years but in a moment this vanished. I was helpless before her. The urge to kiss her perfectly shaped lips was overwhelming. I wanted to explore her mouth with my tongue and then run it down the rest of her body. Once the idea entered my head I couldn't see any other possible ending to the day. But just as my lips were so close to hers that I could feel her breath on my face, Lisa unexpectedly sat up and her chin smashed into my nose. The pain brought me back to reality.

'I feel like we're being watched.' She gripped my shoulder with her hand.

'You are. By me,' I joked, holding on to my throbbing nose.

Lisa pointed at the black window of the pillbox. We both stood up to take a look but there was nothing. The thunder that had been growling in the distance for the past hour bellowed overhead and huge drops of rain started falling so hard they bounced back off the sand at calf height so that our shoes and socks were twice-soaked. Families caught up in the storm began running back to the car park from the beach, belongings spilling from haphazardly stuffed bags. Magnificent forks of lightning illuminated the sky as we pulled on our clothes, and by the time we began running down the other side of the dunes the sky was dark grey.

When we got home, everyone was standing in the driveway at the front of the house, heads bowed beneath the relentless downpour, so they resembled characters in a religious tableau where the object of worship appeared to be Max. The flower beds at the side of the driveway had turned into small, dark rivers that looked as though they were about to burst their banks and a big branch had fallen from the copper beech on to the gravel. Rex was attempting to drag it on to the lawn single-handed.

I was worried that this gathering had something to do with our absence. Lisa and I had been gone for the best part of a day and the shops must have shut hours ago. Even worse, I had forgotten to get the main ingredient for dinner. There were no crabs. But to my relief, when we got out of the car carrying only three bags, I realized we were not the object of any search party and our sopping clothes and wet hair meant we could blend in without too many questions asked. Perhaps there had been a calamity involving the copper beech. Our car certainly looked a little beaten up.

I signalled my confusion to Daisy who was sheltering in the porch, but her attention was resolutely focused on Rosie and Barney who were talking animatedly to Max. I carried the shopping bags to the front door and asked Daisy to take them inside but she stared straight through me.

'Big problemo,' gushed Ava excitedly. 'Dad took Max out for a spin in your car and he was so drunk he crashed into the gatepost and Max nearly died.'

'No I didn't,' protested Max, who appeared completely fine. 'Don't exaggerate.'

'Lived, lived, lived,' muttered Daisy under her breath.

I frowned. Not for the first time, it occurred to me that she worried way too much about her younger brother, when it was obvious Max was one of life's survivors.

'Do you want to help me cook dinner, Daisy? I could do with your help,' I asked, wanting to get her away from Ava.

'She'll only agree if you ask Rex as well,' Ava teased.

Daisy shook her head. She needed to develop a harder shell if she was to survive in this world. I headed towards Barney. In many respects I was thankful for his folly that day. He provided welcome distraction from my own unsteady state of mind. I couldn't believe what had almost happened. I was wary of too much scrutiny in case someone could sense my lurch from euphoria to despair, so I marched over to him and did my best to dredge up anger that I didn't feel. At one point I even found myself trying to put my arms around him, more for my own benefit than his. No wonder he looked confused.

By dinner the storm had passed and we had all found our equilibrium again. As I chopped garlic and crushed chilli I began to relax. I tipped the crabs from their shells and broke up their flesh between my fingers. It was a beautiful evening, warm without being humid, and I went outside to join everyone else sitting around the table on the terrace. The sun hung low and sultry in the sky, casting a benevolent glow over us. The plague of ladybirds had ended as mysteriously as it had started and Max seemed almost relieved that his experiment had drawn to an abrupt end.

'Some of the best scientific discoveries happen by accident when things don't go according to plan,' said Rosie,
cleverly steering him away from his failure to collect up
the last of the ladybirds.

'Like what?' asked Max.

'Mustard gas was accidentally found to cure cancer
cells,' said Rosie.

'How did that happen?' asked Max. He had an enviable
ability to shake off a mood.

Rosie began explaining how American pathologists
analysed the effects of the bombing of Ypres on survivors
after the First World War and found that their white blood
cell counts were always below normal. My attention wandered as she began describing how this was the way it was
discovered that mustard gas damages DNA and kills
nearly all the dividing cancer cells. I stole a glance at Lisa,
willing her to look at me, but she was too busy fiddling
with her camera.

I think it was Lisa's idea to take a photograph of us all
before we ate dinner. She managed to cajole us out of our
seats and on to the front lawn, where she balanced her
camera on top of her big legal briefcase. She bent down to
check that we were all in frame and I stared at the lens,
hoping she was looking only at me. I felt like a teenager
searching for hidden messages in everything she said or
did that evening and liked to think she wanted a photograph to remember the day we had shared together. She
set the timer and ran towards us, wriggling in beside me,
her toes carelessly glancing my instep, mirroring our earlier position on the beach, and I spent hours later trying
to work out if she did this on purpose.

When we sat back down I was relieved to see that everyone had moved from their usual positions at the table so I wasn't next to her. Too much proximity in the presence of others would have been difficult to manage. So I went beside Max, hoping to compensate for my earlier absence. Rex sat down the other side of me and I suggested Daisy sit next to him but she shook her head and said she would go next to Rosie, who had decided she should collect the laundry from the washing line in the front garden in case we forgot it when we left the following morning. Living in the moment was never Rosie's strong suit.

'Come on, Small,' commanded Rex, patting the space beside him. 'It's our last night.'

'You'd better make it one to remember then, Rex,' said Ava.

Daisy blushed.

'I remember every second I spend with Daisy,' Rex teased, but Daisy didn't smile.

Fortunately Max diverted attention away from her, firstly by spilling the Coca-Cola that he was desperate to have as a treat on his last night and then by asking one of those seemingly innocent questions that is in fact so complicated it should be a TED Talk.

'Dad, how can you make sure that when you're old, you remember the good memories and not the bad ones?' he suddenly asked. 'Is there some way you can delete the past?'

'What bad memories could you possibly want to get rid of, Maxi?' asked Ava, putting her arm around him. 'You haven't lived long enough to be bad.'

'Chelsea losing the Champions League, for one,' teased Barney. Three-quarters into a bottle of wine Barney resembled his old self, all good-natured congeniality and wit. He put his arm around Lisa and she didn't shift. I felt a stab of something that felt horribly like jealousy.

'I watched a horror film with Ava and I can't forget it,' said Max. '*The Mummy.*'

'Why on earth did you let Max watch that with you?' Rosie asked Ava.

'I like the way he snuggles into me when he's scared,' said Ava. 'Max is so soft and cuddly.'

'No I'm not,' protested Max.

'You are,' said Ava, pulling him to her.

'It's not a proper horror film,' said Lisa. 'It's just Max is susceptible.'

Daisy looked up from her plate. I noticed how she had separated the crab from the pasta and felt sorry for her for having to pretend to like it, to please Rex. If I had been sitting next to her I would have discreetly removed it so she could save face.

'Are you susceptible, Dad?' Daisy asked me. The way she looked at me made it seem as though it was a question she had always wanted to ask and that my answer could be life-defining, and yet it was meaningless.

'Susceptible to what, Daisy?' I asked in confusion.

Fortunately Daisy was spared by Rosie coming in from the kitchen with news that the storm had blown away all of Lisa's underwear and saved her own. At the time this seemed hilarious. Barney did a whole riff on how Lisa's knickers had been planning their escape for years and had finally made it across the North Sea to a new life in

Holland with a Dutch family who would treat them far better and wash them on a lower heat with the right colours. God, he could be funny.

'You haven't answered my question, Dad,' said Max when it hurt to laugh any more.

I tried to find the simplest way to explain a complicated concept. 'Some people think if you try to push away thoughts about the less obvious background to bad memories, like sound and smells, then they fade quicker,' I said. 'It's like removing the scaffolding that holds the memory in place.'

'So you could watch the scene that frightened you but listen to different music and it would change the memory?' said Rex.

'Precisely.'

Lisa told the story of how I remembered everything on the supermarket list without any prompts and although everyone was impressed I felt wounded that she didn't want to keep the details of our day together secret.

I wanted her acknowledgement that something had shifted between us. I wanted to know if she had really seen someone in the pillbox or whether it was a clever diversion to preserve me from the humiliation of rejection. I wanted a legitimate excuse to spend time alone with her again. I swung from elation to despair like a hormonal teenager. The alcohol softened my resolve and as I stared at the ice cream melting on my plate, all I could think about was how much I wanted to have sex with Lisa. I stirred the ice cream round and round, imagining her hand sliding into my unzipped trousers.

'Dad! Stop it!' I felt the hot glare of Daisy's disapproval and blushed red. 'That noise is driving me crazy.'

'Sorry.'

I needed to get some air.

'Where are you going, Dad?' Max asked.

'I've got to lock the garden shed before we leave,' I said.

'I'll do it for you,' Max offered.

'Don't worry, Maxi, you help Mum.'

Rosie was taking dirty plates into the kitchen and Barney was opening the third bottle of wine that would soon curdle his mood. I got up from the table and wandered barefoot deeper into the garden, ignoring the soggy grass and the sharp twigs blown in by the storm. I could hear Lisa telling glory stories about Barney in a futile effort to pull him back from the darkness: how he was nominated for an award for a piece he wrote about Leonard Cohen for *Rolling Stone*; his star turn playing jazz piano at the Christmas party of some TV show host that I hadn't heard of; the surprise party a DJ threw for Lisa's thirtieth birthday at someone's house in Marrakech. We hadn't been invited to that, I noted.

The padlock on the garden shed was undone. I frowned because I was almost certain that I had left it locked. I pulled open the creaky door and went inside, and found the torch hidden on the shelf in the same place where Rosie's mum always kept it. I switched it on and scanned the shelves with the beam. There was nothing of value inside, apart from the ancient sit-on lawn mower, which I was strangely attached to. I heard something scratching in the corner and wondered if an animal had got trapped inside or whether there were rats again. I remembered a packet of poison in a tin on the top shelf. But when I put up my hand to pull it down six pairs of black lacy knickers

flew off the top on to the ground. For a moment I thought
that someone, most likely Barney, was playing a not particularly funny trick on Lisa. I picked up a pair and
unfurled them in my hand, feeling faintly deviant, and
put the palm of my hand on the flimsy piece of material
that would nestle closest to Lisa's cunt. But it was pockmarked with holes. I shone a torch and saw that it had
been completely lacerated. It must have been done with a
knife, not scissors, because the cuts were too ragged and
irregular. It was the same with the rest of them. I quickly
gathered them up, screwed them into a tight ball, then
got down on my hands and knees and used my bare hands
to bury them in the soil in the corner of the hut where
no one would ever discover them. Who would have
done this?

I came out of the shed feeling nauseous. I couldn't go
back to the terrace until I had regained composure so I
turned left and headed to the end of the garden where the
crumbling flint wall marked the boundary between the
house and the beach beyond. When I reached the end of
the garden I took a couple of deep breaths and felt the sea
air fill my lungs. As my eyes adjusted to the dusky light I
noticed that Ava was sitting on the wall. I quickly turned
to leave before she saw me and tripped on a pile of stones,
stubbing my toe painfully on the edge of a flint. Ava
turned round. She was wearing one of her impossibly
tight T-shirts and I could see the warm orange glow of a
cigarette in her hand. I decided to ignore it. If I told Lisa
and Barney they would use it as ammunition against each
other. As I drew closer I realized from the heavy sweet
smell that it was grass. I cleared my throat to give Ava

time to get rid of the evidence but she didn't make any attempt to hide what she was doing. Even worse, as I drew closer, she took a deep drag and had the audacity to offer it to me.

'Hi, Nick,' she said, sucking in smoke.

'What are you doing?' I asked, trying to sound more composed than I felt.

'Chilling out. You?'

She had always had this very direct way of addressing adults. When she was a child it had seemed amusing and charming but now the challenge in her tone made me feel uneasy.

'I wanted to see the sun slip down below the horizon,' I said, pointing at the sky behind her, hoping she would turn away again. I badly wanted to avoid her gaze. I had a creeping suspicion that it could have been her who had disfigured her mother's underwear. 'Sometimes it helps to be reminded that the sun sets and rises every day, no matter what's going on around you. I realize it can't be easy for you right now.'

I sounded ridiculous, like the confused, drunken middle-aged man that I was. And I was standing in front of the most unforgiving audience in the house.

'Are you going into motivational speaker mode?' she asked.

She stubbed out the roll-up, which should have been a relief except her hands had moved to the hem of her T-shirt. She slowly curled it up to reveal her bare breasts.

'Do you want to see my tits, Nick?'

'Don't do that, Ava,' I commanded, glancing back to the house to check no one else was watching.

'Or would you rather see Mum's? Don't think I haven't noticed the way you look at her.'

She pulled down her top, jumped off the wall and headed back to the house, laughing, before I could think of anything to say.

12

Rosie

Cancer can be a disease of awful retrospectives: the lump that wasn't biopsied; the cough that was ignored; the mole that was overlooked. I pride myself on my ability to detect tiny changes in my patients, yet when it came to my own daughter I failed. It shames me to admit this, but Nick and I saw little to alarm us in the run-up to the seismic events that occurred in the months after our holiday. We had no idea how ill Daisy was and, unbeknownst to us, Max, the only person who might have come clean about what was going on, had been recruited by his sister to help cover her tracks.

There were vague idiosyncrasies, but they were the sweet kind that could easily be turned into family folklore. I remember her dropping a knife on my foot when we went out for pizza on her fourteenth birthday at the end of August. There was a tiny scratch where the blade grazed my toe but she worried for days that I might contract a fatal infection or have internal bleeding, which could lead to a blood clot.

She also developed strong opinions on how things should be done around the house, insisting bath towels should be washed at 60 degrees to prevent them from going scaly and switches turned off at the socket because anything – from the microwave to the mobile phone charger – could give Max and me cancer. Curiously she didn't worry about Nick, even though his mother had died of leukaemia.

'It won't make us ill because the radiation used isn't powerful enough to damage DNA and microwaves are non-ionizing, which means they don't contain cancer-causing agents,' I patiently explained, wishing Daisy would get on with the small stuff like putting her dirty plates in the dishwasher. 'But it will give me a nervous breakdown because my phone isn't charged when I go to work in the morning.'

To be honest, I was more alarmed by her pseudo science than the way she crept around the house checking the sockets after we had gone to bed. When I mentioned these misconceptions to Lisa she laughed and told me that Ava believed the microwave would make her infertile by frying her ovaries and blamed Facebook for peddling fiction as fact. She also listed her current preoccupations with Ava – smoking weed, having sex with her much older boyfriend, coming home late or not at all – which made my concerns about Daisy seem anaemic by comparison. As Nick always liked to say, the only certainties in life were death, taxes and the fact that Lisa's problems would always trump my own.

In hindsight I could see that Ava was at the more extreme end of the spectrum of normal teenage behaviour, whereas Daisy had gone completely off grid. I could tell from the way her usual paraphernalia had gravitated from the kitchen to her bedroom that she was spending more and more time alone upstairs in her room. Her carpet was scabby with wax from the tea lights she arranged in symmetrical patterns on every available surface. Her books, pencil case and calculator sat in a triangular pattern on her desk and she got annoyed if anyone touched them. But I assumed she was doing the normal teenage shift from the public to the private.

She didn't go out much at weekends or hang out with the same friends any more. When I asked her why she no longer saw Ava, Daisy said she needed to concentrate on her work and that Ava had 'gone weird'. I didn't pursue this because in some ways I was relieved the intensity of that lopsided friendship had waned and that she didn't see Barney in his current dilapidated state.

'So let's get this straight,' said Nick languidly, when I mentioned my concerns to him in bed late one night. 'You're worried about Daisy because she's stopped hanging out with a friend who makes her feel bad about herself, she's working too hard for exams and doesn't want to go to a school Halloween party?'

I laughed at my own absurdity and he ran his finger up my arm and across my chest where it lingered on my right breast. I started to tell him some of the things he needed to know before I went on my trip to the US in a couple of weeks: two supermarket orders would arrive on consecutive Tuesdays; the neighbours would have a spare set of keys; sanitary towels and Tampax had been bought and placed in the upstairs cupboard for Daisy. As his finger began circling my breast I lost focus and gave in to the pleasure.

'You always were an easy lay, Rosie Rankin,' he whispered in my ear, hooking his thigh over mine.

I realize people will call me a fool, but I remember that period as one of the happiest in our marriage.

Lisa and Barney continued to distract us with their problems through October, although we were much better friends to Lisa than we were to Barney. I tried to keep in touch with him but he took days to respond and cancelled plans at the last minute, whereas Lisa came by once or twice a week to update us on his lack of progress. She often fetched a bottle from the crates of expensive wine she was storing in our garden shed to prevent Barney from consuming them all. It hadn't stopped him drinking because he still went to the off-licence when she was at work to buy cheap alcohol that he decanted into anything he could lay his hands on. Lisa had discovered this when she tried to wash her hair and realized the reason the shampoo wouldn't lather was because it was vodka. I admired her ability to magic a good story out of misery.

By late October I was working flat out, finessing the presentation for my trip. On the UK side we had almost got as far as we could with the protocol for the trial: the details had been thrashed out and endorsed by the steering committee, the dose agreed, toxicity levels approved, and we had identified more than a thousand patients who wanted to take part. But the euphoria of my appointment had ebbed as I faced the reality of heading up an international team with four different hospitals on three different continents involving thousands of patients.

I had to combine this with my usual outpatient clinics, a weekly multi-disciplinary team meeting and ward rounds. Although my afternoon clinics were meant to start at two and finish at five, more often than not I was still seeing people at eight o'clock at night. The hospital manager had reduced patient time to fifteen minutes to deal with a backlog of appointments but it wasn't long enough to explain complex treatment plans or deliver the worst kind of news. So increasingly when Lisa came round I went upstairs to get on with my work and left her with Nick. It sounds ridiculous, given what happened later, but I was grateful to him for helping my friend.

According to Nick, he gave her all sorts of advice on how to manage her vertiginous finances. Barney and Lisa were equally hopeless with money because neither of them had ever had to worry about it before. He instructed her to cut up her credit card, cancel her gym membership, shop at Aldi, ditch her plan to remortgage their house to raise cash, and set up her own bank account so she had control of their cash flow. To her credit Lisa followed all Nick's advice but his calm reliability fuelled her resentment of Barney, which in turn eroded the last vestiges of any respect she'd once had for him. Poor Barney. He didn't stand a chance.

'Guess where he hid it this time?' I heard her ask Nick as I headed upstairs to make the final touches to my presentation. I paused on the steps, waiting to be entertained by Lisa's answer.

'He kept insisting that he wanted Ava's hot-water bottle with the furry penguin cover in bed with him, even though he's such a rainforest of sweat that I have to change his sheets when I get home from work every night. I got suspicious so I undid the stopper and took a swig.'

'It must taste disgusting, even to him,' Nick said.

I noticed how he had stopped referring to Barney by name but deployed Lisa's at any opportunity.

'It was a little rubbery,' said Lisa. 'But the worst thing was he'd mixed it with orange juice so it tasted like a flavoured condom.'

'Un-fucking believable,' said Nick.

'Un-fucking believable,' agreed Lisa.

'The good thing about an intolerable marriage is that it's easier to leave,' said Nick. 'You're lucky in some ways.'

I couldn't hear Lisa's response but I remember being a little taken aback by their easy intimacy and how Nick knew that Lisa was considering leaving Barney before I did.

I tried to conceal my enthusiasm when Daisy casually told me that Ava had invited her to go to the Year Ten Halloween disco with her the first Saturday of November. We were in the kitchen and I was hunting for the bread knife, which had gone missing again. I could tell Daisy was excited from the flurry of activity: *TICKET!!! COSTUME!!! GREEN MAKE-UP!!!* The exclamation marks on her list caught my eye because they reminded me that Max had asked a question about the significance of the number three that I had forgotten to answer amidst the early-morning mayhem.

Everyone going to the party had to come up with ten songs with a spooky theme for a playlist. Even Barney got involved, sending Ava and Daisy left-field suggestions: 'Bad Moon Rising' by Creedence Clearwater Revival, 'Zombie' by The Cranberries, 'Time Warp' from *The*

Rocky Horror Picture Show. And although they ignored his suggestions I was pleased because it allowed us to feel the sweet caress of shared history between us all again.

Ava arrived late at our house that evening to get ready. She brought Molly, which surprised me a little, because she had never been one of their friends. Molly was loud and self-confident, old before her time, and talked incessantly about the characters in a new show called *Outnumbered*. Ava gave me a quick hug, her skin-tight lurex catsuit slipping between my fingers like butter.

'Great wings,' I said.

'I'm a fallen angel,' she laughed.

There were two other girls who I didn't recognize and a couple of boys in identical Count Dracula costumes, hair dyed white, with fangs stuck on top of their eye teeth and a trickle of red food colouring coming out of their mouths. Nick made snide comments about Halloween being a cynical marketing ploy, but if it got Daisy away from her books then I was satisfied.

Shouts and screams and Amy Winehouse filtered down from the upstairs bathroom as they all finished getting ready. We dispatched Max to report back to us, but Ava pounced on him and insisted he help apply her make-up. When she came down I could tell she had been as good as her word. The bluntly applied eyeliner, the green lipstick smeared above the outline of her upper lip and the blurry asymmetrical stars on her cheeks were grotesque. But the imperfections only highlighted her natural beauty. It was difficult not to stare.

Daisy followed close behind, round-shouldered, wearing a witch's costume from last year that clung to the puppy fat on her stomach like cellophane. She kept trying to pull the dress down over her knees. I felt a wave of pity for her. Sometimes I wished I could edit her behaviour. . Ava slid down the bannister from the top to the bottom of the stairs as she had done in our house since she was a small child, legs flailing. I was grateful to her for the distraction so that the others didn't notice Daisy's self-consciousness. Ava accidentally toppled a pile of my papers and they drifted down the stairs. Daisy apologized for her. *Please don't make excuses for Ava*, I wanted to say. A memory drifted back from Reception when Ava bit a boy in their class and Daisy tried to convince the teacher she was the aggressor, even though the teacher had witnessed Ava sinking her teeth into the boy's thigh. Daisy was always too nice for this world. A thread of anxiety wound around me and then was dissolved by the commotion of Daisy and her friends making their way downstairs.

'This is why I'm hot!' Ava rapped, as she propelled herself down the bannister, the slippery catsuit helping her pick up speed.

It was inappropriate and absurd but it was difficult not to be drawn into the force field of energy she radiated. Everyone laughed long and loud. My gaze lingered on Max's face and I saw he was anxiously looking at Daisy to shore up his reaction. Daisy's face was covered with thick white make-up and her eyes were painted Zombie black so it was difficult to read anything in her expression beyond the fact that she didn't share the joke. Or maybe she wasn't even listening.

They left the house in a mass, hot bodies jostling against each other. Daisy hugged me for a beat too long and I knew she was being brave in the same way she used to be during her first year at school. She didn't want to go. *Stay here*, I should have said. Daisy clearly didn't feel comfortable with Ava and her new friends. But I remembered myself at the same age, turning down invitations to parties until eventually everyone stopped inviting me. One of the Draculas told Daisy to hurry up. I was pleased he had waited for her.

'Coming, Lal,' she told him.

'Have you got your stuff?' he smiled.

Daisy patted her bag.

'It'll be great,' I reassured her.

Daisy didn't reply and I felt bad in case I had embarrassed her in front of her friends.

It still isn't clear to me what occurred that night. There were no adults who witnessed what happened. The blurry sequence of events had to be pieced together in the days that followed by shocked parents and teachers dealing with the aftermath until a clearer picture emerged. And the teenagers involved were unreliable, their accounts either exaggerated beyond all credibility or blurred by everything they had consumed, and even that was never completely clear.

The facts were these: instead of going straight to the party Daisy and her friends took a detour via the park to meet other students from their year – four boys and three girls or five girls and two boys depending on whose account you believed.

They goaded one another into the darkest recesses of the park to mine the Halloween mood, drinking bottles of Baileys, vodka and sambuca pilfered from unwitting parents or bought by obliging older siblings, including Rex. The evidence for this was found the following day when Lisa went to search for Ava's lost mobile phone.

Lal decided it would be really funny to hide in the small copse of trees and jump out to spook unsuspecting strangers who were unlucky enough to be passing by on a late-night jog or dog walk. But no one appeared. Molly later recounted how they hung around the park for a further half an hour until Ava gave the signal and one by one they all crept away in silence until only Daisy was left.

Ava later insisted they hadn't intended to abandon Daisy and had simply forgotten to warn her they were leaving. 'Everything was spontaneous,' she kept insisting. She even tried to convince Mr McPherson, the headmaster, that Daisy was the one who had come up with the idea to go to the park in the first place. Her version of events was contradicted by one of the Draculas, who let slip that they had all regrouped outside Nando's as part of a plan formulated on their Facebook group earlier in the week.

I could see the temptations of such a trick and understood how their stupid teenage brains might find it irresistibly hilarious. But the way Daisy was selected as the victim showed a degree of premeditated psychology that made me certain that Ava had singled her out. I couldn't believe how she could be so cruel and never fully understood her motivation.

It still makes me weep to imagine how Daisy felt at the exact moment when she realized she had been abandoned, although at least she didn't know the extent of their betrayal until later that night when Molly told her it was a set-up. The alcohol might have diluted her fear on finding herself completely alone but it also undermined her sense of direction and she wandered around the park for about an hour until she eventually found her way back to the main path.

Sadness, fear, desperation and rage are the basic ingredients of courage and I like to think it was the melding of these emotions that shaped her decision to go to the party at school rather than return home. Although of course other people, including her head teacher, suspected her motivation was revenge. I can understand why people came to that conclusion, especially given what followed.

It wasn't late when Lisa called. Nick was watching *Top Gear* with Max and I was upstairs cleaning up teenage mess in the bathroom, scrubbing green make-up from the tiles around the basin, collecting bits of tissue smeared with eyeliner and shoving rejected Halloween costumes back into the cupboard. I assumed Lisa was phoning about Barney. A couple of weeks earlier, Nick had to go round to their house in the pouring rain to help carry him upstairs to his room. And once, after he had tried to stop drinking for two days, I had taken him to A&E because he was having hallucinations.

'Ava's gone missing,' said Lisa before I had even spoken.

'They're at the party,' I said. 'They went hours ago.'

'She's disappeared. The head of year called me. She's been lost for a couple of hours but her friends didn't want to say anything until they were sure they couldn't find her.' Her voice was all staccato.

'Have you spoken to Daisy?'

'Her phone goes straight to voicemail. Will you come with me? Please. I can't bring Barney. He's a total mess.'

By the time we got to school, the teachers had called an early halt to the party and switched on the playground lights, spotlighting the cheap decorations: the fake cobwebs, the plastic rats and spiders, and the hastily carved pumpkins with candles already burnt to the wick. Students and teachers dressed in Halloween outfits milled around, the light from their mobile phones flickering in the semi-dark like fireflies.

They searched for Ava haphazardly, focusing on the tight alleyways between buildings one minute and scrabbling beneath shrubs in the flower beds that lined the school perimeter the next. Lisa added her voice to those calling her name in the playground. During the car journey she had smouldered with rage over Ava's selfishness and irresponsibility, expecting her to turn up in a drunken stupor before we even arrived. But now she sounded scared.

'Have you tried her phone again?' I asked, as we walked across the yard.

'It goes straight to voicemail.'

The assembly hall glowed orange in the distance. All the lights had been switched on and inside it was as bright as an operating theatre. I blinked as my eyes adjusted to the glare. A few students drifted around in wilted costumes. There were a couple of skeletons, a pumpkin and too many Grim Reapers to count. They were all unrecognizable. I spotted one of the Draculas, the one who had waited for Daisy, identifiable by his flat, wide nose and flared nostrils. The fake blood was now smeared across his upper lip like a moustache.

'Lal?' I said, waving my hand in recognition, but he swiftly looked away.

'Have you seen Ava?' Lisa asked him as we drew closer.

'The last time I saw her she was with Daisy. But that was a while ago. I told Mr McPherson.' He sounded defensive rather than worried.

'Where's Daisy?' I asked.

He shrugged and gave a quick, tight smile. 'Sorry. Don't know. I haven't spoken to her since the park.'

That was the first mention of the park. I nudged Lisa but she had spotted Molly talking to Mr McPherson, who looked genuinely sinister in his Joker costume. Molly's wings appeared to be vibrating gently, as if she was preparing to fly, but as we got closer I realized that she was trembling. Another teacher who I didn't recognize wrapped a rug around her shoulders and gave her a bottle of water, which she swallowed in deep gulps.

'Everything got out of hand,' she said drowsily.

Lal shot her a warning glance and pulled his fangs out of his mouth. He ducked down beside her and gently held her cheeks between his palms as if comforting a small child.

She leant in towards him.

'It's all cool, Molly, it's all cool. Everyone is cool.'

'There are no insignificant psychedelic experiences, Lal,' sighed Molly.

'Shut the fuck up, Molly,' Lal said quietly.

'I don't understand,' said the teacher. She looked almost as young as her students. 'Everyone was having such a good time. They were all dancing and hugging each other.'

Mr McPherson removed the fake axe from her head and instructed the teacher to go back outside into the yard to tell students to look under the prefab Modern Languages buildings in case Ava had crawled underneath.

'Lal, you go with Miss Matthews,' he instructed.

Lal reluctantly left with the teacher. As he reached the door he turned to Molly and pressed his fingers to his lips.

Still holding the axe, Mr McPherson turned back to Molly. 'You need to tell us everything,' he said fiercely, squatting down beside her. 'And you need to tell us fast. If anything happens to Ava you'll have to live with that for the rest of your life. Do I make myself clear? This is one of those times when you need to make the right choice.'

'Please, Molly,' Lisa begged. 'No one will be angry with you. We just need to find her.'

'My head hurts so much,' Molly said slowly. 'It feels like it's going to burst.'

I noticed the muscle above her right eye was twitching and a pulse throbbing in her temple. When she spoke it sounded as though her tongue was too big for her mouth.

'Look at me, Molly,' I instructed.

Her pupils were fully dilated.

'Have you taken something?'

'I don't know anything.'

It was at this moment that I spotted Daisy coming down the steps into the hall. Her costume was badly ripped around the hem and both her knees were grazed and bleeding. But as she walked towards us in her bare feet I could tell that she was completely sober. I felt proud of her for staying out of trouble. I stood up.

'What are you doing here, Mum?' she asked. She sounded exhausted. 'Can we go home, please?'

'No one's going anywhere until we've found Ava,' said Mr McPherson firmly. 'Can you remember when you last saw her, Daisy?'

When Molly spotted Daisy, she pulled herself on to her feet and staggered unsteadily towards her. Daisy shrank back against me. Molly put out her arms to hug her but missed and concertinaed into a heap on the floor.

'I'm sorry, Daisy,' she said.

Daisy didn't say anything.

'It wasn't my idea.'

'Was it Ava's?' asked Daisy.

Molly looked up at her and nodded almost imperceptibly. 'Do you think she fell off?' Molly asked Daisy.

'Fell off what?' asked Lisa, putting her hands on Molly's shoulders and shaking her like a rag doll.

'The roof,' said Molly dreamily. 'We were all on the roof.'

'What in God's name were you doing up there?' asked Mr McPherson angrily. All the wrinkles on his forehead converged into a single expression of anxiety.

'Chilling,' whispered Molly.

I saw her stomach lurch. She leant forward slightly and projectile vomited on to the floor. Eyes watering, she stared at the pool of sick in wonder. Mr McPherson started running, pulling off his green Joker wig and throwing it to the floor. Lisa and I struggled to keep up with him as he headed into the main school building and leapt up the old stone stairs two at a time.

By the time we reached the fourth floor I felt as though my heart was going to burst through my chest. Daisy was right. I really was unfit. We followed him into a classroom with long benches and metal taps where Bunsen burners could be attached. In the far corner by the window I spotted a metal ladder that led up to an open trapdoor on to the roof. Mr McPherson went up first while Lisa held the ladder steady. I followed behind. It was pitch dark on the flat lead roof.

We could smell Ava before we could see her. The gut-wrenching smell of vomit and shit and urine made us all clasp our hands to our mouths simultaneously. Mr McPherson got out his phone and lit a tentative path towards the stench.

'Oh my God,' said Lisa repeatedly.

We found her on the far edge of the roof, on the side that faced the playground. She was motionless and face down in a pool of sick, her wings flapping in the breeze. It was a long time since I had done shifts in A&E but all the old instincts kicked in.

'We need to turn her over to clear her airways,' I instructed Lisa and Mr McPherson. I saw him hesitate for a second and nodded to give him encouragement like I did with my junior doctors, when they were unsure how to react.

He shifted closer and retched.

'Breathe through your mouth,' I said.

We gently rolled Ava on to her side. Lisa whispered her name, over and over again, like a prayer.

I tilted her chin back and spoke to her. 'Ava, Ava, can you hear me?' I pulled up her eyelids but couldn't assess her pupils because they had rolled to the back of her head. She was completely unconscious. I put my hand on her chest. Her breathing was very shallow and when I measured her pulse it was dangerously low. Severe respiratory depression. Her body started shaking and white foam dribbled out of the side of her mouth.

'She's fitting,' I shouted. 'We need an ambulance right away.'

I heard Lisa scream. It was so piercing that everyone in the playground turned to face the roof in frozen silence.

I was in the middle of my afternoon outpatients' clinic on Monday afternoon when Mr McPherson called. It had been a particularly gruelling session. I had seen a pregnant 27-year-old woman with an aggressive invasive ductal angiosarcoma in her left breast. We needed to discuss whether to go ahead with an immediate partial mastectomy, given the risks of general anaesthesia to the six-month-old foetus. I had to explain that while chemotherapy was the best course of treatment, it increased the risks of growth problems and premature birth. The more I spoke, the closer her husband moved his chair towards her until his body almost eclipsed hers, as if by shielding his wife from the words coming out of my mouth he could save her from the illness itself. My job can be stressful, but it is nothing compared to what my patients go through.

I called Lisa to get an update in between patients. Ava had regained consciousness. She had amnesia and couldn't remember anything from when they all climbed out on to the roof. Her last memory was Daisy sharing a bottle of water with her.

'Thanks so much, Rosie. And I'm sorry. For every-thing.'

My next patient, a glamorous grandmother who always lied to me about her age, had failed to turn up for her first round of chemotherapy a couple of weeks earlier. She confessed to me that she had kept her diagnosis secret from her entire family, including her husband, and had no plans to follow our advice.

I allowed my junior doctor to intervene to explain the benefits of treatment but the more he tried to convince her, the more stubborn she became. She didn't want to lose her hair and eyebrows. He told her there were ways of avoiding this. But she insisted she wanted her family to remember her the way she was now.

Then came the phone call from school. I glanced at my list and happily handed over Mrs K. to my team. She was a notoriously difficult woman who we took it in turns to see, because she regularly accused us of conspiring to give her second-rate care when in reality she was fortunate enough to be on an incredibly expensive and ground-breaking treatment.

I had complacently assumed that Mr McPherson would be phoning to say thank you for my quick thinking on Saturday night. But instead he asked Nick and me to come to school that same afternoon for an urgent meeting. I explained that Nick was at a conference out of town and wouldn't be able to make it.

'Could we come tomorrow instead?'

'This needs to be dealt with immediately,' he said.

His tone was stern, a mark of how seriously he took the evidence of Ava bullying Daisy, I concluded, relieved that the school was going to deal with the issue without our prompting, although I felt bad for heaping another problem on to Lisa's plate. Even when Daisy was waiting for us in his office when I got there, I had no inkling of what was to come. Her face was pale and expressionless. She managed a quick, nervous smile and then looked down at the floor again.

'I've spoken to Daisy's teachers, Mrs Rankin, and they tell me that she's been failing to finish class assignments and falling behind with homework,' said Mr McPherson. 'They also said no one wants to sit next to her because she fidgets all the time. Is that right, Daisy?' He glanced up from his notes to look at her.

'If they say so,' Daisy shrugged.

'But she's up in her room working all the time,' I said, puzzled over the contradiction although I recognized the description. 'It makes no sense.'

'Then perhaps this will,' he said, handing me a piece of paper. 'We've had Ava's toxicology report from the hospital. A group of our students took a drug called GHB. Liquid Ecstasy. It's a legal high. People take it before they go clubbing.'

He said the words unnaturally, as if he was speaking a language he didn't understand, and I guessed he wanted me to translate. Pharmacology had always been one of my favourite subjects. I glanced over it. Gamma Hydroxybutyric Acid.

'It's the active ingredient in a drug that's sometimes prescribed for people with narcolepsy,' I explained. 'It's an illness where people fall asleep all the time.'

He looked puzzled. I continued, secure in my ability to explain complex issues in easily digestible nuggets.

'But if you combine it with alcohol and take a high enough dose it can be fatal. The whole body shuts down. It causes loss of muscle control. Hence the evacuation from every orifice.' I paused to allow him to catch up. 'She's lucky to be alive.'

He rested his arms on his desk and leant towards me. 'Mrs Rankin, Daisy was the one who brought the drug to school but she refuses to tell us where she got it and whether she's taken it before. I know you're a medic and I wanted to make sure that there's no way she's stealing it from your workplace. Perhaps this is why her school work is suffering?'

He kept speaking because I could see his mouth open and shut but I couldn't hear his words. Everyone in the room fragmented as if I was looking through a kaleidoscope. On the right was Daisy, sitting stiffly, jaw set, eyes closed, tapping her foot on the ground and muttering. On my left, where Nick should have been sitting, was a shiny filing cabinet with papers piled on top and a photo in a silver frame of the headmaster with his wife and two daughters. In the centre was Mr McPherson, sitting behind his desk, shirtsleeves rolled up, making accusations that could end my career and leave my daughter with a criminal record. But I couldn't get these scenes to coalesce before me.

'Mum had nothing to do with this,' said Daisy, breaking the heavy silence.

I turned to her in confusion. 'You had nothing to do with this,' I said firmly, convinced that she was trying to cover up for Ava. I turned to Mr McPherson. 'Where Ava leads, Daisy follows. That's the way it's always been.'

'It was sent to our house and I brought it to the park,' said Daisy. 'I didn't even take it.'

'Why did they send it to you?' Mr McPherson asked, but I already knew the answer to that question.

She did it to ingratiate herself with Ava and her friends.

'Lal organized it all. He'd done it before. I wanted to help him.'

'Where did Lal get it?' Mr McPherson asked.

Daisy looked down at her foot as it beat out patterns on the floor. I noticed how she tapped three times on the ball of her foot and then three times on the heel.

'Somewhere on the Internet,' said Daisy quietly. 'He paid. But I agreed it could be sent to us because his parents were suspicious about all the parcels that kept arriving for him.'

I didn't believe her. But later that same day, after speaking to Lal, Mr McPherson phoned me to confirm that Daisy was telling the truth. Lal had even shown him the website. There were lists of hundreds of drugs and even reviews. 'How can this be?' Mr McPherson kept asking. We were all out of our depth.

'When we were in the park Lal gave everyone a full cap. But I poured mine into my water bottle. I didn't want to take it because none of them wanted me to be there. They left me behind.' Her voice had lowered to a whisper.

'I appreciate your honesty,' said Mr McPherson. 'And I'm sorry about what happened to you in the park but I'm still going to have to suspend you from school for two weeks because it was you that brought the drugs into school.'

Frankly, I was grateful for his kindness. For the first time since we had sat down on the hard wooden chairs in front of his desk, I felt my shoulders relax slightly.

'So can you explain what happened to Ava?' Mr McPherson asked Daisy, as if it was an afterthought.

'I was angry with her. She was thirsty and so I gave her the water with my share.'

We went home. Daisy leant her cheek against the passenger window of the car and closed her eyes against the winter sun. I glanced over at her and frowned as I noticed her lips moving soundlessly. If you had asked me to describe Daisy's face to you I could have told you the exact position of the small mole on the left side of her chin, the chickenpox scar hidden behind her right eyebrow, the dimples in her cheeks and the gap in her front teeth. Her features were almost more familiar to me than my own. And yet there was something utterly impenetrable about her that made her seem like a stranger.

'I understand why you did it,' I said.

'No you don't, Mum,' she said softly. There was no challenge in her tone. She sounded defeated. 'You'll never understand.'

I remembered the exact moment after giving birth when the midwife passed Daisy to me and my sense of loss and wonder that she had become a separate being from me. It had been a long hard labour, as if Daisy wasn't quite ready for the world, and sometimes I still had that sense with her. I realized that I had always mistaken her reticence for certainty. Her stillness for calm. And her containment for confidence. She only spoke once more on that trip home.

'Does this mean you won't go on your trip, Mum?'

It took a moment for me to understand what she was talking about. 'I'm not sure,' I said cautiously.

'That would be good in a way, though, wouldn't it? Because of all those illnesses that get spread through the air conditioning on planes. It would be a shame to get sick over Christmas.'

'We'll discuss it all when Dad gets back,' I told her, checking my phone for the hundredth time that afternoon to see if Nick had messaged me. I guessed he was still interviewing the volunteers participating in his research on false memory.

When I got home I went straight to our next-door neighbour's house to pick up Max. Daisy usually collected him from after-school club and he protested about the unexpected change to his usual routine. He kept asking if Daisy was okay and why she had fallen out with Ava and whether she was in trouble – and if she was, was it large trouble or medium-sized trouble.

'I'm guessing it's not small trouble, is it?'

I told him that Daisy had to stay at home for a couple of weeks to sort out a few problems, and although he remained pensive at least he stopped asking questions. Then I called work and postponed my trip to the States.

We didn't spend New Year in Norfolk with Lisa and Barney that year. By this time Daisy and Ava were completely estranged and, as Nick pointed out, hanging out with Lisa and Barney would be like being trapped in an extended version of *Who's Afraid of Virginia Woolf?* but without the laughs. So we stayed in London and invited over Deborah and her husband.

As the month unfolded Daisy seemed to retreat further and further into herself. At mealtimes she got more and more fidgety, plucking woolly bobbles from her sweater, fiddling with cutlery and rearranging food on her plate. She left the table two or three times during a meal to lock herself in the toilet and drove Nick mad by incessantly jiggling her leg, a habit that Max copied, thereby doubling the spillages from the water jug at dinner. Her weight slowly dropped but she was getting taller and I assumed she was just losing the puppy fat she hated.

She fixated more on my appearance – worrying about the tiny network of thread veins on the right side of my nose, the few dark hairs above my lip, the barely visible loose skin under my chin – and dropped heavy hints about highlights, makeovers and wearing the right clothes for your body shape, which suggested she thought mine was wrong.

'Are you trying to turn me into Lisa?' I joked, after she tried to persuade me to get a bob and paint my nails black. I explained that I didn't have much time for self-improvement because I had just been given an extra ward round after we lost yet another junior doctor to a biotech firm.

Although we didn't realize until much later, Ava had been tormenting her on social media. Daisy was blamed for Lal's expulsion from school and a Facebook group had been set up with unflattering photos of her taken at the party, in classes and the playground. There were even some taken in Norfolk wearing her blue swimsuit, gazing adoringly at Rex. Boys and girls from her year posted horrible comments and then one of them added Daisy to the group so that she saw everything that had been said about her.

I tried to tackle Max, to see if he had any idea what was going on, and he responded with long-winded questions about his current preoccupations such as whether it was bad to have bearskin rugs in his virtual Club Penguin igloo because it might look like he approved of hunting, or whether it would be better to clone a stormtrooper with Sith or a Jedi to create the optimum super fighter. 'Optimum' was one of Max's favourite new words that autumn and winter. The other was 'susceptible'.

He had been chosen to play centre midfield for his local football team and spent hours rehearsing scissor kicks in the garden. His first match was scheduled for late afternoon on the last Tuesday of January but the evening before, he announced that he couldn't find one of his football boots. I delivered my usual lecture about putting his stuff in the same place and not leaving things until the last minute, and abandoned my work to track down the missing boot.

I went upstairs to search in his bedroom. Daisy's door was ajar and I glanced through the gap to see her sitting on her bed with her eyes closed talking to herself. I stopped to listen even though I would be accused of being stalky if she caught me. 'Three is a good and safe number,' she muttered and then paused. 'Three is a good and safe number.' As soon as I located the boot, I would go and speak to her.

Max's bedroom was a predictable mess. It would take

days to put everything in the right place. I got down on my hands and knees to search under his bed and found his Norfolk notebook, spine down, hidden beneath an unsavoury hoard of dirty pants, old sweet wrappers, and the filthy missing football boot. This was where he had recorded all the results of his ladybird experiment during our summer holiday in Norfolk five months earlier and I didn't want it to get lost or ruined. The cover was stuck shut with a filthy piece of chewing gum embedded with what looked like the remnants of a ladybird's wing and cat hair.

I loved Max for his uncomplicated nature. I smiled as I opened the notebook. Every page was covered with big complex tables. On the right side was a long handwritten list – curtains, knife drawer, taps, windows – that I initially assumed were the various places in Norfolk where he had found ladybirds. Along the top were the days of the week. The level of detail made me smile.

There were carefully ruled horizontal and vertical lines that must have been drawn by Daisy, judging by their precision, creating dozens of boxes that were filled with incomprehensible hieroglyphics, a blend of lines and crosses. Daisy's initials were at the end of each column and while part of me wished Max didn't crave Daisy's approval so much, the other was happy that she tolerated his hero worship and they got on so well in spite of the three years between them. They were closer than ever.

I flicked through to the middle, noting new categories that appeared: sockets, gas, front door. This caught my attention because there was no gas in Norfolk. I looked at the date. The last recorded time was yesterday at 22.13, an hour and a half after Max was meant to be asleep. I flicked backwards a couple of pages and saw the sign-off time was around about the same every night for the previous month. I forgot about the boot and hid the book inside my cardigan. I would wait till Nick came home and we would speak to Daisy together.

Except Nick never came home.

The end of my marriage wasn't worthy of its beginning. Later that evening, after Daisy and Max had gone to bed, I was in the sitting room with the light turned low, drinking a glass of Barney and Lisa's wine, trying to assemble my thoughts. The notebook lay open in my lap. I was certain there must be a connection between the box marked switches and the way Daisy had to turn off all the sockets at night, but I could find no meaningful explanation. I was desperate for Nick to arrive but he had texted again to say he wanted to write up his interviews without anyone else around.

There was a muffled thumping on the front door. For someone so proud of his memory, my husband was very good at forgetting his keys. When I opened the door, however, it wasn't Nick standing there, but Barney. It was cold enough outside that I could see his breath when he spoke and yet he was drenched in sweat. He leant against the wall of the house as if it was too much effort to stand upright.

'I think your doorbell needs fixing,' he said breathlessly. He pressed it to prove it was broken and I noticed his hands were shaking.

'Is that why you've come round?' I said, making a futile attempt at levity.

'Can I come in?' he asked.

I could smell stale alcohol on his breath. I felt so sorry for him at that moment but I didn't have the energy to deal with his problems and I certainly didn't trust myself to discuss what had happened between Daisy and Ava. One of the few pressing conclusions I had that day was the urgent need to create some distance between our family and the Drapers before they took us down with them.

'Please,' said Barney, sensing my reticence.

'Nick's not here.'

'I know. It's you I want to see, Rosie, or do you not have any time for one of your old friends?'

I gestured for him to come in. He gave me a sticky hug and we headed into the kitchen. I offered him leftovers from dinner and he turned me down, making a tired joke about being on a purely liquid diet. After a few minutes he asked for a glass of wine and when I refused he gripped my arm and said that he needed Dutch courage. I ignored him and found water and a packet of dry-roasted peanuts that I split open on the kitchen table for us to share. He sat down opposite me and started telling me a convoluted story about how he had bumped into Liam Gallagher on the street in North London and managed to secure an exclusive interview that would soon make the cover of a weekend supplement.

'That's great,' I said, too exhausted to challenge his version of events.

He asked about the children and described what had happened to Ava as 'a bad business'. He blamed Lal for everything and said he had hoped that Daisy and Ava would be friends again because Daisy was such a good influence on her. Unlike Lal. 'Especially when things are so difficult,' he said.

I took this as a sign that he was finally acknowledging the toll his drinking was having on his family. He poured himself another glass of water and gulped it down. He sucked his teeth and I noticed how yellow they had become. His head was bowed and his hair was thinning on the top of his head and it made me feel unexpectedly tender towards him.

'You know what's going on, don't you, Rosie?' he suddenly said. 'I mean it's happening in plain sight. And you're a doctor so you're always on the lookout for symptoms, aren't you?'

'I'm not sure I follow you,' I said.

'Nick and Lisa.' He paused. 'You must see it. They've fallen in love. Which is worse than lust, because you can get over desire.'

'Stop it, Barney,' I ordered him, remembering how a patient once said this to me, as if words made her illness real. I could understand now what she had been going through. Because I now felt the same bewildering disjunction between how I believed my life was and how I was being told it was.

'Please don't tell me this comes as a complete surprise,' he said quietly.

There was a catch in his voice that made me scared.

He got up from the table and went over to the kitchen light and fiddled with the dimmer. Then he came back to the table and sat, palms facing down, fingers splayed. He looked up at me and fixed me with his watery blue eyes.

'This is one of the most difficult things I have ever had

to say to anyone. I've debated whether to tell you for weeks and weeks. I kept thinking you would notice something or Nick would cock up. But he's good at deception, knows how to talk the talk. Better than Lisa. She's so transparent. But I can't live like this any more. I need to sort myself out, and to do that I need to acknowledge what's going on. We all do. For the sake of ourselves and our children.'

I felt sorrier for Barney than I did for myself because I knew how difficult it was to deliver bad news to people: the fumble for the right words; the need to make sure there was no room for misinterpretation; the self-critique later because there was never a right way. The tendency to keep talking because the other person is speechless with shock. And yet I don't think I have ever hated anyone more.

When he finished he wiped his brow with the sleeve of his shirt and looked up at me. He blinked away tears but there was no stemming their flow. I had spent much of my life thinking that most bad things that happen aren't as bad as irreversible cancer. But even with the worst diagnosis there is that chink of hope that you could be the one in a million who survives. I have occasionally seen it with my own patients. But he gave me no hope.

'It's not true,' I said in total shock. 'They wouldn't do that to us and our children.'

'Do you know where Nick is right now?'

'He's at work.'

Barney shook his head. 'My guess is they're at the Travelodge in Farringdon.'

He pulled a receipt out of his pocket. I could hardly

read it because my hands were trembling so much but I recognized the last four digits of Nick's credit card. It was dated earlier in the month. Barney put his hand on my arm and squeezed it.

'You don't deserve this, Rosie. You really don't. I do. I blame myself for becoming so unlovable. Lisa hates me, or at least she hates what I've become, so I've played my part. And none of us are immune to the itch, are we? God knows, I've had a few slip-ups in my time.'

'But we're not like you and Lisa,' I said hopelessly.

'We're all animals, Rosie,' he shrugged.

It was so easy for Nick to fall out of love with me. That was the hardest part. There had been no fights fought, no hateful words exchanged, no emotional grandstanding. Nick later said this reflected the lack of passion in our relationship. I argued that we were still tethered by a thread of desire. I wanted to make lists of everything he thought was wrong so that we could come up with solutions. Nick didn't want to put up a struggle because he didn't think our relationship was worth fighting for. He had lost the faith. Or rather he had gained a new faith.

13

Daisy

Dad told Mum it was for the best when he left, although he still tries to make out she was the one who threw him out so people feel sorry for him. He has a limitless capacity for self-pity. Theoretically at least, I guess he was correct, because by the time he came home the evening of Barney's surprise visit to Mum, she had packed two bags of clothes for him (dirty) and left them outside the front door, which was locked from the inside so he couldn't get in. After Barney delivered his news and left, Mum had immediately called Lisa.

'Is it true?' I heard her ask from my listening post in the downstairs toilet.

Three words. Not always a good and safe number. Although I didn't realize it at the time, these would be the last words they ever spoke to each other. I went into the kitchen. Mum put down the phone and poured herself another glass of wine but she was shaking so much that she could only take baby sips. Trying to be brave, I put my arms around her and ignored her instructions that I should go back to bed.

'How could he? How could she? How could they?' she said, over and over again, as if she was conjugating verbs.

I wrapped a coat around her shoulders but she didn't stop trembling. At least I could go through my tapping routine unnoticed: one, two, three, toe; one, two, three, heel; one, two, three, right side of foot; one, two, three, left side of foot. Shoulder, shoulder. The choreography was as perfectly intricate as anything you might see at Sadler's Wells. It didn't dissolve the anxiety but at least it kept it at bay until I could go upstairs and do everything properly.

'I'll look after you, Mum.'

She let me hug her but seemed unaware that I was there. In my head I recited the words to keep her safe, over and over again. I wanted to tell her I understood the pain of rejection but then I would have had to explain what I saw when Rex failed to turn up at the pillbox.

Mum didn't cry that night. I mistook this for courage at the time but now I realize she was in shock. Not long after Mum phoned Lisa, Dad started banging on the door, relentlessly calling on the landline and Mum's mobile until she turned them off. He even tried to beep her using the hospital emergency paging system. At one point I went to the front door and knelt down to shout at him through the letter box.

'Go away, Dad! You've done enough damage.' I must have sounded like a character from a histrionic television soap. The truth was I lacked the emotional hinterland to respond to the situation. My reference points back then were all films and pop songs. I saw the neighbours opposite nervously peering out of their front door to see what all the noise was about.

'Please, darling, let me in,' Dad implored, waving his fingers through the letter box to try and catch my hand.

It was a painful reminder of my lost intimacy with Rex. I blamed him for that too and slammed the lid down hard on his fingers. He yelped and snatched them away.

'She doesn't want to see you ever again. You're a disgrace, Dad.'

'Mummy and I have things we need to talk about. There are issues you don't understand.'

'I understand everything.' I tried to sound as menacing as possible. I wanted him to suffer the way I had suffered since the day I saw him and Lisa in the dunes. I remembered how Lisa wound her way up his body like a snake until her mouth found his cock and his eyes closed and his mouth made weird rictus shapes.

'What do you mean?'

'Does she make you hard, Dad? Does Lisa make you hard?'

'Don't speak like that, Daisy.'

'You disgust me.' I spat the words out.

'Please.' He sounded completely defeated.

Instead of feeling gratified by his misery I found myself temporarily blinded by huge salty tears that poured down my cheeks before I was even aware I had the urge to cry. Eventually he left, head bowed and body stooped like an old man. I went back into the kitchen to tell Mum I had managed to get rid of him, and she gave a tiny nod.

After this, I went up to Max's room to make sure he hadn't heard anything, put my hand on his stomach to count his breaths and recited the special words that needed to be said to keep him safe. Each time I started, however, anxiety about Mum flooded through my body. How could I protect her from burglars without Dad in the house? What if she started drinking and ended up like Barney, with a tummy swollen like a pregnant woman? Or had a nervous breakdown and was admitted to a psychiatric ward and had electric shock treatment and couldn't recognize Max and me any more? Horrible images filled my head and it wasn't until the early hours of the morning that I felt I had completed everything in the right way and could finally allow myself to fall asleep. I think I went downstairs to count the knives in the drawer at least six times through that long night. I don't know why I ever imagined that it would be easier when Mum knew about Dad and Lisa. I never thought the truth could be even more painful than living a lie. My instincts about that were wrong, like I was wrong about everything else.

The following evening Dad came back and sat down at the kitchen table beside Mum in that way parents do when they are trying to present a united front. But really all it did was heighten the sense of crisis. By then the crazy thoughts that Mum was in danger had become over-whelming. I had spent most of the day doing my checks, prayers and tapping, and the periods when I felt normal got shorter and shorter.

When Dad announced, without looking me in the eye, that he was going to move in with Lisa for a little while, all I could think about was the knife drawer behind him. I bit my lip until it hurt so that I didn't cry. I didn't want him to see how painful this news was for me.

'I don't see why you've made me miss my first football

match to tell me you're going for a sleepover,' said Max, irritated by all this unexpected fuss. 'At least let me come with you to show Ava my new Lego model?'

'Explain,' said Mum firmly to Dad. 'Explain.'

'Explain,' I said to make it three.

'I'm moving in with Lisa.' In an effort to downplay the implications of this momentous announcement he made the mistake of sounding almost breezy, as if he was signalling his intention to go and buy Cheerios at the corner shop.

'To help look after Barney?' Max asked. 'That's so kind of you.'

Dad turned to Mum, waiting for her to fall into her usual role of emotional interpreter, but she stared fixedly ahead at a point just north of the cooker.

I pulled Max on to my knee to protect him from the pain coming his way and hid behind his hot little body so I didn't have to witness the moment his world fell apart or conjure up an appropriate facial expression to news I had processed back in August.

'No. We're moving into a flat together. Barney is staying at their house with Rex and Ava. There's a spare room so you can visit us.'

Max tried to grasp these different concepts. Flat. House. Spare room. Us not being Mum and Dad but Dad and Lisa. I felt his body tense in my arms as it dawned on him what Dad was trying to explain.

'You're leaving us?' he finally asked. He sounded timid, like a toddler testing out new words.

'I'm not leaving you. I'm just moving somewhere else. It's not far from here.'

'With Lisa?'

'With Lisa,' Dad confirmed

'If you're not staying here then you're leaving us,' Max said.

'You can come and stay with me whenever you like,' said Dad.

'Will She be there?'

Dad winced and nodded at the same time.

Max shook his head violently in response. 'Never. Not if She's there.'

'I won't love you any less because I'm not living with you.'

Dad held out his arms for Max but he shrank further back into me.

'Do you still love Mum?'

'Of course I love Mum.'

'Then why are you moving in with Her?'

Dad didn't reply. Max ploughed on. He has always been a logical thinker.

'Do you love Her?'

'I love Mum but I'm *in* love with Lisa. It's difficult for you to understand but sometimes human beings develop feelings for each other that are impossible to ignore.' Dad had obviously rehearsed this line. He said it slowly and solemnly as if he was performing Shakespeare.

'If you love Her then obviously you love us less,' Max said, his voice cracking with emotion. He picked up a blunt pencil and drew a pie chart to demonstrate this. In the first drawing Dad's love was divided into thirds. In the second a quarter was allocated to Lisa.

Dad tried to explain that love was infinite.

'Only prime numbers are infinite,' said Max. 'I'm amazed you haven't learnt that. I thought you knew everything and now I realize you know nothing. You are full of shit.'

My head felt as though it was going to explode. It was unbearable that I couldn't protect Max. I needed to be alone to go through all my routines and wanted to bring this to a close.

'He loves Mum but not as much as he wants to fuck Lisa!' I heard myself blurt out.

'Daisy!' said Mum, sounding really shocked and upset. 'That is enough.'

'Well, it's true, isn't it?' I shouted angrily at them both.

Although I needed to blame Dad for all of this, there was a part of me that saw Mum's inability to satisfy him as her failure. If she had been enough for Dad none of this would ever have happened. I still hate myself for feeling this. Max started to cry inconsolably. He wouldn't let Dad near him so Dad got angry with Mum because this wasn't going the way they had planned. Mum stood up and said it was time for Dad to leave. She asked for his keys and at that moment I understood they would never be together again. When Max saw Dad going out the door he ran over to him and wound himself around his leg like a small boa constrictor and I couldn't look because it reminded me all over again of Lisa wrapping herself around Dad.

'Don't leave us, Dad.' He paused for maximum effect and looked up at him with his big dark eyes. 'Please don't leave us. We need you. We love you.'

Dad tousled his hair and unwound Max from his leg, and for a split second I saw him vacillate. He would stay for Max but not for me. I didn't mind. I never felt jealous of Max.

'I can't. I'm sorry,' said Dad eventually, all hollow-voiced, as if he was the one whose heart had been crushed.

Max was wild-eyed. 'Every day I am going to pray that Lisa dies a horrible slow lingering death,' he said venomously. 'Every day, Dad. And if she doesn't then I'll just kill her.'

'You don't mean it, Max,' said Mum, stroking his hair to soothe him.

'I do. I actually do.'

'It's really important that the last memory he has of this experience isn't a negative one,' Dad kept saying to Mum. 'Otherwise it will colour his future recall of the situation.'

At this point I truly thought Dad had gone mad and we had all missed the symptoms.

'Can you just remind me of the positive parts,' said Mum, her voice all compressed, 'because they're not obvious to me right now.'

'It's for the best,' I heard myself say three times as I left the kitchen to go upstairs to my bedroom.

Max told me Dad stayed for a while, frantically searching for his tube pass, passport and photos of us, as if he was fleeing a war zone, which he was. Max followed behind him in silence like a ghostly presence.

My head was full of the bad thoughts about something happening to Mum. The anxiety was of cosmic proportions. I needed to be alone to catch up with my routines. They are all I can remember of the next couple of years. The rituals became like a full-time job with overtime. It was as if the day Dad moved out full time, the OCD moved in full time.

Poor Mum. She was fighting on so many fronts. Dad was possessed by Lisa. I was possessed by my illness. Max was possessed with grief for Dad. I don't know how she kept it together. She tried to be brave in front of us but at night when I passed her bedroom on my way downstairs to check the knife drawer I sometimes heard her crying. They weren't hard tears but a soft, sad keen of yearning for all the lives she would now never live. I heard her once tell a friend that Dad and Lisa had robbed her of her past and future and that all she had left was the present. It sounded terrifying, like being stuck on the edge of a black hole, unable to go forwards or backwards.

Eight years later and I'm sitting in the same place at the same kitchen table doing background reading for uni. We're studying Kazuo Ishiguro this term and although I've finished *The Remains of the Day* and *Never Let Me Go*, I need to nail the themes. I read through the notes sent by the English Department: class; identity; how and why memory is fallible. Dad would love the last one. I do, too, but I won't be telling him because I can't stand the way he's always so desperate to find the common ground between us. Max calls it his enthusiastic Labrador mode. Slightly needy, slightly over the top. Max is good at sounding kind even when he's cruel.

I look at the essay title: 'No one can render their past exactly as it was – Discuss.' I remember a sentence that I underlined in *Never Let Me Go* about the character's self-awareness of the unreliability of memory and am pleased with myself when I instantly find the dog-eared page with the highlighted quote. 'This was all a long time ago so I might have some of it wrong.'

I open up my computer, ready to use this in my opening paragraph. My hands hover over the keyboard and words start to form in my mouth. The butterfly feeling in my stomach starts up again. Everything has changed and yet nothing has changed. Since Lisa sent the letter to Mum the illness has come back big time. I tried to ignore it at first in case I empowered it with acknowledgement. But this was a mistake because instead it gained a foothold. The only advantage I have this time is that at least I understand what is happening to me. I must lack creativity because neither the obsessions nor the compulsions have evolved. The routine goes something like this:

1. I am convinced that something bad is going to happen to Mum.
2. This makes me feel overwhelmed with anxiety.
3. The only way I can stop the worry and prevent something bad happening is by doing all the checking, tapping and saying the special words.

They call it the 'anxiety loop' but 'noose' would be more appropriate. My mouth goes dry and my hands start to sweat and shake, and I realize I am in the throes of a panic attack so I close the screen and the anxiety subsides, although it doesn't back off completely.

This shouldn't be happening because after Mum and Kit left this morning I spent a couple of hours on my routines before settling down at the kitchen table to write my essay. I run through them in my head in case I missed out something: switches, front door, windows and knives; feet and shoulders; special prayer to keep Mum and Max safe. I did them all. Max seems more invincible now so I have updated the version I used to recite to give more emphasis to Mum. If I do all this properly, usually it wins me a couple of hours' breathing space to get on with work before I have to start the whole cycle again. But not today.

I should know from experience that OCD is a hungry master who imposes more rules whenever he suspects his influence is under threat. He is omnipotent and infallible and whatever I do, it will never be enough. I understand all this and still I can't stop. I think I'm going mad.

The small part of me that recognizes all this is completely irrational slips further away from me. I keep thinking about the chain of events after my failure to perform my routines the afternoon I went to meet Rex all those years ago. I'm not taking that risk again. I have even begun wondering whether all the extra attention I paid to Max when I was last ill, checking his breathing every night, and saying a special prayer for him, might have saved him. I crept into Mum's room last night and noted the rise and fall of her duvet and have decided to add this to the back end of my evening repertoire.

It's so exhausting and shameful to live like this, and I can't face telling Mum that I am possessed again because she will be so worried. Even worse, she'll try to stop me. I try to bamboozle the thoughts by moving to the desk in the sitting room overlooking the window on to the street. Sometimes they are distractible. I need to let the outside world in, to see if I can regain perspective. It was a technique my therapist Geeta taught me.

I force myself to look out of the window and observe our neighbours leaving the house opposite. It's the same couple that heard all the shouting the night Dad left. He recklessly bumps down the steps on to the pavement in his mobility scooter while she herds him from behind like a sheepdog. I hear the gay couple who have just moved in next door arguing about whether or not you should peel tomatoes to make a Bolognese sauce. I envy all of them the simplicity of their lives and wonder why I have to live with the fire in my head. Other people have weird thoughts but somehow manage to shake them off. Maybe I should go back to my OCD support group? But everyone I knew there all those years ago has probably recovered and I am the only person stupid enough to have a relapse.

I try to remember some of the arguments that Geeta taught me to challenge the thoughts. *Max doesn't have to do this to stop something bad from happening to Mum so why should I? I have resisted OCD compulsions in the past and nothing bad happened. I cannot control future events with my thoughts.* But instead of believing these statements I find myself writing them down three times over, so they become a ritual in themselves. What I really need is for Max to say the words. More than anyone, he had the ability to help reduce the anxiety. I miss him living at home so much.

I try to call him. Whenever he doesn't pick up after three rings I hang up, so he doesn't realize how many times a day I try to get hold of him. But this time he answers.

'Daisy,' he says, and I can hear the hint of repressed impatience in his tone. 'What is it? I'm going to see you in a couple of hours.'

I tell him I want to confirm the plan.

'We've done all this on Facebook already,' he says flatly.

'I just wanted to double-check.'

'Triple-check, you mean.'

I laugh. I need him to tease me. He says that he hasn't got much time because he's in the middle of something. I ask for details.

'I've just done a home visit with a GP. Stroke. Now I'm off to the library to get in a couple of hours of revision before I meet you and Kit. Is it something that can't wait?'

He's got so short-tempered recently. I try to think of ways to keep him on the phone.

'Did you go out last night?'

'I went to see Wolf Alice with Connie.'

'Good?'

'Good. How are you?' he asks.

'I'm not feeling so great,' I say.

There is a long silence. It's not what he wants to hear.

'There's nothing I can do to help.' I can hear the shrug in his tone.

'Please just tell me that Mum will be fine? If you say it I get a real break from the thoughts.'

'You don't have the power to prevent bad things from happening, Daisy, and nor do I. Even if God existed, he couldn't do that. Shit just happens.'

'I just want you to tell me that Mum will be fine. Can't you do that for me?'

'I'm not getting into that again,' he says gently. 'It's not right.'

'Think of everything I've done for you,' I say angrily.

'What have you done for me?'

'I've protected you from everything. I've shielded you from so much pain.'

I keep pleading but I realize that he has put the phone down on me. He sends a Snapchat to apologize and says it's for the best, which reminds me of Dad, which reminds me of Lisa, which makes me tense and so the whole cycle starts again.

I stare into the street. Luckily there aren't many cars, because if a Vauxhall goes past Lisa comes to mind and I feel anxious and have to go through the routines again. Fortunately it's generally all Volvos in these parts. Kit has noticed my allergy to Vauxhalls and teases me that I'm a car snob.

I check the time. Two twenty-four. In two minutes I can try Mum again. The days go so slowly when you are alone but I prefer it this way so that I can organize my schedule around the rituals. It's going to get difficult now uni has started again. I allow myself to call or text her once every two hours while she's at work, which means I get to communicate with her exactly four times a day until she gets home. I try to vary the schedule so that she doesn't notice a pattern. Geeta, the cognitive behavioural therapist, was really hot on family members who got involved in my rituals and Mum will be alert to this. I never fully confessed the extent of Max's contributions to anyone, and he never grassed me up. She picks up right away but doesn't say anything, which means she is probably in work mode. I feel immediately better knowing that she is fine.

'Can you talk?' I ask, trying to sound businesslike.

'Sort of. Is there something wrong?' Her voice is

muffled and I guess she is in a meeting and has cupped her hand around the phone so no one else can hear.

'Kit and I were wondering if you're coming straight home after work?'

'Not sure. It depends on my list this afternoon.' I hear someone laughing in the background and it sounds like Ed Gilmour.

'I saw the old man from opposite and he was wondering if anyone has Zika at your hospital?'

'No.' I can tell she is distracted. 'Are you okay, Daisy?'

'I'm fine. Don't forget Kit and I are going out tonight to meet Max and his mystery girlfriend.'

'That sounds fun. I might be back late.'

My heart sinks. 'Who are you meeting?'

'A colleague,' she says vaguely. 'Don't wait up.'

I open up the computer screen again. The same helter-skelter of anxiety spins round my body. But this time I realize not only what is triggering it but come up with an antidote. I find some sticky white labels in the drawer of the desk where I'm sitting and cover the letters A, S, I and L on the keyboard in small squares.

I decide to run through every routine one more time before I start work, just to be triple sure, even though my shoulders are red raw from tapping myself and Kit will come home soon and ask me if I have finished my essay and will realize I'm lying when I say I'm still re-jigging the conclusion. There is a new look he gives me now, somewhere between mistrust and disdain, as he discovers that I am none of the things that he wanted me to be while he is still everything I ever wanted.

*

Two hours later I've finished. I haven't written a single word and I'm counting the minutes again until I can call Mum. I'm at my lowest ebb.

A moment of clarity: it dawns on me that if I beat this illness once before, there's a small chance I could do it again. Impulsively I book an Uber (Addison Lee has all the bad letters) to take me to Geeta's office. It isn't far, but I want to hit the road before my old adversary realizes and tries to talk me out of it. OCD finds spontaneity very threatening.

I keep the driver waiting in the street while I run up and down the stairs, checking the sockets, switches and knife drawer three times and see him eyeing me warily as I keep going back to make sure the front door is locked. He interrupts me once to tell me to please hurry up, which means I have to check the door three times all over again. I know I look mad. I am mad.

The big difference with my illness this time is that in an adult the rituals appear even more absurd. My 22-year-old self can't tell the Uber driver that I have to do all this to prevent a burglar getting into the house and lying in wait for my mum when she gets home. Or that this is the reason I avoid going out any more. Whereas when I was fourteen this explanation might have sounded kookily protective. When I finally sit down in the back of his car my sweaty body is so heavy with exhaustion that I'm tempted to ask him to drive me aimlessly around London just so I can sleep.

The one thing that keeps me going is the prospect of seeing Geeta. She is the only person in the world who can help me right now. I calculate that it is exactly forty-five months since I last saw her. We draw up outside the build-ing where she works. It occurs to me that she might be in the middle of a session with another patient, or taking a day off or even have moved offices.

The driver asks me if I'm okay. I'm startled by his kind-ness. I could cry with relief when the woman on reception confirms that Geeta is not only still working at the men-tal health centre but is with a patient right now. I ask if I can see her right away and the receptionist doesn't look remotely fazed, even when I realize that my T-shirt has slid down to reveal the sores on my shoulders.

'Do you have an appointment?' she asks.

I shake my head.

'Take a seat. I'll see what Geeta suggests.'

I sit down as far from the exit as possible to make it more difficult for the illness to make me leave. I look around. The waiting room hasn't changed much. There are a couple of new posters on the wall.

Myths About OCD reads one: 'OCD is no joking mat-ter. The D in OCD means it is a disorder, which means it causes great DISTRESS and DISRUPTION to a per-son's life.'

The posters of famous people who suffered from OCD are still there although their compulsions aren't listed in case they are triggers for patients. But I know them all: Charlize Theron – contamination issues – washes her hands all the time; Billy Bob Thornton – thing about good and bad numbers representing certain people – wrote a song called 'Always Countin''; Daniel Radcliffe – got over a compulsion to repeat every sentence he ever said under his breath – not a good trait in an actor;

Julianne Moore – used to leave her house at a certain time, at a certain pace so the traffic lights would always be green at pedestrian crossings. I have a real affinity with Nikola Tesla, an American inventor who did things in threes or numbers divisible by three.

A woman and a young girl who I guess is her daughter sit opposite. Judging by the state of her hands, the girl surely has contamination issues. Her mum smiles at me and I try to reciprocate. I remember how one of the boys at my OCD support group was so worried he would catch germs that he had to wash all his cutlery and plates five times before every meal, which meant he couldn't even eat school dinners or go out to a restaurant.

Geeta comes out of her office. Her hair is much longer and several shades lighter and she is wearing glasses but apart from this she hasn't changed. The receptionist hands her an embarrassingly thick file of notes with Daisy Rankin written on the front. She walks over to me, hand outstretched as if she was expecting me.

'Daisy. How nice to see you. I've got an appointment right now but if you would like to wait I can see you for a quick chat before my next patient. Sound good?'

'Very good.'

The girl and her mother follow her into the treatment room. Feeling over-confident, I rashly google the BBC, on the basis it contains none of the letters that might make me anxious. The main headline is about Ebola. My body tenses. On an intellectual level I understand the chances of Mum catching Ebola in the UK are negligible. But instead of thinking about the 99.99 per cent of people who won't get ill, I fixate on the 0.01 per cent who might and the certainty that Mum will be one of them because she sometimes has meetings at the hospital where victims are treated. I see her lying semi-unconscious in a hospital bed after contracting the virus. I see the cells multiplying in her body every twenty minutes. I imagine her holding the letter from Lisa and crying tears of blood because she is so upset about what she has told her.

As soon as I have a bad thought about Mum I have to neutralize it by making myself have the opposite thought. So I visualize her on the beach in Norfolk wearing her wide-brimmed hat and the baggy purple swimsuit that highlights her flaws although she thinks it hides them. I imagine her shoulders burnt from the sun because she doesn't have skin that tans easily, all easy smiles as Max turns his trunks into a thong to make her laugh. It almost works. But then I see Lisa sitting beside her and imagine her telling Mum that I saw her and Dad having sex long before the truth came out, and I start to feel anxious all over again. Sometimes it feels as though the worry will only end if I die. I run through a few foot-and-shoulder-tapping sequences. Geeta's waiting room is one place you can get away with this without anyone thinking you're a freak.

'Would you like to come in, Daisy?'

The warm, smooth tone of Geeta's voice is instantly soothing. I follow her into her office and she closes the door. She sits down in her armchair in the corner of the room and indicates I should take up my old position on the sofa. I thought coming back might feel like failure but it feels closer to coming home after a long journey.

Geeta explains that she doesn't have time for a full

session but will try to cover as much ground as possible and book me in for a follow-up appointment in three weeks.

'I'm sorry I can't see you sooner.'

'It's fine. Three is a good and safe number,' I mutter under my breath.

'Do you remember we discussed how there is no good evidence that any number is lucky or unlucky, Daisy?' She says this brightly in a way that doesn't make me feel like an idiot and gives me a copy of research from a scientific journal that proves this. 'OCD hates empirical evidence.'

'I'm having a relapse,' I blurt out as I stuff the paper in my bag. 'I thought it might go away on its own or that I could get away with doing just a few rituals but it's taken over again.'

'Can you talk about the intrusive thoughts or are you worried that if you do they might come true?'

I nod.

She flicks through my notes and peers over her glasses. 'Are they the same as last time?'

'I won't win any prizes for originality,' I say.

'So you're worried about something bad happening to your mum and brother, Max? Are you still ruminating about them being harmed during a burglary?'

Now she's articulated my fears, I can talk about them without worrying this will make them happen.

'Mostly Mum. I imagine terrible things happening to her all the time, like a horror movie on repeat in my head. I'm spending all my time doing the rituals.'

'How many hours a day would you estimate?'

'Around eight.'

'Just because you think something doesn't make it happen,' says Geeta. 'Try to make me pick up my file by using your thoughts.'

I try. Her arms stay in her lap.

She makes careful notes on lined paper and pulls out some worksheets from one of her files.

'Homework,' she smiles. 'I want you to list all your obsessions in the left-hand column and your compulsions in the right-hand column. If you're feeling strong enough maybe you could try to reduce the number of times you perform a ritual. Limit the sequences, for example. The OCD will try and stop you from making changes.'

I take the piece of paper from her.

'Don't fold it into three.' She understands me too well.

I fold the piece of paper in half. She gives me an OCD diary where I have to note what the OCD makes me do, when it happens and how long it lasts.

'Do you have any idea what might have triggered your relapse, Daisy?' she asks. 'Are you feeling anxious about anything in particular?'

Bizarrely, I haven't really considered this. The strangest thing about an illness that involves so much thinking is that you don't necessarily think about the right things.

'It has a tendency to sneak back during times of stress.'

'Lisa sent Mum a letter. I read it.'

'So? What's wrong with a letter?'

'She's dying and wants to see Mum one last time.'

'Why is that so bad?'

'It might set Mum back.' I like the way there's no recrimination for reading a letter that wasn't meant for me.

'She might want to make peace with her old friend before she dies. OCD encourages you to overestimate the likelihood and extent of danger. Try to see it from your mum's perspective. Don't catastrophize.'

'Lisa says there's something she needs to tell Mum before she dies. I've got a bad feeling about what she's going to say and the effect it might have on Mum. There are some things she can't ever know.'

'You can't control the outcome of events with your thoughts, Daisy. It's a trick the OCD is playing on you. Your mum will decide whether she wants to see Lisa or not. And you have no control over what Lisa wants to tell her. Can you give me one example from your life where your thoughts have ever prevented something bad from happening?'

'There was one time when I didn't do my rituals and something happened to Mum.'

'If that happened, it is nothing more than coincidence. There are many reasons why things go wrong and none of them have anything to do with you. When you come next time, we'll talk about this further.' She looks at her watch and then down at her notes again. 'Lisa was a trigger for the illness last time as well, wasn't she? You told me it all started after your dad left your mum for her.'

'This was all a long time ago so I might have some of it wrong.' I apologize to Kazuo Ishiguro for quoting him out of context.

'It's hard work confronting OCD, Daisy. There are no short cuts.'

'There is one.'

She looks interested.

'If Lisa dies it will go away forever. You said it yourself. She was the trigger.'

14

Max

My heart sinks when I get to the pub and see through the window that Daisy is alone. She was meant to be coming with Kit. If it weren't so cold I'd wait outside until Connie gets here but she's always late. I glance at Daisy's feet through the window. Old reflex. She's wearing the expensive R. Soles cowboy boots that Dad gave her the first Christmas after he left Mum. There were some good presents that year: I became the first boy in Year Seven to get a Wii. But every time I played Super Mario it made me miss Dad.

I watch as Daisy taps the toecap on the floor three times, followed by the heel and finally the worn side where the embroidered cactuses unravelled long ago. I count to three and, sure enough, she starts up again. When I look closely I notice her lips moving as she mutters silent incantations. Textbook.

I suddenly remember how Daisy used to read Dr Seuss to me when I was little and made me count exactly how many Bee-Watcher-Watchers there were on each page of *Did I Ever Tell You How Lucky You Are?* If I made a mistake I had to start all over again. Then she copied out all the words in her insanely neat handwriting and tried to make me do the same and got cross with me when I couldn't. Maybe her illness was always lurking in the shadows.

She tried hard to persuade me to come to Mum's tonight instead of going out but I insisted we stick to the plan to meet at the pub because she's spending more and more time at home, and her illness feeds off isolation. The bad part of me – the part that wants an easy life, and wishes I didn't have a sister like this – was hoping she'd cancel. I sigh and the window fogs up with my breath.

I slump against the wall of the pub with my eyes closed. I can't face seeing her alone. Without thinking it through, I send a Snapchat to Carlo and ask him to come along too. Safety in numbers. He gets back right away. *B there in 5.* He's always reliable if it involves meeting a new girl. The fact that Daisy has a boyfriend won't put him off. In fact, the evidence would suggest the opposite. At least in Daisy's current state he doesn't stand a chance of getting with her, even if he pulls out all the stops – which, knowing Carlo, he will.

I take a deep breath and go into the pub. Daisy looks really pleased to see me, which makes me feel really bad. I watch the rise and fall of her chest and realize she's doing the breathing thing to try and keep herself calm. She manages a quick brave smile. She looks so vulnerable that I just want to throw my arms around her, but then I'll crack and we'll go straight back into the old unhealthy habits. The headshrinkers call it 'accommodation'.

Ironically – there are a lot of ironies in this story – I'm in the middle of a mental health component on anxiety disorders so I only get time off from thinking about Daisy when I'm with Connie. I pissed off Carlo by getting the highest score in the group in our most recent test. So I know everything there is to know about how fear and stress reactions are essential for human survival and help healthy people pursue goals and respond to danger. Fight, fright or flight. The body makes three choices before the mind has a chance to think. Daisy would like that. But the threats to Mum that Daisy perceives are not genuine and in her less anxious moments she realizes her worries are excessive. I learnt this week that if she truly believed what she thought all the time (her worst fear was Mum being stabbed by a burglar) the diagnosis would be psychosis. I have always had faith in the power of knowledge. But sometimes you can understand everything and do nothing. It makes me feel so impotent.

'Drink?' I ask casually. I want to keep everything on the level.

'Large white wine, please.'

I look at her empty glass. Always a mistake to neutralize anxiety with alcohol. It actually raises the production of stress hormones. Good observation, Dr Rankin. I wonder if I should try and explain to Daisy but I don't think she would listen and I don't want to draw attention to her illness in case she tries to get me involved. I go up to the bar, hoping that by the time they serve me Carlo will have made an appearance, but when I get back to the table she is still alone. 'Did you get your essay done?' I ask.

'Just re-jigging the ending.'

She has given the same answer for the past month.

'So how's life, Maxi?'

I can tell by the way she grips her glass that she's making an effort not to tap her foot, count in her head, or do the magical thinking. Last time she was ill I was so young that part of me really wanted to believe that she could control what was going on with her superpowers. This time I understand only too well the delusion of the disease.

'All good.'

'How's it going with Connie?'

'Unpredictable in a more settled way. I think.'

'Sounds like progress.'

I would like to explain to her that Connie is the first thing I think about when I wake up in the morning and the last thing before I go to sleep. That sometimes I miss her so much that it physically aches, and when she leaves my flat I lie on my bed and try to find the imprint of her body and musky scent on my sheets. But I have already lost Daisy's attention. She's in retreat from the world again. The illness is stronger than me, stronger than her. It's like watching the tide carry someone you love out to sea.

And there is the guilt that if I hadn't faked the note from Rex everything might have turned out so differently. Although some of the weirdness had definitely begun before the Drapers arrived that summer, it was nothing compared to what happened after that day. Everyone blames Dad when in truth it was my fault. I want to go back to old times, before our role reversal, when I was the younger brother who fell over learning to ride my bike and Daisy was the older sister, always waiting to pick me up, brush me down and tell me that everything would be all right. I would walk through fire for Daisy. I have. But I can't do it again.

I tip my head back and gulp down my beer straight from the bottle so she doesn't notice the way I keep swallowing my emotion, and check my phone to see if Carlo has messaged. Nothing. I don't want to be a beg but I need him here as quickly as possible to dilute us. *WTFRU?* I write. I get nothing back.

'Where's Kit?' I ask, looking for neutral conversation.

Kit is super punctual. He's someone who always sticks to the plan, and I want him on board to take responsibility for my sister so I can focus on Connie and my coursework. Daisy doesn't look up. She runs her finger round and round the rim of her glass of wine so that it makes a high-pitched hum. Someone drops a bottle behind the bar and it shatters on the floor. But I'm the one who's so frazzled that my whole body tenses.

'On edge?' she teases, finally catching my eye, and I see a hint of the old Daisy in the way she smiles and enjoys the irony of me being the anxious one. She starts running her finger round the glass again.

'Please stop that bloody noise.'

She keeps going, faster and faster. I remember counting thirty-one pairs of spinal nerves when we opened up Jean's spinal column and right now it feels as if someone is running a scalpel up each pair of my own. If we weren't in a public place I would wrestle Daisy to the ground to make it stop, like I used to when we were little. Instead I grab the glass by the stem and wine sloshes all over our hands.

Daisy appears startled. 'Sorry. I was miles away.'

She looks at her phone and frowns, and I guess that she's calculating how long she's been here and whether she can check up on Mum. And I understand that if I tell her that Mum is fine she will relax and get some time off from her routines. I've lived through this a thousand times before. It sounds like a David Bowie song.

'Kit's ghosting me,' she says. 'We've had a huge row.'

'What?' This can't be right.

Kit has been one hundred per cent dedicated to her. He buys her T-shirts with personalized messages; if she says she loves the colour yellow he cooks saffron rice; he bought her a first edition of *Howards End* when she got the highest mark in her first-year exams. It's always been too much, not too little, with Kit. Fuck, he's even been living with my mum to please Daisy. Not that Mum is particularly difficult to live with. It's just she can't cook and forgets to do basic domestic stuff like washing clothes.

'I haven't heard from him all week.' She sounds more resigned than upset.

'What's happened?'

'You really want to know?'

'I do.' Although it's not fun, at least it feels vaguely normal to be talking about relationships.

'Kit has a room in a flat with four other guys in Leytonstone. It's his turn to have the biggest bedroom for the next four months and he thinks it's crazy to pay rent to leave it empty. So about a week ago he asked me to move out of Mum's and in with him.'

'So, what's not to love? It's the logical next step, isn't it?'

'I refused.'

'Why?' I ask, although I can easily predict the answer.

'I can't leave Mum. The timing isn't right. I told him I'd reconsider after Dad and Lisa get married. Kit got incredibly annoyed with me. He said I obsess about Mum too much and that she seems pretty relaxed about the whole wedding thing. He said he's serious about our relationship and I'm obviously not and that I'm using the wedding as an excuse.' She gives a self-defeated shrug.

'Have you told Mum about any of this?'

'No, because she would try and stop me from doing all the stuff I need to do to help her and force me to move in with him.'

'And she'd be right to do that.'

'I understand I'm not being rational but there's nothing I can do. It's out of my hands.'

'Do you believe I always have your best interests at heart?' I ask, trying a new tack. Occasionally it's possible to outmanoeuvre the OCD.

'Yes.'

I take her by the hand. 'I think this is one of those times when you have to trust my instincts. Please give it a go, Daisy. Try it for a week, six days if you like. If it doesn't work out you can always move back in with Mum but that way you'll have no regrets. I thought Carlo might be a big pain in the arse before I moved in with him but he's turned out to be a good housemate because he cleans up his shit and listens to cool music.'

I'm trying to make it sound as though the dilemma is all about the usual preoccupations when people move in with each other. Is it too soon? Am I compatible with his flatmates? Do they wash the bath after they've used it? But we both know it isn't.

'When I said no, Kit told me he wanted a break. He said he's finding me too distant and doesn't know what

I'm thinking any more, like my mind is never on him. He wondered if I'd met someone else.'

'Is he aware of his very demanding rival?'

Daisy shakes her head.

'Have you told him anything?'

'I can't. He'll think I'm mad.'

'You are mad.'

She smiles, and I shake my head sorrowfully.

'He's noticed a few things,' she says cautiously.

'Like what?'

'The Vauxhall thing.'

'What Vauxhall thing?' This is a new one.

'I have to do the magical thinking and say all the stuff if I see a Vauxhall because Lisa has the same car. Vauxhalls have become a trigger.'

I burst out laughing. 'That is so fucked,' I say, shaking my head. 'How do you come up with this stuff?'

'It's not me. It's the illness.' Daisy manages a small smile. 'Although it helps to have a good imagination.'

There's a part of her that still has the insight to kick back against the irrational thinking. If only I could lever it open to help her mount a decent counter-attack. *Don't get involved*, the voice says in my head. *This is how it all started last time.*

'So what did you tell him?' I'm genuinely interested because Daisy knows nothing about cars.

'I said that Vauxhalls are badly designed, have poor acceleration, and crap bodywork. I looked it all up on a car website.'

Now I'm really laughing. Daisy giggles too, which makes me crack up even more. And then we can't stop. For a moment it feels like old times.

'I think you should tell him,' I say.

'I can't.'

'Kit's such a good guy. He'll understand.'

'He noticed about three being a good and safe number, and he's fine with that. He likes numbers because he writes algorithms, so patterns and sequences don't faze him. But I can't tell him why I have to do it.'

'What if I spoke to him?'

'No!'

'Be logical, Daisy. If you tell him and he minds then it shows you probably shouldn't be together anyway. And if he doesn't you don't have a problem any more.' And I'm off the hook.

'If I tell him the worries might come true.'

'You told me last time and nothing happened.'

'You're different. You've been involved right from the start. And I feel completely safe with you. Look,' she leans towards me. 'Imagine if I told him and then something happened to Mum. It's not worth taking the risk when everything is so finely balanced.'

'Apart from you.'

'What?'

'You're not finely balanced.'

'Don't do that thing where you try and use humour to avoid talking about my worries about Mum.'

'I don't do that.'

'You do.'

I lean towards her so that our foreheads are almost touching. 'Don't do that thing where you avoid thinking about how much all this affects me,' I say firmly.

'It's a short-term thing, Maxi,' she says, her tone

suddenly gentler. 'We're in a state of emergency because of the letter. I'm doing my best to keep an eye on Mum but she could go and see Lisa at any moment.' She clicks her fingers to demonstrate and even that makes me jump.

'You understand there's nothing you can do,' I say, choosing my words carefully. 'You can't control whether Mum goes to see Lisa. Nothing you do will keep her safe.'

'What do you think she wants to tell her, Max?'

So she's worried about this too. I do a good impression of nonchalance, although I have a pretty good idea: Lisa is going to tell Mum that I wrote the note pretending to be Rex, because Ava has told her, and Mum will finally realize that Daisy's illness wasn't caused by Dad leaving her for Lisa, but by Rex letting her down. Which lets Dad and Lisa off the hook but puts me in the frame. After all, Daisy's therapist said betrayal could trigger OCD and it was after that day the illness got the upper hand. I wish I could tell Connie everything but I suspect she wouldn't be that interested. Last time we hooked up, she forgot to ask me a question about myself. When I pointed out her omission, she laughed and said I was being demanding.

'It might be something completely insignificant,' I say.

'If it's something so important that Lisa can't die with the secret then it's going to be something big enough to have a negative impact on Mum. I'm working so hard to keep her safe.' She pauses. 'You could help, Max. It worked really well last time.'

I urgently need to change the subject. I remember I have the Kahlil Gibran book with the reading for Dad and Lisa's wedding in my coat pocket. They dropped it off at my flat on their way to Somerset for the weekend and wanted me to give it to Daisy. I pull it out and it falls open on a dog-eared page where Lisa has marked the four different sections she wants us all to read with fluorescent pen and written our names along the side in her strange swirly scrawl. I am sandwiched between Ava and Daisy.

'Here,' I say, pushing it towards Daisy. 'They want us to practise. You keep the book because I'll lose it and Lisa will have a shit fit.'

Daisy stares at it but her arms remain rigidly by her sides. 'I can't,' she says.

At first I think she is on a downer about the wedding. I'm not sure if my judgement is off because I'm so pleased Connie has agreed to come with me or if I am caught up in the romanticism of Dad marrying someone who is dying, but I'm not unhappy to read at their wedding. I came to the realization a few years ago that Dad is a pretty selfish human being, and there's something redeeming about his commitment to Lisa in this awful situation.

'Come on, Daisy. Marriage is just a piece of paper. Not even Mum minds that much.' I slide the book along the table towards her and she flinches.

'It's not about the wedding.'

'Is it about seeing Rex again?' I feel that familiar stab of guilt as I say his name.

'I'm more worried about seeing Ava than him,' she says.

'Lisa wants you to read the first section,' I tell Daisy. 'Three verses.'

'You know they did the same reading when she married Barney.'

'Mum told me. If it ain't broke why fix it?' I joke.

She doesn't smile. I push the book towards her and she jumps so much when the edge touches her hand that she tips my beer into my lap.

'Shit,' I say, standing up as it drips into the bag containing my medical textbooks and a couple of files.

'I'm so, so, so sorry.' Daisy tries to mop up the pool of beer with some serviettes.

A couple on the next table eye us warily.

'I can't touch it,' she says desperately.

'Why?'

'I can't touch it because Lisa has touched it, and if I touch anything that she has touched then the anxiety about something bad happening to Mum starts up in my head. Then I'll need to go through all my routines before the others get here. And that will take hours. It's all so exhausting. I just want to make it stop but I can't.'

'You need to break the anxiety loop. Go with it and eventually it will subside. It's like swimming out of a rip tide.'

She is rigid with tension. I take her hand.

'You got rid of it once, Daisy. You can do it again,' I say. I put the book in my back pocket. 'I'll scan the poem and email you a copy.'

'Once Lisa has gone, all this will stop.' She says it rhythmically, three times, with a break in the middle in a way that makes me realize it's one of her special sentences but there is undeniable truth in her analysis. 'How did she look when you saw her?'

'Frail. She's living off juices. I heard them arguing about some quack Lisa is seeing who thinks you can cure cancer by sticking coffee up your arse. So that will speed things up. I reckon she's got a couple of months. If you can just hold out for eight more weeks then it will all be over.'

'Are we bad people for wanting a dying person to die quicker?' Daisy asks quietly.

I remember all those interviews I went through when I was applying to medical school and the ethical dilemmas posed to me to test whether I had the right instincts to make the correct judgement call under pressure. Is wishing one person dead morally wrong if it means saving the lives of three others? I'm including myself alongside Mum and Daisy now. Because if one of us goes down, we all do. Because that's what happened last time.

I shake my head. 'Lisa has caused a lot of problems for us, Daisy. We've been pretty generous to her over the years, given what she did to Mum. And now she's causing problems all over again. She's the one dredging up the past and making Mum revisit the bad times. It isn't Dad's fault that Lisa has written the letter. He'd never let her see Mum. He knows how hard it was for her.'

I try not to look back too much because it's like staring over the edge of the cliff on Mundesley Beach. But I remember once, when Daisy was really bad, and Mum hadn't slept properly for months because she was up every night trying to persuade her to stop her rituals, I had phoned up Dad in the middle of the night and told him he had to come over to give Mum a break. She was getting no sleep, working long hours during the day, and had lost so much weight that her shoulder blades looked like wings.

The doctor had wanted Daisy to go into a children's

psychiatric unit to get some intensive treatment but the only place available was in Birmingham and Daisy wouldn't go. By that time Mum was as pale and gaunt as Daisy. It was like the house of the living dead. I kept cooking and cleaning and generally trying to hold it all together but I had school during the day and homework in the evening. We ate a lot of eggs. Hard-boiled. Omelette. Poached. On a rotation because Daisy liked the symmetry and I could buy eggs on the way home from school.

I could tell Dad was shocked because for the first time since he walked out on us he offered to stay for a couple of nights, even though he hadn't brought any clothes. So he saw how I had to do most of the cooking and Mum's friend Deborah sometimes came round to help with the washing and the neighbours opposite left meals on our doorstep. By that stage Mum hadn't gone out at night for over a year. She brought home papers from the hospital and set up her office in Daisy's bedroom because otherwise Daisy had panic attacks. Often Mum would fall asleep on her bed. Everything fell apart. Everything.

The instant Carlo appears I regret messaging him. Fortunately he is too wrapped up in making an impression on Daisy to read the disappointment on my face. When he takes off his coat I notice he's wearing one of his tight T-shirts that showcases his six-pack. The smell of after-shave hangs over him like a cloud. He is so obvious that I can't understand why girls don't see him coming a mile off.

'Finally I get to meet Maxi's big sister. I've heard a lot about you, Daisy.'

'Have you?' asks Daisy, sounding slightly alarmed because I've told her nothing about Carlo.

'No wonder he's kept you under wraps.'

He shakes her hand and holds it a second too long. Daisy has that bewildered expression that I remember from the last time she was ill. It is when her mind is so consumed by the worries and rituals that everything else fades out of focus. So new situations throw her, which is why she spends more and more time at home in familiar surroundings, where she can tend her anxieties and rituals. Carlo is the opposite of a thoughtful, sensitive person. He doesn't really see himself in relation to other people because he's so self-obsessed. And his self-confidence is so boundless it doesn't occur to him that other people might be riddled with self-doubt. All attributes, I realize, that could be quite useful in the current scenario.

He looks Daisy up and down. I see his eyes flit in a triangle from her breasts to her lips and fight the urge to shove him. I should have warned him if he valued our friendship that my sister was off limits. But then I see that her T-shirt has slid down her right arm revealing an oozing red welt the size of a tangerine just below her collar bone and that Carlo is trying hard to avoid staring at this. No wonder the first doctor she saw misdiagnosed her as a self-harmer. I remember from last time how this sore is like a barometer for her illness. Mum used to monitor it as closely as a newborn baby. Things are worse than I had assumed. The whole area around the point where she taps is red and inflamed and I guess that it's infected. She needs a dressing and possibly a course of antibiotics. Daisy pulls her T-shirt up and the wound disappears.

I glance over at Carlo and can tell from the way he

chews his lower lip that he is probably coming to the same conclusion. I recognize his expression of intent focus from classes.

'So how do you know my little brother?' Daisy asks Carlo. She's trying to make an effort, which makes me feel even more desperate for her.

'We study together, we live together, we party together, we even share the same dead body,' says Carlo. 'It's all pretty intimate.' His eyes keep darting towards Daisy's shoulder but her T-shirt doesn't shift.

'Is he a good flatmate?'

'The best. He's a bloody good cook and that is the easiest way to win a man's heart. He uses spices and shit like that. Impressive.'

'After our parents got divorced, Max basically took over the cooking. Mum can only make one dish,' Daisy explains. 'She undercooks fish and overcooks vegetables. It's a family joke. That's why I'm so thin.'

He crosses his arms and slightly leans back on his haunches to review her. 'Then maybe I could take you out for a meal one day. If Max agrees of course.'

I smile and shake my head at his audacity while secretly wishing that I had the minerals to be like him with girls. I check my phone to see if Connie has messaged. Nada.

'I don't go out that much right now,' Daisy explains. 'I've got a lot of work for uni, and when I'm not studying I'm tutoring to earn money. It's pretty full on. But if you like you could come over and cook a meal for me and my boyfriend.'

It's a great put-down, vintage Daisy, even if it's not quite true, and we all start laughing. I like the way Carlo isn't bothered by the sore on her shoulder, and how he's good at teasing away her anxiety.

'Don't break my heart, Daisy,' Carlo begs.

She looks at her phone. I hate the way the illness always makes demands when it looks as though she might be making a small bid for freedom. I don't want her to break the vibe, so I cave in and reassure her. Surely once can't do any harm.

'She'll either be at work or at home and, wherever she is, Mum is strong and healthy and will live a long and happy life.'

The special words come back easily, like a language learnt as a child. I just need to find the right moment to include the same phrase another couple of times and Daisy will have a reprieve for at least a couple of hours. She looks at me with such gratitude that for a split second I wonder if it's so easy for me to make her feel better why I don't do it all the time.

'Mum is strong and healthy and will live a long and happy life.' As I say it the second time I'm overtaken with a deep sense of shame that starts on the surface of my skin, seeps through my pores, the layers of fat and tissue to my organs, until my entire body feels feverish.

I remember when she was ill last time that I eventually spent almost all of my free time with Daisy, reassuring her and helping her deal with all the checks. If I had friends round I would always have to interrupt football or playing with my Match Attax cards to go and help her, and eventually it seemed easier not to invite them at all. Sometimes I pretended to be ill so I could skip school. When we stayed with Dad and Lisa, he used to comment on how well we got on together, as if this reflected well on his parenting. He had no idea how the balance of our relationship had tilted on its axis and I had become the one looking after Daisy, even though Daisy would maintain that everything she did was to keep Mum and me safe. Mum suspected and mentioned it to Daisy's therapist but Daisy was adamant I wasn't meaningfully involved. That's the insidious thing about mental illness. It's like an iceberg; the most dangerous part is hidden beneath the surface. Now I wish I had told someone, so that I was better equipped to understand how to resist her demands second time round. I realize Carlo is staring at me as if he's waiting for an answer to a question.

'Sorry?'

'What's wrong with your mum?'

He's either being polite or kind or self-interested. Carlo doesn't usually ask questions about other people unless there's something in it for him, and I'm grateful for his sudden attack of basic manners around my family.

'She's picked up a virus from work,' says Daisy. 'She fainted a couple of times. Nothing serious but we need to keep an eye on her.'

'That doesn't sound so good,' says Carlo. 'When did it start?'

It's always a mistake to mention illness to a medic, especially if there's some sense of mystery surrounding the diagnosis, but especially to Carlo, who likes to show off his diagnostic skills.

'A couple of weeks ago. She has low blood pressure so maybe that makes a difference.'

Daisy is a surprisingly convincing liar. We learnt to be

together. However, Carlo isn't listening. I follow his line of sight and see Connie has appeared in front of me. Even though I was expecting her she still manages to surprise me. She's engulfed in an enormous padded jacket that makes her small frame appear even tinier. More significantly, she's bleached her dark hair blonde and cut it short so she looks nothing like the person I described to Daisy an hour ago. Even her eyebrows have changed colour. It's irrational but it makes me feel even less secure in the relationship than I did already. If she was really into me, surely she would have asked my opinion before making such a radical change to her appearance? It's almost as if she doesn't care what I think. It works the other way too. If I cancel plans or I'm late, she doesn't require explanations.

'You like?' she asks, twirling in front of me.

'Why didn't you warn me?' I ask.

'Don't be salty, Max,' Carlo says. 'She looks gorgeous.'

Connie is watching this exchange with the detached amusement of someone used to being the centre of attention. She peels off her coat, one arm at a time, fixes me with her gaze, and I flip from despair to elation. I want to take her outside into the alleyway beside the pub, push her hands against the wall, and rub myself against her like a dog. I remind myself that Connie's here so I can try and normalize our relationship by introducing her to my sister.

'Go get a room,' Carlo mocks us.

Connie ignores him for the most part, which is completely gratifying. She turns to Daisy and introduces herself.

'I'm Connie,' she says unnecessarily, holding out her hand.

'It's unbelievable! You're the exact replica of someone we used to know.' Daisy turns to me anxiously. 'She's the spitting image of Ava, isn't she?'

Of course she is. I'd never thought about it but with her hair cropped short the likeness is obvious.

'Who's Ava?' asks Carlo, anxious to be part of the conversation again.

'She was Max's first crush,' says Daisy.

'That must have been some hot fantasy if you're still repeating it now,' says Carlo.

'I was ten,' I say, desperately trying to win back control of the conversation. 'She was fourteen.'

'So you've always gone for the older woman, have you, Max?' Carlo teases. 'Shy in the streets but a freak in the sheets.'

Everyone laughs apart from me. I don't understand how he has the capacity to make me feel so thin-skinned.

'Here. I brought you a present from work,' Connie says, pulling a papaya from her bag. 'I know how you love them.'

'Thanks, babe,' I say.

'She works at a health food shop,' Carlo explains to Daisy. 'On the exotic fruit counter. Very appropriate.'

I try not to bristle. I have only just learnt where Connie worked myself. It was one of my hard-earned questions.

'I've been working there for almost a year. I want to get into marketing but everyone says working behind the counter is the best way to learn how to sell,' Connie explains to Daisy.

But Daisy's not listening because she's looking at her phone again to see if Mum has been in touch. *Come on, Daisy, make more effort.*

'I think I might go back to New York after that and hang at my dad's for a while. Unless I can get a proper job here.'

'You never mentioned you might leave London,' I say too quickly.

'You can come too, Maxi,' she suggests, stroking my hair.

She knows that's impossible. Even if I wasn't in the middle of a medical degree I had fought hard to win a place on, there's no way I could leave Mum and Daisy at the moment. She leans over and kisses me on the lips. I close my eyes and breathe in to inhale her scent but all I can smell is the heavy stench of my flatmate's aftershave on her coat, along her neck and in her hair. Fucking Carlo. I kiss her back and she slides on to my knee and nuzzles my neck but I suspect it's for Carlo's benefit. Daisy abruptly gets up from her seat on the other side of the table.

'I need to get going,' she says, giving a quick smile. 'It's great to meet you all but I've got to nail the conclusion of my essay.'

I walk her to the door of the pub.

'You tried, Maxi, but it didn't work. I'm so sorry. I'm angsting about Mum. Not a word from her for four hours. I feel so worried I can't concentrate on what anyone is even talking about.'

'Please. Don't go, Daisy.'

'Watch out for Connie. She's going to crush your heart.'

'I'll walk you home,' I say impulsively.

286

I can't leave her in this state. I go back to Connie and Carlo who are deep in conversation and tell them I'll catch them up at the party later. I put my arm through Daisy's like I used to when we were little and start walking. I pick up speed. There's malice in my stride. I curse everyone who is keeping me apart from Connie. Mostly I curse Lisa because I blame her for all of this.

Daisy tugs on my arm.

'There's something I need to tell you, Max,' she says.

15

Nick

Instead of a hen or stag party, Lisa and I find ourselves attending a healing retreat in Somerset the weekend before our wedding with 'friends' Lisa has met at Gregorio's Surviving and Thriving support group. There's something I never thought I would hear myself say. Still, life with Lisa has never been a straight line and I love her for it (mostly).

I mounted a reasonable defence, arguing that Gregorio and his merry band of snake oil salesmen had already hijacked our honeymoon and personally I would rather opt for a couple of days in Norfolk or dinner with the friends we salvaged from our messy divorces. When Lisa resisted, I spent half a day researching luxury spas up and down the UK so I could present her with a more seductive alternative, but no amount of massage and meditation could convince her we should go anywhere else.

'It's not about the place. It's about the people,' she insisted, pushing a leaflet into my hands. 'This could be a turning point for me.'

I can't ever say no to her. Especially now. So I tried hard to pretend to be enthusiastic about the healing properties of systemic constellation, tachyon, and Tibetan pulsing, even though I had no idea what Gregorio was talking about. The only upside is that I'm relieved of juicing duties for the next three days. Everything at the retreat is focused on abstinence. There are three plant-based meals a day and optional green juices. I say a silent prayer that I had the presence of mind to stock up on packets of ham, sausage rolls and Pot Noodles at the motorway service station, otherwise I would have starved or shat myself senseless. Gregorio is so preoccupied with our bowel movements that I am convinced he has an anal fixation. After breakfast there are various therapy sessions, alone and in groups, coffee enemas for the chosen few, and more plants for lunch.

There's no alcohol, no sugar and no coffee. The worst thing, however, is that during daylight hours Lisa and I don't spend a single minute alone together, although she gets plenty of attention from Gregorio because he does the advanced Spiritual Awareness workshop that Lisa attends with one other woman, whilst I'm with everyone else in the beginner class run by a man called Reyansh from Essex via Pune who insists on calling me Niko. When you don't know how much time you have left with someone, every minute together counts.

It's all so relentlessly awful that yesterday I put the processed ham on the radiator for the day, to provide an optimum environment for bacteria to multiply, and ate it this morning, hoping that I would get food poisoning and be confined to bed or sent home. Then I realized that Lisa would end up spending even more time with Gregorio so I made myself sick.

'What are you doing, Nick? Everyone is waiting.' Lisa comes into the bedroom.

You wouldn't guess she was ill unless you knew. She's a little pale and walks more slowly perhaps, but that highlights her natural grace. She has an ethereal quality that makes her more beautiful than ever. I see the way Gregorio looks at her and know that at least we both agree on that.

I encourage Lisa to lie beside me on the bed. She flops down, leans into me, and I enfold her in my arms. For a moment we are perfectly happy. I wonder if I could suggest we cut loose to the four-star hotel up the road and order juices from room service in a deluxe suite. I resent every minute that we spend with these strangers.

I dared express this sentiment at the group session on the second day, after Gregorio encouraged us to share our fears and worries. I was rewarded with a public mauling by him for my 'self-sabotaging beliefs and selfishness' because the collective energy of the people in the room was a vital part of Lisa's recovery. He informed everyone that his regime has pretty much stopped the cancer in its tracks.

'Pretty much doesn't sound very scientific,' I pointed out. 'Do you mean you have ended the replication of the faulty DNA and therefore prevented the cancer cells from multiplying? Because that sounds as likely as Canute holding back the sea.'

'Nick has a number of roadblocks in his subconscious,' Gregorio told everyone calmly. 'We're hoping to dismantle these over the next few days.'

No one said anything. I would argue their energy has been totally sapped by a diet more suitable for a rabbit and their minds addled from lack of sleep. Also, you don't want to get into a row with someone who has persuaded you to share your darkest emotional secrets with a room full of strangers.

Except they aren't strangers to Lisa because she has met most of them before, at the support group I refuse to attend, which makes me the bad guy. I am beginning to wonder if Gregorio is the leader of a cult but I can't even google Cultwatch to check because they've taken away our mobile phones.

'Didn't you hear the Tibetan chimes calling us to the day room?' Lisa asks me. She makes no effort to get out of bed so I stay put.

'Only in my nightmares,' I mutter.

'Please can you try a bit harder, just for me?'

I hug her tight. She should be eating food that gives her energy and protein for cellular regrowth. I could cook delicious meals for her instead of endless juices. But Gregorio is not a logical thinker. Everything is about feelings rather than knowledge. It's as if thousands of years of scientific progress have been thrown out of the window. It's completely terrifying.

'You have to work on resisting those self-sabotaging beliefs, Nick,' says Lisa, pretending to be Gregorio.

One of the few things that give me hope is the way she ruthlessly imitates his slightly nasal mid-Atlantic drawl. She peers over the edge of the bed and finds the half-eaten packet of sausage rolls and threatens to grass me up to him.

'Don't shirk the work, Nick,' she says, using one of Gregorio's jingoistic phrases.

'Please, Lisa,' I say dramatically, getting down on my

hands and knees on the floor beside her, 'the sausage rolls are helping me rediscover my true spiritual nature! He'll make me do a thousand sun salutations as a punishment or, even worse, attend sessions of Tibetan pulsing through the night.'

We both start laughing, and I feel completely content. I cherish these moments as never before. I forget the way the carpet crunches with the remnants of dead insects and dried dog biscuit and trace my finger around her lips. I wonder if we could have sex. Gregorio has banned it because it saps our essential energy, which is as good a reason as any for trying.

'This weekend is a vital part of my treatment. Gregorio says it could be the tipping point so we need to give it our best shot. He thinks the juicing and enemas are really starting to work. He sees real progress after the first six weeks.'

'I think we should go back to the oncologist we saw in Norwich for another opinion,' I say, trying to rein in my emotion. 'So he can monitor your progress and confirm that Gregorio's right, because I'm not sure his treatments have been peer reviewed.'

'He's curing me of cancer. The juices and the positive thinking are working. I feel amazing. Gregorio is amazing.' She looks radiant. Her eyes always go watery when she mentions his name.

'Lisa, you're a trained lawyer. You spent your entire career weighing up facts and on some level you must know this isn't possible. Rosie trained for nine years before she was allowed near someone with cancer. What qualifications does Gregorio have?' I try not to sound as panicky as I feel. I keep thinking that if she had followed the oncologist's advice, she would have started conventional treatment five weeks ago and the cancer cells might have had a fight on their hands.

She turns to me. 'You have to believe, otherwise it won't work. Please don't question him because it makes me feel anxious, and anxiety inhibits the healing process.'

The irrational logic reminds me of Daisy, long before she was ill, worrying that the Tooth Fairy wouldn't come because she kept thinking she wasn't real.

'If you imagine how it is to be healthy, you will be healthy,' she says, getting off the bed and pulling me up. 'Come on. They'll all be waiting for us.'

She takes me by the hand and we head out of our bedroom and back downstairs into the sitting room below. We are in a large Georgian country house, on the crest of a valley just outside Shepton Mallet. The windows at the front all have long views across gentle valleys and hills, where sheep graze peacefully on a diet not dissimilar to the one Gregorio has prescribed for us. In the idyllic garden, there are trees with arthritic branches and thick, sturdy trunks that I now regard as friends for the comfort they give me when it all gets too much. They have a sense of permanence now surely lacking from my own existence.

It is home to some wacky local aristocrats, whose attendance has been heavily discounted. Unlike ours, which cost almost a thousand pounds – to pay for facilitators, who are apparently 'all world-class leaders in their field'. How many Tibetan pulse experts are there in the world? I questioned Lisa. Especially after I learnt the practice isn't Tibetan at all. Their field is probably smaller than a handkerchief.

Lisa describes the interior of the house as 'shabby shabby'. It basically looks as though someone has tipped the entire contents of a Marrakech riad on it. There are dusty, faded throws that smell of joss sticks and cat pee draped over every available surface, lamps veiled in colourful fabrics, moth-eaten kilims on floors, and woven cushions that give me immediate allergies.

We go into the huge sitting room where the rest of the group are sitting cross-legged on cushions, waiting for us. Jenna, who competes most with Lisa for Gregorio's attention, is in the lotus position with her hands meditatively clasped together.

'Girly swot,' I whisper in her ear as I walk past.

Lisa nudges me. 'For God's sake, Nick! Grow up.'

I sneeze loudly.

'It's fine, Lisa,' says Jenna, patronizingly. 'I feel sorry for Nick for not being open to the possibility of expanding his bandwidth.'

'I'm resolutely stuck on Radio 4,' I confirm.

Gregorio sits with his back to the window so his tanned naked torso is strategically washed in late-afternoon sun. The owners of the house, Hamish and Rowena, are on his right-hand side. They wear brightly coloured flowing clothes and jewellery with stones as big as walnuts that make them look like exotic birds. Apart from Lisa, they are probably my favourite people in the room because a) whenever Gregorio is out of earshot they refer to him as the Wizard of Oz, and b) over breakfast this morning they questioned Lisa about her decision to keep her cancer diagnosis secret from Rex and Ava, something I am seriously concerned about now their arrival is imminent.

'Gregorio says the negative energy from their worry could jeopardize my recovery,' Lisa explained.

'But the positive energy from their love for you could help the healing process,' argued Rowena.

It's a measure of how bad things have got that I appreciated this intervention. I am seriously beginning to think the reason Gregorio has instructed Lisa not to tell her family is that he doesn't want other people questioning his methodology. Or worse, going after him when his treatment fails.

I learnt in our first session that Hamish and Rowena suffer from anxiety and memory problems following years of hard partying. Gregorio diagnosed a blockage in their subconscious. When I asked if he wanted me to fetch a plunger, they laughed hysterically.

I explained that the nerve pathway affected by Ecstasy is the serotonin pathway, and serotonin regulates mood, anxiety, memory and perceptions. Gregorio looked interested when I mentioned perception but his face darkened when I said that Ecstasy users have significant reductions in the way serotonin is transported in their brain and that this could account for Hamish and Rowena's symptoms. I also pointed out that there's been consistent research showing Ecstasy users put themselves at risk of impaired hippocampus-dependent memory function.

'The hippocampus is where new memories are stored. No one knows how you can reverse those effects.'

'This is the kind of negative thinking that Lisa complains about,' Gregorio admonished me. 'The subconscious is the body's hard drive. It can be rebooted just like a computer.'

'Well, let's hope Hamish's is an AppleMac.'

I've never heard so much bollocks in my life but I don't say any more. It's the Dunning-Kruger effect: the less you know the more likely you are to perceive yourself as an expert. There is another woman who has recently been diagnosed with breast cancer called Sonia, who is also very nice. Her parents live abroad and she has no one to look after her. She told the group that she's worried she won't be able to cope with the juicing regime on her own so, without even consulting me, Lisa promised she could come and stay with us. Everyone apart from me applauded Lisa's generosity. I was panicking about anything, from how I could carry eighteen kilos of fruit and vegetables on my bike to what would happen if Lisa died and I was left looking after Sonia? My heart was beating so fast that I imagined I could see it through my T-shirt. I have lost all control over this situation.

Easily the most annoying couple is Jenna and Hal, who are competitive with Lisa and me about their superior progress in discovering their true spiritual nature together. Hal has an attitude of patronizing sympathy for Lisa because of her bad luck in choosing a self-sabotaging partner like me (his words, not mine), and Jenna offers to stroke and massage Lisa so much that I think she's probably bisexual. Or maybe I'm just hopeful. Sex has been so off the cards that I wake up in the morning horny as a teenager and Jenna has a great arse, pert and full without being overbearing. I'm literally mesmerized by the upside of her downward dog.

I take my place on the cushion that doubles up as a dog bed for Rowena and Hamish's flatulent old Labrador. Gregorio begins with some breathing exercises.

'Inhale love and exhale gratitude,' he instructs us.

I'm relieved I can close my eyes so I don't have to look at his wiry little body any more. His smooth chest and tiny feet give me the creeps. I can't believe that less than three months ago I actually felt indebted to him for helping Lisa come to terms with her illness. He prattles on for a while about how the sea is his spirit guide, although he has that irritating habit of calling it the 'ocean' to highlight his mid-Atlantic credentials.

'If you swim with the power of the ocean, rather than against it, then anything is possible,' he says portentously, as if he has just discovered relativity. Everything he says is so irritatingly banal.

He introduces the theme of this morning's session: evolving the subconscious. At least I more or less understand what he's getting at. Yesterday it was systemic constellation, which involved dismantling negative and unseen energetic forces across time and space. It sounded like the plot of *Star Wars*. I discovered that Lisa's cancer was her grandmother's fault, for walking out on her marriage, and got sent out of the room for pretending to be a Jedi warrior when we were doing role play to alter the course of history.

Gregorio goes on for a good twenty minutes about how most human behaviour is driven by the subconscious and that if you harness its power you can make whole and complete patterns for change. I don't disagree with this basic premise. I just don't like the way he claims all this came to him one day as he was meditating in front of the ocean, when he is sketching the principles of cognitive behavioural therapy, which is older than me and available on the NHS. I show admirable self-restraint in remaining silent. I count how many hours there are until we can leave. It's less than twenty, which fills me with the kind of positivity that the Tibetan pulsing failed to trigger.

'Please can you all hold hands,' says Gregorio solemnly. 'We're reaching the apex of the weekend. After forty-eight hours of intensive work nourishing mind, body and soul, we are now ready to start sharing the positive energy we have released to overcome the issues that have brought us all here.' He stares pointedly at me.

Rowena squeezes my right hand in a gesture that I hope is sympathy rather than an attempt to transfer positive energy. Jenna takes my left hand and I swear I can feel her finger rub the palm of my hand. I think about her body as a way to counteract Gregorio and feel a vague sense of loss that I will never sit behind her in another yoga class.

'Jenna, please can you swap places with Sonia,' orders Gregorio.

He isn't a mind-reader. I feel a bit dirty admitting I have anything in common with Gregorio but we obviously share the same taste in women.

'Bad memories and experiences create blockages so our energy can't flow freely, and we get sick. If we release that stuck energy then our problems will start to be resolved.'

His tone has gone all Darth Vader. I open my eyes and see his Adam's apple bob up and down with the effort to lower his voice.

'The subconscious mind is way more powerful than the conscious mind, and if it can be programmed there are no limits to what you can achieve. You will open yourself up to more self-love and healing. It is the imbalance between the conscious and subconscious mind that causes disease.'

I see Lisa nodding. I imagine the cancer cells in her body planning a big hedonistic party where they can all divide and reproduce without any threat to their existence.

'Before we move to the next level does anyone have any questions?'

Hamish and I both put up our hands. Hamish says that he's not sure he has made as much progress as everyone else because he's still waking up with his heart racing. When Gregorio doesn't say anything Hamish tentatively wonders if he should sign up for another intensive weekend of work.

'The answer is in the question,' responds Gregorio sagely. He turns to me. 'Nick, Nick, Nick,' he says in his most patronizing tone.

'Greg, Greg, Greg,' I say. 'I want to make sure I am understanding you correctly. Are you suggesting that Lisa's cancer can be cured by hope marinated in organic vegetable juice?' It's an extraordinary statement. I feel as though I have walked into the New Testament and Gregorio is playing the role of Jesus in the feeding of the five thousand, but this might be because I am so hungry. I gamely continue. 'So if she dies, is it because she didn't believe enough? Or drink enough kale juice? So that she thinks it's her fault? Because that's not just irresponsible, it's cruel.'

Gregorio's chill eyes narrow.

'Science and technology undermine our innate wisdom and leave us at the mercy of experts, who reduce our power to self-heal, and pharmaceutical companies, who conspire to make us dependent on their drugs,' he says. 'I am simply a facilitator to help release the body's innate capacity to do what it does best.'

'I know who I would choose,' I mutter.

'Perhaps, Nick, you should consider the role you have both played in creating the conditions for Lisa's blockages.'

'Greg, you've lost me,' I say, adopting his passive-aggressive habit of using my name every time he addresses me.

'Perhaps you should assess the psycho-emotional roots of her illness, Nick. Cancer is caused by negative emotions, trauma and unfinished business.'

'Don't you think the fact that Lisa's mother and grandmother both had breast cancer suggests there might be a genetic component to the disease?' I struggle to remain composed. I tap my bare feet nervously on the floor like Daisy used to do.

I try to remember how Rosie explained it all. I wish she were here because, unlike me, everyone always listens to Rosie. People warm to her. Eight sets of eyes bore into me as I struggle to articulate how cancer strikes across generations. It feels as though I am fighting for my life in the scientific equivalent of Max's favourite childhood book, *The Hunger Games*. Then it occurs to me that actually I'm fighting for Lisa's life, which makes me feel sick with nerves. I get caught in cul-de-sacs about DNA repair genes. There are dangerous bends in the road when I lurch from explanations about the difference between protective tumour suppressor genes and oncogenes. But I really lose people during a long stretch about gene mutations. It strikes me that the problem with contemporary scientific knowledge is that human beings need a basic narrative of how life works, and this is too complicated for most people to understand.

'If Lisa had done the family constellation therapy years ago, this destructive cycle could have been broken,' says Gregorio serenely. 'We would have seen the emotions that hadn't been expressed by her grandmother, and the destruction would have stopped.'

'I can't believe that anyone is seduced by this crap,' I say. I look towards Hamish and Rowena for support but they resolutely stare into the middle distance.

'Relationships are like plants, they need good soil to grow, especially at the beginning, and from everything that Lisa has told me, the roots of your partnership were nourished in deception, lies and other people's misery,' says Gregorio. There is a nip of triumph in his tone that I hope Lisa notices.

'That's got nothing to do with her illness.'

Lisa blushes bright red. Everyone turns to me. Rowena is no longer holding my hand.

'Lisa understands that her illness is in part the result of the pain you both caused the people closest to your heart – her best friend, Rosie, her ex-husband, Barney, your daughter, Daisy, who was made ill by the negative energy surrounding it – and the poison that seeped into her relationship with her own children. If you can accept this, you will all begin to heal together.'

I can't believe that Lisa has shared intimate details of our relationship with this ridiculous man. I'm stunned into silence. I turn towards her but she won't catch my eye. For a moment I think I'm going to burst into tears at the absurdity of it all. But then Gregorio might think he has made a breakthrough. Or even worse, won the battle.

'I think perhaps you should all do some family constellation therapy together,' Gregorio suggests. 'What do you think, Nick?'

'This is what I think.' I get up, stride over to him and shove his shoulders as hard as I can and, because he's sitting in the lotus position, he can't unravel his legs fast enough so he topples backwards like a skittle.

For the first couple of hours on the drive back to London we don't speak to each other. We've never had a big disagreement before so there's no well-rehearsed format where we shout a while, recriminate, and sulk. We haven't yet reached the distrust-disillusionment phase of a relationship where words are weaponized to inflict maximum damage. So I flail around, trying to read Lisa's body language for clues, and even in the way she blinks and sniffs I sense her disapproval.

Eventually she falls asleep with her back to me, head resting against the passenger window. When the traffic snarls up I gently run my hand down her back and feel the gnarled bony undulations of her vertebrae through her heavily quilted jacket. She's starving to death. It's unbearable.

She's warned Rex and Ava that she's doing a detox but

they are bound to notice that she has lost too much weight, especially Ava, who hasn't seen her mother since she moved to Portland a year ago. She's arriving a few days early to spend 'quality time' with Lisa, and I'm staying well out of the way in case I'm turned to ice by her cool disdain. Ava very noisily and publicly sided with Barney after their divorce and I can tell from the emails, where she makes comic mockery of our wedding by referring to it as The Big Day, that she means to cause trouble. She's threatening to bring her musician boyfriend, who is apparently the reincarnation of Kurt Cobain, although when I look him up I see his band has less than fifty Spotify streams. Hopefully my irritation with Ava will cancel the guilt I feel for Rex, whose quiet failure to launch is most definitely connected to the way he ended up looking after his father through the dark days of our abandonment.

I take advantage of Lisa sleeping to stop at the drive-through McDonald's on the M4, where I buy a double Big Mac and fries, which I eat too fast. Sometimes I wonder if I'm trying to eat for two. I notice my stomach now presses into the steering wheel. A few miles later I pull up on the hard shoulder and am violently sick. As I heave into the hedge I wonder what kind of man I am that I can't persuade the woman I love to take my advice over that of some pseud she met at her yoga studio less than four months ago?

As I retch the answer becomes glaringly obvious: on some level Lisa trusts him more than she does me. There is nothing I can say or do that will change her mind. In fact, it's worse than I thought: it isn't that she truly believes

Gregorio's treatment will work, it's more that he has made her feel she deserves to be ill.

I wipe my nose and mouth with my sleeve.

Any certainty ebbs away and I'm left facing myself on the hard shoulder with cars noisily speeding by but not loud enough to drown out the voice in my head telling me that I'm a fraud, and a fool whose children don't care about me because I failed to resist the itch and made my daughter ill. When I get back in the car and turn on the engine Lisa is awake. I pretend the wind has made my eyes water.

'I invited Hamish and Rowena to our wedding,' she says. 'I hope you don't mind.'

'Of course not. The more the merrier.'

I smile but it feels like a grimace. Frankly I'm relieved she still wants to go through with it. We embark on a neutral discussion about the wedding. At what point will the children read from *The Prophet*? Should I buy crabs the day before? Where will everyone sleep? I answer all these questions with my customary decisiveness.

When we get back to the flat, I realize that we don't have enough fruit and vegetables for Lisa's regime the following day. I can't go out early tomorrow morning because I'm doing a talk at the Ministry of Justice on how to avoid misleading witnesses with poor questioning techniques. So I end up cycling like a maniac to The Whole Foods Market and get to the shop just as the man with the luscious lips and beard from the exotic fruit counter is closing the steel shutters. Gasping for breath, I approach him to see if he will take pity on my predicament but instead he locks himself in and threatens to call security.

'I know you,' he shouts. 'Go home and look after your fiancée instead of hanging around here, you fricking freak show! In any case she doesn't work on Sundays.'

'That's not very peace and love,' I shout back.

But he's gone inside. I curse him and I curse Gregorio. Hippies can be such bloody fascists. I remember a late-night Caribbean shop, which sells exotic fruit and vegetables, close to my old home. I get back on my bike and pedal fast, ignoring the red traffic lights and one-way streets, along a route so familiar that I could cycle it in my sleep, wishing – as I do whenever I'm under pressure – that I could return to the ease of a world where I'm still married to Rosie and my children believe in me like they once believed in Father Christmas.

Sometimes it makes me dizzy to consider all the different lives I could have lived if I had made different decisions along the way. If I hadn't taken magic mushrooms would I have got together with Rosie? If Barney hadn't turned into a drunk might I still be married to her? If I hadn't been so distracted by the girl in the fruit shop would I have noticed how Gregorio was more than a karmic joke? At the moment I think a lot about the life that will now be unlived because the future I had envisaged with Lisa has been stolen from me twice over: firstly by the cancer and secondly by Gregorio.

He has already been in touch with Lisa, emailing one of his positive messages just before she was meant to drink her eight o'clock juice: *Life is a mirror and will reflect back to the thinker what he thinks into it.*

When I arrive outside the Caribbean grocer, instead of breadfruit and cassava, I find a kitchen shop selling twenty types of unaffordable copper-plated saucepans. I get back on my bike and cycle to my old home, as if this was the plan all along, wondering the best way to ask Rosie for advice. She's had her fair share of patients who ask to postpone chemotherapy in favour of intravenous vitamin therapy, and she was always so reasonable and sympathetic. 'If someone is promising a cure that costs money and a premise that sounds too good to be true then it's probably a scam.' She always said the same thing. I used to find it boring but now it seems comforting. A sensible woman, my ex-wife. Sometimes I wish I had married Lisa first and Rosie second. She's the kind of person you want to be with in old age when survival rather than sex is the first thing on your mind when you wake up in the morning.

It's more than seven years since I last had the front-door keys to my old home but I still reflexively put my hand in the pocket of my jeans to find them. Even after all this time, it feels odd to be ringing the doorbell like a stranger. I look round nervously in case the neighbours see me, but the street is quiet. I suddenly realize that it's close to eleven o'clock and that Rosie might not welcome a late-night visitor when she's got to be at work the next day but, to my surprise, Max answers the door and tells me that Rosie is out.

'Who with?' I hadn't expected this.

'I don't know, Dad,' he says flatly.

'Why are you here?' I still sometimes feel left out when I think of the three of them under the same roof together.

'I'm helping Daisy with something.'

I push the door but it doesn't open and it takes me a couple of seconds to realize Max has his foot against it.

'Can I come in?' I ask.

Max looks at the wooden floor, and shifts from one bare foot to the other, clearly uncomfortable with the proposition.

'Please.'

'Does Mum know?'

'I need to talk to her about something urgent.'

'It's really late, Dad. Daisy's about to go to bed and I'm going to a party.'

'I'll wait until you go, and if Mum's not back I'll leave at the same time.'

If I sound desperate it's because I am. Max reluctantly acquiesces. It's the first time I've been here since I stayed for a weekend to help out when Daisy was ill. Not that Daisy would let me near her. According to the therapist she saw, I was a major source of her anxiety. So I stayed in the kitchen and cooked meals that I froze with labels giving cooking times and helpful suggestions for vegetables.

Feeling more ill at ease than I anticipated, I follow Max into the small hallway. My old home looks much the same and yet there is something missing. The hall is painted in the same dark purple, a colour I jokingly christened 'womb' when Rosie chose it. The books on the shelves are stacked in the same order. The bowl on the hall table still has the same collection of random objects, including a Chelsea key ring. As I edge into the kitchen I note the white laminate cupboards from Ikea that I installed ten years ago. I feel a surge of affection for the green-and-brown pottery teapot that Rosie and I bought during a summer holiday in Andalucía. And for the wooden fruit bowl that Barney and Lisa gave us as a wedding present.

It takes a few minutes to put my finger on it and then it occurs to me that I am the thing that is missing: there is no evidence that I ever lived in this house or play any role in the family that considers it their home. The photo of our wedding that used to hang in the hallway has been removed, as have the black and white pictures of me in the snow with Daisy and Max; instead there are photos of the three of them on holiday in Greece. My jacket that hung on the hook beside the bookshelf has gone; even my favourite cookery books have disappeared. Every trace of me has been eradicated.

'Where am I?' I ask Max.

'What are you talking about, Dad?' Max asks curtly.

'It's as if I don't exist. There's no reference to me anywhere,' I say.

'What do you expect? You haven't lived here for years.' He is uncharacteristically brutal. 'Don't be so needy.'

I ruffle his hair like I used to when I came home from work and he shakes me off. I see Daisy's jumper hanging over the back of a kitchen chair and hear the sound of footsteps going upstairs. Max quickly turns over the pieces of paper on the kitchen island so I can't see what they've been writing. Maybe it's a surprise to do with my wedding. A speech perhaps. He sits down but doesn't offer me a seat. I notice his left hand is inexpertly bandaged up, but when I ask him what happened he doesn't respond.

'You know she saw you, Dad.'

There's a flinty edge to his tone, or maybe I'm feeling oversensitive after Gregorio's pummelling. I recall the fracas in the Indian restaurant when Lisa and I took him and Daisy out for dinner and wonder if they've had another argument. His phone beeps and he picks it up. I watch his elegant hands flutter over the keyboard and remember the way he used to grip my thumb in his fist when he was a baby and cry when I tried to unfurl his tiny fingers. I want to tell him this when he finishes messaging, even though he'll find it mawkish. My emotions bubble up so close to the surface these days. Rosie would be proud of me.

'Who saw me where?' I ask in confusion. I have no idea what he's talking about.

Max frowns at his screen, ignoring me. There is a finely etched vertical worry line between his eyebrows. He must be under a lot of pressure at the moment. I resolve to take him out to dinner before we leave for Mexico. As I wait for him to finish messaging I spot one of Daisy's essays beside her computer. It's all about memory in the novels of Kazuo Ishiguro and I feel proud that my daughter has inherited my interest in the subject. I pick it up to start reading but don't get further than the title because I notice four letters on the keyboard of her computer have been inexpertly disguised with bits of paper. I try to remember the QWERTY layout but can't identify the hidden letters.

'Daisy saw you and Lisa having sex in the dunes when we were on holiday in Norfolk that summer. She was in the pillbox, watching through the window.'

His voice is hard. I struggle to process his words because I am blindsided by this revelation. And I can't make any sense of what he has described because it's neither the complete truth nor a complete lie. It is a mutation of fact. The backdrop is correct, Lisa and I were in the dunes that day, but the action bears no resemblance to reality.

'Why was Daisy there?' I flounder.

'I don't see how that's relevant.'

'What she says. It's an untruth,' I splutter, using a word Daisy and Max invented as children. 'How could she even get inside the pillbox? The entrance was choked up with sand.'

'She described everything in perfect detail, Dad. How your trunks were hung out on the marram grass beside Lisa's clothes, the way your underpants were pulled down your thighs and her black knickers were tangled round her ankle.'

He paces up and down the kitchen before coming to stand so close that I can smell the beer on his breath. As he leans over me I'm suddenly aware of his superior physicality. I feel acid rise in my throat but manage to swallow it back down.

'Just because someone tells you something with confidence, details and emotion, doesn't mean it happened. In fact, the greater the level of detail the less likely it is that the memory is accurate. I've spent most of my career doing research about this.' I try not to babble.

Max does an eye roll. 'Can you imagine what that did to her, seeing her dad screwing her mum's best friend? She was only thirteen. And then she had to keep your sordid little affair secret for six months until Mum found out. No wonder she got so ill. That's why she tried to hurt Ava. She wanted Lisa to suffer like you'd made her suffer.'

I am stunned. He might as well have punched me in

the stomach. My breath leaves my lungs and I gulp for air like a fish out of water.

'She said Lisa was lying beneath you on that tartan rug we used to have and that she looked straight at her.'

'I remember Lisa saying that she thought she heard a noise, but we were a fair way from the pillbox. She even checked through the arrow-slit window when we went past, but there was no one inside.'

'So you're not denying you were there.'

'I was there. We were there. But what Daisy describes. It's not true. I wasn't even wearing swimming trunks. You have to believe me, Max.' I hear the pathetic desperation in my voice and the fury in his.

'I saw her when she came back to the house. She had been in the dunes because her legs were bleeding from the marram grass, and I could tell something bad had happened.'

'It's a partial truth,' I concede. 'She might have been there but she's confused about what she saw. Please. Let me explain.' I struggle for air as if I've just been for a jog.

'How would she remember exactly what you were wearing?' Max asks.

'There's a photo of us all taken that same day. She might have seen it.'

'Why should I believe anything you say when you've lied so much before?'

'I want to tell you what happened, Max.'

I can hear the desperation in my voice. I close my eyes to better remember the details of that afternoon but also so I don't have to see the contempt in his eyes.

'Lisa and I went swimming. We went up into the dunes

to dry. That's why our clothes were hanging on the grass. She lay on her back and I lay on my side next to her and we talked. We were close enough to touch. She heard something, and when she sat up she hit my nose with her chin. Do you remember, I had a cut on my nose when I came back, Max?'

'You told me you did that on the kitchen cupboard.'

'I didn't want anyone to realize we'd gone to the beach.'

'If you say so.' His tone is laced with sarcasm.

'My relationship with Lisa didn't start on that holiday. It happened later.'

'I'm not looking for a history lesson, Dad.'

'People don't always remember things accurately. The question isn't whether our memories are false, it's how false are our memories?'

'Why would Daisy tell me this if it wasn't true?'

'I don't know.' I pause for a moment. 'She was ill. Sometimes people with OCD have messed-up memory processes.' When he doesn't say anything, I continue. 'Think about it. Not even Daisy trusted her own memory, because otherwise why did she have to check the windows and light switches all the time? How many times a night did she count the number of knives in the drawer? She wasn't in her right mind.'

His phone beeps again. My head starts to throb and I rub my temples.

'Mum's not coming home. I think you should go, Dad.'

I spot some fruit in the bowl and ask if I can take it.

Max shrugs and turns his back to me. 'You're truly pathetic,' he says coldly. 'Trying to use your daughter's illness as an excuse.'

I get back on my bike and head home, wishing I met adversity with courage and fortitude, like some of the patients Rosie used to describe to me when she came home from work. Unfortunately my children are right. I'm self-pitying and weak-willed. I'm also scared. I'm scared of losing Lisa; I'm scared of what she wants to tell Rosie; I'm scared of what Max has just told me and that I'll lose him too; I'm scared of being alone; I'm scared of all the regrets I will have when I'm an old man, mindlessly wandering through the landscape of my mind and finding it devoid of anyone who loves me.

16

Rosie

Here's the strangest thing: not only do I match with Barney on Tinder, I don't realize it's him. Firstly, his profile pic looks nothing like the man I last saw sobbing in my kitchen seven years ago. And secondly, in an effort to wean myself off Ed Gilmour, I have become aggressively active, indiscriminately swiping right, ignoring my own rules and responding to men who send messages with asinine amounts of exclamation marks and don't know the difference between *their*, *they're* and *there*. It's a bit like picking dishes off the conveyor at YO! Sushi just because they vaguely resemble something I've enjoyed before.

So I probably mechanically swiped right to Barney simply on the grounds that he had a nice face, dark hair and was currently active within a mile radius of my office. *It's a match. You and Bernardo have liked each other*, the notification reads. At one point I find myself trying to keep thirteen conversations going at once and start copying and pasting the same responses to everyone. I've learnt over the past year that men lose interest if you don't message back quickly. One falls by the wayside when I realize that I'm dealing with a *Star Wars* fetishist who wants me to dress up as Princess Leia (his bio about being a Jedi in the sheets and a Sith in the streets should have been a giveaway).

'Fancy bumping into you here!' reads the next message.

My body tenses. I've always been terror-struck about coming across someone who knows me on Tinder. Not because I fear judgement. The breakdown of my marriage was about as far from conscious uncoupling as you can imagine and dissected by all sorts of people. I once even came across a mother at Daisy's new school who told me about the 'bastard husband' of a friend of a friend without even realizing she was describing my marriage. I made sympathetic comments until it dawned on me that I was empathizing with myself. My colleagues were brilliant because they let me immerse myself in work, which gave me a different identity from the role I would never have chosen as 'the wronged woman'. Deep down most of us would prefer to be 'the other woman'.

People were kind and well-meaning but the scrutiny was relentless. *You're better off without him . . . There's plenty more fish in the sea . . . You of all people can cope with something like this.* Actually, I couldn't. At the beginning I had work to distract me. But when Daisy got really ill I had to take six months off and got through the night by planning my own funeral. I made lists in my head of music that I would want played ('One More Cup Of Coffee' by Bob Dylan), potential readings (anything by Emily Dickinson), and imagined what might be said of me in the eulogy (a good woman felled by a weak and vain man). It was strangely calming, and usually I was asleep before the climax where my coffin was lowered into the ground. One thing my patients have taught me over the years is that sometimes you learn to live best when you're looking death in the face.

So it's not judgement I fear when I read this message, it's more that my match might be the husband of a friend or patient – or even one of Daisy's friends who has lied about his age. So I'm relieved when I look at the profile photo more closely and recognize that Bernardo is Barney. His dark curly hair is a little greyer and his face thinner, drawing attention to the glasses perched on the end of his slightly crooked nose. I remember now that he broke it two weeks before he delivered his bombshell to me. Nick told me how he'd come home black and bloodied after a two-day drinking binge and I didn't question why Lisa had told him rather than me.

I would love to say that I was one of those women who intuited what was going on under her nose and cleverly pieced together the evidence before unmasking her feckless husband in a witty, dramatic sting. However, I very much wasn't. There was no long list of festering grievances between Nick and me. I trusted him. I trusted Lisa. I loved them both, which made the sense of loss and betrayal more exquisitely painful.

I look at Barney's bio: *writer, biker, ukulele player*. Unbelievably, he's not the first ukulele player I have matched with.

Ukulele? For real?

He sends back a picture of him playing in a band where every member apart from him has a beard and wears a fedora.

What u doing here? He writes back. Casual but friendly.

I check his location and see he's four hundred metres closer to me than when he first messaged.

316

Same as you, I say.
Want to go out for a tonic water?
When?
Now.

I check the time. It's eight o'clock on a Sunday evening. I was planning a night in and I would be breaking my rule about not meeting up with anyone the first time we message. But, strictly speaking, Barney isn't a stranger or a real Tinder date. Daisy and Kit have gone to meet Max and when I check in with Ed Gilmour he says he's busy. So I take the plunge.

Where?

He suggests a pub within walking distance. I suspect he's probably already there. He was always brazen.

Barney tried to contact me repeatedly the first year that Nick and Lisa moved in with each other. I ignored all his calls and messages and eventually blocked his number. That first winter, I stayed at home every evening, watching the news without properly listening, feeling totally wiped out. Not even the drama of banks collapsing and workers with ghostly expressions carrying boxes of belongings from offices that no longer existed could hold my attention. And while Barney was probably the only person who could have come close to understanding my sense of loss and shame, I didn't want to speak to him. I didn't want to see anyone who reminded me of Nick and Lisa.

Besides, I could tell Barney was still drinking because every couple of weeks he sent exactly the same message: *Don't shoot the messenger.* He assumed I was angry with him for being the bearer of the worst kind of news. But I was more furious because Lisa would never have left him for Nick if he hadn't become a drunk. She always fell in love with the idea of a person rather than their reality. While Barney was on his uppers, Nick's star was rising. He had written a science book that managed to cross over into the mainstream and there was talk of a TV series, although it never materialized.

I had little idea what had become of Barney over the intervening years. He moved out of the area and bought a flat in Haggerston, where Rex and Ava lived with him and started new schools. I only knew this through Daisy and Max. After a lot of persuasion from me they eventually spent the odd weekend with Nick and Lisa, but they never crossed paths with Rex and Ava. There was too much history between them all. So all ties between Barney and me were severed.

Occasionally I was reminded of him. When I decided to eradicate all traces of my marriage to Nick, I found a postcard with a photo of flashing neon breasts by the artist Adele Röder in my bedside drawer. *Saw this and thought of you, Barney.* He always loved trying to shock me. When Amy Winehouse died, one of his old interviews was reprinted in *Rolling Stone*.

I see him as soon as I go into the pub, at a table in the corner. He's left me the most comfortable space on the upholstered leather bench and bought me a Bloody Mary. I'm touched that he's remembered it's my favourite drink. He gets up to greet me.

'Hi, Rosie.'

'Hi, Bernardo.'

He smiles and goes in for a kiss on the cheek but I try to give him a hug and we end up awkwardly caught in a half-embrace with him nuzzling my right ear. We unfurl and there is a slightly uneasy moment where we step back and stare, gauging what is familiar and what has changed in that way people who haven't seen each other for years make inventories of each other. Adjectives go through my head like ticker tape. Thinner, balder, more wrinkled. He speaks first.

'Thinner, balder, more wrinkled,' he says. 'You were always very transparent.'

We both laugh.

'You look great, Rosie. Better than ever.'

'Thanks. So do you.'

'Divorce suits us.'

'There has to be some upside.'

There's another silence. We've already run out of words. But it's not uncomfortable. I notice he's wearing an old white T-shirt with a faded picture of The Rolling Stones on the front. Nick bought the same one when he went to visit him in Tokyo, when Barney was covering the Bridges to Babylon tour. It billows around the area that used to be filled by his stomach. He sees I've noticed and pats his tummy.

'It got so bad I ended up in hospital. They drained three litres of liquid from my stomach. It was like bursting a waterbed.'

'Sometimes the liver can't cope any more.'

I wonder if he got cirrhosis, and whether his liver has regenerated, but don't want to end up embroiled in a doctor–patient type discussion. I check the whites of his eyes and his fingernails: neither looks yellow.

'Rex and Ava came to the hospital with me. It was the lowest of all my low points. I checked in to rehab a couple of months later and haven't touched a drop since. I still go every week, though. For maintenance. It never leaves you alone.'

'Congratulations,' I say. 'That's such a tough thing to do.'

'I exercise a lot too. It's probably another addiction but at least it doesn't screw things up for other people. And it's useful now I'm back in the dating game. Fit forty-somethings go down very well.'

'So how's that going?'

'Knackering. It's not how I imagined middle age would be. At least it's not boring. But I find the choice over-whelming. It's not great for someone as indecisive as me.'

'Are you one of those men who secretly swipe right while you're on a date?'

'Guilty.' I had forgotten how disarmingly open Barney is. 'But I won't do it when I'm with you.'

'We're not on a date,' I remind him.

He asks me what I'm up to and I explain that we're about to start the final phase of the clinical trial I was working on when we went on holiday together for the last time and that there are hopes of a real breakthrough.

'It's really something to decide to dedicate your life to the same thing for ten years,' he says. 'I'm not sure I could commit to anything so long term.'

'People think making fundamental change is all about making one big decision but actually it's all about the little decisions taken along the way.'

'God, you were always so terrifyingly impressive, Rosie,' he says.

'But it didn't make me irresistible, did it?'

'They fell in love. Or rather they fell in love with the idea of each other. We didn't stand a chance. And I was a mess, which didn't help.'

He sounds more wistful than bitter and I am relieved, because of all the curdled emotions of divorce, bitterness is the worst. I ask him what he's up to and he tells me that he gave up journalism and retrained as a piano teacher and has a part-time job in a secondary school close to where he lives. He's also been asked by one of his former interviewees to ghostwrite an autobiography. His name won't be on the cover but he's going to get paid a lot of money and wants to take a six-month sabbatical to get it done.

'That's a lot of plans for someone who can't make decisions,' I tease.

'It was a lot of decisions for someone who can't make plans,' he says, in between tiny sips of tonic water. He looks up and gives me a long, hard stare. 'You know, Rosie, if someone had asked me who would be the person I would be least likely to find on Tinder, I would probably have placed you pretty close to the top of my list. I never had you down as a risk-taker. It's like the Wild West out there.'

'Maybe the alternative is riskier. I did a lot of being alone. Daisy was ill for a long time. And I have a first-class degree in coping with rejection.'

He arches his eyebrows questioningly. It is such a familiar gesture that it almost hurts. I remember an Easter egg hunt in Norfolk where Barney wanted to hide eggs in improbably tricky places. He climbed to the top of the copper beech that lost its branch in the storm, high enough that we couldn't see him through the leaves, and then got such bad vertigo that we had to get a fire engine to bring him down. This in turn reminds me of a wedding where he was best man and got so drunk that he went to the loo with the microphone still attached to his lapel and Lisa went to find him and they didn't realize everyone could hear them argue. He used to make me laugh so much. I'm suddenly overwhelmed by everything that has been lost. I feel old before my time, like my mum in the last years of her life when everyone she knew had died and she was only left with the memories. 'Memories are good but the real thing is better,' she always used to say.

'What was wrong with Daisy, if you don't mind me asking?'

'She was eventually diagnosed with OCD,' I explain. 'I knew something was wrong after Nick left, but didn't understand what was going on for ages. I blame myself. I was too caught up in my own drama. By the time I found out, it had taken over. It's an insidiously covert illness.'

'God, that sounds awful.'

'It gets worse. She didn't get the right treatment at first and deteriorated so badly that I had to give up work. She'd lock herself in the toilet and refuse to go to school and lost so much weight the doctor thought she had anorexia. It felt as though on top of everything else I was losing my daughter too.'

'It must have been so hard dealing with all that on your own, Rosie.' He puts his hand on my forearm and leaves it there, tucking his thumb absent-mindedly beneath the sleeve of my sweater where it touches the soft flesh on the inside of my elbow. The best communication doesn't involve words.

'They were tough times. Max was great. He spent lots of time with Daisy but sometimes I think he lost his childhood in the process. Our GP got to the bottom of it eventually and Daisy got referred to someone who did cognitive behavioural therapy and taught her to manage her problems by changing the way she thought. It took almost two years but she turned things around for her.'

'And Max?'

'He's into his second year at medical school. He's great. Just the same.'

'I miss your kids,' he says. 'I felt so bad for the way Ava treated Daisy, and Max was very sweet to me on that holiday in Norfolk. I wasn't in a good place. I could feel Lisa slipping away from me but there was nothing I could do to stop it.'

'He was born intuitive,' I say.

His hand still rests on my arm. I notice that neither of us has taken more than a couple of sips from our drinks and wonder if he's also trying to make his last as long as possible. His face is so familiar and the conversation so easy that it makes me smile. He grins back. I can't imagine ever not knowing him again. But one thing I have learnt the hard way is never to make assumptions.

'Nick called me up last week. Totally out of the blue,' Barney says. 'I didn't recognize the number so I picked up.'

'How long since you've seen him?' I ask.

'Not since he came over the night I got beaten up. I

can't even remember him being there so I don't know if it qualifies. That whole period is a bit of a blur. I had a lot of blackouts.' He gives a hollow laugh.

'Maybe it's good you can't remember it all.'

'Sometimes stuff comes back to me, even now, but I've no idea if it's real or not. That's the worst part.'

'Like what?'

'Weird shit. I have this memory of being in a pub like this and some guy saying that he'd found my wallet and recognized me from the photo on my driving licence. But then I never carry my driving licence, so how could he have been sure the wallet belonged to me? I'll never know. Last year I bumped into someone I used to work with and she said I'd once turned up at her flat at two in the morning and spent the night on the sofa, but I can't remember any of it.'

'Did you sleep with her?'

'She didn't mention it and I didn't like to ask. But if I did it would have been crap. So you're right, perhaps it's best not to know.'

'So what did Nick want?'

Barney laughs. We both understand Nick would only call if he needed something.

'It was difficult to tell at first. He started talking about his research on people who have false memories about traumatic events in a way that made me think he was trying to ask me a question without being specific about what he wanted to ask. I'd forgotten how you always have to second-guess him. It means it takes twice as long to get to the point where you understand what it is he's driving at. He's the king of circumvention.'

'Remember, I lived with him,' I laugh.

'He told me Lisa has been diagnosed with cancer. Did you know?'

I nod. Barney blinks back tears. I give him a serviette and he dabs his eyes and blows his nose. I see the barman shoot an anxious glance over at us because he doesn't want a scene. He rings the last orders bell.

'Even after everything that's happened I still care about her. I thought he was calling out of a sense of respect for my history with Lisa. But when I asked if I could see her he said she doesn't want anyone to know. He swore me to secrecy and said they are planning to tell Rex and Ava when they get back from their honeymoon. It's crazy.'

'Some people like to deal with illness on their own so it doesn't define their life. I see it at work all the time,' I try to reassure him.

'It's worse than that,' says Barney. 'She's got involved with this organization that claims you can cure cancer with juicing and coffee enemas. It's completely crazy. She has a healer who has basically insinuated himself into every area of her life. He's the reason they're going to Mexico on their honeymoon, and he's even going to the wedding.'

I'm totally floored. We've all lost patients to the secret powers of alternative therapy but I can't believe that someone as intelligent as Lisa could fall prey to a quack.

'So what medical treatment is she having?' I ask.

'None. Apparently this guy has made her think that she got cancer because of all the negative energy around the start of their relationship.'

'So why didn't we get ill?' I ask. 'Or Nick?'

'He says it's impossible to reason with her. Gregorio has got into her head and she doesn't even leave the house unless he's approved the decision. He wanted my advice on how to persuade her to go back to the oncologist. He asked me how I got her to do things that she didn't want to do when we were married.'

'So what did you recommend?'

'I told him you were the only person Lisa ever listened to.'

The barman comes over and tells us he's closing up. I look around and see the chairs on all the other tables have been upended and we are the last people there. We go outside on to the pavement and stand shivering by the door, neither of us sure how to disentangle ourselves from the evening.

'I'm sorry I never responded to your messages,' I say.

'I understood. I understand. It was probably for the best.'

'I felt too fragile.'

'It was a smart decision. I would probably have done something stupid and regrettable. I liked the symmetry of a revenge shag. I even thought about it when I came round that evening.'

We start walking down the street towards the tube. He has the same slightly shuffling gait. Our elbows nudge each other as we fall into step.

'So what's been your worst date?' he asks.

I think for a moment.

'There was a guy who wanted me to pee on him.'

'I don't understand why people aren't up front about their kinks,' says Barney. 'It's so unlikely that you would accidentally match with someone who happens to be into the same thing.'

'It's a bit public to confess to something so niche, isn't it? Someone you know might see you. It's not exactly like playing the ukulele.'

Barney laughs. 'So how did you get out of it?'

'I told him very politely that, contrary to popular opinion, urine isn't sterile and while bacteria are healthy for your own biological ecosystem they aren't necessarily meant to be shared with others.'

'He might have thought you were doing role play as a doctor.'

'What about you?'

'A woman was sick going down on me. I had to wash my pubic hair with shampoo for a week afterwards to get it back into peak condition. But my friend had his car stolen, which is worse.'

We've reached the bus stop.

'Do you want to come back to mine for another tonic water?' Barney suggests. 'I promise I won't ask you to piss on me.'

I set off before first light to avoid awkward questions from Daisy about where I've been or where I'm going and reach Norfolk as dawn is breaking. The veil of fog that swaddles me for most of the journey lifts as I reach the coast to reveal frost-bleached hedgerows and sugar beet that stand as stiff as meringues. It is a landscape imprinted on me since childhood and its familiarity encourages me to keep faith with the decision I made in the early hours of the morning.

For the umpteenth time I feel for my bag on the passenger seat to check the manila envelope is still there. The letter inside has been folded and unfolded so many times that the ink has faded on the creases and there are words missing. I don't know why I've brought it with me because I can recite it word for word. But like a talisman it quells my nerves and strengthens my resolve.

On the other side of the sugar-beet field, I catch sight of Winterton Beach. The sea is a hyperactive froth of cross-currents and eddies. I open the car window to hear its roar, remembering how Daisy used to wake up in the night begging us to turn down the volume of the waves and Nick would lie beside her with his hands over her ears until she went back to sleep.

The summer after Daisy and Ava were born Lisa and I came to this beach every day for six weeks. We breastfed our babies and swam in the sea as part of what Lisa dubbed The Scorched Nipple Policy. Rex was just three and we helped him construct ambitious marine zoos with seaweed walls to contain crabs and tiny molluscs he found in rock pools. We read trashy magazines and giggled over their advice for getting rid of pregnancy bellies and kick-starting post-partum sex so our husbands didn't stray. *Why do they assume men stray and women don't?* Lisa would ask in outrage.

She bought half-bottles of Prosecco and we invented ever more absurd excuses to celebrate – me squeezing into my pre-pregnancy jeans, Daisy learning to sit up on her own, Lisa getting chatted up by the lifeguard. Mum was still alive and only too happy to help cook and wash clothes while we wallowed in our new babies. Truly, it was one of the happiest periods of my life.

As I drive through the gate where Barney clipped the wing mirror of our car, to park outside my old home, the memories come in waves, buffeting me so relentlessly that I feel almost seasick. I try to float across them like Daisy learnt to drift over her thoughts. I see the garden shed and recall my dad, who died when I was seven, sitting in a green-and-white striped deck chair, listening to cricket and shouting out scores to Mum, as she pricked out vegetables at the table. And I remember the last meal we ate at that table, the day the ladybird epidemic ended, and how everything felt louder, brighter and edgier than it should, for reasons I never really understood.

It is eight years and six months since I was last here. I walk slowly towards the front door, sniffing the air like a dog recognizing its old hunting ground, and lick my lips, knowing they will taste of salt. I turn the door handle and find it isn't locked. Losing this house was a self-inflicted wound. I was the one who suggested to Nick that he keep it in exchange for our home in Putney, to reduce the upheaval for Daisy and Max, and he readily agreed. He was hyper-emollient in those early days, alert to any opportunity to build bridges with his children. The fug of lust had clouded his judgement and he hadn't realized how Daisy and Max would view his departure as a double betrayal. For a long while they refused to see him and it took months before I could persuade them to spend a weekend with him and Lisa.

It was the right decision, given what happened to Daisy later that spring. She went back to school in April after Nick left but she didn't stand a chance. She was exhausted all the time so I took her to the doctor and he thought she might have glandular fever. When tests came back negative he wondered if she had an eating disorder. She had lost a lot of weight and spent mealtimes fiddling with her food rather than eating. But the weeping sores on her collar bones were more indicative of self-harm.

She had terrible dark thoughts about something bad happening to me and often I sat up with her until the early hours of the morning so she could share what was going on in her head. A couple of times I caught her wandering around the house in the middle of the night, turning lights on and off and opening and shutting kitchen drawers. I would beg her to stop, and when she couldn't I sat at the kitchen table sobbing while she counted the knives, over and over again, just so she wasn't alone. Max could have coped with moving house, but not Daisy.

I cautiously push open the door and stand on the threshold, staring into the hallway, nervously turning the manila envelope in my hands. Lisa's familiar spotty wellington boots and Nick's old walking shoes take centre stage in the space where the old fireplace once stood, and their coats and jackets hang on pegs. For a split second I'm puzzled why Lisa's belongings have replaced my own. This lurching adjustment used to occur a lot the first couple of years after Nick left me, especially when I woke up in the morning. Then I remember.

I wonder what my mum would have thought of how things turned out. She adored Lisa for the same reasons the rest of us did: she never allowed her shitty childhood to undermine her optimism and zest for life. She had this ability to transform dull days into something memorable and create fun from the least promising circumstances. I remember Nick seeing her, the morning after his magic mushroom experience. Lisa came over with Barney, and as she stood in Nick's kitchen bathed in the early-morning sun, he started worrying he was tripping again because everything about her was so radiant. It occurs to me now that maybe I had lost him to her before he even belonged to me. Mum always warned me to watch out for her ruthless streak. 'What Lisa wants, Lisa gets, no matter who she tramples along the way,' she always used to say. 'She's a survivor.' But I never dreamt I would be the one who ended up being trampled.

It is eerily quiet. I know that Nick is in London today, because he is buying Max a suit for the wedding, and that Ava lands tomorrow. So this is my only opportunity to see Lisa alone until she gets back from Mexico – and from what Barney said, by then it could be too late.

I walk through the hall. I can't resist poking my head round the door on the right that leads into the dining room used by my parents at Easter and Christmas. It has been transformed into a sitting room with a large L-shaped sofa in front of an inglenook fireplace that must have been hiding behind the ugly electric fire.

I head into the kitchen and the big revelation is a modern-looking conservatory where the washroom and back wall used to be. My eye is immediately drawn to the views down through the garden to the cliff and the beach beyond. There is a new gate that leads straight into 'The Wild', as Max used to refer to the scrubland betwixt land and sea. Lisa has done all this so much better than I ever could.

A collage of photos hangs on the wall beside the fridge

and I go over to take a look. There are pictures of Lisa and Nick on holiday, sometimes together, sometimes with friends, including a couple I see regularly who have never mentioned they still see them. I admire their diplomatic skills. There is a picture of Nick on a camel, staring into the middle distance with a strange intent look that I recognize but don't miss. The shelf on the left is full of self-help books: *The Spiritual Power Of Empathy*, *The Complete Crystal Bible*, *How To See, Hear And Feel Your Angels*. It makes me smile to think of the effect their presence must have on Nick.

'Hello, old friend.'

I jump. The voice is so familiar but it has a desiccated quality that I recognize from my patients. I look in the direction that it has come from. All I can see is the back of a huge cane recliner. The joke used to be that Lisa always had to get in the first word. She speaks in a calm, measured tone that makes it sound as if she has been expecting me, even though I have turned up unannounced. I walk towards the bed and find her propped up by an arc of cushions.

'I was beginning to think you wouldn't come.'

I'm glad she's spoken first because it gives me time to recover from the shock of her appearance. Her face is hollow, her cheeks pale, and her eyes are sunken, although their cat-like shape and vivid green colour are unnervingly the same. She has put lipstick on, and for all that it highlights her beautifully shaped lips, the contrast with her skin tone is too severe. She's wearing a sweater but it hangs off her like a child in oversized school uniform on the first day of term. There's a half-finished glass of green sludge on the table beside her that resembles pondweed.

'I know I look like shit. You don't have to pretend.'

'That's because you're drinking shit,' I joke.

She laughs weakly.

I hadn't really planned how to greet her. So my reaction is an instinctive one; I sit down beside her on the edge of the bed, careful not to make the mattress bounce in case her back is sore, and lean over and hug her gently. She's as bony as a chicken carcass.

'Don't worry, I'm not breakable,' she smiles. She hugs me back but there's no strength to it.

'The house looks great. You've done such a good job.'

'How do you always look for the best in people, Rosie?'

'It makes life easier,' I shrug. I cradle her hand with my own as if I'm holding a baby bird.

'You always knew the right way to behave in any situation,' Lisa says, squeezing my fingers. 'Whenever I'm unsure what I should do I try to imagine how you would handle the same situation. I was a better person when I had you as a friend.'

'I'm not here to talk about the past,' I say firmly. This is one of the few lines I have rehearsed. Barney's best piece of advice was to take the emotion out of the situation by viewing Lisa as a patient rather than a friend. 'We've all moved on. Truly.'

'Having cancer is like time travel. There's so much time to think and I go backwards and forwards, pondering everything that has happened and all the possible scenarios to come. I only get time off when I'm asleep. So I've been thinking a lot about the consequences of my behaviour towards you and my monumental selfishness.'

'It wasn't just your responsibility. It was Nick's too,' I remind her. 'We all have the right to happiness.'

'Not if so many other people pay such a heavy price. I'm so sorry, Rosie, for everything that was lost. I'm sorry for all the deceit and lies and the way it affected our children, especially Daisy, and the way I made her so ill. Most of all I'm sorry for the loss of our friendship.' She slumps back into the cushions.

I have waited seven years for Lisa to say something like this. Although I don't respond the cynic in me wonders if she has rehearsed these words with Gregorio because, surely, some of the content of the letter was his idea. But as she struggles to speak it dawns on me that the person she is apologizing to is not the same person who was wronged years earlier. It is a strangely liberating discovery. I realize I no longer wish the past could be different, and while I don't believe in the power of forgiveness because of its religious connotations, I do believe in the freedom of forgetting.

'It's fine. Really.' And it is.

Lisa's body relaxes. Her hand feels cold so I pull the rug up to her chest and tuck it in around her.

'I'm like an old lady,' she smiles.

'How are you feeling?'

'Better than I was.'

'I should have brought you Prosecco and lifeguards.'

'Is that what you usually prescribe for your patients?' she asks.

'It's as likely to work as the regime you are following,' I say dryly. 'And it would be a lot more pleasurable.'

She doesn't ask how I know, although anyone could guess from the piles of fruit and vegetables everywhere and the dirty juicing paraphernalia, not to mention the jars of murky coffee.

'My healer, Gregorio, has a holistic approach to deal with the symptoms and the cause of the illness,' Lisa says. But she hesitates like someone speaking a foreign language.

'Have you spoken to other people he has cured?'

'He's shown me testimonies.'

'It's all anecdotal, Lisa. When we do a trial we recruit thousands of people to get the most accurate results. It takes years and years, and then it has to be rigorously investigated and replicated by the scientific community to make sure it is a true result. Even when patients start medication we share information about their progress with their GP, nurses and all the members of my team, to make sure we all agree that we are giving them the best possible chance.'

'He's helping me deal with the guilt.'

'You didn't get ill because you went off with Nick,' I say gently.

'And what I did to Daisy?'

'Daisy is fine now.'

I explain to her about the clinical trial I am running and how a last-minute space has opened up, I tell her that the oncologist she saw in Norwich can refer her to me and she could start immunotherapy treatment within the next three weeks. I try to keep my voice calm and steady as I explain the basic science behind the treatment. But I also mention that she won't lose her hair.

'You know me too well,' she smiles, her wispy papery skin wrinkling around her eyes.

'You'll need to get some blood tests done before you go on your honeymoon but we can arrange for the results to be sent to me from Norwich. The oncologist who saw you is a good friend. He's a lovely guy. He'll help sort out the paperwork.'

I check the time. Nick will be here soon and I don't want to cross paths with him. I urge her to consider my proposition and let me know her decision before the end of the week. Neither of us speaks for a while. We both look out of the window, staring at a landscape almost devoid of content. I wish we could swim in the sea together one last time.

'You would do this for me after everything I did to you?' she asks.

I nod.

She doesn't cry. She's never been the self-pitying type.

'Everyone is entitled to a chance. You're no different. Don't let Gregorio make you think you deserve less than this.'

I ask Lisa if there is anything she needs before I leave and reluctantly pour her another glass of sludge.

'Rosie. Before you go, there's something I have to tell you.'

The words are lifted from her letter. I had assumed this promise of intimacy was no more than bait to lure me here because it so closely mimicked the dynamic of our friendship. From the moment we met as sixteen-year-olds it was tacitly agreed Lisa always had the best secrets and it was my privilege that she chose to share them with me.

When we drifted apart, after she gave birth to Rex and I was still studying at Leeds, she used this exact phrase when she got back in touch after fourteen months of radio silence.

Lisa must sense my reticence. She awkwardly shuffles to the edge of the wicker recliner, chewing her lower lip with the effort, and pulls herself upright. She puts her hand on my shoulder.

'I get so light-headed,' she says wheezily.

'It's your diet, not the illness,' I say. 'You're sodium deficient. We can sort that out too.'

Now that she is standing up I can see how brittle she is. Her thighs are probably the same circumference as my calves. I walk close behind her as she heads towards the kitchen table so that I can catch her if she falls.

'I'm not asking for your sympathy, because it's what I deserve.' She passes me an iPad. 'Nick is up to his old tricks.'

I look at the screen. It is full of photos. The first dozen are all the same girl dressed in a T-shirt with spaghetti straps brushing her short brown hair. It's a strangely intimate scene. At first the pictures have an intrusive quality, as if she is being photographed unawares, but as I scroll along she turns to the camera and smiles. I would guess she is older than Daisy, perhaps late twenties. It's difficult to tell. More photos of the same girl follow. This time she stands behind a shop counter. Lisa gives a running commentary.

'Nick isn't good in stressful situations. He likes all the attention to be on him. And cancer is like a jealous lover. It never leaves you alone,' she says.

'Where did you get these?' I ask, still puzzled about their relevance.

'He's a middle-aged man. He doesn't understand that we share the same iCloud account. He's obsessed with this girl.'

She scrolls through more pages and there are pictures of the girl with one arm around Nick's neck and the other inside his shirt. I feel like a dirty voyeur.

'Why are you showing these to me?'

'I want you to understand that, whatever I decide, it has nothing to do with you. I know you will see it as a personal failing if you can't change the course of history here. But I'm finding my own way through all this, like you had to.'

As I leave the house I get a text message from Barney.

No more becoming strangers.

17

Daisy

It's Dad's wedding today and I'm back in my old bedroom in the attic of the Norfolk house. It has been reincarnated as Lisa's yoga studio and apart from the view from the window overlooking the sea there's nothing to remind me of how it used to be – which is good, because otherwise I might be engulfed by all the memories.

I just have to get through the next couple of days and then everything will get easier. I have said these words so many times over the past week that I've decided they deserve to be officially annexed to the end of my special incantation. Although, strictly speaking, they should be copyrighted to Max because they were his promise to me after I finally blurted out what happened all those years ago.

I hadn't planned on telling Max. I guess I was desperate for him to understand why I was so worried about Lisa seeing Mum and the effect it would have on her to realize for the first time that Dad had been having an affair with Lisa for months. But mostly it was a panicked reaction to the feeling that Max is pulling away from me. Unusually, he didn't interrupt once, except at the very end, as we reached the front door. *I'm so sorry, I'm so sorry,* he said, over and over again, until he started to remind me of me.

His face did that corrugated expression that I recognized from our childhood when he was trying to stop himself from crying.

I was about to give him a hug when he suddenly lifted his arm and smashed his fist so hard into the wall that I thought he'd broken his knuckle. I don't know what was more shocking: the way blood started to seep out of his hand, or his anger. He did it again. I grabbed his arm. *Fuck medicine. Fuck Dad. Fuck Lisa!* he yelled. Max has never been an angry person. But if this was his reaction to what I'd told him about Dad and Lisa, I was right to be worried about Mum's. I persuaded him to come into the house so I could bandage his hand but really I didn't want him to leave until he had calmed down. For the first time in my life I was scared of my little brother.

The walls of my old bedroom are now covered with mirrors so it feels as if I'm under surveillance from myself. A statue of Buddha sits beneath the window, mocking me with his serene half-smile, and there is a futon where one of the bunk beds once stood. The wallpaper has been painted over in grey, but when I put out my hand I can feel the triangle of marks from the last time I was here. I close my eyes and read them like Braille, waiting for the urge to make patterns. But the anxiety has subsided since Dad let slip shortly after we arrived this morning that he and Lisa are going on honeymoon to Mexico for a month.

'Four whole weeks!' I said ecstatically, compensating for his apparent lack of enthusiasm.

Dad shot me a suspicious look. He probably thought it was another example of me being contrary but I was genuinely pleased, because while they're away I should get some proper time off from the thoughts. I felt so good that I took a mug of tea from Lisa without even worrying that the fact she had touched it might trigger the obsessions. I wish Max had been in the kitchen to witness my progress but he had disappeared to check on Connie, who had taken to her bed with a migraine shortly after we got here.

Max is being so spiky. It's like I lit the flame of hatred in him. He's furious with Dad and Lisa. But there's also the effort of trying to please a girl who doesn't want to be pleased. I don't think Dad notices anything. He's too busy arguing with the spiritual healer about where the wedding should take place, with Lisa over her juicing diet and with Max over his refusal to wear the suit he bought him. I see the vein in his temple throbbing when he presses the lid of the juicer. He's even angry with the curly kale. He's never been good under pressure.

I sit on the futon bed and get out the diary that Geeta has instructed me to fill in each day until my appointment. I list the obsessions – same old, same old – and add up how many hours I have spent on each compulsion the past couple of days, noting that although things haven't got much better, equally they haven't got any worse. Flatlining gives me a glimmer of hope, because there's something to build on.

I decide to do one of the exposure and response prevention exercises. This means I have to think about one of my obsessions and then see if I can resist doing the rituals for fifteen minutes. Under Obsession I write: *'Thinking something bad will happen to Mum.'* I look at my list of how to fight back and focus on number nine. *'Let the thoughts pass without acting on them and their strength will weaken. The more you practise the easier it will become.'*

I set the timer on my phone. I'm glad I've got this room to myself. It was bad enough spending two hours on the train with Max and Connie, pretending that I had a bad stomach so I could lock myself in the toilet to run through my stuff without any interruptions. For once I was grateful for the thoughts, because I can't bear how Max is so in thrall to her. He behaves like an over-eager puppy and I can tell she finds the devotion irritating. Why on earth would he bring a Tinder date to Dad's wedding? Maybe he should do some of my exposure and response prevention exercises to reduce *his* obsession. Except then he'd realize I'm seeing Geeta again. I haven't told him, because he's made it pretty clear he wants nothing to do with my illness.

While I'm waiting for the alarm to go off I decide to distract myself by checking out the cupboard on the left of the fireplace where we used to store our clothes. Yoga mats in pastel colours fill the lower shelves but those above waist level are stacked with boxes containing our old toys and books. All our childhood holiday memories are bundled into this cupboard. I decide to do a forensic inventory of the contents – in case there's something I want to take back to London with me – and start removing boxes and lining them up on the floor.

I find Max's dinosaur figures; my entire collection of Sylvanian badgers; a box of books by Dr Seuss that Max and I read obsessively; and even the containers with the dead ladybirds from last time we were here. I pull out *Did I Ever Tell You How Lucky You Are?*, smiling as I remember how I used to make Max copy out the words of this story, over and over again, and the expression of nervous intent on his face as he desperately tried to get it right. He always pressed so hard with his pencil that he broke the lead. I skim-read the story again and it occurs to me that the Hawtch-Hawtcher watching the Watch-Watcher watching the bee probably has OCD. I recall other childhood preoccupations: the way I couldn't get into bed until I had flattened the sheets; how I forced Mum to say 'I love you as wide as the biggest ocean and as tall as the tallest tree' before I went to sleep; and how I had to have three cuddly toys in bed with me at all times. I have always been a worrywart. This is a breakthrough, but I don't have time to process its ramifications because someone bursts through the door without knocking.

'Small!'

I jump and the book slips through my fingers. It's years since anyone has called me that. Rex strides towards me open-armed, dressed in an oversized stripy hand-knitted jumper and threadbare jeans. I stand up to greet him but he stops in his tracks.

'Fish in a tree,' he says in mock alarm, using a phrase poached from Dr Seuss. 'You're the same height as me.' He has filled out so he properly inhabits his once rangy body and his curly hair is thicker and wilder than ever, but he's unmistakably Rex. 'It would be difficult to do a crocodile roll with you now.'

I'm surprised he remembers. That summer seems like ancient history. We meet in the middle of the room and hug clumsily. I quickly disentangle and step backwards a couple of paces.

'Do you speak?' he asks.

'Sorry,' I say. 'It's been almost eight years.'

'Since you last spoke?' he teases. 'I've never had that effect on a girl. I'll take it as a compliment.'

The heat rises in my face and I feel like the shy girl who used to do exercises to get rid of my fat knees and stomach wrinkles in the hope that Rex would notice me. I even find myself sucking in my tummy.

He smiles, as if he understands everything, but of course he knows nothing.

'How was your journey?' I ask, fumbling for a question that gives me more time to scan his face. It's disconcertingly familiar, apart from a long scar across the top of his left cheekbone. I try not to stare but then worry that I've spent too much time looking at his lips, which are the same shape as his mother's, reminding me of what I saw in the dunes, so I look away. I try to imagine what Max would say. He always has a good selection of facts to fill a vacuum.

'It involved a boat, four different trains and a bus. It would have taken me less time to go and see Ava in the States.'

'Boat?'

'Ferry, to be precise. I'm living on an island off the coast of Scotland trying to work out what to do with my life. It's a longer project than anticipated. I've already been there for three years and there hasn't been much progress.' He gives a quick smile.

He's much less sure of himself than I remember. But I can't work out if that's because his dreams have shrunk or because I'm less in awe of him.

'What do you do?'

'During the day I'm a part-time tree surgeon who suffers from vertigo, and in the evening I work in a local pub – even though I don't drink. Not after what happened to Dad.'

'That's a lot of contradictions.'

'They say it's best to confront your fears.'

'They do.' My responses are getting more and more inadequate.

'That's why we're all here, isn't it?' He gives a wicked grin.

'I guess,' I reply, although I hadn't thought of it this way and can't tell if he's being serious. It was always difficult to tell when Rex was joking.

'Aren't you going to ask what happened?' He reaches out for my hand and presses my fingertips to the scar on his cheekbone.

I run my index finger along its outer edge and it feels cold and gristly like bacon rind. 'How many stitches?'

'Nine.'

Good number. The alarm goes off on my phone. The fifteen minutes are up. I pull away from him and walk over to the bed to turn it off.

'Sorry.' I apologize.

'You still say sorry too much, Small. But I find your consistency reassuring.'

I realize that a quarter of an hour has passed without me even thinking about whether I need to thump my shoulders, tap my feet or check the curtains (except I would have to adjust that part of the routine because Lisa has replaced them with a blind). Rex is at my side. I see him eyeing the papers on the bed and I sit down on the futon to gather them up. I don't want to talk to him about what happened to me. It's not that I don't want him to know, it's more that I'm relishing this small break from the thoughts.

'So why do you think they're getting married after all this time, Small?' Rex asks as he sits down beside me.

The bed is so low and his legs so long that his knees and head are on the same latitude. There's a pinch of bitterness in his tone. He obviously has no idea that his mother is ill, which makes me feel bad that I do.

'They don't exactly epitomize the running brook, singing their melody to the night, do they? They're pretty tense.'

'What's with the poetry?'

'It's a quote from the reading we're meant to be doing,' he says.

'I haven't looked at it.'

'Me neither.'

'And what's with the pigmy hippy and the endless juicing? Mum looks so gaunt.'

He doesn't wait for an answer. I remember how he always liked to range across subjects, hurtling from one idea to the next before returning to the beginning.

'I wasn't going to come. I'm only here because I wanted to see you and Max. I've missed you guys. Sometimes I think that holiday in Norfolk was the last time I felt truly free. Ava's like Mum, she specializes in reinvention. But I was never any good at new beginnings. I almost drowned in all the endings. Although at least it wasn't at the bottom of a bottle of whisky, like Dad.' He stares at his feet as he speaks and hooks his arms around his knees.

346

'There was too much bad history,' I say.

'Not between us.'

Either he's forgotten or he doesn't comprehend what he did to me when he didn't turn up that day. I can't work out if he's being provocative or emollient, or simply never realized how painful it was to feel so abandoned by him.

'You and Ava disappeared into thin air.'

'After we moved to Haggerston I never went back to school. Someone had to be with Dad all the time. Even when I popped out to buy milk, I didn't know what I was going to find when I got home.'

'That must have been so scary.'

'Off the scale. Eventually he got sober, but it stays with you. Now it's not so much the fear that he'll relapse, more that I could end up like him.'

'We're not condemned to repeat the mistakes of our parents,' I smile.

'Let's drink to that.' He raises an imaginary glass in the air and laughs, but it catches in his throat.

I look at him in the mirror. His eyes have a faraway look. It feels shameful to tell him that I probably understand his anxiety better than anyone when his fears were grounded in reality, while mine are make-believe, like scary fairy tales you tell children to get them to behave. One of the worst things about OCD is its irrational toddler logic.

He keeps talking.

'One time I went into the sitting room and found him lying on the sofa in a pool of blood. His eyes were open and he was staring at the television. It was *Jools Holland*, and The Divine Comedy were playing. Blood was pouring out of his nose like a geyser. I tried to sit him up but he pushed me away and I fell sideways on to the glass coffee table.' He strokes the scar on his cheek. 'I held him until the ambulance came. I got it into my head that if I let go he'd die. I couldn't find the television controls and the music was playing really loud. My blood soaked into his T-shirt, and his into mine, until you couldn't tell who was hurt. Dad can't remember any of it. Nothing.' He shrugs.

I put my arm around him and he leans into me. His wool jumper scratches my arm. We sit there in complete silence, like survivors of a natural disaster. I've never felt so close to anyone in my entire life. Not even Max.

'Where was Ava?'

'On a school trip. I tried to protect her from the worst. We didn't tell anyone how bad it all was in case they took Dad away from us. That was my biggest fear. He'd lost everything else by that point, so it would have killed him if we'd gone to live with Mum and your dad.'

'At least you did the right thing.'

'I did the right thing for Dad, but maybe it wasn't the right thing for me. But one thing I've learnt is that life isn't about doing the right thing. It's about not doing the wrong thing.'

He rests his head on his knees as if it is too heavy to hold up. His left hand sits on the bed beside me. I touch it with my finger. It feels dry and calloused like a rocky outcrop.

'Tree surgeon's hands,' he explains.

I leave my hand on top of his and remember how I used to write his name in tiny letters in my homework diary, and stalk him on Facebook, and try to invent

348

sentences in essays where the first three words began with the letters of his name. And even though I would like to stay like this forever, because the sense of connection is so intense, I realize this is more likely the goodbye that we were denied before.

'Shall we go and join the freak show down in the kitchen?' Rex suggests when he eventually lifts his head.

This makes me laugh because it's so true. We're a motley crew. Apart from our dysfunctional family, and crazy Gregorio, there's a couple I have never met before called Rowena and Hamish. I felt an immediate bond with Hamish, because I can tell from the way he can't sit still and paces up and down the kitchen that he's a fellow worrier. I even saw what Geeta used to call 'the patron saint of panic attacks' – a brown paper bag – in his jacket pocket.

'I can only do short bursts,' I warn.

'Me too. Although I've finally found something in common with your dad,' Rex says as we go down the stairs.

The old stair carpet in different shades of mud has disappeared and instead there are painted floorboards, which act as a tannoy, announcing everyone's comings and goings.

He lowers his voice. 'I think I want to kill Gregorio.'

'For a spiritual healer he inspires a lot of hatred,' I giggle.

'Ava thinks he's great but I think he's full of shit,' whispers Rex.

'He can't be full of shit after all those enemas,' I say.

'I have learnt one thing from him,' says Rex.

I cock my head quizzically as we push open the kitchen door.

'I would say, as a good rule of thumb, it's best not to offer someone an enema within the first fifteen minutes of meeting them.'

'What do you think is an acceptable amount of time?' I ask.

'Forty-five years?' Rex suggests.

I quickly divide the number by three, but there's no emotion attached to the calculation, even when the result is one of my favourite numbers. It's more like remembering an old friend. Giggling with Rex, like the person I used to be, I head into the kitchen and see Ava for the first time. I remember how still she was when she was taken away from school in the ambulance and wonder if she is thinking the same thing – except of course she can't be, because she was unconscious at the time.

She stands cool and poised. She's wearing a denim miniskirt and crop top but even though she looks like a waitress, and I'm wearing a new dress, she still manages to make me feel immediately frumpy.

I'm embarrassed rather than nervous to see her, because my life has stood so still while hers has expanded so much that she's moved to the States where she has a job working for a music production company and a live-in boyfriend who apparently looks like Kurt Cobain. At least this is what Dad said. I have no idea what Kurt Cobain looks like. She is gracious, with a haughty manner that could be construed as patronizing.

'Daisy, how lovely to see you again.' She kisses me on both cheeks in a friendly godmother doing her annual duty call kind of way. I want to remind her that before she unfriended me from her life we used to practise French kissing on peaches, share Facebook passwords and compete over who knew the most trivia about Justin Bieber.

'I'm about to make tea, would you like one?' I offer as I switch on the kettle.

'Not after what happened last time I accepted a drink from you,' jokes Ava.

I feel myself blush.

'So what happened?' asks Hamish in his nervy staccato voice from the opposite side of the kitchen table. He pulls at the gold trim of his velvet waistcoat with one hand while the other runs through his hair until it stands on end. 'Would you like to share with the rest of us?' He speaks like someone pickled in group therapy. He's probably the oldest person here, but he has an unworldly innocence that makes it impossible to hold anything against him. Rowena slaps his hand to stop him from picking at the trimming but he immediately starts shredding the skin around his nails instead.

'Just jokes, Daisy,' says Ava, ignoring him.

This is the phrase she used when the headmaster got both of us in his office to try and get to the bottom of what had happened that evening. It's an echo of our former life and for a moment the rest of the room recedes. I see Lisa at the end of the table, drinking juice, with Dad on one side and on the other, Gregorio, tiny and shrivelled like a walnut.

I turn my back on everyone to face the kitchen cupboards and switch on the kettle. I am once again the teenager who was abandoned in the park by people I wrongly assumed to be my friends. Although everyone made a fuss about the Facebook page they set up afterwards with pictures of me exploding from my Halloween costume, like a tomato bursting its skin, and the comments about my blubber, I have never felt more alone than that moment when I discovered that I was by myself in the wood. When I stepped out from behind the tree all I had left were the thoughts.

I wonder if Ava has told her boyfriend what she did. Dad always says that everyone re-constructs memories to favour themselves. I've even overheard him describing how he saved Lisa from a dysfunctional relationship with an aggressive alcoholic. I am pouring boiling water into the mug. It spills over the edge to form a small steaming pool on the kitchen worktop but my reactions are sluggish. Suddenly Dad is beside me. He prises the kettle out of my hand and, before I have a chance to resist, presses me to him like he used to when I was little. I remember how I used to put my feet on his to dance a slow waltz around the kitchen. As we cling to each other I hope that Dad and Lisa's happiness outweighs the misery they caused the rest of us.

Max comes into the kitchen. There's a wild, dark look in his eyes. Connie isn't with him. He asks for painkillers.

'Mum is strong and healthy and will live a long and happy life,' Dad says, patting my back.

I understand he's trying to be comforting but it's weird hearing him recite my special words when he's never done it before.

'Can we get this show on the road, please?' barks Max impatiently. 'Connie's not feeling great.'

'Come on, let's do this, people,' says Gregorio, getting up from the table and clapping his hands so all our attention turns to him.

Of course Gregorio has won the argument about where the actual ceremony should take place. After spending yesterday scouting for locations he declares the most auspicious setting to be the flat roof of the bunker in the dunes, which is so brilliant in its inappropriateness that I almost have begrudging respect for his flawed intuition. He mistakes the awed silence around the table for reverence and bows his head. I can't understand how someone as rational as Dad has allowed this man to worm his way into his life.

'I'm wondering if the garden might be better?' Dad nervously intervenes. 'It's pretty cold out there. What do you think, Lisa? Perhaps beneath the magnolia we planted together?'

'Actually, Mum planted that tree,' Max growls.

'Don't throw shade on The Big Day, Maxi,' says Ava. She feeds off tension like those fish on the ocean bed.

'I think Gregorio knows what he's doing,' Lisa says smoothly, sealing the deal. That's Lisa's way.

'The negative ions from the ocean will fill us with positive energy and the six sides of the pillbox represent enlightenment,' says Gregorio enthusiastically. 'And I've already built a sacred circle from shells. We won't find anywhere with the same spiritual energy.'

I should show him the research paper that Geeta gave me, proving there's no scientific evidence that some numbers are luckier than others, but he's too busy explaining to Lisa how the sacred circle represents eternity. I'm slack-jawed at his capacity to promise immortality to a woman dying of cancer. It makes my warped logic about protecting Mum with my routines seem practically scientific by comparison. For a moment I almost feel sorry for Dad.

'That's perfect,' says Lisa dreamily as she wafts away from the table. She wraps a pale-pink shawl around her long-sleeved cream wedding dress. With her pale skin and wilted gestures she resembles a beautiful faded rose. Dad reaches out to put his arm around her but she slides through his fingers. She's so thin that the biggest risk on the beach is she might get blown away in the breeze.

'You look lovely, Mum,' says Rex.

She really does.

'Shall we head out together, Maxi?' suggests Ava in her syrupy tone. 'Like old times?'

I realize how much we were all relying on Max to see us through this. Although he's younger than the rest of us he's always been the linchpin. But he's even more on edge than me.

'If you're sure we're going right now, I'll fetch Connie,' he tells Ava.

Gregorio stands up. He's wearing long, flowing white and purple robes with huge sleeves and has painted weird hieroglyphics on his arms.

'I didn't realize we had to come as extras from *Life of Brian*,' Rex jokes.

Hamish starts muttering something about the Knights of Ni and how they should have bought Dad and Lisa a shrubbery as a present and looks all hangdog when

Gregorio accuses him of belittling the spirituality of the occasion.

When Max returns with Connie we head outside. I don't understand why she agreed to come when she clearly wants to be here even less than the rest of us. We troop through the back garden, past the shed towards the gate that leads to The Wild. Crocuses and daffodils poke their heads through the soil and a warbler serenades us with his soulful song. I'm uplifted by the way I notice all this because not only does it mean I'm living less in my head but it shows I've learnt to look for the signals that might help me repair the broken part of my brain.

It's warm for March. Dad always says it gets hotter every year. But this year he's right. The weather is one of his specialist subjects when conversation between us flags. The sky is cobalt blue, the spring sun hangs low and defiant, and it's difficult not to feel the promise of summer in the air. Even at my sickest, the sun could force my obsessions into the shade. Rex and I are at the front of the pack and we gradually pick up pace until the rest of the group is well behind us. The last words we hear Gregorio utter involve instructing Dad and Lisa to face east during the ceremony because the sun represents their new beginning.

'Does he ever stop?' asks Rex.

The dunes lie ahead. They seem bigger than when I was last here. I spot the white lozenge-shaped roof of the pillbox right away because it's the same one I see in my dreams. Rex effortlessly starts to scramble up the sandy knoll and I can't help wondering if this is how it would have been if he had turned up all those years ago. I can't get any purchase in my slippery-soled shoes so he waits for me, sticking out his arm to haul me up like a stubborn donkey through the deep sand. As we get higher our legs sink up to our calves, slowing our progress to the summit. I grab on to the marram grass for support and wince as it cuts my hands.

At the top we stop to catch our breath and survey the landscape around us. The North Sea is on one side and Mum's house on the other. I'll always think of it as her house. Thinking about Mum being alone reminds me that I've fallen behind with my routines. As Rex circles to take a panoramic shot on his phone I run through the special words in my head but they are an afterthought, like an insurance policy you've suddenly remembered to renew. There's no emotion attached. For today, at least, I've managed to break the loop. I turn round to check the progress of the rest of our group. We're way ahead of everyone else. Max and Connie are just stick figures in the distance.

Rex takes my hand again and we track across the tallest dune towards the pillbox. It's buried so deep that it looks as though it's being slowly entombed in the sand. Only the top quarter of the arch at the entrance is visible, making it completely impossible to crawl inside. It used to be a challenge to climb up on to the roof but now it's no more than a step up. We jump in and out of Gregorio's shell circle like children, recklessly kicking the cockles out of the way, shouting to make ourselves heard above the noise of the wind and the methodical crash of the waves below. That sound was the soundtrack to our childhood.

'It's like returning to a crime scene,' says Rex breathlessly as we survey the broken circle.

'What do you mean?'

'I used to meet girls here. You guys used to spy on us all the time. Remember?' He looks away shyly but it's more that he's conscious of the absurd gulf between the over-confident seventeen-year-old with the big dreams and the uncertain twenty-six-year-old standing before me now.

'Why didn't you come that day?' I suddenly ask him.

The question hangs in the air. I fix my gaze towards the sea, wondering at the way the horizon looks as though it has been drawn with a ruler. It feels like ancient history, as if I'm asking about something that happened centuries ago when Vikings landed on this beach, but there's a wistful tone that Rex picks up on.

'Which day?'

I turn and search his face for answers but there's that blank look men adopt when they worry a woman is about to make emotional demands they can't respond to. I think back to my thirteen-year-old self, waiting inside the pill-box, and remember how euphoria curdled into despair when Rex didn't arrive. I can still conjure up the dank acid smell inside the pillbox, and recall the pathetic way I played house by burying the rubbish and sweeping the floor with a piece of driftwood. Most of all I remember my anger and distress that Dad and Lisa had robbed me of the role I was meant to be playing. I remember it all in such detail that I wonder if a version of me remains buried inside the pillbox along with my old white knickers.

'I waited so long for you. It felt like a lifetime.'

'You've completely lost me, Small.' Rex turns his head

and narrows one eye, as if he's trying to corral his memories in case he's missed something. 'Nope,' he says finally.

'The two sentences you wrote on that note were pretty specific.'

'What note?'

'The one you left under the lamp beside our bunk bed.'

He shakes his head emphatically. 'I've got no idea what you're talking about. What did it say?'

'It said to meet me here at three p.m.'

The temperature dips a little as the sun slips behind a cloud and I shiver. Rex suggests we take shelter in the basin in the sand until the others arrive. He keeps walking and I follow him. I never imagined that I would return to the spot where I saw Dad and Lisa wrapped around each other, but maybe coming back with Rex appeals to my love of symmetry.

'So what did it say on the other side of this note?'

I wait a beat. The words are still coated in shame. We've reached the hollow in the sand. It's more concave than I remember, hollowed out by the wind over the intervening years. Rex steps down and pulls back the swathes of marram grass as if they're curtains and we step inside.

'You make me hard.'

It's good he's in front of me so I can't see his face, but I feel his grip tighten around my hand.

'For real?'

'Verbatim.'

'I would never have written something like that to a thirteen-year-old. You didn't even have breasts back then, Daisy. No wonder you didn't want to see me for all those years. You must have thought I was a complete pervert.'

'I thought you liked me.'

He hears the unevenness in my voice.

'I did like you. But never in that way. You were like a little sister to me.'

'I'm sorry.'

'Don't say sorry all the time.' He sounds almost irritated. He pauses for a second weighing things up. 'But I was here that day, Small. I spent the whole afternoon with the girl from the caravan site. We always met in the same place. In this hollow in the sand. Maybe you heard us. I hope you couldn't see much. That could have been a little disturbing to someone so young.' He snorts with embarrassment at the memory.

We glance over at the window of the pillbox at exactly the same instant. I frown. It's much further away than I remember. And the angle is slightly offset, so I couldn't have been facing the scene head-on. I realize right away that those close-up shots of Dad and Lisa's face weren't accurate. It wasn't possible to have seen the sweat on her face or the way his trunks wrinkled around his ankles. The realization makes me feel sick, as if I'm the one with vertigo. It dawns on me that it wasn't Dad and Lisa at all. It was Rex and the girl. How could I get this so wrong?

The fragments come back in the wrong order, as if they're on shuffle, so I have no time to absorb one before the next reveals itself. Some of the memories must be reliable: the animal noise, the instructions to fuck harder, stronger, faster. I know this is possible because Ava and Rowena have reached the top of the pillbox and their words are carried to us on the breeze.

I feel breathless as I try to catch up with all the

permutations of this revelation. This isn't what Lisa was planning to tell Mum. It wasn't my failure to perform my rituals that meant that I didn't protect Mum from Lisa. Dad is flawed, but not as malevolent as I had assumed. In fact, no more flawed than the rest of us. Thoughts fly through my head like the wind coming off the sea.

I remember what Dad says about our memories being unreliable and how the point of them is that they help us define how we act next. And I realize that I need to speak to Max and tell him I got it all wrong.

'So if not me then who?' asks Rex.

I've almost forgotten he's here with me. 'What do you mean?'

'If it wasn't me who wrote the note then who was it?'

I think of Max's angry frustration the other night. And I know that it was him.

18

Nick

Black holes are stars that have collapsed under their own gravity. They produce gravitational forces so strong that not even light can escape. This is how I feel as I stand on top of the old World War Two pillbox holding hands with Lisa inside Gregorio's sacred seashell circle. Fortunately Gregorio doesn't stop talking and everyone's too busy trying to fathom out what he's rambling on about to notice that I am trapped at an event horizon, unable to go forwards or backwards. For a minute I wonder if he has cast a spell and turned me to stone.

'May your love be as constant as the never-ending waves that wash up on the shores of human consciousness,' he says loudly, turning to take a deep bow in front of the North Sea, before bending down to scoop up sand in a giant conch. 'Each grain of sand represents a unique decision, event or feeling that helped shape Nick and Lisa. Let's take time to feel our quantum consciousness manifest itself through fractional vibrations of these tiny particles.'

The way he mixes scientific terminology with his quantum bunkum is shameless. I'm riveted by his creepy manicured nails, carefully topiaried hair and beard. He resembles a human bonsai. The thought makes me smile for the first time today. Lisa grins back. I try to focus on her. My eyes move but my body remains stubbornly frozen, even though it's a benignly warm spring day. She looks radiant in her long cream dress. Her hair is pulled off her face and twisted into a bun garlanded with wild flowers that blow in the breeze. And the spring air has brought colour to her cheeks and lips. My gut twists and the wind makes my eyes water but I can't lift my hand to wipe them. Tears pour down my cheeks and I see Rowena and Hamish dab at their eyes with handkerchiefs.

Gregorio continues. I zone out. For once I'm grateful to him for his ability to spout utter nonsense. In fact, I hope he never stops. I have the urge to prostrate myself at his feet, cling on to his robes and ask for redemption. I want to confess to everything and submit to his authority. I want to believe in him like I used to believe in myself. I close my eyes so that I don't have to witness Daisy or Max's bitter indifference any more.

The irony that, after everything we have gone through, my children hate me for what I haven't done, rather than what I have done, isn't lost on me. Maybe it's no less than I deserve. I simply can't account for what Daisy told Max. I'm an expert on how emotion and stress influence the formation of memory. So I understand that sometimes people fictionalize memories to protect themselves from recalling experiences that threaten their beliefs about themselves, or exaggerate a miserable experience to make their fight back seem even more impressive. But the sweet, flirty connection between Lisa and me on the beach that day bears no resemblance to what Max outlined. It's like

Daisy eerily turned my sexual fantasy into her reality. My professional opinion is that she has filled in the narrative gaps with sleights of mind based on what she imagined happened afterwards. The failure of episodic memory to replicate experiences is an adaptive design to create order out of chaos. And Daisy's teenage years were very chaotic.

I wonder how much of the past eight years of her life has been constructed through the prism of this inaccurate memory. It's no coincidence that the OCD really took hold after the holiday in Norfolk. It must have undermined her shaky confidence after Ava dumped her and undoubtedly accounts for some of her hostility towards Lisa and me. I remember the mutilated underwear that I found in the garden shed and how she told Max she gave Ava the spiked water hoping she would die. No wonder she felt so protective towards Rosie.

A few hours ago I thought this injustice, this mangling of fact and fiction, was the worst thing that could ever happen to me. Now I know better. Because since then I have learnt that what Daisy and Max don't know is way worse than what they think they know. God, I've turned into Gregorio, talking in riddles! I'm not a religious man but for a moment I close my eyes and pray for oblivion. My misery is unremitting and all-consuming. As Gregorio might say, I am caught in a cosmic vacuum. I hear someone giggle weakly and realize it's me.

I was sitting beside Lisa on the edge of the cane recliner in the conservatory when Daisy and Max arrived from the train station earlier today. I stood up awkwardly, partly because I was dressed in a suit and tie ready for the ceremony, but also because I hadn't seen or spoken to Max since the other evening. I noticed his left knuckle was now expertly taped up, like a boxer's. I didn't ask any questions. I could feel the force field of his aggression repelling me. I've grown immune to Daisy's barbs over the years but this was something new and therefore more unbearable.

Lisa got up excitedly to welcome them, compensating for my stiffness. The wedding has given her an injection of energy and she has spent the past few days organizing the house with Ava and obsessively doing paperwork. There are vases of lilies everywhere that spook me with their funereal whiteness and heady scent. She has also finally agreed to see the original oncologist before we leave for Mexico. I'm encouraged by this renewed zest for life and the way it suggests Gregorio might be losing sway. I was even quietly confident that if the appointment with the doctor goes well we might cancel the honeymoon in Mexico in favour of a mini-break in the chemotherapy unit in Norwich. For a few days it had felt like getting married was the best decision I had ever made.

I hugged Daisy as long as she would let me and did a round of hollow back-slapping with Max, feeling almost irritated that he could be so angry with me about something that hadn't even happened. Still, I felt grateful to my children for coming at all, and tried not to be hurt that they hadn't bought us a card let alone a present. Lisa immediately herded Daisy and Max deep into the kitchen to show them some old photos that she had dug out during her clean-up.

'Look at the four of you in the bath together. So sweet, don't you think?'

I didn't hear their answer because I was suddenly aware of another person, stranded amidst the bags that Daisy and Max had dumped by the kitchen door. I had almost forgotten that Max had said he was bringing a girlfriend. In fact, with all his virtual dating, I wasn't completely certain he was even in a real-life relationship. Frankly, I had been more curious to meet Daisy's boyfriend; however, he had called off at the last minute. Although I had initially been grumpy about Lisa's decision to widen the invitation to include outsiders, I now understood their vital role in diluting tension. So I went forward to welcome her with a dose of cheery bonhomie appropriate to the father of a new boyfriend.

I saw her a couple of seconds before she noticed me. Even before she looked up from her phone I knew it was Connie. There was something about the tilt of her head and the curve of her neck. So I had the agony of panicking not just about my own response but also her reaction. At least I had the presence of mind to step forward so that my body obscured hers. She was wearing a short dress with long sleeves and the brooch that I had bought as a gift for Lisa but had impulsively given to her after she happened to mention that she was interested in Indian art. I still don't understand why I did that, because her tastes were so inconsistent that it was like meeting a new person every time I saw her. Her likes and dislikes were fickle. Her thoughts untethered.

She had dyed her hair and cut it even shorter since my last abortive attempt to find her. She looked up from her phone and saw me. Her face didn't flinch, apart from a tiny muscle that flickered just below her right eye. She betrayed nothing. I recognized myself in her ability to dissimulate.

'You.' That was all she said.

I stuck out my arm to shake hands, but really it was to prevent her coming any closer. My own mouth was fixed in a rictus grin, the corner of my upper lip curling nervously.

'Let me show you your room,' I offered. My voice quivered.

I could see Gregorio watching from his perch. But he was too busy imbibing Connie to notice my discombobulation.

I closed the door behind me and we walked up the wooden stairs in silence. I took it slowly – to allow us both to adjust to the gruesomeness of the situation. I tried not to look at the way her hips swung in front of me and her dress clung to her buttocks. I remembered that first time her finger drew a line down my forearm when I was buying papayas. It had felt like a religious experience, as if I had been brought back from the dead. We had gone out dancing and had drunk so much, the only way we could stay upright was to cling on to each other.

As I reached the top of the stairs I bit my lip so hard to quell the desire rising through my body that it started bleeding. I haven't always been a bad father. I read my children every book in the Narnia series without skipping any pages; I never missed a school play or parents' meeting; I cooked wholesome meals, which included ingredients from the five main food groups; I did my share of the dirty work – the nappy changing, the night shifts – and the endless mopping up of spilt drinks, tears and mud. I accepted my responsibilities like a foot soldier taking orders from *The Good Parents' Handbook*. But discovering that I am sleeping with the same girl as my son pretty much negates anything positive I have ever done. People have rotted in hell for less.

She turned towards me as we reached the landing. I pointed at Max's bedroom. We went inside. I couldn't decide whether to shut the door behind me or not. In the end I left it ajar. We stood in breathless panic for a moment, unable to speak. The pollen from the lilies sitting on the chest of drawers hit my lungs and I hoped I might suffocate.

'I didn't realize,' she said.

'How could we?'

'I need to leave right away.'

'You can't. It will attract the wrong kind of attention.' I put out my hand to rest it on her cheek.

She pushed it away. 'You're fucked up, Nick.'

I nodded in agreement, but she had already dropped her bag on the bed and gone back downstairs to find Max. And after that she didn't leave his side.

I remind myself I'm in the middle of getting married. At least a sacred shell service doesn't require much interaction. It's all about Gregorio. The wind is getting up and I worry that Lisa might get cold. I glance across at the arc of people watching us make our vows and realize that, with the exception of Rowena and Hamish, there isn't one of them who I haven't let down. I turn to Gregorio, grateful for the distraction, as he holds our wedding rings towards the sun and tells the guests how their circular shape represents the perpetual love between Lisa and me. 'It has no beginning and no end. It is round like the sun and the moon.'

Gregorio slides on the rings. 'I now declare you man and wife,' he says.

I kiss the bride chastely, eyes closed, trying not to think about Connie. She's standing so close to me that, if I wanted to, I could reach her with my hand. I wonder how I will sleep through the night knowing she's in the room next door.

Confetti unexpectedly flutters around our heads, landing on our hair and shoulders. I look up at the blue sky and close my eyes against the sun. I'm touched that someone thought to buy some. My mood is so fragile that the tiniest gestures have huge impact. For an instant I feel euphoric with life's infinite possibilities, once I have got this day out of my way. Lisa laughs and shakes her head to get rid of the confetti but it doesn't come out. When I pull away from her to gently brush it from the sleeve of her wedding dress I realize that it's not confetti at all. It's dead ladybirds. I frantically try to get rid of them, but their dried feet hook on to us like burrs, and friction makes the wings stick to Lisa's satin dress. I catch Connie's eye for a split second. She steps backwards, taking care not to disturb the shells. Max opens another Tupperware container and uses both hands to throw more fistfuls of ladybirds at us. Bumbling Hamish assumes it is some lucky tradition connected to Gregorio and joins in. I open my mouth to shout at Max to call a halt to this weirdness but a ladybird sticks to my tongue. I spit it on to the sand and wipe my lips. They feel dry and shrivelled. Gregorio jumps around waving his conch, desperate because everyone's attention has moved away from him.

'Stop it, stop it,' shouts Lisa as the ladybirds rain down on us.

I keep trying to sweep them away.

'Stop it!'

I assume her anger is directed at Max, who now stands in front of us to pour the last remnants over our heads. Daisy tries to remonstrate with him, pulling the containers out of his hands. But Lisa is shouting at me.

It's not an original approach. I start drinking almost as soon as we get back to the house. Some wit has turned on 'Hotel California'. The Eagles got it wrong. You can't actually drink to remember because alcohol interferes with the ability to form long-term memories. The more you consume the more you forget. So I drink with the specific aim of disrupting activity in my hippocampus.

The mood has soured. After a short-lived détente, Lisa and Ava are bickering again. I hear Lisa telling her to go steady on the drink and Ava countering that it's a bit late for boundaries when she checked out of parenting eight years ago. Lisa warns her that she doesn't want to end up like Barney.

'Don't worry, Mum. There's nothing I would do the way you and Dad have done it.'

Instead of being pathetically pleased to have been invited to our wedding, Hamish and Rowena now look like they would rather be anywhere else instead. They lean into each other for support, like a couple of ancient buttresses, as it dawns on them that when it comes to the hierarchy of dysfunction, we reign supreme. Shortly after this I catch Hamish breathing into his brown paper bag. When I try to put my arm around him, he jumps away warily like a dog that thinks it's about to be kicked.

I can't help thinking about my last wedding day in all its utter lack of complication. The biggest dispute was over whether we should offer a vegetarian option at dinner or use the spare cash to buy more alcohol. But that brings into relief the problem with my relationship with Rosie: it was too anaemic. If I had stayed married to her I would have turned into the pillbox on the beach, slowly being entombed in sand. Boredom is a slow form of death, isn't it?

Everything with Lisa has taken place in glorious unpredictable Technicolor. It has all been hard fought and you would have thought for that reason, I might have defended it better. She comes towards me. Her face is serene and lustrous, as if it has been lacquered, and the long satin dress makes it look as though she's floating.

I raise my glass to her. 'To my beautiful angel.'

Lisa takes the drink from my hand and places it on the top of the fridge, well out of reach, smiling ethereally. We embrace like two soldiers who have managed to escape a battlefield without any obvious flesh wounds whilst the rest of our unit has perished. I pluck a ladybird wing from the sleeve of her dress and long to make love with her one last time.

None of this casts me in a good light. There is no justification for what I've done. Contrary to the popular folklore perpetuated by people like Gregorio, the worst of situations doesn't always bring out the best in people. I have been under a certain amount of pressure with Lisa's diagnosis and refusal to accept treatment. It's fair to say that I haven't been thinking straight. It doesn't take an accomplished psychologist to point out that sleeping with a woman twenty years younger is an unsophisticated attempt to dodge death. It's like time travel. It's like mainlining serotonin.

I'm aware suddenly that Ava is taking a photo of us that she plans to tag 'The Big Day'. She shows me the picture on her phone and I stare at my face. I see a man with crêpey skin around his eyes, cheeks mottled with age spots, and thinning hair (but not so you'd notice if you hadn't met him before). Someone who used to be ambushed by desire at inappropriate moments, during lunchtime meetings with postgrad researchers and schoolteachers, but who is now pathetically grateful when he wakes up with an erection in the morning. I see someone who is an efficient machine when it comes to producing academic papers on memory function in prestigious journals including *Nature* and *The American Psychologist* but who has failed to deliver on his early promise and has had to settle for circling the edge of his dreams without completely fulfilling them. And that's the weakest kind of man: the man on the eternal hunt for small crumbs of comfort amidst the wreckage of middle age.

It's an unlucky twist of fate, meeting Connie, but I don't believe in coincidence. Extremely improbable events are surprisingly commonplace. It's just bad luck that all the different elements of my life fused together at the same time.

We all like to find patterns as a way of trying to understand our world, to give us the illusion that we control it.

We spend hours every day trying to make sense of it all, and most of us recast our experiences into a reasonable life story that can be told down through the generations. Life's biggest struggle isn't for food and drink, it's the struggle for narrative harmony.

I feel in my pocket for the speech I have prepared but I don't trust myself to read it in front of Connie and Max. I scan the room, looking for them, but they've disappeared. Any relief is fleeting as I panic that Connie might bend under the pressure and tell Max what has happened.

I have to speak to her. I can bear anything but this.

19

Rosie

I have waited all week to hear back from Lisa, relentlessly checking inboxes, phone messages and junk mail in case I have missed something. She's getting married this afternoon and is meant to be leaving for Mexico in the next couple of days. I'm not entirely surprised by her radio silence. Lisa always takes things to the wire. But I'm under pressure from work to confirm the final list of participants in the trial and my colleague in the States has a queue of other women willing to sign up right away. Time is running out.

I know from previous experience that the longer a patient takes to come to a decision about treatment the less likely the answer will be positive. Sometimes it's a difficult call: it's not obvious whether the outcome of one regime is any better than another, or the side effects are so cruel the patient will have no quality of life. But for Lisa, it's a no-brainer. It's the choice between doing something and nothing. Possible life or certain death. In fact, the juicing regime could kill her before the cancer does because of the risk of sodium deficiency. I went to Norfolk armed with the facts, to convince her of this, but I didn't need to bother because she knew most of it already.

After some crazy healing retreat, Lisa had done her own due diligence and had reluctantly conceded Gregorio was at best deluded and at worst a quack. She told me she was planning to dump him after the wedding. She had spent so much of her life looking after herself that I should have realized she wouldn't fail at this point.

Either way, Lisa didn't need much convincing of the superiority of the treatment I was offering. I explained it was a Phase III trial, which means problems with dosage and toxicity have been ironed out. She sounded really interested when I told her that even some of the Phase I patients were still alive, because these were the sickest recruits who chose to embark on a risky, unproven experiment when they had nothing to lose. She was so enthusiastic that I thought she was going to sign up then and there, and I was the one who insisted she should sleep on it.

'I'm so pleased for you, Rosie,' she said. 'How amazing to do something so positive with your life. To leave something behind.'

I can't badger her. It's never right to hassle or heckle patients into a decision, even if you believe it to be the right one. I can give my considered opinion, based on the options available, and if someone asks what I would do in their shoes I can tell them. But my job isn't to force treatment on patients, it's to support them through the process and respect their decision. And despite our long history, Lisa is no different.

I sit at the kitchen table and draft an email on my phone, just a couple of lines asking how she is feeling, in the hope it might trigger a response to the bigger question, but in the end I press 'delete' because it's her wedding day and maybe she wants to forget she's ill. I know how awful it is to feel your life has come to be defined by a single catastrophic event, and the relief when you're distracted from it for a few hours.

I haven't told anyone what I have done. It's slightly murky ethics, offering a place on a trial to a friend, even though Lisa fulfils all the criteria. But it's more that I don't want any narrative to develop that casts me in the role of heroine coming to the rescue of the woman who has wronged her. I don't want to spark some apocalyptic debate on the nature of darkness and light, good and evil, wrong and right. I want to help her because almost everyone deserves a chance.

Let me be clear here: I'm not offering Lisa a lifeline because I care. The memories of the good times we shared were recast many years ago in light of what happened between us. So if I suddenly remember a hilarious moment, like the competitions we used to have on the beach – to see who could replace her underwear with a bikini top and bottoms the fastest without removing any other clothes – I now see Lisa's comic gyrations and flashes of breast and buttocks as partly a performance for Nick. Everything has been tainted.

When she told me Nick was up to his old tricks she wasn't looking for sympathy or advice, she was trying to tell me that the way he had treated her was no different from the way he had treated me, which allowed me to reach peak indifference about them getting married just in time for their wedding day. I'm doing this for Lisa because I don't care any more. And that feels liberating.

*

It's Barney's idea to spend the day of the wedding together. *Just in case*, his cryptic message reads. Just in case of what? I wonder. Just in case one of us gets the urge to go to Norfolk to make a scene when Gregorio asks if any man knows any reason why Nick and Lisa shouldn't be lawfully joined together? Or Barney is tempted to hit the bottle for the first time in seven years? Or I take to my bed and never get up again?

'Just in case you're tempted to go on Tinder,' he says when he arrives with a case of non-alcoholic beer, a DVD of *Blue Valentine* and a playlist of songs that he promises will make us relieved not to be married, which I correctly guess includes a lot of The Smiths and Joy Division. Barney was always good at turning an unpromising day into a memorable one.

'You know, if we were young we'd just get drunk and stoned,' he says, following me into the sitting room.

'If we were young we wouldn't be in this situation,' I point out.

He commends me on my ability to be rational.

I tell him it was probably one of the reasons my marriage failed.

He thinks I'm joking – but I'm not – and then he pulls an already-made joint out of his pocket, saying, 'Here's one I prepared earlier,' like a *Blue Peter* presenter. We smoke it together and I choke and tell him that it makes me feel old, not young. But actually it makes me feel nothing, and sometimes that is the best feeling of all.

I had forgotten how easy it is to while away time with Barney. Because he can't sit in a room without music playing, and I don't want to get into a state of existential gloom by listening to his playlist, I pretend the speaker is broken and we put on old records and sing loudly and out of tune to every single David Bowie album in chronological order, using hairbrushes as microphones. And we agree that it is the soundtrack to our lives. I ask him if Nick was unfaithful to me and he mutters something about what happens on tour stays on tour. He makes me dance for hours and we take selfies and I have to wrestle his phone out of his hand because he really means to send them to Nick and Lisa.

Once we have exhausted ourselves we put on *Morning Phase* by Beck and wrap ourselves around each other, heads resting on the other's shoulder, and sway in time to the beat for the whole album without speaking a word. It's easy to create sweet notes on a bum day, especially when it involves old friends. I feel his hand drift inside the back of my T-shirt and his cock growing hard through his jeans and we end up having sex on the sofa. It's strange sleeping with someone I know so well. There's none of the risk that I'll call him by the wrong name, discover he voted for UKIP or lives with his mother. Sleeping with Barney is like coming home to a house with a warm fire after a long cold walk.

Afterwards I offer to cook a late lunch from leftover chicken and rice that I have in the fridge, and Barney suggests we have a piece of toast instead.

'It's because you think I'm a crap cook, isn't it?' I ask him.

I don't want to tell him there's no bread. I'm lying on my side on the sofa, head resting on his chest, eyes closed, my fingers tracing patterns on his stomach, and he warns that if I go any lower we'll have to have sex again.

'I don't think. I know,' he counters. 'The idea is we get through the day without killing ourselves. I'm not eating that chicken unless you get your infection control team to vet it first.'

I think we fuck again and then fall asleep, but it might be the other way round.

'Why didn't we do this years ago?' Barney asks sleepily at one point. 'We're so good at it.'

When I wake up I go into the kitchen, dressed in Barney's T-shirt. I pull up the top, so the collar covers my nose, and inhale his scent, wondering at its familiarity. I don't think about anything apart from the good time we have shared together. I don't presume that we will meet again, although I would like it if we do. I look around for my phone to check my notifications because I feel like seeing Ed Gilmour later. There's nothing like dating apps for forcing you to live in the present.

It's still dark outside and I glance at the kitchen clock and am astonished to discover it's almost six in the morning. Barney had a mad plan that we should each make a speech at midnight and toast our future happiness apart, but we must have slept through the night like the middle-aged people we are.

I feel strangely flustered by this loss of time, as if I've missed the clock strike twelve at New Year or have fallen asleep in the first hour of a long-haul flight and woken up as the plane lands ten hours later. I want Barney to leave as soon as possible, because Kit is coming to fetch his stuff from Daisy's room. And besides, I generally don't like spending the day with someone I've spent the night with.

I've left my phone in the sitting room and don't want Barney to know I'm checking Tinder so I decide to log in as guest user on Daisy's computer. I find it under a pile of papers on the kitchen table. The essay she has been writing for the past four weeks is still unfinished. I lift up the screen and wait for the computer to come on. I notice she has covered up some of the letters on the keyboard with pieces of sticky paper that I attempt to peel off. She's an expert in procrastination but even by Daisy's standards this is original.

I turn on the computer and log into my emails and am both surprised and delighted to see that Lisa has finally sent me a message with an attachment, just half an hour ago. I have the brief hit of self-satisfaction that comes with managing to convince someone to do the right thing. I open the attachment to check she has filled in every-thing correctly but it doesn't contain a scanned copy of the consent form. Instead there's a picture of a poster that she used to have hanging in her bedroom in Norfolk. I recognize it immediately. Lisa was obsessed with the Pre-Raphaelites because their messy lives resonated with her own, but I was always disturbed by this picture of Ophelia being swallowed up beneath the murky waters because it was like watching someone drown. There are two words written across the bottom of it. *Thank you.* Fol-lowed by a flurry of overblown Lisa-style kisses.

At least it gives me an excuse to write back to ask when she is going to send the consent forms. But as I type her name into the email I realize that the letters Daisy has covered up spell LISA.

I understand what this means right away: Daisy's

having a relapse. After Nick left me and we spent months exchanging angry emails about why Daisy and Max wouldn't stay with him, Daisy finally revealed that the real reason she couldn't go was that if she touched something Lisa had touched, it made her so anxious about me that it would prompt round after round of compulsions. Lisa was a trigger for her OCD. It was obviously utterly illogical, and Nick really struggled to grasp that I wasn't trying to poison the already shaky relationship between him and Daisy. It marked the moment that I truly knew Daisy was possessed by the illness.

I look at the picture on the screen and the hidden letters and am gripped by a fear that starts in my stomach and spreads through the rest of my body until it feels as though I'm on fire. For a moment I can't move. I can't hear myself think and I furiously rub my temples to try to work out the connections between the hidden letters on the keyboard and the picture that Lisa has sent.

I head back into the sitting room to frantically search for my phone and eventually find it stuffed down the side of one of the sofa cushions. Barney doesn't stir. When I turn it on I see that there are three missed calls from Daisy at around three o'clock in the morning and a text message asking me to get in touch because she's worried about Max. I think of the notebook I found in Max's bedroom revealing how involved he was in Daisy's illness and realize he is the missing link.

The past has never seemed more present.

20

Max

I wake up in the morning and stretch my arm across the bed to reach for Connie, wondering which part of her I will touch first. The only other body I know as intimately as hers is that of my cadaver, Jean. The thought makes me smile. Sometimes, when I can't sleep at night because I'm missing her too much and the dark thoughts that she might be with someone else gather overhead, I soothe myself by doing an imaginary inventory of her body as if I'm in an anatomy class: I visualize the shadowy dimples above each buttock, the dainty map of wrinkles on her elbow bone, the soft downy hair in the nape of her neck, and her bony right ankle with the tiny scar from a child-hood ice-skating accident. Somehow, the knowledge that I know her best calms me down and makes her mine again.

As soon as my fingers touch the warm tangle of sheets beside me I realize that she has gone. And almost imme-diately I understand that unless I find her right away we will most likely never see each other again. I sit up, get out of bed and throw on yesterday's clothes in a single motion, managing a quick glance through the bedroom window to see that it's getting light outside, which means it must be around six thirty. The curtains are wide open. Did I mention I have never slept with them closed since the summer Daisy first got ill?

I stub my toe on the edge of the chest of drawers as I stumble through the door and head down the stairs, two at a time, still fumbling with my T-shirt. If I'm fast enough I might just catch her. The front door is ajar, giving me confidence that I'm on the right track. I pull on the first pair of shoes that I find in the porch, which happen to be leather sandals belonging to that mad hippy friend of Lisa's. I feel the imprint of his foot in the sole and it repulses me.

It's still half-dark, so that the shrubs either side of the driveway are shadowy, monstrous shapes whispering taunts in the breeze as I edge down towards the front gate. When I reach the road I turn left, simply on the basis that this was the route Barney chose on his reckless road trip with me all those years ago. But luck is with me this time. I hear the low rumble of a car engine and in the far distance I see a neon sign flashing on the roof of what must be a taxi come to collect Connie. It's parked beside the field where Barney saw the judgemental cows. Country music plays in the background.

I set off on a very slow jog down the road, hobbled by the dark and the straps of Gregorio's child-sized sandals cutting into my feet. *Mustn't shout out. Mustn't shout out. Mustn't shout out*, I tell myself. Because Connie will hear the desperation in my voice and it will push her even further away from me. I have been mad with jealousy since I discovered the truth about her and Carlo. I decided right away not to confront him because he would have questioned my indignation. Last term he watched a couple having sex in the flat opposite through half-drawn curtains and when I suggested this demonstrated a certain moral ambivalence he argued that, on the contrary, he had managed to resist the urge to film them and post it on YouPorn.

But last night, when it was my turn to pose a question to Connie, I made the mistake of asking her if she was being distant with me because she had slept with Carlo. She said she was fed up with my insecurity and my stupid games and suggested I should try to find a girlfriend closer to me in age because: 'Frankly, it's getting boring.' She lay down with her back to me and refused to let any part of my body touch hers.

I couldn't sleep and ended up going into the kitchen at around three a.m., where I sat on Lisa's wicker recliner drinking beer and watching episodes of *True Detective* on my iPhone, finding comfort in its nihilistic prophesying about everybody being a nobody. My phone died six minutes before the end of episode seven. So I ransacked the kitchen drawers searching for a charger and, hidden beneath a bunch of clean tea towels, I found a plastic file containing paperwork with Mum's neat handwriting across the top and Lisa's original letter to her. I sat down on the recliner, heart racing, as I tried in my drunken, exhausted state to work out what all this meant. But it didn't require *True Detective* powers of deduction to conclude that Mum had been to see Lisa and offered her a place on her clinical trial. I couldn't believe it. This would completely tip Daisy over the edge. I felt furious with Mum, but of course she had no idea what was going on with

Daisy, so I turned my sights on to Dad and Lisa and sculpted my hatred until it had turned into something cold and hard.

At some point I heard a sound in the kitchen and looked over the edge of the recliner to see Daisy open the drawer where the knives used to be and then head upstairs again. I remembered how Dad had recited Daisy's special words yesterday in a pathetic effort to get close to her. The noose around my neck tightened. I went up to bed and tried to wrap myself around Connie but she shook me off, like Barney shook me off when I tried to explain to him about the ladybirds eating the aphids all those years ago. I had tried to talk to her about Daisy's illness yesterday afternoon but she explained in an apologetic tone that she wasn't invested enough in my family to want the back-story. It's not that she has fallen out of love with me. She was never in love with me.

The early-morning damp and cold wrap themselves around me. I pick up pace and soon I'm close enough to hear someone speak. But now I'm here I panic about what to do. I curse my decision to invite Connie to the wedding. Far from cementing our relationship, it has exposed all the cracks. I thought with her by my side I would feel invincible. Instead I feel as out of control as I did in the car with Barney. I'm paranoid the real reason she wants to leave is because she's aware Carlo will be home alone.

The taxi driver sits patiently with his window wound down, singing along tunelessly to 'Jolene'. I hear raised voices. To my complete surprise Dad is standing at the rear of the car, fully dressed, his back to me. His arms windmill in the air as if he's remonstrating with Connie.

It's something he does when he's not getting his own way. In my sleep-deprived state I guess that he caught her leaving and is trying to persuade her to stay. My mood lifts slightly. It's a stroke of luck that he found her, because otherwise she would have been long gone. Although his gesture is futile – no one can will a relationship into being – I'm touched by his attempt to help: after years of Mum picking up the pieces, he's finally there for me.

It's getting lighter. I expect them to turn round and see me at any moment. I still hold out hope that Connie will relent when she sees me. I am fleetingly distracted by the sound of a flock of geese flying overhead, which is why I don't remember the exact choreography of what happens next. But when I look at Dad and Connie again the night has lifted enough for me to see clearly that they are embracing like a drunken couple holding each other up for support. Connie whispers something like, 'Lisa knows,' but my attention is more taken up by their body language. Neither wants to let the other go. Her sleek head nestles in his shoulder and his lips are pressed to the top of her head like he's giving her a blessing. His eyes are closed. Eventually, she untangles herself and gets in the taxi. Connie has never shown this kind of emotion towards me. It is a simple statement of fact.

I turn back before they can see me and throw Gregorio's sandals into the side of the road so I can move faster. Instead of going back to the house I follow the track down to the beach. There is no plan beyond the need to keep moving.

The dawn sky over the sea has started to bleed different shades of red and pink, but behind me it's still dark. I remember Mum telling me that one of the best things about Norfolk is that, because it faces north-east, you can watch the sunrise and sunset from the same vantage point. I wish she were here now because I'm overtaken with the feeling of being both too young and too old to understand the world around me. Mum has an amazing ability to make sense of the incomprehensible. She always knows the right thing to do.

Overhead the geese continue to honk their way across the sky, looking out for each other like family should. I walk without purpose. When I reach the beach I head for the bunker in the dunes. The circle of shells from yesterday's wedding is still there. I kick each one over the edge of the roof, even though it hurts my bare feet, and I'm denied any destructive pleasure because they lump soundlessly on to the sand below.

I sit down facing the sea, with my legs dangling over the edge, like I used to as a child. Its slate-coloured surface is calm and beguiling as it emerges in the early-morning light. When I scan the beach I realize I'm no longer alone. A small figure appears in the right-hand corner of my sight line. The offshore wind blowing from the sea stings my eyes and blurs my vision but after a few blinks I realize that it is The Second Mrs Rankin, as Ava refers to her mum. Everything Ava says is pickled in self-defensive irony. But I envy the freedom she won by turning her back on all of us.

I have endlessly replayed this image of Lisa walking across the sand but, contrary to what Dad maintains, the detail remains stubbornly the same. She's stooped over, head bowed against the wind, walking slowly but decisively towards the sea, her hands deep in the large pockets of Dad's coat. She pauses roughly halfway between the dunes and the water to get down on one knee and examine something in the sand. She pulls off her gloves. I put my hand against my cheek and realize how cold it is.

The full moon overnight means all sorts of crap belched on to the shore in the high tide. Lisa picks something up and puts it in her pocket. I later discover that it's a piece of sea glass and wonder if she planned to give it to someone. When she pulls herself up again she walks with renewed purpose towards the water's edge, leaving the gloves lying on the sand. She stops and stares a while.

She shrugs off Dad's coat from her shoulders on to the damp sand. She's wearing the same dress from yesterday and stands as still as a mast while the floaty satin billows in the breeze, then, almost as an afterthought, removes her shoes and walks towards the sea. *Hardy types, these Norfolk folks*, I think, as she steps in and lets the waves break around her calves. Mum is the same. She would swim if she were here. But The First Mrs Rankin has been usurped by The Second Mrs Rankin and can no longer come back to her childhood home.

I'm puzzled why Lisa lets the sea lap at the hem of her dress because Dad is fanatical about the corrosive properties of saltwater. The waves are breaking so close that the dress is quickly soaked by the spray. She half pirouettes, turns her back to the water and stretches her arms in the air. At first I think it is some weird ritual Gregorio has taught her. He's always banging on about how the sea cleanses your soul. But then I realize that she is pulling off her dress until she stands in her bra and knickers. I feel embarrassed to be watching her, like some dirty Carlo-style voyeur. She unhooks the bra and throws it with the dress on to the sand and I see her breasts swinging slowly with the effort. I noticed how weak she was yesterday when she tried to climb up the dunes.

If I were Carlo I might go down to the water's edge and try to seduce Lisa as a way out of all this. But my entire life I have always done everything right. I have never lied about being ill when I wasn't. I have never cheated at school. I have never got any grade below A in a public exam. I have never been unfaithful to a girlfriend. Or logged on to a friend's Facebook and sent porn to all their contacts. I have not done any of these things and yet where has it got me?

I watch Lisa, wondering if she is attempting to dig her feet into the sand beneath the waves so that she can stand steady. I used to do this as a child. The currents beneath the surface are strong enough to take down a heavy man, let alone a frail woman. But instead she keeps walking, legs apart, cowboy-style, taking small toddler steps further into the water, arms out to the side to maintain equilibrium. I watch and wince. Her ankles will be numb. The air temperature can't be any more than four degrees, which means the sea must be about eight. The water laps at her waist. Suddenly she cartwheels beneath the surface like a synchronized swimmer doing a sideways dive. It's difficult to tell whether it's by accident or design. I wasn't expecting that. I stand up on the roof of the pillbox to get a better view.

She comes up and shakes her head like a dog. A wave crashes over her and for a second she disappears again. I blink a couple of times and see her break to the surface a few metres further out. I'm pretty sure she's doing front crawl but it's difficult to tell because she slips in and out of view as the waves rise and fall. The current is strong and for a while it looks as though she's swimming on the spot. She stops for a moment and tries to stand. But it's too deep so she flips on to her back, arms flapping beside her. I swear she's staring straight at me. She disappears and when I see something in the water again I wonder if it could be the bobbing head of a seal. When I was little, Daisy used to terrify me with tales of women who turned into seals called Selkies and how they used to swim as far as they could and cry seven tears into the ocean to attract a Selkie male.

I look up at the huge sky. It's burnished red and orange. I remember how I used to be able to comfort Daisy by demonstrating her insignificance in the world. It's incredible how she thinks she has the power to control events with her thoughts whereas I feel so utterly impotent. Life is something that just happens to me: Dad going off with Mum's best friend; Daisy's illness; Carlo's treachery; and the scene I just witnessed in the road. Whatever was happening there, the intimacy and intensity of that moment between Dad and Connie had nothing to do with me.

My chest tightens until it feels as if someone is slowly squeezing my neck. I am back in class with Carlo sitting beside me, the scent of Connie still on his body as the lecturer talks. *'Anxiety comes from the Latin* angere, *to choke.'*

I am nineteen years old. I know too much and too little. I don't have a belief system beyond a desire to mend broken people and take care of my mum and sister. When

I look out to sea again Lisa is swimming in open water, arms moving as methodically as a metronome further and further away from the shore. Should I go in after her? I weigh it up in my mind as if I'm in an ethics class.

It's a simple equation: if Lisa survives, Daisy doesn't. And she will take me down with her, because I can no longer tell where she starts and I end. This is our chance to cut free from each other.

I stare at Lisa in the same shocked way that Daisy stared at her from this same location that afternoon eight years earlier. We're back at the beginning. But this time I'm writing my own story. I see a hand waving but I can't tell which way she is facing any more.

She slips under the water.

Acknowledgements

Heartfelt thanks to my editor Maxine Hitchcock and my agent Jonny Geller, and all the good folks at Penguin and Curtis Brown. I'm truly fortunate to work with such wise and dedicated people. Big thanks to Phil Robertson for keeping the faith and digging me out of the troughs. I'm indebted, as always, to my first readers Helen Bairamian, Helen Townshend and Henry Tricks for their honesty and encouragement. Thanks to my daughter Maia for allowing me to exploit her proofreading skills, and my husband Ed for putting up with it all. For feedback on early drafts and encouragement when I needed it most, thanks to Charlotte Simpson-Orlebar, Annabel Mullion, Lisa Goldstein and Annie Woolf.

Finally, thank you to the wonderful medics who helped me with my research: Professor Ian Smith at the Royal Marsden, and Sarah Halford from Cancer Research UK. And to all those OCD sufferers out there, I hope this shines some light on a much misunderstood illness.

For more information on OCD get in touch with OCD Action at www.ocdaction.org.uk.

Reading Group Discussion Points

1. Were you aware while reading that some characters' narratives were unreliable? If so, at what point did you start to realize this? Why do you think people mis-remember significant events?

2. We have insight into Daisy, Max, Rosie and Nick's points of view in this book. Why do you think the author chose not to include Lisa's?

3. How do you think the four points of view worked as a narrative device to explore the novel's main themes? Did you identify with one character more than the others?

4. In the novel the children inadvertently intuit the sexual tension between some of the adults, describing them as 'susceptible'. Do you think the behaviour of the adult characters has more to do with circumstance or character?

5. How much did you know about OCD before you read this novel? Discuss the depiction of mental illness and addiction in the novel and how they impact on the narrative.

6. What does the novel have to say on the nature of forgiveness? Do you think that it is more difficult for children to forgive than adults? Is Rosie motivated by forgiveness when she offers treatment to Lisa? Is it self-serving or altruistic? What is Lisa's motivation for sending the letter to Rosie?

7. Discuss the representation of social media dating in the novel. Do you think dating on Tinder provides a good

escape for Rosie, or does it create more problems than it solves?

8. Twenty per cent of husbands leave their wives during illness, compared to two per cent of wives leaving their husbands. Why do you think this might be? Did you have any sympathy with Lisa when Nick's behaviour became apparent?

9. The strongest bond in this novel is the bond between Daisy and Max rather than between the children and their parents. Why do you think this is?

10. Rosie accepted there would be no day of reckoning with Lisa. Do you think an apology could have changed the outcome of the story? Should Lisa have been in touch with Rosie sooner?

11. Who betrays who in the novel? In your opinion which is the worst betrayal?

12. Daisy believes Lisa is determined to take them all down with her, and even wishes her dead. Do you think Lisa is fairly or unfairly judged in this story?

13. What do Nick's feelings towards Lisa's illness and treatment say about his character? In Nick's position how do you think you would behave? Was he right to criticise Lisa's choice of cancer treatment, or should he have supported her?

14. Does Rosie owe Lisa anything once she knows she's dying? Do you believe, as Rosie says, she agrees to the letter's request because she doesn't care any more?

15. Why do you think Lisa brings about her own death at the close of the story? Do you think any of the other characters could be held responsible?